UNDER THE WAVE AT WAIMEA

Under the Wave at Waimea

PAUL THEROUX

HAMISH HAMILTON
an imprint of
PENGUIN BOOKS

TO SHEILA, *ʻo koʻu alakaʻi*

HAMISH HAMILTON

UK | USA | Canada | Ireland | Australia
India | New Zealand | South Africa

Hamish Hamilton is part of the Penguin Random House group of companies
whose addresses can be found at global.penguinrandomhouse.com.

First published in the United States of America by Houghton Mifflin Harcourt 2021
First published in Great Britain by Hamish Hamilton 2021

001

Printed and bound in Great Britain by Clays Ltd, Elcograf S.p.A.

The authorized representative in the EEA is Penguin Random House Ireland,
Morrison Chambers, 32 Nassau Street, Dublin D02 YH68

A CIP catalogue record for this book is available from the British Library

HARDBACK ISBN: 978–0–241–50444–4
TRADE PAPERBACK ISBN: 978–0–241–50445–1

www.greenpenguin.co.uk

MIX
Paper from
responsible sources
FSC® C018179

Penguin Random House is committed to a
sustainable future for our business, our readers
and our planet. This book is made from Forest
Stewardship Council® certified paper.

Out of the water I am nothing.

— DUKE KAHANAMOKU, legendary Hawaiian surfer

PART I

Under the Wave
at Waimea

The Island of No Bad Days

T he one wild story that everyone believed about Joe Sharkey was not
true, but this was often the case with big-wave riders. It was told he had
eaten magic mushrooms on a day declared Condition Black and dropped
left down a forty-five-foot wave one midnight under the white light of a full
moon at Waimea Bay, the wave freaked with clawed rags of blue foam. He
smashed his board on the inside break called Pinballs and, unable to make
it to shore against the riptide, he swam five miles up the coast, where he was
found in the morning, hallucinating on the sand. More proof that he was a
hero; that he surfed like a rat on acid.

His being found on the beach at dawn near Banzai Pipeline was a fact,
and he'd taken LSD, not mushrooms. But so much of the rest of his life had
been outrageous, and sometimes heroic, glowing with sensuous happiness,
that his fellow surfers never questioned whether the wave had been a monster, or if he'd been on it, or broken his board, or swum alone to Pipeline, nor
did they accuse him in pidgin of *bulai* — lying. Sharkey had shown himself
the equal of the best of them. When he'd first been asked about the Waimea
story, he'd been young — eager to make an impression, and prone to embel-
lish. In time he learned that exaggeration was always a side effect of fame
and fiction a feature of every surfer's reputation, the yearning to be a dog off
its leash.

The appeal of surfing to Sharkey was that it was improvisational, a question of balance; of staying on your board on a radical feathering wave, a
dance on water, at its best a display of originality, perhaps not a sport at all
but a personal style, a way of living your life, a game without rules, incompa-
rable. And some of the greatest rides, on the biggest waves, were never seen
by anyone except the surfer. The surfer rode the wave, the wave blobbed

softly, and it was over, the epitome of performance art. The surfer paddled to shore, the wave was gone, there was no trace of the ride — something like a fabulous death.

His lover, Olive Randall, knew the truth, because (being new to his life, and English, and a nurse) she'd asked in her forthright way, "So what about it, then, you grinning numpty?"

And she looked for more. Sometimes — the way the earliest humans studied a stranger — she examined his body to read his history and know him better. He slept naked, and often in their first month together she woke beside him and searched for meaning in the ink on his skin. Much of the imagery was obvious, some of it obscure, a great deal was a record of risk; his disfigurements were those of a warrior, battle scars and scabbed wounds and the sutures from wipeouts and jellyfish stings and face-plants.

In the early hours of muted sallow daylight his tattoos were mottled like bruises, but after sunup they were sharpened, as he lay, facing away from her, his back exposed, a great blue wave covering it like a dragon's mouth, fanglike foam on its jagged crest tipping past the top of his spine, the well-known print of the Japanese wave at Kanagawa that most people recognized, except that in this depiction Sharkey was surfing the great curved face of it. In his tattoo he was crouched on his long board, one arm extended, as he had surfed a forty-five-footer at Waimea or the great wave at Cortes Bank. But Cortes was so far offshore — a submerged island more than a hundred miles in the ocean west of San Diego — only the boatman had seen him, and few people knew that it was one of his triumphs.

Tribal slashes of black, licks and ribbons, covered his upper arms and del-toids, and the syllable *Om* in complex Tibetan brushstrokes on each decliv-ity of his shoulders. His arms — "full sleeves" — were enclosed by bands of sharks' teeth, stylized, triangular. A snake circled his left wrist like a bracelet, an ouroboros, its tail in its mouth. On his right arm more sharks' teeth, a frigate bird on the back of his hand — his power animal, he called it — flat-tened, his wings outspread, also serving as the image of a compass. Some were faded, some were fresh, all had meaning.

Hawaiian dots, many of them like pinpricks, a constellation of them on his fingers, and balancing that pattern the Southern Cross on his right foot, below an anklet of dolphins. Tattoos hammered into his skin, rat-tatted with blunt inky spikes in Tahiti and Samoa and poked into him with a chattering needle in Santa Cruz and Recife and Cape Town; Devanagari script from India, a lozenge that looked Egyptian, single words, like the name on the meat of his thumb — an old girlfriend? Olive had finally asked him, but no. "My mother," and he seemed lovable saying that.

"Your mum," she said. She cocked her head at him and kissed him. "Your muvva."

Perhaps, she thought, the whole of his life was inked across his body, that she'd know him better by studying his skin. He was hearty, and twenty-four years older, but the lover she'd longed for, passionate but secure and successful enough not to intrude in her privacy. She wanted to be loved, but not possessed. Sharkey was too self-absorbed and fanatical about surfing to be possessive.

He stirred; he seemed to know, hyperalert in his nakedness, that he was being observed — and perhaps felt her warm breath on him. Then he turned over and saw that she was wide awake, hovering; he kissed her, embraced her, her small warm breasts fitting his hands.

Sharkey loved to sleep, because his sleep, like the saturation of a drug, was so much like drifting in the ocean, toppling and bobbing like flotsam, and he was, as they said in Hawaii, a waterman, the Shark.

In his house in the woods, on a bluff above the sea, he lay buoyant in sleep, levitated in noiseless night and darkness. There he hovered, tremulous with the ripple in his sinuses of small snores — hours of that, until in the aqueous shallows of slumber the day got into his dreams. Someone must have mentioned surfing while stoned or asked him if the story was true, or repeated it to him — of his eating mushrooms and paddling into the surf at Waimea in the dark, and the rest of it, swimming on his board out to sea for safety and ending up thrashing ashore beyond Pipeline, the old tale haunting him in his dreams.

He was so expert a big-wave surfer that stories like that — his own fictions, the wilder exaggerations of others that were attributed to him — added to his fame and made him a legend. His admirers were the most inventive, eager to improve upon their hero.

The dispute in his dream unsettled him, because there were always doubters. But he smiled when he woke from it, because he was so young in his dreams and, awake, he knew he was sixty-two. And at once he was aware of Olive's warmth and her nakedness, and he turned over and slid toward her. She parted her legs to welcome his searching hand and enclose his body. Then he lay in the dark against her, as on a wave, and rode her while she clutched at his arms as though climbing through a hold-down, and in their delirium their bodies were phosphorescent, lit with desire.

He sank to sleep after that, then floated, drugged and wrung out by the convulsive lovemaking, lying on his back, his mouth half open, like a castaway, adrift again.

As the sky above the treetops paled at his uncurtained window, he stirred

— the light seeping into him, reddening his eyelids — and he settled lower into his soft bed in a body-shaped pod of warmth. In the rising light the dream came again, more vivid now, in full color; he was flat on his board, paddling in turbulent water, and anxious — the anxiety woke him — and he blinked, recognizing his room, and was free of the dream.

Every morning he woke and was content, knowing the whole day was his. He flung out his arm, snatching at emptiness — Olive was no longer beside him. She'd risen, one of her early starts, to work at the hospital. Their love-making now seemed unreal, a ghostlike hold-down in the dark glimmer of dawn. But he could smell her body on the sheet, which was still damp where she had lain.

Sharkey stretched, he yawned like a dog, he roared with satisfaction, then kicked away the sheet and swung himself off the bed, swallowing air, roaring again. His voice alerted the geese outside on the lawn, which replied in urgent squawks, startling the peacock into a fit of screaming. Now the sun was a hot blade at the window, and a dewy blue stillness of thick dampened petals sweetened the morning.

In this blossom of solitude he remembered the night before, and he fell back on his bed to recall the details of the evening.

It had been party at a beachfront house overlooking the surf break they called Off the Wall. "Party" meant a small room crowded with shrieking young people, the heat and smack of their sweat, the sustained pressure of their bodies and bare legs, jostling boys with big shoulders, girls in shorts, a woman with purple and blue fish scales tattooed on her upper arm, a ring in her lower lip, others with nose rings and wearing T-shirts with slashes. A TV screen on the far wall showed surfers on the boil of curling waves.

Sharkey stood marveling, believing that he was anonymous, liking the sight of this great health and the suggestion of recklessness in the heat and noise, the shouting girls, their brown toes, the wild-eyed groups, all of them contending.

A tall girl nearby with sun-scorched hair and a stipple of tattoos across the tops of her breasts and a swimmer's pale pickled-looking fingers looked up, smiled at Sharkey, broke away from her shouting group, and approached him.

She screamed "Hi!" to be heard above the din and stood, confident, just his height in bare feet, looking him straight in the eye.

Sharkey nodded. "How's it?"

"What was your secret, when you were starting out?"

Her shouted question got the attention of some boys, who drifted over to hear his answer.

But he said, "Ask these guys. It's their party."

"You were killing the Pipe before any of us were born," one of the boys said.

Sharkey was cautioned. *You're old,* they were saying.

"Did you have a long board then?"

"A wooden board that looked like my mother's front door," Sharkey said, and swigged his beer. "We all had longer boards in the seventies. Even Gerry and Butch."

"Who's Butch?"

"Van Artsdalen. An outlaw. A wild man. A waterman." But none of this registered. "Even Jock had a giant board."

Hearing his name, Jock Sutherland waved and said, "Balsa-wood core," and withdrew, going shy, as he bowed his head and vanished.

"This guy killed it today," the tall girl said, putting out her long arm and snatching at a young man's shirt. "Double overhead A-frames!"

His neck was looped with leis, which flopped as he twisted aside, and he smiled but kept his eyes on Sharkey. The flowers bulked under his chin, and the respectful way the others awaited his reaction Sharkey took to mean that he'd been a winner.

"How old are you?"

"Nineteen," the boy said, tugging the garlands away from his chin, the flowers from his mouth.

Sharkey could imagine him shacked inside the Pipe, cutting back, whipping around, the hotshot moves that won points these days. With this in mind, Sharkey said, "I remember when it was considered a victory to just stay on that wave without wiping out. No other moves."

"Tell him your secret," the tall woman said, and it sounded like a taunt.

"You know how it works," Sharkey said.

"It's a dogfight now," one of the other boys said.

"Okay," Sharkey said. "It wasn't a dogfight then."

The tall woman said, "What was it?"

Her tone was that of someone asking an aged veteran about a long-ago war, of antiquated weapons and maneuvers, former days, and again Sharkey understood that they saw him as an old man.

"There weren't many of us," he said. "But it's always a dogfight in the lineup, you know that. And there were plenty of locals — it's their territory. Remember, the Hawaiians killed their first tourist."

Someone whistled.

"Captain Cook," Sharkey said.

They were slow to respond; they leaned back and opened their mouths wider, as if to listen more clearly. Sharkey realized that only a few of them

— the tall woman and perhaps one other — knew who he was, and so when he spoke it was in a protesting tone.

"If you're in the lineup, be respectful — take the wave that nobody wants, the one with no exit, that breaks in front of the reef. Be willing to fall. On the Pipe, the hardest part is making the drop, because it's so steep. And you might just get dumped on the reef. Or worse."

One of the boys at the back asked, "What's worse?"

"Underwater tunnels. Those caves. I've been put in a cave."

Even the boy wearing the piled garlands of flowers was listening now, but Sharkey could tell from the attentiveness of the others that they were spectators and not hard-core surfers, and probably saw a guy talking because he was half drunk and old, and old people never listened.

"And there's the hold-down."

"The two-wave hold-down," someone said.

"The three-wave hold-down," Sharkey said, protesting again, asserting himself. "Three bombs hitting you. Under the wave at Waimea."

"That's suffocation," the boy said, speaking through the thickness of lei blossoms.

"But you keep climbing up your leash," Sharkey said. "Up the heavy evil wave."

The tattooed young woman said, "You still surf the Pipe?"

"I choose my days."

"How about the Eddie?" one of the boys said. "You compete in the Eddie?"

"I surfed with Eddie Aikau," Sharkey said. "I knew Eddie Aikau. Yes, I surfed in the Eddie. I surfed with Eddie's brother, Clyde. I can still handle big waves — know why? Because it's straight ahead, less stress on my joints. No kick-outs. Economy of movement."

Why am I lecturing them? he asked himself. *Am I trying to impress them?* He smiled, pitying himself, finding himself laughable.

"Waimea's awesome," the young woman said.

Except for the winner and his garlands, they had to be tourists and first-timers, though Sharkey could not tell whether they were dazzled by what he said; if not, he was making a fool of himself with all his talk.

Aware that he was boasting — and why was he boasting to these youths? — he said, "Phantoms, off V-Land, is gnarly. Jaws is even bigger. So's Mavericks. And there's the Cortes Bank, off San Diego. That's killer."

Speaking again through his flowers, the garlanded boy said, "You surfed Cortes?"

"You've been everywhere," a toothy boy said, looking hungry and a little surprised. He didn't know Sharkey either.

"In your day," someone started to say.

"My day," he said, and shook his head.

I'm old—I'm ancient to them, Sharkey thought, not hearing the rest of what was being said. *I'm craggy, I'm gray, and they think I'm past it.* And it was true—he was lean, and sinewy rather than thick-muscled. He was deeply lined and leathery from decades of sun, with bright lizard eyes and a lizard face and long skinny hands, and many of his tattoos were sun-faded and others indistinguishable from bruises. *I am unknown to most of them. I am the past.*

"My day is every day—today and tomorrow," he said. "I've been there" —and he pointed at the TV screen, which was showing a man on a big wave in Portugal. "Nazaré. Used to be unridable. It's a gangbang now. Try Chile —the wave they call El Gringo. That's a wave. Try El Quemao—more dangerous than most—not just huge but it breaks on a dry rocky reef."

A traveler's tales, boasts about destinations like playing cards, snapped down in a game of trumps.

"In Portugal?"

"Lanzarote, Canary Islands. I smashed a helmet in half there," Sharkey said. "Shippies—Shipstern Bluff, Tasmania. A slabbing wave, a mutant. It creates steps. I air-dropped off the steps."

You don't know me, he wanted to shout. *I'm not old!*

They stared at him as though looking at a stranger, staring at a corpse, implying with their eyes the idle notion "You won't be here much longer."

One of them turned aside and said, "He reminds me of that guy a long time ago who ate mushrooms and then surfed Waimea at midnight."

Briefly he hated them. Then he laughed and murmured, *They don't matter!*

He thought with wonderment, *I'm old.* When did it happen? It wasn't sudden—no illness, no failure; it had stolen upon him. *It could have been while I was surfing, going for smaller waves, becoming breathless and needing to rest as I paddled out. Or maybe on the days I stayed home, making myself busy, unaware of time passing, and then it was sunset and too dark to go anywhere except to bed. I hadn't really noticed except for the ache in my knees some days. And growing old is also becoming a stranger, with a different and unrecognizable face, withering to insignificance, ceasing to matter. Nothing more will happen to me. So soon, so soon—and how sad to know that I will only get older.*

Naked, shaving with his electric razor, buzzing it over his cheeks, he padded to the front room and threw the sliders apart, letting the day into the house, the air like silk slipping across his shoulders. He returned to the bathroom, brushed his teeth, spat out the suds, and walked to the kitchen. He swung a kettle of water onto the stove to boil, then found a pineapple and slashed at its sides, revealing its pulpous yellow, and carved slabs of its flesh and chunked them on a chopping board. He put a pinch of Dragon Well tea into a pot and filled it with the kettle of hot water. Last, the pineapple chunks in a bowl. And the tea and the bowl he took to the lanai, to sit and study the day. He was barefoot, he was content.

The ghost of a wind barely fluttered the leaves on the pak lan tree as he listened to the surf report: "... head-high sets in the morning, rising to twelve- to fifteen-foot faces in the afternoon, with a high-surf advisory expected for north- and west-facing shores. Light winds today and tomorrow. A storm in the central Pacific heading our way will deliver brisk and breezy conditions over the weekend."

Hearing the radio voice, the geese squawked again, and when Sharkey had finished his fruit and drunk his tea, he took a bowl of pellets downstairs to the sloping lawn — the five geese following — and scattered it slowly, watching the big birds contend. The biggest gander he fed holding pellets in his cupped hand, and the eager bird coming close stepped on his foot, raking his instep with its fangy claws and leaving a deep scratch and a mudstain. As Sharkey nudged him away, the peacock emerged from the frangipani grove, and the two black Muscovy ducks sidled toward the scattered feed, pecking cautiously. Mourning doves settled and strutted, looking for a chance to seize some grains, and the chatter of all the birds brought a pair of small scrawny chickens — jungle fowl — from behind a clump of dusty blue bamboo.

He watched until all the food was pecked away and the geese had gone through their particular sequence: having finished their pellets, they headed down the lawn and began tearing at the short grass with their beaks, as though moving on to the next course. It seemed the pellets made them hungry for grass, and then they'd all take turns drinking at the basin. They too had a routine.

No soft descriptive words came to him, but the fond feeling did, that he had found a place he loved; that he was so happy living on this island he could die here — such a life taught you how to die. The mood of satisfaction in his mind was a summation: *I don't want more than this.* He knew he had everything he wished for; he was too superstitious to say so, for fear it would seem like smug boasting and what he had would vanish.

And that thought was underscored by a shama thrush, its warbling so melodious it held him still until he could see the bird itself flash from a branch to the ground, where it found an insect the geese had raised, jubilantly beating their wings. One peck and the thrush was back on its branch, its long tail twitching, warbling again.

All this time — rested, resolved into a calm, restored body — he was smiling at the warmth of the day, the beauty of the night-dampened trees, the glitter in the blaze of sunrise. He was whole again. Feeding the birds on the lawn put him in mind of the chickens in the coop. He dug a bucket of pellets from the grain barrel on the lanai and walked down the hill to the grove of trees, where a screened-in coop — once a work shed — held a dozen hens. They fluttered and screeched when he entered. He filled the feeder with pellets and found six eggs in a nesting box, small smooth ones, off-white, and delicate, like lumps of carved ivory.

Heading uphill across the lawn to his house he saw a new hibiscus blossom on the bush by the path, the knob of a tree fern swelling to unfurl into a frond, the pencil-shaped culm of a bamboo shoot protruding from the edge of a clump, the new spear of a palm slanted from the top of a trunk, a yellowish curled leaf of a monstera in the midst of elephant ears of the thick vine, gardenias blown open on a bush, and more, to the sigh of the ironwood boughs at the periphery of his lawn.

He had planted everything but the ironwoods, he had watched it all grow bigger by the week. He was no gardener, you didn't have to be here, a broomstick jammed into Hawaiian soil would become a tree and bear fruit. His plants and shrubs had taken hold and bulked on the hillside, and he marveled at his luck.

It all looked edible, and much of it was — the thick bamboo shoots, the blossoms and leaves of the nasturtiums, the golf-ball-sized lilikoi, yellow-skinned red-fleshed passionfruit that he pinched open and ate or Olive juiced. And the sweet finger bananas that grew by the walkway, the mountain apple tree with its ripe fruit of pale crispness, the Java plum tree, the heavy avocados, each one swinging on a stem.

He lived in a garden, enclosed by fruit trees. He drank his second cup of tea, gloating on the pleasure of it all, the trees growing more fragrant as the sun warmed them, his birds contented and fed, no longer squawking for food but strutting on the grass, and some of the geese resting, their heads tucked under their wings.

The drawn-out boom of the waves at Waimea a mile down the hill, the muffled rumble, then the collapse, like crockery shattering, the sigh and retreat of the heavy water, was a continuous rehearsal of slow bursts. It was as though the ocean were being filled somewhere far-off and the big bulky ripples of its filling were slamming the edges of the shore, rising higher, brimming against the beach, the sea like an enormous swilling pot, the fury somewhere over the horizon pushing its disturbance to its rim.

Light offshore winds would mean almost glassy conditions, wave faces burnished to velvet.

Sharkey sat in silence. The silence was composed of the racket of mynah birds, the cheeping of green sparrows, the chitter of finches, the dry rustle of the palms, the clatter of their fronds, the distant sound of the surf — now a chug-chugging, now a suck-squeeze and a drenching crash, a vast sieving of ocean, a bolster of water butting against sand and rock, growing louder, beckoning with a loosening boom.

He'd woken with the assurance that the whole day belonged to him. Olive was at work: her absence helped. There was never any question of his doing anything he didn't want to do. He told himself that he'd earned this solitary splendor: he'd worked, he'd sat unwillingly at his laptop and tried to please his sponsors; but now all that was over.

It was not a question of retirement — apart from a few years lifeguarding, he'd never had a real job, and so there was nothing to retire from. The life he was leading was the life he had always led. To those who said, "You've got all the answers," he smiled, and when they added, "You're selfish and spoiled," he replied, "It's called being happy."

"Here's the secret," he said. "I don't want more than I have — therefore I have everything. It's the economy of enough."

He was content; he'd found the best place to live — a little farm on the North Shore of this island; and the best way to spend his days — surfing. When the surf was up, as on this sunny day in January, he knew he'd spend the whole morning catching waves, and after lunch, and maybe a nap, more waves.

"You're such a wanker, you never think of anyone but yourself," Olive said after a week with him. It was not an accusation but statement of fact, marveling one night as he speared the last slice of mango from the bowl that sat between them.

"Yes, I have to, because no one thinks of me," he said. "It's a mistake to think that anyone cares, or gives a shit about your welfare. People think only of themselves. You have to do the same."

Olive had a what-about-me? frown on her face, but exaggerated and self-mocking.

She said, "That party where I first met you, I saw a stonking big geezer get down on his knees when he saw you. That got my attention."

"So you noticed he was old."

"Yes, but he truly respected you as a surfer. And so did that popsy he was with."

He had known English Olive for a month. You meet a new person and become lovers and, talking in bed, you become someone special again, interesting in your vividness, as your life is reviewed, and all your stories are fresh and indisputable. Olive still did not know him, but there was time.

"Big-wave surfing at night, by moonlight. The magic mushroom story. Surfing from Maui to Molokai in a storm. The exotic travel — all the hype," he said. "Too bad they don't know the truth."

"They'd be disappointed?"

He shook his head. "No. The truth is better — what really happened is messier but matters more."

"They wish they had your confidence."

"You have confidence. You came here alone — you got a job at the hospital. You did it all yourself. You're *akamai*."

"Pardon?"

"Super-smart," he said. "We have the word here, but we don't have much of the real thing."

Her *akamai* story had impressed him as proof of her power and conviction. She had come to Hawaii from London with her boyfriend, Rupert, for a visit, just ten days in Waikiki. He'd stayed in town and she'd taken the bus to Hale'iwa, had lunch — an avocado-topped mahi burger and lemonade, sitting in sunshine — then boarded another bus, intending to travel around the island. But approaching Waimea Bay, looking down from the bus, she was dazzled by her first sight of the waves, wide and glittering, walled by cliffs of lava rocks; the green valley behind it lush, like the gateway to Eden. Getting off the bus, she stepped into air perfumed by blossoms and walked to the beach, where she sat on the slope of sand under a pale blue heat-bleached sky, sadly watching the waves breaking, the waves seeming to speak a language she believed she could learn — almost tearful, because she knew she'd be leaving in a few days.

From the bus window on the way back to Waikiki, she saw a bumper sticker on a beatup car: NO BAD DAYS. She kept the memory from Rupert. The flight to Heathrow via Los Angeles took eighteen hours. They arrived before dawn, the taxi rattling through greasy streets, heavily dressed people jostling at bus stops to keep warm, frowning like bewildered refugees, resigned to rain, the black solidities of London house fronts, the mute unwelcoming English look. Rupert groaned, saying he had a meeting at the bank later that morning. "And the hospital awaits you, petal."

On their arriving home after a holiday, Rupert always told the same joke: "Wipe that smile off your face, Ollie. We're back in England." He said it that morning and looked at her. "Bloody hell, you're still smiling."

Later, she told Sharkey she had been thinking, *I want to live on the island of no bad days.*

She did not tell Rupert she'd come to a decision. She knew he'd oppose her. Within a month she'd resigned from St. Thomas' Hospital and was back in Hawaii, applying for a job at Kahuku Medical Center and living near Rocky Point, alone.

Sharkey finished his cup of green tea, and the recollection of the talk with Olive made him smile, because it suggested that he'd had fame, and that his fame would grow, and that something would come of it. But he knew that was not so. All this time he dabbed at his foot, where the goose had clawed him. He glanced at his hand, and seeing that he had blood on his fingers, he licked it off. The wound wasn't serious — just a claw mark.

Olive had left a note for him on the counter, one word in her neat nurse's hand, all caps — WANKER.

It was a love note, her perverse way of complimenting him, an English thing, teasing the one you love most.

He was content. He was now convinced that the beauty of his life was a certainty that nothing more, nothing greater, would happen to him; that, at peace, he asked for nothing; that he was only on another wave, sliding, climbing, paddling up its back, hovering at its lip, tipping and then racing through the tube — a man surfing, moving in an easy crouch through turbulence, all the time reading its features and its froth, anticipating its alteration, keeping a fraction ahead of his roll, just a man on a board, flying across the swelling slope of heavy water.

2

Epic Surf

His dreams prepared him for the day, nothing in his mind was accidental; the wave that rose in his sleep broke on his waking and swept him into the morning.

He was already in his shorts, and the day was so warm he didn't bother putting on a T-shirt. His board was strapped to the roof rack from yesterday. He drove down the hill to Three Tables Beach, and parked, and waxed his board. He studied the sets rising outside the break they called Rubber Duckies, the way they lifted and rolled in, staying whole and smooth-faced until they smashed against the wall of lava rock at the shore and cascaded down its fissures.

That rock wall, with its spikes of eroded and pitted boulders, was the reason most surfers avoided this spot. There was no beach, no sand, nowhere to crawl ashore. In places it had the look of a shattered Gothic steeple, carved to sharpness among broken gargoyles and stone ornaments. Surfing on the Côte Basque, Sharkey had seen such gray steeples in Brittany, and there the beaches were rocky too, looking tumbled with old cathedral stone. Linger a fraction too long here at Rubber Duckies, or wipe out at the end of a ride, and you were dashed against the spikes of bulking lava. He had seen surfers lacerated on the stones, their arms and faces torn and bloody from a badly timed run and a face-plant. He always surfed alone, and the danger, the knowledge that mainly kooks surfed here, assured him of solitude.

But he saw two surfers seated on their boards on a swell. He paddled out, duck-diving beneath incoming white waves, tucking the nose of his board down, and joined them in the lineup. He greeted them as he sat, legs dangling in the water, rising on the incoming swell like a man on a horse.

"How's it?"

They nodded and he took them to be newcomers, mainlanders, or per-haps foreigners.

"Were you out yesterday?" he asked. "It was okay. But it's coming up."

One said, "First time," with an accent, probably Brazilian.

They had no idea who he was, and he smiled, enjoying the novelty of their not knowing him, of his bobbing on the wave with them as a stranger.

And so instead of taking the next good wave he hung back and swayed on the swell, letting it lift him, so that he could watch the other two paddle into the wave and surf it. One of them missed it; the second tipped himself into the face and caught a ride, surfing it almost to the rocks. And when the man lost his balance at the end and a wave behind him slapped his back, he snatched at his board and saved himself by swimming hard away from the pitted lava rock, blackened from the seawater streaming across its serrations.

Straddling his board, rising and falling, riding the swell like a horseman in the sea, majestic on his steed, soothed Sharkey almost as much as catching a wave. He sat watching the other two surfers until, as he guessed would hap-pen, the bigger of the two misjudged the distance and dismounted too late and wound up struggling in the foaming rock pools beneath the black cliffs.

The second surfer dithered and called out to his friend, whose board had dinged the rock, snapping off its fin. Then both were foundering, slapping the incoming waves, kicking themselves away from the cliffs, until they managed to edge toward the beach about sixty feet away and the more for-giving sand. One man was injured, the other one helping him out of the water, the boards tumbling after them. They sat on the dazzling sand above the tidemark and conferred, and then climbed higher up the beach, the first man limping.

They'll be fine, Sharkey thought, glad to see them go. *And if they're scared they'll never come back.*

With the surf to himself, Sharkey sat on his board and waited for a wave, and when he saw one rising behind him he lifted his board into the froth, paddling like mad, and leaped onto the board and stood and braced, his arms out, and rode it, twisting beneath the overhang, then cutting back to ride the whole smooth sculpted hollow of the wave's face, spanking the glissade with his board. The wave was his, the whole cove too; the others wouldn't return. Someone should have told them to be careful here — there was no beach for the waves to break upon, only the scabbed edges of the low cliffs and the black fangs and sharp talons of the eroded lava rock.

Paddling back to where the waves were rising from the incoming swell, he remembered another story attributed to him, how he'd kept paddling one day until he'd found himself five miles offshore, among the late whales of April, and drifted with the cows and the calves on the southwesterly rip current, the Waimea Express, all the way to Kaena Point, and come ashore where the albatrosses nested.

"Is it true?" people had once asked.

"Just a story," he said. They weren't convinced, yet no one had asked lately.

Anyone who did not surf had no idea how even the most basic maneuver took such strength and balance; how for long periods in a pounding shore break he was still driven by anxiety; how so many of his good friends had died — drowned in a hold-down, got hit by their board and knocked unconscious, got caught by their snagged leash. But it all looked so simple from shore, people invented improbable feats and heroics. They did not understand that simply to ride a big wave was a miracle of poise and strength.

In his dreams he was always on an empty wave like this. With the waves to himself, he surfed for the next two hours in the sunshine, and on a whim, for a better view of the green cliffs, he paddled out for almost a mile, near where whales filled the ocean's surface with the misty plumes from their blowholes. He looked back to the island and gloried in the sight of the steep green *pali,* a vertical drop that was a wall of tangled trees and black rock. There was too much of it to be visible close up — you needed to be offshore to take in the whole panorama of spires. He was the only surfer out today at this break, the sole owner of this view.

After ten good rides he took one more, carving a turn toward the sandy beach down the shore at Three Tables, where the injured surfer had lain, where his friend had helped him away. Sharkey dropped to his board and paddled to the low waves flopping against the sand. He sat and looked at the sea until fatigue overtook him, a great heaviness penetrating his body, and he stretched out, using his board to pillow his head, and he slept with the sun on his face, his back on the hot sand.

Flattened against the beach, in that posture of floating face-up, he slept, buoyed by the sun heating his body, levitated again in slumber. He was cooked in dazzling light. When he woke, sand adhering to the sweat on the side of his face, he yawned, as two young surfers strode past, their boards under their arms.

"How's it?"

They acknowledged him with grunts but no more than that, and for the second time that day he thought, *They don't know me* — had no idea that the lanky figure stretched out on the beach, propped on one elbow, was the big-wave surfer Joe Sharkey. He smiled at the notion of his anonymity, the novelty of it, the restfulness it offered him. It gave his day the order he wanted, without interruption.

He carried his board to the car and strapped it to the rack, then walked up the road to the supermarket, bought a sandwich and coffee at the deli counter, and returned to the beach and sat cross-legged for lunch. A month before he'd seen a monk seal wriggle ashore just here and hump itself up the steepness of the beach, away from the waves. The doggy thing had folded its flippers against itself and slept for three hours. He'd watched it the whole time, in a mood of protection, and it was a reminder of his animal sleep in his animal life.

With that thought he looked up, hoping for a whale, but the pod he'd seen earlier, spouting plumes of mist, had swum southwest, out of sight in the direction of Kaena Point. Backlit by the afternoon sun, the point was a dark headland, afloat in the gleaming sea.

Satisfied with food, warmed by coffee, bathed in sunshine, he snoozed again, sweating and seal-like, and when he was rested he got his goggles from the car and swam out beyond the rocks, upraised on sea foam like tabletops, that gave the beach its name. He drifted awhile among schools of darting fish until he saw, just below the surface, a green sea turtle nibbling at the moss that clung to the pitted rocks.

The turtle was not alarmed, though its side eye widened on the flat of its head when Sharkey approached. It set its hooked parrot beak against the rocks, nagging at the weedy growth, and it rose and drifted with the incoming swell. Sharkey saw how its flippers were positioned like wings, which it slowly beat in the luminous water, and doing so it seemed to soar without effort, a slimy green manhole cover tipping itself weightlessly out to sea.

That's how I fly in my dreams, Sharkey realized, seeing the turtle lift itself away from the spiked shelves of black rock and move its flippers slowly, angling itself, not a manhole cover anymore but big and buoyant, rising like a fat beaky bird with four wings.

The swell had increased; the waves were much higher than they'd been in the morning — one pushed Sharkey so near the rocky reef that he had to fight to avoid being tumbled against it. So he dived into the swell and swam out, but as he did his foot struck the sharp face of the reef, and he knew from the sting of saltwater that he'd slashed his toe.

Positioning himself at the widest opening, he body-surfed through the slot between the rocks on a rolling wave and made it to the beach in one ride. There he sat, clutching his toe, until the blood stopped flowing through his fingers. And he laughed, seeing that the cut was near the wound the goose claw had made.

No one was surfing the toppling white crests at Rubber Duckies now, no one was swimming; the waves were twice the size they'd been earlier in the day — the surf forecast he'd heard in the morning was proving accurate. Fifteen-foot faces here meant higher waves at Waimea, just around the point of land in the next bay.

Rather than drive to the parking lot, which was probably full of tourists' cars anyway, Sharkey unstrapped his board from his roof rack and carried it along the road to the path beside the guardrail that led to Waimea Beach. His toe ached from the cut he gotten on the rock, but he mocked himself — a sore toe! — and was soon distracted by the boom of the breaking surf before he saw the great sliding rollers swallowing the surfers, who looked tiny in the blue slopes of the waves.

Flattened on his board, sledding down the steepness of the wave-washed sand, he entered the water paddling, using the riptide at the right-hand side of the bay to help him into the huge incoming swell and the density of foam. He ducked under three large waves and, still paddling, got himself beyond the break, where five other surfers in the lineup were riding their boards.

Perhaps one of them spoke to him, but if so Sharkey didn't hear it. The waves collapsing on the inside rocks at Pinballs drowned out all other sounds, and anyway the other surfers were too anxious and watchful to take their eyes away from the blue bulge of the swell and the sets, now rising to what was known in Waimea as epic, or nearly so, dangerous to anyone except the most experienced big-wave surfer. But even experts drowned here, toppled and pinned to the bottom by a succession of crashing waves. If this swell kept rising they'd certainly hold the Eddie contest — when the faces of the sets had to be sustained at thirty feet and above, and even better if they were forty.

Those young surfers he had met at the party last night — were any of them in the lineup now? He scanned the faces of the surfers near him, and as he did two of them pushed off and were engulfed, tumbled, fighting to balance. Another wave in the set rose behind him, and beyond it, as he adjusted, a likelier wave. A surfer ahead of him slipped sideways, out of sight, like a naked man tumbling from a building, and Sharkey propelled himself into the wave lifting his board, and when the nose of his board protruded into its lip, he jumped and squared his feet for balance and crouched and rode it, skidding slantwise on the curling face, into the moving trough.

His wave was wicked froth spilling over him as it barreled, and he angled his board to right across its face, the dark water below him ripping like a muscle of blue. Then he was streaking down a steep hillside that was carrying him forward and fast in a precipitous skid. It took all the strength he had in his legs to stay upright and to keep the board jammed against the moving slope of gleaming water, and just as he thought he was free of it, a shadow fell over him, the peak of the wave toppling him into a swallowing barrel and speeding him sideways. He shot through it, enclosed by a glittering narrowing cone. He rode it until it swelled and subsided under him, and he was released as the wave broke utterly and flattened and washed and pooled against a wave draining down the beach, allowing Sharkey to float almost to shore. He dropped off his board and pushed it onward to avoid a wave now breaking behind him and threatening to swamp him.

Out of the surf zone, he fell to his knees. All his strength was gone in the effort and exhilaration of that one great ride. He carried his board up a dry sand mound on the beach and gasped with delight. He was exhausted and knew that a good part of that fatigue was the result of anxiety when, in the middle of his ride, he had felt the ache in his lacerated toe and feared that adjusting his feet for the pain would put him a fraction off-balance and send him off his board. He would be buried. High, dense, and unforgiving, it was the sort of wave that would push him down, and the waves behind it would keep him down. The thought of it, together with his unexpected fatigue, kneeling alone on the beach, his lungs burning, made him briefly tearful.

As a younger man he might have gone out again, but this ride was enough. And he saw that the risk he'd taken was real — the slice in his toe had opened and had begun to bleed again, probably from the effort of holding the board down against the force of the wave. That injured toe and clawed foot might have been his undoing.

He had proven himself and felt reprieved, and now the daylight was fading, the last of the sun snagged in low clouds floating on the horizon, beyond Kaena Point, the early sunset of winter, hardly six, when the sun sank and glowed in a green flash in the sea.

Going home, he passed an improvised sign, FRESH FISH, and pulled onto the grassy shoulder of the road, where a man was sitting on the flap of his pick-truck, kicking his feet, a plastic cooler next to him.

"What have you got?"

"Got plenny ahi," the man said, lifting the lid of the cooler. "I catch 'em myself today morning."

"Looks nice."

"Is primo. Good for sashimi. Look — big, da fish."

The fish slashed into thick bleeding slabs was as red as beef.

"Give me five bucks' worth."

Wrapping two steaks in a square of white paper and folding it into a parcel, the man salivated, as people do when handling fresh meat, and handed it to Sharkey. Accepting the money, he said, "Is so *ono*," and touched his lips to indicate its savor.

Then Sharkey was home, on his lanai, drinking a beer as the last of the light slipped from the sky. The cloud was pulled apart and smokelike, appropriate to the fiery glow beneath it, and soon there were more flames, blazing to pure gold, and at last a quenching of pale pink and fading blue, the light cooling over the horizontal seam of sea and sky.

He sat, listening to the occasional grunts of the geese. The chickens had taken to the trees to roost for the night. Before he finished his beer he saw the headlights of Olive's car reflected on the stands of bamboo, and he rose to greet her, but when he did he felt a stab of pain in his wounded toe, and he favored it, limping slightly as he approached her.

"Darling," he said.

"You had a good day?"

"My mother used to say that to me."

"What's wrong with your foot?"

"Dinged it on a rock. Goose clawed it too. How was your day?"

"Busy." And she knelt to examine his toe. "Ouch. That's a deep cut. I'll bandage it."

"Later."

"We had a surfer with a gash on his leg."

"Might have been a guy I saw at Rubber Duckies. A *malihini*. Small world."

"Brazilian. It was slashed to the bone."

"A lesson," Sharkey said. "Want a beer?"

"No. I'm shattered. I've been tired all day. Was that you this morning, you beastly little man, having your way with me?"

"That's me — the incubus."

Olive yawned, saying, "I'm hungry, though."

"I have eggs — got them this morning. And I bought some ahi along the road from a guy. There's salad too. I'll make it."

"Okay — let's have a shower."

They took a shower together, soaping each other, and after they'd dried themselves, Olive sat with her whining hair dryer and brush while Sharkey peppered the ahi and seared it, then sliced it thin and arranged it on the salad. He heated the smaller frying pan, cracked the eggs into a bowl and beat salt and pepper into them, and poured the mixture into the pan, scraped lightly at it and grated cheese on it, then folded it and divided it in half. Olive had put the mats on the table, and he joined her with the two plates.

They ate quietly, and when they finished they sat without speaking, and as though to explain her silence, Olive said, "I'm so fagged."

"The gate's open," Sharkey said. "I'll get it."

Walking in the darkness on the loose stones of his driveway, he felt the ache in his toe sharpen with such suddenness he stumbled slightly from the pain and wondered if he'd stubbed it.

He closed the gate and, limping back to the house, saw Olive watching from the lanai.

"I think I stepped on something."

Olive shone a small flashlight on it. "You're really unlucky. Two punctures, near your cut. I told you to let me bandage it. That's a ghastly centipede sting. Poor toe."

"Poor me." But it was only his toe, and he was someone who had known broken bones and slashes from crown-of-thorns starfish, and stinging stonefish and razor coral. And he smiled, thinking it was the toe the goose had stepped on and clawed, the one he'd cut on the lava rock, and now the centipede.

"Poor you." Olive hugged him.

"I'm happy," he said. "Nothing hurts if you're happy."

They went to bed. Olive was asleep almost immediately. Sharkey lay awake, slowly subsiding as he reflected on the day. It had been a good day, waking from a dream of flying and making love. The contented geese, surfing at Rubber Duckies, swimming at Three Tables. He'd seen whales and had an inkling of their long eerie calls from underwater. He'd spotted a green sea turtle. He'd surfed a monster wave at Waimea. He'd bought and seared an ahi steak. He'd drunk a beer by the light of a dazzling sunset. His toe ached slightly still — perhaps more than slightly — but that pain was a reminder that he was fully alive.

A perfect day. He'd spent many days like this. He hoped for more.

3

The Great Pacific Garbage Patch

Early evening in the dusty exhausted light on the North Shore, the purply-pink sunset puddling at the far end of the ocean, and then the green flash, the gulp of the sun as it winked beneath the water. Sharkey turned from this splendor to watch the twitch of the waitress's shorts. He stood to see more, then self-consciously looked away, and just beyond the window a white-faced owl was spooked from a monkey pod tree to flap into blackness. As a mass of flies found his sweaty head, he batted at them with his free hand. And Olive was on the line.

"Liv," he said, the phone clapped to his ear.

The waitress's tight-fitting shorts were white frilly knickers, her T-shirt was artfully torn, a disk tattooed on the nape of her neck beneath her swinging ponytail, a spidery tattoo wrapped around her ankle.

"That was the second transfusion we did today," Olive was saying. "I was in triage . . ."

He looked away from the waitress and said, "Sounds like you had a big day," hoping to take up the slack.

And now he turned to look at the froth accumulating at the edge of the beach; but it wasn't froth, it was flotsam, junk, plastic bags pulsing just beneath the surface like the odd beanies of blobby jellyfish, and a condom like a sea creature, and he was disgusted and angry, thinking, *Everything that is wrong with the earth has a human origin — they are the problem, befouling the planet.* The trash was a reproach to him for leering at the waitress.

"So I'm running late. I'm in my car. I won't be much longer."

"You know where I am. Aloha." And, clicking off his phone, he gave his full attention to the waitress. He loved her lips, he loved her feet, she was

small and solid, had dimpled knees and tousled hair that had worked loose
from the clip that held her ponytail. She had everything. Most of all she had
youth.

"Can I get you a drink?"

"A beer, please."

She drew her whole face into a puckered grin, like a child's awkwardness
before an adult.

"I know who you are."

He said, "I'd like to know who you are."

"I'm nobody."

"You're a surfer," he said, and — hesitating, laughing like a bashful boy
— reached, squeezing the hard meat on her well-developed shoulder.

"Yeah, but I'm a surf bunny. It was too big today for me."

He said, "I was out. Pipeline was cranking."

She laughed, full-throated, appreciatively. "My boyfriend thinks you're
awesome. His father thinks so too. He says he used to see you in the lineup
when he was a kid."

And that was that — the boyfriend, the admiring old man — she could not
have put him in his place more neatly, without any effort. *I'm a bystander,*
he thought. *Everyone is spoken for, or too young. I should be glad with what I
have, which is a whole life, yet the animal in me is always hungry.*

"Want a glass?" she said when she came back with the beer, the bottle on
a tray.

"I think beer tastes better in a glass," he said. "You need to get your olfac-
tories going, dip your nose in it — you know, smell it."

"Old factories, I guess so," she said, suddenly flustered, and he was reminded that he should not be so glib. She was sweet, in the island way. He
knew the stare of incomprehension, as though he'd lapsed into another language or was mocking her.

Olive slid past the waitress as she was bringing the glass, saying, "Here
you are," and claimed him by kissing him hard, saying to the waitress,
"White wine."

"And one more of these," he said, pouring the last of the bottle and handing it back to her.

"They told me you were out here," Olive said.

"They're so young," he said, seeing the waitress now head inside to the
bar for the wine. "Here's a story. A reasonably attractive young woman is
sort of lost. She's a surfer, better than average but not a headliner. She gets
dumped by her boyfriend. Bummer. And then instead of a new Brazilian
bathing suit she buys herself a thirty-dollar pair of frilly knickers and puts

them on her smiling ass, and men clamor to talk to her. She meets an older man, with money. Just this change of clothes, this one thing, and her whole life is transformed."

"In England it wouldn't happen that way. Some posh bloke might be tempted, but as soon as she opened her mouth she'd be slagged off as an oik."

"An oik," he said.

"A scrubber."

He faintly understood. He said, "An American would pounce."

"Because Yanks are randy little monkeys," Olive said. "Most men are."

"But you like me — and we're so different."

"Yes. Utterly." She leaned at him; she said, "I like friction."

"That's the good news," he said. He pushed at the half-rolled blind of split bamboo. "They call these chicks in Singapore — these shades."

"I forget you've been everywhere."

"I had to, or I would never have found this place. And now that I'm cured of travel, I don't want to go anywhere."

"What about the surf in Indonesia? In South Africa? The eighty-foot waves in Portugal? What about Jimmy's, the break on Christmas Island? That you named after Captain Cook?"

They were new enough to each other that she deferred, and listened, and asked for more.

He sipped his beer. He said, "There's enough here, all the surf I need or want."

"There's Joe's."

Joe's, the left-breaking wave at Sunset, named by others for him. The waitress returned with Olive's glass of wine and another beer for Sharkey. He said, "And there's Joe's."

Surfing had turned him into a traveler; he had taken his board around the world, to the places Olive had named, and to Brazil and Tahiti and Cornwall too; to the break just beyond Hue on the midcoast of Vietnam, to San Sebastián, and to the harbor at Hanga Roa in Rapa Nui. He knew the world by its surf breaks, by its bands of surfers, a compulsive and secretive and single-minded tribe of barefoot, big-shouldered gypsies.

"Cheers," she said. But he was frowning. "What's wrong?"

"I was looking at that junk on the shore. There's junk at Joe's. There's junk everywhere."

"It's so gross."

"There's a whole mess of it in the mid-Pacific, an evil wheeling tangle of marine debris — rope, plastic, chemical sludge, a floating junk pile, getting bigger. Some of it gets loose and floats here." He pointed to a fragment of plastic bobbing in the water. "We're part of it. The great Pacific garbage patch."

He finished his beer and ordered another and became sullen, pouring this third beer, telling her how every crisis on earth, from pollution to overpopulation to poverty and ill health, could be ascribed to humans. He sipped and said, "We're the problem."

"Something cheery, please," Olive said. "I've had a long day in triage." Seeing the waitress, she called out, "Please bring me a beer." Then she said, "One cheeky bastard in the ward decided to flash his old job at me."

"What did you do?"

"Laughed," she said. "It would have been against hospital protocol to kick him in the goolies."

"No!" Sharkey said. "Disturbing!"

Just then the waitress handed Olive a bottle of beer and walked away laughing at Sharkey's horrified reaction.

Olive said, "Sometimes the sight of people laughing alarms me."

"Ever notice, rich people don't laugh a lot — it gives too much away," Sharkey said. "And it's sinister when they do. You know it's a form of boasting."

"The poor actually cackle and hoot. They have nothing to lose," Olive said. "You want to laugh with them."

"The word 'juices.'" Sharkey had finished his third beer and was signaling for another. "Juices can seem dreadful."

"Bodily fluids," Olive said.

"'Fluids' is worse," Sharkey said. He watched the waitress pour a bottle of beer into his glass and drank a third of it, staring at Olive, nodding as he swallowed.

"Are you saying you hate those words because deep down you're aroused by them?"

"Deep down they disgust me," he said with such sudden force that Olive drew back. "Litter. Graffiti. Stretch limos. Garbage in the ocean. Sewage spills." He put his glass down. "I think of them and I can't swallow."

"Steady on, Joe."

But he was gesturing and insistent, with a drunk's deafness. "Surfing in the Philippines that season I got horribly sick, I couldn't understand it. The waves were awesome. Heavy evil barrels, all ours," he said. "I was stoked, yet I got sicker."

"Right," she said, and looked closer. He never opened a book, but he always had a story that got her attention. He wooed her with his stories, like a traveler returned from a long journey, wishing to be a hero, seeking a listener.

He swallowed the last of his beer and took a glass pipe from his shirt pocket, mashed a pinch of weed into the bowl with his thumb. As he squirted a flame from his lighter he took a deep hit, throwing his head back and gulping.

"Then a local guy told me why no one else was there. We were surfing on an outflow from a sewage culvert!"

"There goes my appetite."

"I surfed Midway," he said. "It's just up there, end of the chain — three hours away. The waves aren't great, but it's amazing for bird life. Everywhere you look there's albatrosses nesting on the ground, thousands of them. And dead chicks. The mother albatross flies five hundred miles to scoop up a colorful scrap of plastic floating on the ocean. She flies back and jams it into the chick's throat."

"Crikey," Olive said softly, but Sharkey was still talking.

"All the problems on earth, the ones that threaten our existence, are caused by humans," he said, palming the pipe; and she was reminded of how a few drinks, or a hit, made him pompous.

"If they threaten our existence, then isn't that a good thing? Our extinction will solve the whole business."

"Not fast enough," he said, slurring his words. "Instead of eliminating litter and nuclear waste and dirty air and traffic, and all the rest . . ."

"Eliminate people."

"You got it," he said, and wiped his mouth with the back of his hand. "Lose them. Not a few. All."

"I must be in the wrong profession," Olive said. "Grafting away in a hospital. Making people healthy."

"You're easing their pain. That's noble. I'm thinking of something else."

"Zero growth."

"That's a start," he said. "Negative growth. Progressive depopulation."

"No one's having babies in Germany or Italy, or Russia, or Japan," she said.

"India's overflowing with them," he said, and still talking disgustedly he raised his empty glass, signaling to the waitress. "So's China, so's Africa. It has to stop. I like the idea of shrinking cities, cratered towns, empty villages — huge areas of hollowed-out houses and collapsed communities — thanks" — the waitress was filling his glass again — "grass growing where there were once streets, wolves roaming in the old broken neighborhoods," and he smiled and giggled a little as the waitress hurried away. "Frilly knickers."

"You're drunk." He was toasted, he was deaf and doll-like, sure of everything, precise in his movements, meaninglessly cautious.

Instead of replying, Sharkey sat back and stared at the ocean. The surface had gone black but it was dimly visible and rutted; the southerly breeze created low furrows that caught the edge of moonlight, the flop of the shore break, the distant sea like wrinkled tinfoil, all of it distressed.

"My father was in 'Nam," he said. "He's in a chopper, heading to Khe Sanh, his first week in the war. A young soldier is strapped next to him, and he sees he's scared, and my father says, 'I'm going to give you some advice, kid.'" Sharkey paused and Olive became attentive. "'When you get to the firebase, consider yourself already dead. With that in mind, you'll be fine.'" Sharkey filled his pipe again and spurted a flame into it.

Olive closed her eyes and intoned, "Consider yourself already dead, and you'll be fine."

"Hunter Thompson loved that."

"You knew him?" Olive said eagerly.

Sharkey jerked his thumb as a yes and said, "He was such a drunk, such a stoner. Always stayed in a luxury suite, either in Waikiki or at the Kahala, half-eaten meals all over the place, bottles of brandy and his stash of *pakalolo* nearby. Coke in his shirt pocket in a twist of paper, usually the same shirt. He didn't know squat about surfing, yet he had an instinct for risk. He loved seeing big strong men compete, especially in sunshine — marathoners, football players, surfers. And he was dazzled by the availability of drugs here, though he misunderstood the culture. He made it into mumbo-jumbo and cannibalism. Hawaiians battling each other and cursing. His idea of sport."

The trill of tickled strings of a ukulele drifted past them from inside the bar, and in the nearer distance the wavelets shimmied in the pale moonlight, mimicking its rhythm, or so it seemed to Sharkey, his heavy head saturated with smoke.

Olive said, "The *Lono* book."

"Hunter used to tell me that he envied me," he said. "His alias was a kind of compliment. Whenever he checked into a hotel, no matter where in the world, he gave his name as Mr. Joe. He made a point of telling me that. He was a great guy, a kind of tragic figure — timid, for all his partying. He liked hanging out with me. Imagine — and he wrote about ten books. I haven't even read five books. He told me once, 'Surfing a big wave is like writing a book and just as intellectually demanding. Joe, I'm a surfer!' I didn't know whether to agree or not. But I did say to him, 'It's all in the head.' He shot himself because he thought he was falling apart physically. Because the world had gone rotten."

He was nodding again, remembering, and he had kicked off his sandal and begun to massage his foot. "Wrecking the planet. The things I've seen. Damming rivers. Dynamiting fish. Oil spills. How much do you really care?"

"When I'm at the beach," Olive said, "and I see a plastic bag or some bits and bobs of rubbish, I always pick them up. The small things we do can save us."

"Have another drink."

"That's my limit. That's your limit." She wagged her finger. "Brain damage."

"I'm not drunk," he said, clutching his foot.

Seeing he was agitated, she took his hand and said, "You're the luckiest man in the world. You've been everywhere. You've made money doing what you love. You still get a shit-ton of wonga from residuals on endorsements. You have your mother's trust fund and a massive house. And you have me. Why on earth are you rabbiting on about death and destruction?"

"Too many people," he said. "People are the problem."

"What's wrong with your foot?"

"Nothing."

"You keep rubbing it."

"That bite," he said. "It's itchy, like an old beesting." He scratched it again. "Actually sort of pleasant to dig at it," and he kicked off his sandal and raised his foot. "And that other thing — the cut."

Holding his foot firmly, she used her thumbs to examine his big toe. His foot was long and brown, his twisted toes curled like a flipper.

"Two claws — or fangs — that's a centipede signature," Olive said, and chafed one thumb against the reddened bumps. "Papular urticaria — these are the papules. An allergic reaction to the bite."

"Thanks, doc. It feels better already."

Olive was peering closely. "Envenomation. I'll clean it again when we get home. This could ulcerate or go septic. You need to put something on it. Your poor foot!"

He toed his flip-flop and slipped his foot in. "There were no centipedes here until humans came. No pigs, no goats, no mongooses, no mosquitoes, no feral cats, no dogs. Humans are the problem. Humans are an infection on the earth."

In his pitch of indignation he sniffed and wrinkled his nose, then drank again, and he used his knuckles to clear spittle from his lips. He became self-conscious as he did so, turning aside to see whether anyone had noticed him.

As he turned, a big brown fat-faced man grunted at him, and Sharkey, startled, jerked his head away as though he'd been slapped.

But the man laughed and said, "How's it, brah?"

Tattoos on his neck, a cluster of scars raked beside one eye, a low rattling laugh — Moe Kahiko. His hand seeking a fist bump, was so tattooed it looked like a blue glove. The man had come from behind him and was now crouched beside him like a snorting wordless animal hoping to be petted.

Bumping the tattooed fist with his own, Sharkey recovered from the surprise and said, "I'm good, brah."

"You scared him," Olive said.

"Nothing scares this braddah," Moe said. "They tell me you stay out here on the lanai with the wahine." Moe smiled, showing his discolored and broken teeth. "I try say aloha to my braddah."

"You catching any waves?"

"A few. Da kine. Too much da wind."

"I was out at Rubber Duckies yesterday."

"Was insane," Moe said.

"A *malihini* did a face-plant on the rocks. Cracked his leg. Olive fixed him at the hospital."

"Today was big but more worse da wind."

"Moe, this is my wahine, Olive."

"Nice to meet you," the man said, and clutched at Olive's hand, enclosing it with his two thick tattooed ones as though trapping a small bird.

"Besides being a great surfer, Moe is a wall-builder. He did the walls at my house with his team of Tongans."

"No walls nowadays." Moe shook his head, saying, "Business is junk all over the island."

"What about the North Shore?"

"Here is more worse. It the junkest."

Sharkey had the ocean on his gleaming face, blue eyes and fine lines from the years of sun flashing on the water, a bony mask, the leathery skin shrunk to its contours. And the other man, stocky, with a fleshy face, like a feature of the earth, big dirty feet and blackened fingernails and tattooed fingers, his knuckles bruised from handling the lava rocks he fitted onto the walls he made.

Sharkey said, "Moe, you should advertise."

The man sniffed and considered it and dismissed it with a grunt.

"If I did that, people around here wouldn't like me more than they already don't."

Laughing at each unexpected word, Sharkey said, "I'll remember that. Want a drink?"

"Gotta go, brah." He rummaged in the pocket of his shorts and brought out a bulging plastic bag. "Dis for you. I smoked one pig — take it. Is da kine."

He hugged Sharkey and when he turned to go bumped a chair, stumbled a little, and walked off, lightly cursing.

"See?" Olive said. "Some people aren't so bad."

Sharkey sat back and stared at the ocean again. The surface had gone black but it was dimly visible and rutted; the onshore breeze swept low furrows, their edges moonlit, the nearer water gulping and dark, the water in the distance at the horizon like ripped cloth, all of it distressed and dreamlike.

"I used to buy *pakalolo* from him," he said. "Then I went elsewhere."

The pretty waitress appeared again, holding menus under her arm.

"Can I get you guys something to eat?"

Drawing a deep delaying breath of equivocation, as though just coming awake and reminded of where he was, Sharkey looked to Olive for an answer.

"I'm not hungry," she said.

"Yeah, I'm good."

The waitress slid the check next to his drink, saying, "No hurry. I'll just leave this with you. *Mahalo.*"

When the waitress had gone, slipping among the cluster of tables, twitching through the hanging strands of beaded curtains in the doorway, her ponytail dancing, Olive said, "You're not as gloomy as you sound."

"How do you know that?"

"I see you staring at the waitress's glutes. Isn't that a sign of hope and belief?"

"A mere glance at the wonder of nature and Hawaiian nutrition. God made those curves too."

"She's all tits and teeth. And you're drunk, mate."

"Just a little."

"Instead of pigging it here, let's have a drink at home," Olive said, and seeing that Sharkey had become subdued, she hugged him. He held on, he kissed her. She said, "I don't trust anyone until I see them drunk. I didn't trust you. And then I saw you plastered. You were nicer, just a little giggly. And I realized I was safe. Hey, let's go."

4

Drunk on the Road

The night-blooming jasmine, a leggy hedge of it next to the parking lot, filled the air with a flare of sweetness that matched the moonglow on the distant headland, Kaena Point, giving it the look of an outstretched paw in the sea, the shadowy mountain and ridge behind it like a recumbent lion.

Sharkey murmured these images in sentence fragments and pointed at each — the jasmine hedge, the headland, the mountain, the moonlight on the water, now eclipsed by a swelling cloud — and then he bent over to scratch his buzzing toe.

"My foot is killing me."

Olive had turned her back to the sea and the mountain ridge and the cloud. She said, "How did Moe cure you of buying his weed?"

Still working on his toe, feeling the burr of his fingernail on it, Sharkey said, "It was crazy." Then he stood and stamped the dust of the parking lot, flexing his toes. "I was in Half Moon Bay, surfing Mavericks. I'd been away for weeks — hot romance and big waves. One night I get a message to call Moe. I'm thinking, *What?* He never called me on the mainland before."

As he opened the car door and slid behind the wheel, Olive said, "I think I should drive." As she spoke, rain began to fall, plops and whispers on the nearby leaves.

"I'm fine. It's just —" He lifted his right foot and wagged it.

"Your poor toe."

"And a goose stamped on my foot. What was that word, 'venomed'?"

"Envenomation."

He repeated the word in her English accent and then, "I love it. Now look." Sliding behind the wheel, splaying his fingers, Sharkey showed her his car key, and with precision, inclining his head, he fitted it to the slot and started the engine. "We're good," he said, and switched on the headlights. "Leave your car here. We'll pick it up tomorrow."

Pearl-like raindrops began to scatter across the windshield as though flung by an unseen hand. He tapped the wiper lever and started the blades. The patter was like the *tut-tut* of a warning, because a moment later the windshield was awash, water streaming across the wiper blades as they slapped back and forth, two gleaming fan shapes on the window.

"Where did this dirty weather come from?"

"Wind's from the south," he said. He eased the car out of the parking lot into the road, moving slowly, angling his head to see through the flicking wipers. "*Kona* weather."

"Moe," she said, to prompt him. "The phone."

"Yeah. Moe. He says to me, 'I done a bad ting.'"

"Pig English," she said.

"Pidgin."

And she knew from his pauses and his drawl that he was telling the story his own way, slowed by beer. Drinking made him solitary and slow and deaf, the combination of beer and weed simplifying him. He became ponderous, punctuating his speech with pauses. He narrated in one-sentence paragraphs, each one like an announcement, ploddingly — "with care," someone might say, but Olive knew he was drunk. Though she felt safe with him when he was drunk, his drunkenness turning him into someone milder; he became a person she did not know well. An inner self was released with alcohol, as though he needed to be pickled to come to life. And drinking, far from impairing him, increased his concentration and made him more deliberate.

"I done a bad ting."

Repeating himself was another feature of his drunkenness — and most people's — but she could see he was distracted, negotiating the narrow bridge out of Hale'iwa, squinting at the lights of an oncoming car, past the wipers smashing at the rain. But once he was beyond the beach park and moving faster on the straight road, he resumed.

"I says, 'What is it?'"

"He says, 'I don't want to tell you.'"

Olive laughed at his mimicry of the forlorn voice on the phone.

"He says, 'I was getting some deliveries from the Big Island. Two, tree packages a week. Da kine, all taped up, all plastic inside, no can smell 'um.'

"I'm thinking 'packages from the Big Island' means *pakalolo*. But of course who am I to raise an objection? He knows I'm one of the more serious stoners on the North Shore."

"Which is why I'm wondering what made you give up buying from him."

"I'm coming to that."

He was leaning forward to see, the strain of peering through the splash and beat of the wipers giving him a false smile.

"Take your time," Olive said.

"'Two, tree packages a week for one haole guy. Maybe it more better if I not send 'um one week to my mail can.' I can't see much through this rain," he said, raising his voice to be heard over the drumming on the car roof. "'Maybe more better if I send two, tree to you.'"

"Your mail can?"

"My mail can."

"But you're in California."

"That's the whole point. Moe comes up with the brilliant scheme of diverting his packages of *pakalolo* to me."

"Addressed to who?"

"To me, from his grower."

"Is that legal?"

"I said —" Growling at the rain, Sharkey then sighed. "That glare is driving me nuts." He winced again. "I said, 'Did you send them?'

"'One, I send. Da kine.' I'm in Santa Cruz at a pay phone, putting coins into the slot, holding an old-fashioned black receiver, and I can't believe what I'm hearing. A package of *pakalolo* sent to me through the U.S. Postal Service.

"'You sent a pound of weed to me?' He says, 'No. Small, the box.' I said, 'If I'm busted I'll lose my house. I'll have to do time for that amount. They'll kick me off the tour.' He says, 'I know I done a bad thing. I neva inten' fo' do it. But I wen' wrapped it okay. Cannot smell.'

"I says to him, 'Moe, for God's sake, don't do it again.' And then he starts to make a whinnying noise and I think, *What?* He now sounds like a small boy with a big problem.

"I go, 'What is it?'

"'It nevah come! Maybe too small, the mail can.'"

"Careful," Olive said, seeing that a car ahead had pulled over but not completely. It was tipped against a storm drain, part of it still angled into the road.

Sharkey tugged at the steering wheel, squinted ahead, cursed so softly it could have been a prayer, and swung his car around the protruding vehicle. She was reassured by his efficiency.

"The package of *pakalolo* he's sent me hasn't arrived. His plan was to intercept it and keep sending the weed to me — because after all I'm not home. But on the day of delivery there is no box of weed in my mail can, as planned by the genius.

"I says, 'Are you sure it was sent?'

"'Guarantee. My braddah have the receipt.'

"'So where's the *pakalolo*?'

"'I dunno.' And he made that whinnying noise again. 'I know I done a bad ting.'"

"That's mental," Olive said.

"I assumed it had been seized. They have sniffer dogs. A big wrapped box from the Big Island can only be weed. A dog smells the box and they pass it to the feds. Dealing weed in that amount through the U.S. mail is a federal offense. I guessed it was a pound, maybe more. I could be facing serious jail time."

"God, what did you do?"

"I cannot see a thing," Sharkey said, flicking his high beams onto the rain-swept road. "I didn't want to cut my trip short — the surf was huge — so I kept calling home. Moe's always mournful. The package is nowhere to be seen, two weeks after it was sent priority mail from a neighbor island."

"Weren't you worried?"

"Petrified. I could not believe anyone would do anything that stupid." He slapped the steering wheel. "Jail! Big fine! Seizure of assets!"

"So what happened?"

"I can't see through this rain," Sharkey said, beginning to shout — and his shout matched the force of the rain, which was a harsh sound. The rain was an odor too — of earth and roots — and with the window cracked open for air the dampness inside the car drenched them.

"The package of weed," Olive said, to prod him.

"I was in suspense for a month." Sharkey leaned closer to the windshield. "Moe thinks it's been picked up by the feds. What I didn't tell him was that I've been having my mail forwarded to the mainland, to the post office in Santa Cruz. And I'm pretty sure they know something about well-wrapped packages like that." He leaned again. "I cannot see a damned thing."

His talk, his story, nagged at her, when all she wanted was for him to sit in silence so that she could use the drama of the weather to claim his attention, like music swelling behind a spoken epiphany. She felt that his inattention, his halting way of telling the story, had left them exposed to the fury of the storm. She had needed to fortify herself to endure it, but, distracted by him, she was startled by the way the car was thumped by potholes. Every phase of the rainstorm was a surprise and — it was true — all she could see in front of them was the rain-splashed windshield. It was as if they were in a cage and saw nothing beyond the bars.

In the headlights of some oncoming cars, the wet road was briefly visible again. Passing the surf break they knew as Chun's Reef, Sharkey saw the waves rising and dumping at the edge of the road, the froth pooling in the shallow broken pavement.

"Surf's up," Olive said, because he was stalled in his story.

"Junk waves," Sharkey said, lowering his head toward the steering wheel to see the road better. "My foot is really killing me."

In the dense and dirty nighttime rain, oncoming cars were licks and blobs of light stroked by the twitch of the wiper blades. Then he was driving blind again and could not see past his hood ornament. The drop of his wheels into the road ruts jarred his teeth; more cars, more headlights. He drove into the light as helplessly as into darkness.

"No sign of the package of *pakalolo*," he said, gripping the wheel, fighting the potholes. "All this time I'm waiting for a visit from the feds. Then one day I go to the Santa Cruz post office and there it is, a small, well-wrapped box, innocent-looking, about the size of an old video cassette. Maybe a pound of weed, compressed in a brick."

"Contraband," Olive said, and averted her eyes from the glare of the on-coming cars rounding the curve at Waimea.

"Yeah. I was so spooked I destroyed it — burned it and buried the ashes. And I left Moe in the dark. He could have ruined me."

"You didn't tell him?"

"He doesn't deserve to know. He's a useless shit, like everyone else. Oh God —"

Sharkey was still talking when there came a sudden shattering crash that was both a succession of loud bangs and an urgent thump on the chassis. The rapid three-part noise was like a tree branch collapsing onto the car, so explosive that Sharkey's chest smacked the steering wheel. He lost his grip, he foundered. At once a low portion of the windshield splintered into his lap, pricking his arms with shards. Olive squawked in fright, her hands flying to her face.

Stamping on the brake and swerving onto the roadside, Sharkey came to rest and clutched his face, babbling in confusion, and then Olive saw a twisted bike and a motionless man who'd hugged himself into a bundle.

"Jesus," she said as she shoved her door open. She crouched over the man, seizing his wrist for a pulse. The rain flattened her hair, plastering it against her face. Her shoulders were skinny in her soaked clothes. Even in the rain the smell of alcohol coming off the man was strong. In the light from Shar-key's car, Olive could see a gaunt face drained of blood yet serene and un-marked, as if made of wax. Except for the eyes — wide open and dull and disappointed — it was a martyr's death mask of surrender.

"He's gone," she said in a small voice. Sharkey was staggering from the car, groaning with effort. "The man's dead," and she raised her anguished face to Sharkey, who knelt next to her, frowning.

Cars slowed down, the drivers gaping. A policeman stepped out of a blaze of blue lights, raking the scene with a flashlight.

"That your car?"

Sharkey said, "It was an accident."

"He must have been riding toward us," Olive said. "I just checked him. No discernible pulse. I think he'd been drinking."

"He was on our side of the road," Sharkey said.

"Don't move him." The policeman began talking into his phone. "De-Souza. Code One — serious. I'm going to need an ambulance at Waimea. We've got a collision. One man down." When he clicked the phone off, he said to Sharkey, "You okay?"

"I'm good."

"Let's see your license and registration." Working his flashlight over him. "Was you buckled up?"

"Sure," Sharkey said, and Olive looked away.

"You're Joe Sharkey," the policeman said, moving his flashlight from the license to Sharkey's pale face and bleeding arms.

"That's me."

"I seen you here at Waimea, way back, on a big wave. My old man surfed Waimea. Ray DeSouza."

"'Ray-Ban,' we called him."

Her voice cracking with anger, Olive said, "What about this poor man?"

"You knew him?" The policeman turned away from Olive to concentrate on Sharkey, who lowered his arms and stood in the rain, nodding. "Was one great guy. Wish he was here. He pass."

"Bummer."

"For the love of god," Olive muttered, peering down the road as though for relief.

Now the siren of a distant ambulance overwhelmed the chugging of the waves.

"Let's get out of this rain," the policeman said. "Sit in my car. We'll go to the station for a statement as soon as they take this guy away. I got to empty his pockets, check for an ID. You okay?"

"I'm fine."

"You're limping."

"Banged my foot in the accident."

Onlookers had gathered, a small crowd, all dressed alike, in T-shirts and shorts, barefoot. The dead man was dressed that way too, but his clothes were muddied — whether from the crash or before, it was impossible to tell. Olive knelt and took the man's pulse again, and slipped her hand into his and held it, pressing it softly, wishing for a miracle.

"Wipeout," someone said in a low voice.

Another muttered, "He wen' *make*."

Then they sat, side by side, Sharkey and Olive, behind the divider grate of the squad car, and were soon taken away, up the long hill to Wahiawa.

"What are you going to do about that man?" Olive said.

"Sister, we seen that buggah before," the policeman said.

At the station the policeman went to the counter. "Joe Sharkey," he announced to another man in uniform behind the desk. The man rose to shake Sharkey's hand. "I heard we got us a Code One. Officer DeSouza was first responder, so he'll take your statement."

Sharkey gave his statement — the rain, the darkness, the potholes — and as he spoke, pausing, offering more, he recreated the circumstances of the accident, and the seconds of impact became episodic, a whole halting narrative. "I saw him at the last minute," Sharkey said. "I tried to swerve but he came straight at me." Olive frowned. "He was cycling down the wrong side of the road." Olive sighed, turning away. Detail upon detail, the story fattened and became fiction.

"Probably drunk — he stank real bad," the policeman said. "We seen him a coupla times near that squatter camp on the bypass road." He smiled at Sharkey. "Was you on the Pipe today? Was epic."

"So who is he?" Olive asked.

"We don't know. He was carrying a fake ID. I just ran a check on it. No hits."

"I was out," Sharkey said. "Got some good rides on triple overhead bombs."

"Sweet."

Sharkey stood abruptly and went outside. On the veranda of the police station, he stared into the rain, which was still pelting past the streetlamps, glittering in gold drops as it fell. Olive walked over to him, facing the downpour. She lifted his arm and draped it on her shoulder.

Sharkey said in the night, "I ran into a drunk homeless guy," and Olive began to cry.

"Give you a lift," the policeman said, and opened the rear door of his cruiser. On the way back to Hale'iwa, he monitored his crackling radio, and only spoke once on the way: "Gonna be epic tomorrow too." He dropped them at Olive's car, saying, "I'm Ronny DeSouza — you ever need anything, get in touch," and bumping fists with Sharkey said, "The Shark!"

Olive took the wheel and drove to the house. She watched Sharkey cross the lanai to the wicker sofa, where he sat, his hands on his knees, palms facing up, as if in a yoga pose.

"I ran into a drunk homeless guy."

"You said that already. You pranged that poor bloke on his push-bike."

It was not his repeating the statement that bothered Olive. It was the sentence itself, and his tone — relief tinged with resentment — when what she expected him to say was "I killed a man."

She approached him, not so much to console him as to console herself. He stared into the night. He looked supremely relaxed, in a posture of reflection — he might have been composing a poem in his head, she thought. She went closer and saw that his body seemed uninhabited.

5

The Search for the Hundred-Foot Wave

Y ou're so happy," a journalist had said to him once, a woman from a surfing magazine, wearing a T-shirt with his face on it and lettered DA SHARK! She meant, *You're impossible* — and she seemed to be complaining, because she wanted a different story. "And you're younger than I thought."

"Days you spend on the water are not deducted from your life," he said, and laughed. "Surfing keeps you from growing old."

A life of happiness was too easily summed up, and who cared? In books, in gossip on the tour, in life generally, a happy man was a rarity — usually someone minor, one-dimensional, shallow, careless, often a fool. And with surfing's emphasis on struggle and risk, they were dopers, they were stoners, they were beer drunks, but they were happy when the surf was up. He did not contradict the interviewer. He smiled and snapped his fingers as he did in idle moments, mouthing a song.

Bum
Bum
Bum
Biddly-bum . . .

Yet for a long time — years perhaps — a shadow had been creeping across his life. This advancing darkness had been preceded by ominous mutters, and a sticky damp as of stinking fingerpads, the prickle of hairy hands, a rising odor — an animal smell, or that of a desperate tramp — overripe, like decay. It was the sense that a creature had been stalking him, and he took this shadow to be a premonition — of what, he could not say.

Engrossed in surfing, the pure frolic on water, he hadn't paid much attention, and when he mentioned it to Olive soon after he met her, she had not taken any interest. You couldn't scare a nurse, nor impress a nurse with a horror story or a mention of a bad smell: their working lives dripped with blood and wounds and puke. One of the traits he loved in Olive was that she could cap any gruesome tale with one much more macabre. She'd seen people in every form of distress, humans trapped and suffering — the ailing, the maimed, the dying; drowning victims, battered wives, dope-sick tweakers.

If Sharkey mentioned a surfer who had planted himself headfirst on a reef, she could counter with the head trauma of a motorcyclist tipped into the path of an oncoming car. She was unshockable in the face of physical injuries. If anything, the sight of a mangled body made her more efficient, more studious and attentive — as she'd been the first day he'd seen her in the house at V-Land, reviving with the kiss of life a boy who'd overdosed — so Sharkey's stories did not mean much to her. Human cruelty was to her the great offense; it was all the worse when it was bloodless, and so "I hit a drunk homeless guy" was an outrageous statement, one she found hard to forgive or explain.

Sharkey had not noticed anything unusual. In his improvisational life, the awkward or intrusive incidents that had preceded the collision had at the time seemed unremarkable, more annoyances than portents. He was as confident in his daily life on land as he was on the water, where he could ride any wave that lifted him.

Surfing was the pulse and passion of his life, not like a sport that involved catching a ball or swinging a bat, and not a recreation either. It was a way of living your life that only other surfers understood — even the posers and punks who'd somewhat spoiled it; and good waves took precedence over everything on land. When the surf was up Sharkey was on it, no matter what else was happening. And nothing was compatible with surfing — no job, no enterprise, no other event. Surfing had dominated his existence, made him a hooky-playing student and a wayward son but a happy man. At just the point he was criticized by his disapproving mother — then a recent widow — for spending so much time in the water, when he had seemed so self-indulgent, he had begun to win surf contests and make money, on the tour and from appearance fees. He was well known at sixteen, a champion at seventeen, famous at twenty, a winner of the Pipeline Masters and the Eddie at Waimea, holder of the Triple Crown.

"Being on the water is all that matters," he said, "and surfing is the best way of being on the water."

Surfing was easy, everything else was hard; but he had been blessed. He was the luckiest man he knew, a success as a teenager doing something he loved, later living on endorsements and on the inheritance from his dead mother's investments, in the most beautiful place he'd ever seen — and it was a surfer's privilege to know the loveliest coastlines of the world.

He'd come with his parents to Hawaii as a ten-year-old, after bumping from one army base to another. His father, who had risen through the ranks, was promoted to colonel when they arrived at Fort Shafter, and was soon assigned a regiment and sent to Vietnam to command them as advisers, arming and training ARVN soldiers and Montagnard irregulars — the Degar people — in the Central Highlands to fight the Vietcong. Two tours, with frequent trips home, and on the second he'd been wounded, not by the enemy but in an accident, a hard chopper landing in Danang that crushed his spine. He was treated in Saigon, then airlifted to Tripler Hospital in Honolulu, where he died of liver failure.

"A sad memory," Olive had said.

"He was someone I didn't know anymore. Not the big intimidating colonel but a thin yellow man connected to plastic tubes, gasping to breathe."

By then Sharkey had been in and out of two schools and was failing at a third.

His father's death confused him, angered him, made him reckless. He found refuge in the waves. His mother, distraught, collected the insurance and, unexpectedly, a large inheritance from her husband's family — cash, a stock portfolio, real estate on the mainland. There was money now where once there had been a man.

Her money kept his mother suspicious of suitors, and single. She had boyfriends, but she steered them away from her teenaged son, who was doing so poorly at school. Yet the boyfriends persisted in trying to befriend the boy, as a way of ingratiating themselves with his mother. They were either too stern or too indulgent, and Sharkey found them ridiculous in their attempts to interact with him, as though auditioning for the role of father and husband. It was known that Sharkey's widowed mother was wealthy. She moved to a bigger house in Manoa, but by then Sharkey had been expelled from Punahou School and was struggling at Roosevelt High.

It had never been easy for him to be the son of an army colonel; it was even harder to be the son of a rich widow.

"I'm not going to marry again," she said. "I wouldn't do that to you, Joe. I wouldn't do it to myself. A woman with money would be a fool to get married."

So in addition to the role of son he assumed the roles of husband, friend, confidant, lover almost — he held her, he soothed her, he listened to her complaints — and he was oppressed. Some days he wished she would die, and he was ashamed of that feeling in himself. Knowing that she was a burden on him, she said frankly that if he looked after her and kept her safe and remained her companion — "companion" meant everything: her friend, her walker, her support and comfort — he would never have to work; that on her death he would inherit everything she had. Just hearing that, he saw her small coffin.

This promise made her contemptuous and him cynical, but it bound them together in a bitter bargain, each one trying to prove the opposite of what they felt. Some days the power was hers, other days his, and in that seesawing way it was like a love affair — or something resembling the lingering end of an affair, each one hanging on, insecure, fearful of letting go, and resentful, as when his mother didn't get her way she wept, and he wanted to scream, not at her but at himself.

He tried to please her and of course he failed: she would not allow him the satisfaction of pleasing her, because that would make him confident, and she might lose him. Sharkey understood her manipulation, and there were days when he saw her — stiff permed hair, makeup that gave her a floury face — propped up in the armchair where his father had once sat, and he pitied her for the drunken buzz in her tiny head. She reminded him of an animal holding still so that it will not be seen, like a rabbit stiffening on a shadowy late-afternoon lawn but standing out, the more obvious for its stillness in the breeze. She sat, and she drank.

He was saved by the sea, he thrived offshore. He found a school friend, a surfer, a misfit like himself, who introduced him to the moves and vouched for him at the beach, where he was guided by an older surfer — Uncle Sunshine. His form of rebellion was to swim away, and in time to surf the most dangerous waves, to build his confidence and to scare his mother; in doing so, he made his reputation. His mother did not understand enough of surfing or the power of the waves to be scared, and that frustrated him. Sometimes his mother insisted on attending his surf meets, taking photos of him while sitting in a folding chair under a wide-brimmed hat, on the sand — the only surfer parent on the beach, watching with admiration, possessing him by showing up, by her very presence keeping the girls away — the girls half fearful of the widow and half respectful of the loyal son, but also mocking both.

All this time he was a student, first at Radford with the other army brats, then — with their move to Manoa Valley — at Punahou, where he was intelligent enough to do little work and still manage to pass but was soon expelled for smoking *pakalolo* and finally sent to Roosevelt, where he was one of the few haoles, failing in his studies and bullied by the tough local boys. Hating school, he escaped to the beach, surfed most days, and longed to go away, to be free of his mother. He dropped out of Roosevelt and devoted all his days to surfing. He traveled to the mainland, and at Mavericks he saw his first epic waves — sixty-footers — and later added Jaws on Maui and Cortes Bank to these monsters, and still searched for a hundred-foot wave to ride.

By then he was on the world tour and had his first tattoos. He traveled — to Portugal and Spain, and Bali, his mother saying that she wanted to follow him; but the effort was too great, the flights too long. He managed to exhaust her. She stayed home, like a wife abandoned, and welcomed the attention of men. She queened it with her suitors, amused by their promises and flattery, and in this ideal situation fell into a casual decadence, drinking too much, indulging herself, encouraging the men just so far and then rejecting them, reverting to a sudden iciness that was itself perverse.

Sharkey traveled the world, wherever there was surf — and there was surf on almost every coast, at the edge of every continent, on most Pacific islands. You could not be a big-wave surfer, or surf year-round, without being a traveler.

And when he began to make money, in contests and from endorsements and appearances — he was still in his twenties — he became defiant; and his mother knew her hold on him was weakening. The money was modest, but it pleased him that it came so easily. Being away from her made him independent, and she objected; she wanted her boy back, not realizing that in her stubbornness she had made him succeed; her selfishness had kept him away, and being away from her had made him a man.

His mother complained of obscure aches and pains, which Sharkey disbelieved, regarding her complaints as attention-seeking. In what seemed like an act of revenge his mother broke her hip, became an invalid, and died. He inherited everything his mother owned — money, property, the investments, the stock portfolio. And he knew a greater freedom, more travel, continuing success as a surfer, more latitude in his search for the hundred-foot wave. He had always guessed that he would not be wholly free until his mother was dead. He was released, to fall in love, but the feeling that he had wished his mother dead — that had he believed her in her misery, he might have lengthened her life — this guilt never left him. That, and something else he could not undo.

Saying he was too grief-stricken to view her body, he received her ashes by mail and scattered them off Shark's Cove on a day of big surf that would disperse them, perhaps dissolve them. As the dust of her remains left his fingers he was given life, a fortune, a long career as a surfer that was easily summed up.

He was interviewed often, and always he was described as a natural waterman, with effortless grace and bravery, able to ride the biggest waves, imitated by many, admired by nearly everyone, envied, and praised, but not loved — surfers were too selfish and single-minded to be loved. He had achieved his goal of riding a one-hundred-foot wave, which was not a wave but a life on the water.

This was what most people knew of Sharkey, the account of his life that he offered to interviewers, such as the young woman from the surfing magazine who said, "This is the hardest assignment I've ever had. You have everything, especially that thing that makes you impossible to write about — you're happy."

But, like most of what people tell you about themselves, little of this was accurate. Because the messy essentials, the painful, shaming episodes, were left out; this version of Sharkey was misleading, and incomplete, and much of it false.

6

Portents

"The unexpected happens — a comic or odd blindside," Sharkey was saying to Olive, "and at the time you smile. Then afterward you understand that events give off power. The vibes affect you. And when you see that they were warnings and omens you get the shudders, like coming off a big wave you'd ridden mindlessly and you think, 'Man, I could have died.'"

Staring at him as if he were someone approaching her on a sidewalk, as though trying to decide if he was a man she knew, Olive said simply, in a small, certain voice, "But it was the bloke on the push-bike that died."

"It's all *pau*," Sharkey said.

She still stared at him, wondering at the word, meaning "done," and waiting for more.

"I should have seen it coming," he said. He smiled to think that he hadn't paid attention to the portents. He'd been tapped on the shoulder but he hadn't turned around. "I ignored the warnings. It cost me."

"Cost that poor bloke his life, you mean." Her disbelief was concentrated in her squinting tone.

"Totally freaked me out," Sharkey said, looking away.

"What are you talking about?" Yes, she thought, he seemed like a stranger, one speaking in a different language, a foreigner, oblivious, half deaf. So, trying to make him understand, she spoke as though to a child.

He did not have words to describe to her how he felt — that after the accident his life seemed to stall, to falter and then to skip backward. And that he seemed to separate from himself and become a bystander to his own life, watching without comprehension but amazed that he was offered this perspective, as his own shadow. The experience was pleasantly bewildering, because there was no threat. It is not dangerous to be your own double, he thought. But it was illogical, like a dream, full of absurdities, vaguely shameful. He watched like a passive onlooker as this deepening stillness took hold, sinking to a tedium he found restful, especially after the hallucinatory suddenness of the accident. That crash had been a seismic sucker punch, like a reef rising up to knock him from his board and hammer the board apart.

Now inert, dull-minded, becalmed, and enlarged by the tedium, the way indolent people grow fat — but the fatness was in his head — he recalled a slow succession of awkward incidents. Though strange, they had seemed fairly normal by Hawaii standards. The North Shore, he liked to think, was the edge of the known world, the absolute limit: beyond it was unreadable ocean, strange lands.

But after the accident these little episodes seemed to have the weight and meaning of portents. None had occurred on the water — water was his element; all had happened on land, many of them after he'd just come ashore.

It was as though — he imagined — he'd been singled out, and someone, or some sentient force, had been speaking to him; and he hadn't paid attention. Had he listened, heeding the warnings, there might have been no accident. There would have been no revelation for him, and no story, nothing to tell. If he'd been alert and known the implications, his life would have been undisturbed and remained the fiction he contrived to make it.

An accident is a surprise, unanticipated, a happenstance. But this, he now saw, had been foretold, because there was a meaning in all events and it is their accumulation that gives them form and meaning and makes them readable. It was not a single thing, it was many, and they made a pattern that sprawled and became logical and had a meaning.

He now knew exactly when it had all begun — the day, the time, the place. He had been driving from the post office at Waialua a few minutes past four o'clock on a Friday — the office had just closed for the day — and he'd seen a woman at the bus stop near the playground at the Waialua Elementary School. She'd been conspicuous, burdened by a large black bag. She was attractive at a distance, and when she signaled to him, he slowed down to look. Up close, she was fleshy, with greeny-gray eyes and a sensuality in her direct gaze, seeming to challenge him, not only with her eyes but with her full lips, even her posture, leaning at him. She was alone.

She had gestured to him with a tennis racket. That was to him her distinguishing feature. Without the tennis racket she was a brooding dusky woman, heavy for her height, standing by the road. With the racket in her hand, she was a tennis player, probably with a powerful forehand, heading home after a match at the school's courts. And that was another thing — her being so near the school, an hour after the end of classes, suggested she was a teacher.

She was wearing a floppy-brimmed hat and white tennis shoes and loosely fitting shorts, and her black bag was full — of what? He could not see. But his calculations gave him confidence; even as he was slowing down he had decided who she was — a teacher; how she'd spent the past hour or so — playing tennis; that her car was at the garage — why else would she be at the bus stop? Sharkey believed himself to be a shrewd judge of people; a surfer who traveled widely had to be insightful in sizing up strangers, because a surfer, naked on a foreign beach, could so easily be preyed upon — the boys with rusty spears who had assaulted him on a shore in New Guinea were just one instance.

He raked at the clutter on the passenger seat — his hat, his keys, a water bottle, a pair of pliers, a damp towel — and tossed them into the backseat as he drew up and slowed beside the woman.

"You want a ride?"

Without a word — pressing her lips together in effort — she fumbled with her bulgy bag and the tennis racket and pulled the door open. She got in, seating herself heavily, then snatching the door shut hard enough to rattle the window, looking too fussed and preoccupied to reply.

Starting away, Sharkey said, "Where are you headed?"

The woman grunted and, lifting her free hand, pointed into the windshield.

"I'm going to Hale'iwa," Sharkey said.

Instead of responding, the woman sat back, resting her bag on her fat knees and placing her tennis racket on the bag.

"Playing some tennis?" Sharkey asked, and glanced at her.

The woman scowled, lowering her head, and Sharkey saw that she had pitted cheeks, a smudge of dust on her chin, and her thumb, curled on the tennis racket, was dirty, the nail tip black. Her shorts too were not clean, with a stain like a rime mark of an old spill that had dried. And now he remembered like an afterimage from the bus stop that her tennis shoes were ragged and unlaced.

But the tennis racket was new and well strung, and she clung to it like a prestige object. It was this that gave her plausibility, even authority, though she remained silent — and at first her wordlessness helped her, the way a silent person can seem assertive, making us jabber. But Sharkey was less sure now. He had seen her dirty thumb, her bad skin, the stain on her shorts, and something else, a thin high whine of stink that might have been hers but could also have been a hum from Waialua Creek, which they were passing.

"Because if it's not Hale'iwa" — he needed to get this straight — "I'm not going farther than the community center."

She said nothing — no whole words — but a gasp of impatience like an unformed word was audible to him, and when he looked again at her for meaning he saw she was moving her lips, mouthing words. Her lips were cracked, dead and peeling skin on their fullness.

"Do you understand what I'm saying to you?"

The woman made a sudden noise, a honk of objection, the sort of sound a startled duck might utter. Hearing it, Sharkey became anxious. Then he knew, or was almost sure, she was in the grip of a drug. He knew drugs. She was toasted and mute, with the obvious slowness and density of someone under the influence, grunting and obtuse and vague, less like a drunk than like someone who'd been clubbed on the head. And she'd probably slept in those clothes.

As he was passing the side road to town she honked again and made as though to grab the steering wheel.

"No!" he shouted, and pushed her arm away, shoving the tennis racket. He repeated it, fiercely, but the woman hardly reacted — she hugged her bag and repositioned the racket.

The tennis racket! It conferred respectability, suggested health and sports-manship; and yet now he was sure she didn't play, she was merely fumbling with it, she must have stolen it — what a fool he'd been. But he didn't laugh, because he knew that someone drugged was someone dangerous, capable of anything, grabbing the steering wheel and sending him into a tree, howling at him, accusing him of — what?

"Give me money," she said — her first words.

He said, "I'm giving you a free ride."

"Money," she said, licking her cracked lips with a gray tongue.

"No money," he said, and became more watchful, fearing she'd use the racket on him, or yank at his shirt with her dirty hands.

"Give five dollars."

He wanted her out of the car; his heart was beating fast. She seemed to swell in her seat. He prepared himself for her lunging at him, chopping at him with the racket, and he raised his right elbow to ward off any attempt she might make.

"And now I'm going to drop you off," he said, approaching the community center, glad that no one was in front of it to witness what might be a tantrum.

"No," she said, and used her tennis racket to point down the road.

"Please get out of my car." He took a deep breath. "I'm being righteous — *pono* — you get it, lady?"

"No."

"Get out!"

"Five dollars," she said.

"No."

"Give money."

Sharkey reached across and lifted the latch and pushed the door open, and still his elbow was raised to fend off any objection she might make.

"Fucken howlie."

She batted at his arm with the tennis racket, but so feebly he snatched it from her and threw it past her into the gutter, facing her, daring her. He waited for her to use her hands on him, but she reached for her bag, tugged at one handle, and opened it — and he could that it was crammed with filthy rags and greasy scraps of paper, a tangled mimicry of possessions. She gripped the bag and hoisted it, hitching herself forward on the seat and sliding out of the car. Before Sharkey could pull the door shut she bowed as though in respect to thank him and spat at him casually, without force, leaving a gob of slime on the doorframe and a gleam of spittle on her chin.

"Go home, bugga, back to mainland," she muttered. "You weevil fucken howlie."

"You're zorched, lady!"

Sharkey was breathing hard as he drove away, telling himself that it could have been worse, that she could have physically attacked him while he was driving and caused an accident. And when his head cleared he laughed, thinking how before he'd seen her clearly the only feature of her that had caught his eye was her tennis racket. And he laughed at "weevil" too.

That might have been a portent — she was witchlike enough — and was that party another, where he had met that arrogant boy? The boy who had no idea who Sharkey was, had stood up straight, the better to be seen among the surfers and hangers-on. He was so sure of himself, so confident of his ability to take any wave, the others saying, "He da weenah!" although the room was full of bowlegged and leathery old surfers who'd been riding waves long before that boy had been born.

The boy garlanded with leis seemed to imagine that he gave off a glow — of youth, of virility, of success and sunshine — and heads were turned toward him, his mass of blond curls and blue eyes. He was as yet too young to be tattooed. But for him no one else in the room mattered. He was new to attention but already so used to it that he expected it, believing he deserved it, and would have been puzzled if anyone else in the room had been praised.

Sharkey was fascinated. Something about that callow kid, he thought to himself — he couldn't take his eyes off him. What was it? A tug of recognition, someone he vaguely knew, a way of standing — his posture, a resemblance to . . . who? Sharkey watched, nagged by not knowing why he was watching, but perhaps in the way a man stares at a much younger and beautiful woman who he knows is indifferent to him, who he will never see again

— a glimpse of the unattainable, a black pearl the size of an acorn in a velvet box in a jeweler's window.

He had gone away smiling, thinking, *That boy has no idea of the disappointments that lie ahead of him. He believes that he can ride any wave he wants, entice any woman with a nod, find any surf break in the world. And why,* Sharkey thought, *am I so rueful?* He knew him. *I was that boy.*

Those two incidents a few weeks apart. And there were the dogs. Sharkey was sitting in his house drinking a cup of coffee he'd just brewed and heard a thumping, heavy paws beating on wood, two dogs loping past the window on the wood planks of the lanai, their heads lifted just above the sill as they bounded past.

He had hurried out to chase them away but they were off the lanai by then, side by side, a pale one and a dark one, short-haired, no collars. What was stranger than their sudden appearance was that they had not barked. If they hadn't been so heavy he would not have heard them, so there was something ghostly about their suddenness, bursting into view, then vanishing. They'd run with their mouths gaping, their thick tongues twisted out of their jaws, in pursuit of — what?

They had bounded up the hill, out of sight, when Sharkey remembered his geese, and he ran barefoot up the grassy slope, snatching a rake he'd seen leaning against a rail. As he ran, a flock of birds came his way — the two ducks, three geese, the peacock, even some startled chickens, all apparently flushed by the dogs. But when he got to the top of the hill the dogs had gone; he could not tell whether they'd fled left or right, off his property.

Peering at the bushes for movement, for a clue, he remembered the old gander, which had not flown downhill with the others. He called out and within seconds heard answering squawks — all the birds came to be fed except the old gander. For nine years the gander had been his companion, he'd raised him from a two-day-old gosling, and the greedy affectionate bird had never missed a feeding.

Sharkey searched in the thickets and gullies of his property, expecting to find the torn body of white feathers or the cowering bird itself. He found nothing. No sign of the bird at all gave him hope that it was not dead, but it was a wan hope. He searched part of each day for a week, and after that week his hope was gone. Whose intrusive loping dogs? He did not know and never found out. They'd come silently, heavily, red-eyed, like dogs in a dream. Another portent.

Around the same time, which was in the month that preceded his hitting the man on the bike at Waimea, a woman confronted him in the supermarket, Foodland, at the bottom of the hill. She was attractive — lovely eyes, a surfer's body, her hair girlish in braids, vaguely familiar — but in the moments she began speaking to Sharkey her anger made her ugly and unknowable. She was fierce-faced, affronted, her pretty mouth twisted in threat — he could tell that as soon as she spoke she was preparing to attack him.

"You don't reply to my letter!" She stepped in front of him. She was loud, unembarrassed, and when bystanders paused to gawk at her she shouted, "You must think you're too good for me!"

"I didn't get a letter," Sharkey said, wondering if she was joking, backing away, trying to get out of the store.

"I put it in your mail can a month ago!" Shouting, she reached for him. "I asked for a simple favor and you didn't reply!"

She had the animal threat face, the bared teeth, the wild hair, the recklessness of someone enraged, and he believed she was going to hit him, or scratch him — her arms were raised. Though he could block her attack, he could not easily stop her. He felt obvious, the foolish target of a woman's anger — some bystanders began to laugh, and they hooted louder when he ran.

Before he got away he heard the woman say, "You've forgotten all the people who helped you," and the yelp, "Karma!"

In his car, driving up the hill, he wondered if that was true — and wondered too if he would see the frantic woman again, or was she gone, like his goose and the crazy woman with the tennis racket?

None of these incidents on their own would have alarmed him, and even taken together they were not strange enough to portend anything dark. But he reflected that all this happened before the accident that killed the drunk homeless man. Now they seemed full of meaning, with the shadow of significance. What troubled him was that he had not been able to read this meaning at the time, and even now he could not say what they were about, only that they seemed linked. Yet he was convinced they held a darkness he was too busy to discern.

He thought, *If I had put them together, might I have avoided the accident?* And he answered himself: *No.*

But he remembered the other incidents, trivial at the time: the old goose stepping on his foot and muddying his toes, gashing his foot on the lava rock, the centipede bite that had left one toe throbbing, stubbing that same toe, on his right foot, the one he used on the accelerator and the brake.

All this, then the accident.

7

Picking Up the Pieces

Without his own car, and with Olive needing hers — the insurance appraiser still had not examined the wreck, which had been towed to the front of the house and left there, the shattered window, the crushed and torn-open hood filling with rain and fallen leaves, a feral cat asleep on the backseat — without a car, he had begun to walk down the hill, or ride his bike, often with his surfboard under his arm, as he'd done when he'd been a teenager; and it did not dismay him. He was reminded of his youth, of skipping school, of happy days, pedaling, walking, hitching rides, being heedless, seeking waves.

Only four days since the accident but stunned by the event, he felt his life turning around and drifting backward into the blur and simplicity of the past, when if anyone had asked him what was going to become of him, he would have said, "Who knows?" He didn't ask. In his heart he had believed in his strength and his luck; he was convinced that he'd be all right. He kept this certainty to himself because he didn't know anyone who felt this way, certainly none of his friends. Nor had he ever told his mother: he didn't want his mother to say that she'd always believed in him — which was untrue — and then take credit for his success. An older Hawaiian man had guided him, the tough waterman who went by the name Uncle Sunshine. He was surprised when Uncle Sun said, "You got the juice. You got the moves" — surprised and dismayed, because now he had to live up to it, and this praise, which was also a prediction, was a burden.

His mother had asked him what his plans were.

"None," he said. "But I'll be fine."

"Because you have no ambition." She had a way of snapping at him and then turning her back, and in those days of her early widowhood, with her back turned, she left the house with men. *Imagine* — pursed lips, a little-girl voice — *I'm dating again.* Her late husband, the Colonel, was screaming from his grave.

But Sharkey did have ambition, it burned in him, because it was his secret, seeing himself in his dreams atop the boil of a massive, still-swelling wave, climbing to stand on his board and in a crouch riding through the barrel, his trailing fingers reading the wall in the pipe of rolling water, and at last twisting his board into the lip of foam, and after a swooping cutback speeding through the shallows of a breaking wave — then loud cheers, hoots, yells, and "Joe Sharkey!" shouted over the loudspeaker.

No ambition? He was bursting with it, it trembled and enlarged him and made him incoherent. How could he tell his mother, or anyone, that in his heart he was already a hero? He had always wished for it, his small boy's dream of bigness and power. His father's urging him to become a soldier meant that he had to prove himself as brave, or braver, in another dangerous profession, and the risks that surfing demanded made it heroic. His ambition to ride the biggest waves, to be celebrated for it, meant he could not say those words to his mother or anyone — they'd see a skinny boy and laugh, they'd ask "How?" and they'd pity him for being deluded. Some might mock him, as they did all dreamers. Yet he lusted for glory.

Pedaling his bike after the accident, he was returned to that dream; and he knew that he had succeeded — the years had proven it. He was now sixty-two, a well-known big-wave surfer, a champion. He had become the person he'd always wanted to be — too superstitious to speak the word "hero," but he knew that no one had matched him on the tour. He did not need to call attention to his surfing excellence or any of his feats — there were plenty of people to do it for him, even if not as many as before. There were the record books too; and he was a brand name — flip-flops, boards, leashes, shirts, trunks — though many of these products were no longer in the stores. Newer names, younger surfers, had taken his place. He didn't want to think of them as the punks he saw at parties these days, it seemed envious and unworthy, but they did seem younger, flashier, more callow, without any idea of how surfing had emerged; and now and then when Sharkey said, "When I was a kid I met Duke Kahanamoku," they merely nodded or murmured, "Sweet."

"He flashed a shaka at me," he said. "One day he saw me swimming and said I was like a monk seal — water dog. It was like a blessing."

The paradox of surfing fame was its elusiveness, that it was local, like a tribal rite enacted in water, part of an oral tradition. Like all passed-down stories, surfing tales became distorted, exaggerated, improbable, and many were forgotten. When Sharkey had started all those years ago, surfing was seldom filmed, hardly recorded, and few pictures were made of it. It was witnessed by the guys in the lineup, or some people on the beach with binoculars, delighting some onlookers, and then gone, becoming talk, anecdote, and casual boasting. These days there were wide-angle films, scuba divers rolled with the wave and photographed surfers inside the barrel, a whole surf meet was a permanent record. But not when he'd begun.

And so he was well known to the older surfers and a name to some others, but he was almost unknown to the grommets, the younger ones — an old guy, a presumptuous stranger at the parties, hardly noticed when he shopped at Foodland to buy groceries, just another leathery geezer in flip-flops.

He had never ceased to surf. He had his favorite breaks and beaches, he owned twenty boards, he could still manage the biggest waves — was better surfing straight ahead on a monster wave than hotdogging and stressing his knees on a smaller one. He laughed to think that the pack of boys doing air-reverses, trying to impress the surf bunnies at Sunset, had no idea who he was. But it rankled too, because they had no memory of his achievements. He was mentioned with the handful of others as one of the first of the big-wave surfers, but the point was never made that he was still riding big waves, that he surfed nearly every day, that often after dark, after the younger guys had gone ashore to find a girl or drink beer, he was in the thick of the boil at Waimea, often alone, and no one knew, no one saw him streaking in moon-light down the face of a wave.

He was ageless in the water, on a wave. On land it was a different story, the anonymity of old age — though sixty-two wasn't old; Clyde Aikau and Jock Sutherland were still surfing, and they were older. His on-demand virility in the sack had never failed him, what Olive called "your hurricane fuck." But the sun had turned him to leather and the sun-brightened hair of his youth was now gray, and there was less of it. He was sinewy, almost gaunt in his leanness, beaky, with deeply freckled hands and a mass of ink on him, the look of a lifer in prison, or an old sailor. He resembled so many of the aging surfers, battered by waves and the hard drinking and drugging of the past, his whole life showing on his face and his body.

The great waves he'd surfed so well had rolled toward shore and broken on the beach, and there was no memory of them now except in the talk of the other reminiscing surfers — and they had trouble with the truth. The waves kept coming, the younger surfers riding them, and now bigger money and more hype and high visibility.

As a teenager on the Pipe, he had surfed big waves alone, unobserved, to the empty beach. That was the mystical quality of surfing — the self-posses-sion and obscurity. For all the talk today, and all the glamour, no one rode the waves any better. He was consoled by the idea that he wasn't alone: Ha-waii was full of old surfers who were forgotten.

So he was heartened — absurdly, he knew — when the insurance man rec-ognized him and apologized for being a week late in looking at his car.

"I never realize it's Joe Sharkey's car," the man said, and covered his face with his hands, like a shamed boy.

"You a surfer?"

"Not in your league."

That was nice, not for his ego but because he had the man's attention, and his respect would mean the whole messy business would be finished fast and efficiently.

"How does this thing look?"

"It might be fixable," the man said. "But I'll need to see the accident re-port. And we'll have to get an estimate for the damage on the car."

He was a man of about forty, in a white shirt and tie, as rare on the North Shore as a woman in a dress wearing high heels. He was a claims adjuster, he said, he lived in Pearl City, he sometimes surfed at Ala Moana, his wife was in real estate, two children — and Sharkey thought, *The other world.*

His name was Ben Fujihara. He said he'd stop at the police station in Wa-hiawa on his way back to town to get a copy of the accident report.

"In the meantime, here's a list of approved body shops. You can drive it, the car?"

"All the bodywork on the front end is busted up, and the windshield's smashed. But it runs." Sharkey was studying the printed form. "I could try this place in Waialua — Aloha Garage."

"Let me know what they say," Fujihara said. "We'll look at their estimate. Oh, and" — he held out a small white pad — "would you mind signing this?"

"Is that some kind of form?"

Fujihara said, "Your autograph. For my boy. He'll be stoked."

"Does he know who I am?"

"I'll tell him."

When he had gone, Sharkey drove to Waialua, where at the body shop a man rolled from beneath a car and smiled, wiping his hands on a rag.

"How's it?" he said. A name patch, KEOKI, on his pocket. "Park that bad boy over there. You here for one estimate?"

"Yeah." He bumped the man's grease-stained knuckles with his own, say-ing, "Joe Sharkey," and waited a beat for a reaction.

"Nice car," the man said. "Lexus. Ninety-seven. They make da kine good that year, braddah. Sales were bad so they put everything into that year's model — more better parts, more safety, extra padding for quiet, leather. Good product."

"It's been carrying surfboards for the past sixteen years. And I had a little accident. What do you think?"

"If fix," he said, and with an expression of sorrow shook his head from side to side, "it look humbug."

"I'm here for an estimate," Sharkey said.

The man frowned. "She totaled."

"No — I just drove it here from my house. It needs bodywork on the front end and a new windshield. Pop out the dent in the door and fix some dings. It runs fine."

The man was smiling, as though at Sharkey's stupidity, being patient, taking no interest in what he said, waiting for him to finish.

"I make a report — it's totaled," the man said. "Then you get your money."

"And what happens to this one?"

"I buy it."

"So it's not totaled?"

"You don't get it, braddah."

"Yeah, I do, Keoki." The insurance company would compensate him — and he'd buy a new car. And Keoki would get the car he admired and would fix it. "You want my car."

The man had not lost his smile. There was a streak of grease on his neck, his fingernails were black, his hair dusty and matted. As the two men stood face-to-face, in silence, a woman in denim overalls approached them, rolling a wheel she might have just repaired — the tire was new, with shiny black treads.

He had first taken her to be a thin boy, but he saw that her hair was piled into her baseball cap. She was dark, thin-faced, Filipino, with large dark eyes, and seemed too small, too thin, for the fat tire on the big wheel, but she controlled its movement, balancing it on top with the flat of her hand. In contrast to Keoki, her overalls were clean. Steadying and stopping the wheel, she looked at the car as though wishing to claim it.

"Totaled, right?"

"So this man says."

She made a knowing face, widening her eyes.

"Georgie, he wants it, eh?"

"That was one primo year," Keoki said.

"You wen' buss up someone, yah?"

Sharkey was startled by her confident statement, having taken no more than ten seconds blinking at it to size up the car. He said, "How do you know?"

"*Koko,*" she said.

"Whaaa!" Keoki wailed. "Where you see *koko*?"

And the woman approached the car and with a thin hovering hesitant finger pointed daintily to a smudge of brown like a scabbed blister on the jagged rip of the front fender.

Sharkey said, "You mean blood?"

"Poor buggah blood," the woman said, and used her finger to flick a stray wisp of hair over her ear.

"Cannot," Keoki said, and turned away in disgust. "No can buy 'um."

"How much you want for dis?" the woman said.

"I guess you're not superstitious."

"This car *kapu,*" Keoki said. "It a bad ting. It stay wid human blood. *Koko* bring trouble"—and it sounded worse in his pronouncing it *tchrouble.*

"How much?" the woman said.

Sharkey said, "I don't know. If it's totaled, you do the math. The estimate to fix it, subtracted from the Blue Book value. I'll sell it to you for that, or best offer. I'll buy a new one."

"Suppose was da poor buggah head?" Keoki said, rocking in his greasy overalls in a clumsy anguish. "Da head is sacred kine. Full of *mana.* Da *mana* is on the car, but it a curse, yah. Why you no tell me you hit one buggah?"

"It was a drunk homeless guy on an old bike. Maybe a tweaker."

"He wen' *make?*"

Sharkey sucked his teeth, tossing his head at the same time, sound and movement indicating yes.

"Josie, you take da car. I no want 'um." He grimaced, averting his eyes from the smudge of blood.

"Deal." With the heel of her hand, graceful but firm, she pushed the wheel she'd been steadying beside her, and when it was rolling trotted next to it to a car canted upon a red upraised jack.

When Sharkey, half laughing, told Olive what had happened at the garage, she said, "Are you surprised? Hawaiians have a thing about blood and bones—any body part of a human is power. And potential trouble. That was the first lesson I learned at the hospital here."

"*Tchrouble,*" Sharkey said. "Funny. He'd really wanted the car."

"You reckon it strange that he had respect for the dead? Fancy that."

"Maybe. But the guy's in a garage, with a wrench in his hand."

"For most people on earth—don't you know this?—the dead don't die. They're always with us."

Sharkey smiled at her seriousness. "He was afraid."

"Fear is one way of showing respect," she said. "But you're Joe Sharkey. 'No fear' is your motto."

"I'm getting me a new car."

"You so deserve it," Olive said, then looked away, shaking her head.

That became his mission for a week, going from dealership to dealership, Olive joining him on the afternoons when she was free, talking to salesmen, taking test drives, and assessing the suitability of the car to take a roof rack for his board. Some of the salesmen knew his name, and Olive stood aside and watched with distaste as they smiled, glamoured by the visit of the big-wave rider. They were older men, some of them surfers themselves, eager for the boast of Joe Sharkey buying a car from them.

Buying a car was a novelty, and a diversion. He'd believed that his old well-maintained Lexus would last another few years, or longer. He had not contemplated replacing it. But the accident had changed everything, and he found himself the object of attention, the experience he'd known in bazaars around the world, hawkers calling out, "Look, look, sir," and appealing for him to buy. He enjoyed the attention for the power it gave him to look or to turn them down.

He settled on a sleek, black, bullet-shaped SUV, the chrome grille set like a scowl, the rear end rounded and buttocky and businesslike, the whole vehicle hunched forward, nose down, as though for speed, with a roof rack that could accommodate two boards, a head-turner, unexpected and welcome, a gift.

"Another toy," Olive said when he drove it home.

She would have said more in mockery, except that on arriving he complained of a severe headache. And then instead of driving it, cruising to Hale'iwa, he left it parked in the garage. For two days straight she found him lying on the sofa, his hands on his face. Back spasms, he said. Insomnia.

"I can't believe it," he said, talking into his hands, and explained that it was too painful for him to drive.

"I was expecting something like this," Olive said. "You keep forgetting you were in a serious accident."

But, his back knotted, his neck throbbing, he remembered now: the gouts of rain, the splashing windshield wipers, the bright blobby glare and in that glare the explosion of sound and light and shattered glass, the broken bike and the baglike form flung forward against the window.

Except for the cuts on his arms he had not hurt himself. Then he had only sighed, seeing the sodden corpse of the man, and instead of a tremor of guilt or fear he had felt a towering vitality, the dizzying conceit of having survived, standing in the rain, a whole man, slightly bewildered at the sight of Olive crouching over the dead man, her fingers on his wrist, saying, "He's gone."

Sharkey had not been injured; he was surprised, feeling weirdly strengthened, as though having come through a testing ordeal, proven himself, the sense of having surfed a big evil wave that had tricked and toppled him, the joy of bobbing up after a hold-down and paddling to shore.

Driving from the dealership with the new car he'd felt the first of the back spasms, the tugs on his head, hot wires of pain wrapping his neck, seeming to yank his eyes from behind, and, fighting this, his lower back came apart.

"I almost didn't make it," he told Olive — and it was true, he'd just missed hitting a cyclist on Nimitz and nearly sideswiped a car on the H-1, his hands greasy with sweat gripped the steering wheel — pain in his eyes, pain in his finger joints.

Once, long ago, in Indonesia, surfing Mentawai Reef, he'd contracted dengue fever — a week of pain in his joints, his temperature 103 degrees, thirst, headaches, and low spirits. It was less like a sickness than a bereavement, like sorrowing, a fatal melancholy that was also physical anguish.

That was how he felt now. "Can't drive" was an understatement — he couldn't sit or stand, and even lying on the sofa he was in pain, as though he'd broken his back. At night the fever headache kept him awake and, weakened by sleeplessness, he felt sharper pain in the daytime.

The Valium Olive gave him for the back spasms depressed him and sent him to sleep, but he seemed comatose, and when he woke, unrested. A week of this, but even when he was well enough to stand, or shuffled to the car, he felt the pain again in the driver's seat.

"I guess I'll do the driving now," Olive said, knowing how he hated to be driven and thinking it might encourage him to deal with his pain and drive.

But he accepted her offer, and though he still surfed or swam, there were days, medicated, when he was slow and sleepy and felt like an invalid, people he knew at Foodland or on the beach surveying him with surprise and saying in their gauche overfrank way, "You look terrible, man," or "You okay, brah?"

Yes, he said, insisting. It was a bug. It was going around. He'd be fine.

8

Intrusions

To feel ill on a sunny day in the islands, to sicken under a cloudless blue sky, his eyeballs burning with fever, was a peculiar form of torture. Hawaii was not its stuffy rooms, its offices or interiors — it was its outdoors, where he lived, upright, barefoot, and all work seemed wasteful. Sharkey's element was water, sunlight beating on the sea, its heat flashing against his face, and everything else a confinement.

I am an animal, he often murmured to himself, *I am a sea creature, a water dog, flipping from wave to wave.* He seldom lingered in the house. He woke and walked outside each morning and only then did he take a deep breath to taste the day, inhaling the purring aromas of the flowers beneath the lanai, the flutelike blossoms of pak lan, the orange trumpets of pua ke-nikeni, the traces of jasmine, and licking all their syrupy perfumes on his lips suggested something crushed, seeping sweetness into the air, the first fingertips of day. He was vitalized by his outdoor life in this water world.

But this particular morning, seeking a reassurance of health, he swung his stiff legs off his bed after another night of headaches and back spasms — he'd resisted the Valium, which left him dry-mouthed and zombielike — and he went outside and was so dazzled by the bright light he staggered back, the sun like a sword blade. Some deep breathing, the pranayama he had learned in yoga, helped settle his head, and by degrees he felt his strength return, a noticeable assertion of health, and he vowed to go surfing.

Lying in bed in the daylight clouded his mind and drained his energy, desiccated and demoralized him. He needed to restore himself, to rehydrate by being in the water; he wanted to make a bold move, by surfing — to slip away from his aches and trick his illness. Simply to feel ill seemed to him a mistake, it was wrong; being decisive was the answer, action was the cure.

He was glad that Olive was at work when he woke, because he knew she'd try to convince him to take it easy. "Relax," she'd say, and he'd have to listen.

Though they'd been together only six weeks, she was now part of his life; the accident had created a bond, it was something they'd struggled through, a shared experience of sudden death. Because of this he knew how she'd react. He had learned from his mother, from his solitude, that it was possible to hold long unsatisfactory conversations with people he knew well — even though they might be absent. He had one of those frustrating dialogues this morning, rebutting all the arguments he'd heard before, the times he'd been sick. He often felt that Olive became her true self when he was ill or out of sorts — "a bear with a sore head," as she said — because it put her in charge, and in a position of strength she mothered and manipulated him in ways that made him frantic to get well.

"I'm going surfing."

"That's the last thing you should be doing."

"It'll make me feel better."

"It'll set you back. You need rest."

"I need action — the Miki Dora way." And he nodded. "Miki once said that no problem is so big or so complicated that it can't be run away from. Great surfer. I had one of his long boards. Da Cat."

"Go back to bed."

"You're so bossy."

"Because you're such a stubborn plonker. Look, I'm a nurse. I know what I'm talking about."

"And I know what's good for me."

"Always the narcissist. But you look ropy, like something the dog sicked up. The dreaded lurgy."

"I can look after myself."

"You need rest, maybe medicine."

"I hate medicine. I avoid it. Medicine makes people sick. You're a nurse and you don't know that?"

And more, sparring and nagging, and Olive wasn't even in the room. She was six miles away at Kahuku Medical Center. Yet he was playing out the dialogue, responding to her, as he pureed a mango smoothie and changed into his board shorts and T-shirt and then threw handfuls of pellets to the geese. While they pecked and squawked he sat and drank the smoothie, still murmuring in reply to Olive's objections.

The glare made him unsteady. He had to put on his sunglasses and stretch again before he was able to hoist his board onto the roof rack, and even so the simple task seemed unusually laborious. But this was the cure. He needed to surf, and if this lifting of the board was harder than normal, the reason had to be the new car — the SUV was higher than his old car, the new roof rack sat on different towers and bigger clamps; it was more of an effort to hoist the board at that angle.

"It's just a question of getting used to it," he said, talking in his head, as though in reply to Olive, who would have challenged him — "See, you're having trouble lifting it" — had she been there.

He smiled to think how we carry on conversations with people who are absent, who loom large in our lives, justifying our actions to them. He often found himself responding with force or irritation to the objections of his mother, though she'd been dead for years, opposing her through force of habit, feeling nagged.

How the dead rule our lives from the grave, he thought, remembering Olive and *The dead don't die,* and laughing out loud at this gave him a jolt of vitality.

Pausing just before he got into the car, he glanced at its shine, its newness, the sleek bullet shape — and his surfboard strapped on the roof rack made it sleeker. Going closer, he saw his face in the side window, someone he scarcely recognized — a much older and frailer man, and though he told himself that his aged appearance was the result of his illness, he knew that face awaited him in the future, a preview of himself as an old man. Surfers aged badly; it was the sun burning their flesh and the erosion of strong waves — pitiless nature. Surfers remained physically strong but they looked like hell, like old homeless coots, their bodies dried and hollowed like driftwood, and for the same reason, bobbing in seawater, rubbed by salt, cooked by sun.

Behind the wheel, starting the car, moving up the driveway, he said (as though to a stranger who'd remarked on his worn and weathered face), "You know how long I've been doing this? Almost every day since I was a teenager at Magic Island, playing hooky from Roosevelt. Every day in the water, the sun and waves beating my face."

He'd seen faces like this on old half-broken men on the coasts of Africa and Asia, but he was so disturbed by his own that he tried to verify it in the rearview mirror. The mirror was crueler, clearer than the side window with its dusty soft focus. He saw a brown pinched face and anxious eyes, and while still peering he oversteered, saddened by the sight, and saw his expression change as the right side of the car caught the edge of a terracotta planter and cracked it, raking the front fender, digging a furrow into the new paintwork.

"Shit!" He was further shamed by his eyes in the mirror, registering helplessness, as though rebuked. Then he leaned back and saw a cartouche of his foolish face.

To blunder was one thing; to observe yourself blundering in this way was worse. And when he backed up he raked the car again and swore louder. Then he averted his eyes from the face that grew older and uglier in those seconds.

I'm sick, he told himself. *I'm going surfing. I'll feel better in the water, I'll get well.*

The surf at Waimea was head-high and clean, but even so he decided on the simpler predictable break at Pua'ena Point in Hale'iwa. He felt better driving down Kam Highway and promised himself a good day. When he parked he vowed not to look at the scrape on the fender, but a man on an old bike near the wall at the parking lot called out to him.

"Nice ride. Too bad it mess up. You hit one tchree?"

Sharkey shrugged, unstrapping his board, telling himself he didn't care; but his annoyance was like heat suffusing his body and pressing against his eyes. The man had one leg slung over the bike, and the very sight of the rusted bike, the man clinging to junk, made Sharkey furious.

But he said, "I like it the way it is."

"Da fender *kapakahi.* It look humbug."

Tucking the board under his arm, making for the beach, Sharkey heard the man call out behind him.

"I know one guy do body work. He stay *mauka* side of 'Ehukai, near Ted's Bakery. Can fix, brah."

The man was still muttering as Sharkey knelt to fasten the leash to his ankle, and then he dropped onto his board and paddled out. So as not to betray his weakness to the man he had marched to the shore and now paddled, asserting himself. But he had not gone far when the effort of it slowed him. The water was chilly, like cold metal against his skin, and the twist in the small of his back that Olive called a spasm kept him thrusting hard with his arms.

Easing up, he lost his momentum and was pushed sideways and slowed by the slap of a low blunt wave like a speed bump. He tried to right himself, lost his grip, and the board crushed with a chewing sound against a coral head. He felt through his fingers on the board the scrape of his fins and hoped they hadn't snapped. Another set of waves lifted him and helped him straighten, but the force of it took all his attention, so that he couldn't tell whether the fins were damaged.

He headed for the empty wave of the break, glad that he had it all to himself, because he knew he would be struggling. The sets kept coming, and he rode them, straddling his board, waiting for a likely one, misjudging several before he caught the crest of a good one and was swept up, paddling, and then canted on the face of it, and he stood to surf it. But just as he mounted the board, positioning his feet to angle it, the thing slipped from beneath him, and he could tell as he toppled that two fins were gone and the third broken.

He thrashed to regain his board and hugged it and paddled to shore in dark water as the sun was blurred by rags of drifting cloud. He was cold again, and cursing his board and the sharp coral head he'd hit, and the wave that had swung him sideways.

His board seemed heavier for being damaged and useless, he had to stop twice on the beach to kneel for rest, and the second time he saw a man on a bike pedaling away — the man who'd spoken to him near the wall.

It seemed odd for anyone on such an old bike to be pedaling so fast, and he smiled at the urgency of the man, because he himself was feeling so winded and slow.

But then, nearer the car, he knew why. His side window had been smashed, his expensive sunglasses stolen — that was all — and the thief was gone.

After he'd strapped his broken board to the roof rack and started out of the parking lot he looked for the man on the bike — he was certain he was the thief. He saw no sign of him, only the obvious fact that it was easy for anyone on a bike to vanish down a narrow dirt track that led through the mass of ironwood and kiawe trees banked by guinea grass on the far side of the road.

Still, Sharkey gunned the engine, hoping to catch a glimpse of the thief, and as he imagined sideswiping him and knocking him sideways off his bike, the effort of pressing his foot on the accelerator caused a stabbing pain in his big toe. He could only relieve it by easing up on the pedal. And it was then — his foot throbbing, the car slowing — that he saw the last of the thief, his dirty shirt, his rear tire, disappearing through the bank of guinea grass at the roadside and enfolded and hidden by the dense trees.

Sharkey's foot was so sore that even if he'd been able to park near that pathway, he knew he would not have been able to chase the man. He howled in frustration and drove home slowly, infuriated by the broken glass at his feet. In his garage he swung his legs out and saw that his toe was swollen, probably aggravated by the seawater and his awkward stance on the board. And the reddened bulge still bore two marks like eye slits, the piercings of the centipede's jaws. So the bite of the centipede had become infected, enlarged, mottled pink, pale yellow, and purple, like a poisonous creature inhabiting his toe, making him clumsy, causing him to limp and stumble.

"It's like a carbuncle," Olive said later. "I'll have to lance it and drain it. You'd better stay out of the water."

Sharkey did not mind the pain of the narrow blade slicing his flesh; the cut was like a flame, cauterizing the wound, a ritual of punishment and forgiveness. He'd always regarded incisions and tattoo needles, blood-drawing and stabs, as small deflowerings, always with a blossom smear of crimson. He liked Olive's medical term, "bloodwork."

But he was still angry. "He broke my window for a pair of sunglasses. I could have killed that guy."

Olive lifted her face and looked at him with wonderment that became a disbelieving smile.

"He excites my contempt, as my dear mother used to say."

"My mother never said that."

He limped more thumpingly now, his bandaged toe chafing in the thong of his flip-flop. He took such care that his overcautious gait dragging and hesitating to protect the toe caused him to stumble, and in one of those stumbles he fell.

He'd been shutting the henhouse door with one hand, latching it, and holding a bowl of eggs with the other. He missed hooking the nose of the latch to the fitting's eye, and leaning away and attempting it again, he snagged his sore toe on the overhang of the brick step. It was as though his foot had caught fire. He raised it and lost his balance and toppled forward, the bowl breaking on the bricks, the eggs smashing in a mass of yellow mingled snot-like yolk and goo and fragments of shell.

He cursed again, louder than ever, and heard his helpless howl echo in the gully below. The chickens squawked back at him and he heard their racket as blaming.

His days were fraught with accidents, many of them minor, like dropping the bowl of eggs — but such clumsiness made him feel old and futile. Some were more serious — he left a burner on the stove alight and scorched a pot (Olive: "That's a sure sign of senility" — she was joking but he was stung). More serious still, he very nearly hit another cyclist, swerving as he reached for his cell phone, horrified that he had come so close that the man called out and pedaled after him, catching him at a red light and thumping the car roof, screaming, "Howlie!"

So after all these years that was what it had come to. Over fifty years in the islands, years of big-wave surfing, of beer-drinking on the beach, and handing out free weed, and party-going. He wasn't Joe Sharkey of Waimea fame, or the Shark, or Braddah Joe, or Joe-Boy or Uncle Joe. He was a haole, another white guy in a new car, an unwelcome alien.

And because he was injured and couldn't get into the water, and his new car was unreliable — possibly a lemon — he did not go far. He rolled down the hill to Three Tables and sat in a beach chair with binoculars, looking for the blowhole vapor of a whale offshore.

While he was sitting there one day, a man approached him, a fat man carrying fins and a face mask.

"Saw three whitetips," the man said. "Under that ledge."

"Really."

"You got three types of sharks here in Hawaii — your tiger shark, your great white, and your whitetip. But your whitetip is mellow. They just stared at me, like 'Who's this guy?' and I swam right past them."

The man was pale and flabby, with rented fins and a mask, and he stood beside Sharkey, his feet planted in the sand, still talking about his encounter with the sharks. He was earnest in a salesman's way, selling his information, and now he was talking about the configuration of the clouds in the distance.

Sharkey stared with defiance. *He thinks I'm a tourist.* With his bandaged foot and his binoculars he might have looked the part, but how did that square with all his tattoos? He became indignant, insulted to be unrecognized and, worse, having to listen to this ignorant man lecture him, telling him what he knew.

"Why are you giving me a fucking weather report?" Sharkey said. "I've lived here my whole life."

"Take it easy." The man was rattled by Sharkey's sudden outburst. "All I said was I saw some sharks."

"I've seen a million sharks! I'm a shark!"

Backing away, the man said, "Know what, pal? You got a problem. You need help." And walking off, attempting to be brisk, he sank and stumbled in the sand, a clumsiness that — Sharkey saw — spoiled the effect of his scolding.

The next day a young man with a camera approached him. Sharkey believed he had recognized him and was going to take his picture. He was not sure whether he should cooperate or snub him. But the man said, "Mind taking my picture?" and handed him his camera. Sharkey obliged; the man lingered, standing too close.

"This sand is so coarse. It's not like this in Louisiana, where I come from. We got a more powdery kind of sand — real soft. But this stuff is amazing, the way it feels on your feet, gritty-like. I guess it's a different kind of sand altogether. I thought there was only one type of sand. But there's more. The way I see it . . ."

I have traveled the world, treading the sand of a thousand beaches, Sharkey thought, *and this man is lecturing me, like that other man with the sharks, not listening, no questions, just assuming that I am, like him, another tourist from the mainland, an old retiree on an island vacation.*

He laughed at the thought, throwing his head back, but in an obscure way he was hurt — as he had been with the stumbles and the broken eggs and the theft and the misunderstandings — and that gave his laugh an edge of bitterness. These intrusions upon the serenity of his life amounted to assaults;

made him overcautious, even a bit timid, and here he was in his beach chair on the sand, his sore toe upraised, and the young man still drawling.

Ludicrous. But there was an element of the ridiculous in the bewilderment of sadness. What were these intrusions telling him?

"You think that's funny?" The man beside him was fierce, blinking, his jaw chewing his anger.

And Sharkey realized how he had been laughing.

"No, I don't," he said, sounding suddenly fearful. "Not at all."

9

Repetitions

H unter Thompson used to repeat himself."
"Queen Anne's dead," Olive said.

"What?"

"An expression," Olive said. "You've told me that before."

"And what he said was often about me."

"So you've said. You're a mesmerizing raconteur."

"Always stayed in a luxury suite, either in Waikiki or at the Kahala, half-eaten meals all over the place, bottles of brandy and his stashes of weed nearby. Coke in his shirt pocket, usually the same plaid shirt."

Olive stared at him. He wasn't fazed. She said, "And he always checked in under the pseudonym Mr. Joe."

"I think you know why."

Squinting at him as though he'd just teased her, but with a half-smile of forgiveness illuminating her face, Olive began to speak in a hot whisper of impatience. "Look—"

Sharkey cut her off, saying, "But Hunter was a fan and a recreational socialite. He didn't know squat about surfing, but he was reckless and had an instinct for risk—for the drama of sport, for physical effort."

"Right," Olive said. "He looked you up."

"He looked me up." Sharkey was staring into the shadows at the corner of the room, as though by speaking earnestly he might bring the man to life and see him emerge from that darkness. "He'd been given my name by a big-wave rider."

"So you told me." Olive wondered where this was going—the urgency, the story she'd heard before. She said, "Absolutely spellbinding."

She had a wary guarded look, watching him through heavy lids, the look she might have had for one of her patients who'd come to the emergency room with slashes on his arm and a story about how he'd fallen down —*fallen down?* Or the man with deep scratches on his face, in handcuffs, charged with shooting his wife, saying, "I was cleaning my gun." But she listened rather than contradicted what was obviously a story, watching without seeming to doubt or mock, because there was no telling what the injured person might do.

"Hunter used to tell me that he envied me. His pseudonym was a kind of compliment." Sharkey smiled in the direction of the shadow, as though meeting a ghostly gaze. "Mr. Joe."

Listening, Olive thought, *At what point will he realize that he is rabbiting on in a blatant parody, almost as though he's testing me to challenge him?* In speaking of the past, describing his surfing exploits, he had told such extraordinary stories that even the blandest retellings sounded like boasts. Yet the offense of boasters was not the oversized, obnoxious stories but that they were bores, because boasters repeated themselves and couldn't keep their stories straight, being essentially untruthful in their exaggeration. And they never listened.

What she longed to do these days of his talking was to face him and say, "For the love of God, park it!"

But Olive was too watchful, too cautious, to make an objection to Sharkey, because that was the other trait of boasters — their insecurity, their thin skin. Yet Sharkey had seemed to her to have a healthy ego, and she wondered at this monologue about Hunter Thompson that she had heard before.

"'Writers are surfers,' he said. He was a great guy, a kind of tragic figure really, who liked being around stronger men — outlaws, pirates . . ."

"Bikers," Olive said. "Gun nuts."

"You got it," Sharkey said, and seemed to relax, though he did not look at her, was still peering across the room.

What was going on? Didn't he remember?

That was all he said that evening. But it was enough — too much.

Out of the blue another day he began to talk as though someone had flicked a switch. They were at the table, using chopsticks to eat the bowls of ahi poke and rice that Olive had brought from Foodland on her way home from work. Sharkey put his chopsticks down and sat forward and stared past her.

"I was at this surf meet at Mavericks," he said. "When it was over—I came second, a money prize—I drove up the coast and had an urge to look up an old girlfriend. Not just an old girlfriend but a great passion, the kind that makes you wild and irrational. I'd been divorced for about a year—my wife never watched me surf." He made a resentful face, pushing out his lips.

"'People don't care about me. I'm nobody to them. All they want is to get close to you.'"

Olive said, "San Francisco."

He nodded. "Mission District. You're going to think she was some airhead surf bunny I'd known years before that I'd nailed in the back of my van."

"I don't think that."

"She was a college professor I'd met in a coffee shop in Santa Cruz. She was small and kind of sallow, with one of those drowsy, hungry faces, pretty in a girlish way but not unusual, with greeny-gray eyes, the sleepy kind. She looked like a grim little monkey and she was combing her hair at the table when I saw her."

"Without a mirror."

"I mean, what woman combs her hair without looking in a mirror?" Sharkey said. "I sat at the next table, and there was something" — he sniffed, twitching his nose — "in the air. She seemed to give off a warm damp odor of sexuality. Maybe a pheromone, but it smelled to me like bark mulch, something of the earth, something swampy. She seemed to be freaked by my leaning into her space and she went to a table outside. I followed her and pestered her — teased her, that was always my method."

"When boys tease you it's usually because they're attracted to you."

"Someone told me that once."

"I know."

"It worked. It wasn't love, it was desire, an animal urge to possess her. I hung around, I told her I was single, I talked about places in the world I'd been surfing — Cornwall in England got her attention, South Africa too. We had sex that night and the next morning. That great swampy smell got stronger. I wanted to eat her, I felt like a cannibal. We left bite marks on each other. I was half mad. I couldn't leave her. I almost cried when I had to fly back to Hawaii, and I'd wake up at night and smile, thinking of her. I went back two weeks later. By then we'd talked a little on the phone, but I hated the phone. When we were together she said that she'd found out who I was, that I was married, that she was angry. I told her I was divorced. But she was demented too, the same desire. We had this full-on physical thing, fastened to each other, thrashing, insane. Later she called me, she cried, she wanted me, she threatened to kill herself, she raged at me. I needed to surf, yet I was still obsessed with her. I began to understand what addiction is like, how meaningless it is when people say, 'It's bad for you. It'll kill you. You'll have to give it up.' No — I wanted to devour this woman. Crazy, I remember the obsession more than I remember the woman."

"Then it ended."

"In the worst way," Sharkey said. "And a long time afterward I saw her in San Francisco. We had lunch. She was pinched and disappointed, a little old woman with white hair. I barely made it through the meal. I thought —"

"No magic."

Now Sharkey raised his eyes to her. "You've had that experience?"

"You've told me that story before."

"When?" He looked bewildered, as though she'd tricked him into talking.

"The thrill is gone. No magic."

"So you know?"

"You left out the part where she was going to drown herself in your swimming pool."

"Motel swimming pool. I told you that?"

"The cure for an unhappy love affair, 'Wait twenty years.' That's what you said."

"Sunny Jim" Olive sometimes called him, and had often said that his great surfer smile and his beautiful teeth and sunburned and satisfied face, even the scar on his cheek from the old dog bite, showed he didn't worry — she meant he didn't reflect, but that seemed like an accusation. He would have said himself that he wasn't a worrier and not reflective but active. All he wished for were sunny days and big waves.

"I'm not into sitting around, man," he'd said. But he was sitting now, and in his enforced idleness, resting his back, allowing his sore foot to heal, he became reflective, remembering vivid images rather than stretches of time that involved his saying, "And then . . . and then . . . ," which he hated.

"I had two boards in South Africa. I asked the African guy who drove me to the beach to help me with the second one. He says to me, 'I don't carry.'"

Olive said, "Sometimes a whole year or a whole trip or a whole relationship is summed up in an image, or an injury, or a something someone says. 'I don't carry.'"

"One thing that stands for everything."

"But you told me about that too. Your African driver. It was Jeffreys Bay."

His fingers flew to his cheek as though he'd been slapped. He'd told her those stories before? It was bad enough to repeat yourself and be boring, but the look on Olive's face was one of pity, as though she was hearing an old man blab about the past. Repetition was the trait of the bore, and it was lazy-minded, arising from indifference, or contempt: to the bore, all listeners were the same, and repeating a story meant that it didn't matter whom he was telling it to, filling the air with his talk was a sort of compulsion, the bore being above all an impatient listener, whether a celebrity bore or a hero bore.

But the other implication, that he hadn't remembered telling the story before — that shamed him too, as much as his being a bore. He had been quietly proud of his memory. His good memory had made up for his poor education, and no one knew or cared that he'd dropped out of high school. Travel had taught him, and he could recall the peculiar curl in the contour of a barrel and the slope on the face of the wave that drove him to go left on the heavy wave at Teahupo'o in Tahiti, and the soft lips of his first lover, Nalani, whom he'd kissed in the darkness of an old van after school, and the down, like golden leaf fuzz, in the declivity in the small of her back. He remembered names; his memory for details he'd been told was phenomenal. He often said, "I forget nothing" or "I am cursed with total recall," when he felt his head was buzzing with trivia, his whole life and all its sounds and images crowding his brain. Some memories he would have been happy to delete, many things he wished to forget — scenes and accusations that visited him at night — but he was burdened with them.

Or so he thought. Now it seemed that by some obscure puncture his memory was leaking, as Olive was reminding him, and that he had no access anymore to his memory. He associated the smiling droning bore with the celebrities he'd known. One characteristic of the celebrity — so many of them idolizing surfers — was that he or she was on familiar, even intimate terms with the whole world.

That was the oddity of fame, not that everyone seemed to know you but that you were always confiding to strangers, speaking in general, everyone a potential ally or well-wisher, as though on a lifelong campaign, the guest of honor at every table, the brightest light at every party, always the talker among rapt admiring faces — it seemed that way. You were everyone's friend, holding conversations with the multitudes, and so you had no real friends, but that didn't matter, because the intensity of one intimate friend, or a loving wife, was an obstacle to talking to the world. The world was your friend.

The surfer celebrity was the sort of hero who strode into a room, smiling, with confident eyes, and a hush fell, and the celebrity spoke to the room and did not linger; after the talk — no questions — the celebrity departed. Because of being known so well as a power figure, the celebrity was like a visiting friend — his history in everyone's mind, no introduction needed, and he launched into his talk so self-assuredly that it could pass for the authority of preaching. No one answered back, there was no defiance or disrespect; the celebrity's presence indicated agreement, since he was the superior elder brother, not to be challenged.

Sharkey had spent his big-wave-riding years as one of these golden men, and though he'd become over time friendlier and more detached, he was sought out by other celebrities, surfers, or visiting musicians or writers — rockers and names.

One of these was Hunter Thompson, himself a talker — a shouter when he was drunk — and seldom a listener, gravelly voiced and unpredictable, attracted to the recklessness and tribalism of surf culture, the available drugs and the drinking, the stew of hangers-on, the promise of sex — sex was like a handshake here, a way of getting acquainted. When there was no surf there was nothing to do except raise hell.

Hunter had become Sharkey's friend. Everyone in Hawaii knew Sharkey; everyone elsewhere knew Hunter, it seemed. In the fractured days after the accident, in what he thought of as his convalescence, Hunter Thompson was often in Sharkey's thoughts — he mentioned him to Olive, he talked about the derangement of celebrity, the famous person, known to all, looking for listeners.

"In actual fact," Olive said again, with as much tact as she could, "you've told me that before."

The softened words still stung Sharkey, especially as Olive had listened to an hour or more of his talk, and he realized that he'd bored her, as Hunter had often bored him, telling the same drunken stories in a hotel room or over the phone from Woody Creek at three in the morning. But his embarrassment was brief; he quickly forgot what he had told her and how she had responded.

"He liked me. We had plans."

She nodded and decided not to say, "So you've told me."

She was surprised by his solemn, reflective tone, as though he'd just remembered these incidents and was imparting them with reverence for the first time. She knew they were old settled memories that he'd told her before. Why he was repeating them she had no idea, but if she commented too often he'd be self-conscious; so she listened, as though hearing them for the first time, because he spoke in tones of discovery and wonderment.

Sometimes her patients, stunned by a drug or waking from surgery, behaved in this muddled way, and so she listened to Sharkey, trying not to seem clinical or detached, to his earnest recollections as he walked her backward through his memories, as though on a path they'd traveled together. He seemed to believe that everything he said was a stark revelation, while she squirmed, pitying him for his obvious repetition. None of it was new to her.

At what point would he realize he'd told her all this before?

"Earthquakes," he said, and a smile flickered on his lips. He did not hear Olive's shallow sigh. "Great occasions for meeting girls — I mean, hooking up. They run out of the building and cower in a street or in a doorway. I get next to the chicks, hugging them during the tremor. There's no rush on earth like it — better than a wave. 'Quake foreplay, 'quake sex."

"San Francisco," Olive said.

"We were in the doorway" — he hadn't heard her — "and the car alarms are going off and the windows breaking — glass shattering in the street —

and we're snatching at each other, insane, like it's the end of the world. And that's how the world will end, destruction and orgies."

"And you spent the night with her."

"Another time," he said, gabbling now, his eyes fixed on his sore foot, which he was flexing, "I'm in a hotel in Bali — surf meet at Uluwatu — and there's a fire alarm. Everyone is evacuated and standing in the dark in their bathrobes, seriously worried, except me. I put my arm around this gorgeous woman and reassure her, and she thanks me as I stroke her. There's no fire. But the sudden event, maybe fear, has bonded us. I head back to her room with her and we get it on — panic sex."

It gave him such pleasure to relate these ridiculous stories, as though for the first time, that she stopped saying she'd heard them before.

"Getting married? Big mistake. 'Why should I have to share you?' 'Why doesn't anyone talk to me?' Good thing we didn't have any kids. Her family wanted them, so they could have them to themselves. Big pressure, because her family was involved. Women in Hawaii live close to their families, so they're always making bad decisions, and the family sorts it out. Kids, bills, all the crises. They ended up hating me."

"You were young."

"And I was young."

Olive withdrew, she took refuge in her work, but on her return home Sharkey was glad to see her so that he could lead her back into his past, all of it known to her now.

"We used to paddle into the big waves. Then they towed us. These days the young guys paddle into bigger and bigger waves. It's the boards. Smaller, lighter. And the guys are more intense."

He had wooed her with his stories once, and now she was near to being repelled, except that she was so sorry for him in his plodding in circles.

"My mother wanted me to stop surfing. She saw me lose a contest — I was just a kid — and she mocked me. But when I became successful she boasted about me to her friends. She was weak and hypocritical. Yet I was so sad when she died."

Olive was surprised by his solemnity — it seemed stagy and forced. But he was frowning, as though he'd just remembered these things and was speaking about them with reverence for the first time. Why he was repeating them now she had no idea, but if she mentioned that, he'd be self-conscious.

When he'd wooed her with stories, he'd held her attention, because all of them were fresh, and her eyes had brightened as he spoke. He was a good talker, and it surprised her that, storyteller that he was, he had never written a line — he was stumped with a pen, he'd doodle a little, then crumple the paper. But it didn't matter. He had stories.

Testing him, because she'd suffered all day with the memory, she said, "You killed a man a few weeks ago. You don't even know his name."

He shook his head, as though correcting her. "Ran into a drunk homeless guy."

She roused him early the next morning, before he could protest. She said, "You're coming with me, don't eat," and he sat stunned and sleepy in the car.

"'Nobody heard him, the dead man,'" she said on the road.

"Which one?" Sharkey said.

"It's a poem. We learned it at school."

"Poem," he said, expelling the word in a flat breath, as though it were meaningless.

"The dead man moans,

I was much too far out all my life
And not waving but drowning."

"Dead men don't moan," Sharkey said. "Dead men are gone."

Olive looked sideways at him and, seeing that they were near the emergency entrance of the hospital, decided not to reply. Sharkey allowed himself to be checked in, Olive doing the talking. He was booked for an MRI and assigned a cubicle. Olive left him in the care of a nurse, and glancing back, she saw him being handed a flimsy hospital gown and cloth slippers. When she stopped in after lunch he was cross-legged on the bed; and the next time she looked in he was being wheeled back to his cubicle, a big man in baby clothes but still smiling.

After the long day he crept to the sofa on the lanai and, like a cat folding itself, curled into a ball of repose. He resumed staring at the setting sun, in the posture of the previous day.

He began to speak.

Olive said, "Park it," and then quickly, "I think you've told me that before."

Waiting for the results, because Olive asked for the specialist at Queen's to read the scans, Sharkey sat, sometimes curled and catlike, sometimes in his yoga posture.

"The doctor cleared you," Olive said in a disbelieving whisper two days later.

"What doctor?"

Instead of answering that, she said, "I'm worried about you."

"Olive — the fretter."

His lazy boast, always, was that he never fussed, and he was contemptuous of anyone who claimed to care, as though they were revealing a weakness.

"The best doctor at Queen's read your MRI."

"What doctor? What MRI?"

"'He's good to go,' he said. You're fine."

Sharkey smiled as though at a child too small to understand and needing to be humored. He said, "Of course I'm fine. Listen, there was no hospital, okay? I've been surfing awesome waves."

Was it the conspicuous humiliation of the hospital gown, having to submit to the tunnel of the machine, or the long, almost all-day delay in Emergency? But he remembered nothing of it.

She said, "Except for the hospital and the tests, you haven't left the house."

He began to laugh, but softly, and then he stopped and nodded, as though he'd become aware that he was mocking her for inventing the trip to the hospital and the scan.

He glanced at Olive in pity for not understanding him, as though she were someone adrift in a sea of uncertainty and seeming to believe she was safe, just bobbing in circles and liking the rise and fall of the swell and never realizing she was lost. All this time, his soft, accommodating smile.

The sun was setting again into the seam of the horizon, the last of the light flashing on his face. He was remembering the barrel of a wave. Olive was watching him. When he turned to her, she was horrified by the sight of him: his wide-open eyes were unlit, dull, and disappointed, his face waxen, no light behind it. She remembered the man on the road, his martyr's death mask of surrender. Then Sharkey resumed talking in the darkness, another story she'd heard before.

10

Hapai

While Olive worked every day at the hospital, Sharkey sat as though immobilized, yet smiling his sleepy smile — repeating his stories and imagining that his days were full of sunlight and big waves. She could not convince him that his life was emptying, narrowing, closing in on him — closing in on her too. He was unworried, yet she felt the onset of uncertainty that extended to her body as a physical imbalance, at times producing dizziness, a feeling at moments of vertigo. Was it loneliness that provoked the sensation that she was toppling forward?

Often in this mood she was weakened by a wave of nausea passing through her. She wanted to tell him, "I am not feeling well. Therefore I'm alive." In the house with him she became mournful — lonely, a feeling she seldom had when she was alone — and at times she went outside or back to the hospital to cure herself of loneliness among her friends.

"You stay okay?" Luana, the shift nurse, asked.

"A little pukey."

Luana hugged her, big warm damp arms and hair thick with coconut oil. "You take something, sister. It's a shame."

"It's a sign of life," Olive said, thinking of Sharkey's delusion of health in his weird confinement of repetition.

But Luana's question had startled her — she had not thought she'd looked so obvious in her discomfort. Olive's nausea was unusual. She had arrived early so that she could meditate awhile before she signed in. But life goes on, she thought, emptying her mind, and was heartened: if she was sick, she'd get well.

She sat in a lotus posture under an awning on the roof, with a view of the sea, and she inhaled the day, using her breathing exercises to clear her head and settle her stomach. It seemed to work; a sensation of weightlessness lifted her. But when she lay flat on her back in a corpse pose a new thought intruded: there was nothing like this variation in Sharkey's day-to-day — no friend, no yoga, no questions. He sat smiling. Was he holding his breath? His past crowded his present, and the rest was a void. She knew that much of what he'd claimed he'd done was boasting or invention, but that was how heroes lived, inhabiting their own myth with such conviction that other people were persuaded. Yet most people's lives, no matter how humble, were marked by incident, the rise and fall of hope, the swelling of self-belief, the looking for more, and always the waking to a new day.

Olive saw that Sharkey's repetitive life, more serious than a delusion, was like a terminal illness.

Yet the man was functional. He ate, he slept, he limped in his garden, feeding his geese and chickens, plucking blossoms, squinting at the sun. Perhaps this was how prisoners or monks lived their lives, shuffling in narrow spaces, pausing often, adjusting themselves to their confinement, like animals in zoo enclosures, learning how to repeat their small steps: pacing, drowsing, blinking, head-bobbing, vegetating — functionless behavior, with the shallow breathing and slowed heartbeat of someone buried alive.

And if you interrupted them in their pacing, asked a question, you got the same answer, and perhaps a monologue — something circular, the thought that had been stewing in their mind.

Or was she imagining his condition, exaggerating his passivity and drowsy routines? He was an energetic surfer, but he was a panting animal too. A lion pounds after its prey across the savannah and seizes it by the haunches to devour, roaring and tearing with its teeth, and gorges itself, and then lolls and naps, yawning under a tree, days of this, long periods of grunting repose. The monk seal on a wave, the water dog of the Hawaiian coasts, tossed in surf, diving for food, rolling in the swells nipping at fish, until at last exhausted, noses to shore and bumps up the hot sand above the tidemark and sleeps. He was that lion, he was that seal.

Tending to his chickens, he seemed himself: gathering eggs, feeding his geese and ducks, picking lilikoi and avocados, making his meals. Something might not be working inside him, a nerve circuit might have died, yet he was alive. But the stories, the smile, the head-bobbing — her worry was their sameness, and her anxiety wearied her.

He took no notice of her. He was asleep when she set off for work; he was tired on her return, so she saw only the limp man, doddering in his fatigue, and was often grateful, because she was tired too and hadn't the strength to rouse him, even less to listen to another story she already knew.

Her weakness was like a reproach — her need to sit down to look at her laptop (she'd always done it standing), or bracing herself to clutch her tablet to look at a patient's history, or to read a temperature or a heart rate or bloodwork. She'd climb a flight of stairs and feel lightheaded and need to steady herself on the handrail — and then the griping in her gut and the intimation that she was about to heave, her mouth filling with saliva.

Just as quickly it would pass and she'd regain the confidence that it was nothing, or something she'd eaten, a chunk of bad ahi, or — powerfully — that it was a visceral reaction to her worrying about Sharkey; how nothing had been the same since the accident. But she was cautioned too, and thought, *I'm probably in worse shape than he is.*

With her it was physical, and these days laid her low, napping in the nurses' room at the hospital; with him it was a dropping of his spirit, a diminishment, seeming like obstinacy, the great flame of his being reduced to an afterglow, like the ocean after sunset, blackening, going cold. There were no words for his condition; for hers there were plenty: she was weak and nauseous and easily fatigued, she felt disgusted and sad and futile.

She was no use to him; he said he didn't need her. She was superfluous, except at work.

And that was the great thing about a job, the sustaining illusion that you were necessary, and if you didn't show up, the work would never get done. It was the conceit of your being essential. Except for a spell as a lifeguard, Sharkey had never had a job. He knew nothing of deadlines and emergencies, nothing of budgets, of money. He lived in his passion for the water: if the surf was up, he was up, in his car or on his board, all other promises were broken, all other urgencies faded into insignificance, his whole attention was fastened onto his being on a wave, even in rain and wind, sometimes in starlight, sometimes in moonless darkness.

So the conditions of the water had always determined the rhythm of his days. The tidal variations were so small — a few feet at most in Hawaii — they hardly mattered; but the swell and the shapes of the waves were the pulse and beat of his vitality. And when, between the big swells, the surf subsided, Sharkey swam, he free-dived off Shark's Cove or spearfished; he did not sit. Either he was active in the water or else he lay in the sand, chewing air or lightly snoring, the coarse grains clinging to his skin, the sand heating his back. And when he was rested he rolled himself down the beach to the water and flashed into the bluey-green depths among the parrotfish and shoals of manini and the needle-nosed sea eels.

He ate what came to hand — the sweet eggs from his chickens, mangoes and avocados and lilikoi from his trees, breadfruit when it was in season. He drank green tea in the morning, one strong coffee after lunch, beer at night. He browsed when he was hungry, yawned and dozed when he was tired, and when he was aroused he rolled against Olive as though body-surfing a warm wave, entered her, and rode her until they both lay ashore on the bed.

But since the accident he'd shown no interest, as though the shock to his system that had made him repetitive and forgetful had also short-circuited his libido. Once, when she mentioned this, he said, "We made love yesterday." But they hadn't.

These days he was asleep when she returned from work; he'd drunk a few beers, he'd eaten, the house was frosted with moonlight and skeletal in semidarkness. When he saw that the surf report was for clean conditions he was up early; otherwise he was unresponsive when she left for the hospital.

Nor had he noticed that she was wakeful, sometimes retching, and it annoyed her that she could not get his attention with her seemingly fragile health. Scrupulous in taking precautions, sometimes a pill, sometimes a patch, she knew she could not possibly be pregnant. She wanted to scream at him (as patients sometimes howled at the hospital), "Don't you see I'm sick!" But really she wasn't sick enough, and didn't want to be so sick that she needed him, because what use would he be? He'd been no help at all to his aged mother. He told her, *I saw her losing it.* He'd say, *When I get like that, hit me with a brick — shoot me.*

One morning when the surf was up and he was alert, moving quickly, slapping the pockets of his shorts for his keys, his board already on the car, she said, "Joe — wait."

"Yeah," and rattled the keys in his impatient hand.

"You're better off alone."

He looked at her, irritated, deaf with detachment.

"Can't find my new sunglasses!"

As soon as he started to swear, she left. And driving to the hospital, always the same road, feeling the potholes with her hands on the steering wheel, she repeated the sentence she'd practiced, the tactful farewell — *You're better off alone* — then thought, *No.*

"I'm better off alone," she said in the mild mumble she used in the car, talking to herself — talking, because saying something aloud helped her remember, filled her with resolve.

Luana always asked how she was feeling, and because Olive said, "Fine," and Luana didn't believe her, Luana kept asking, as on this morning.

"I was wondering," Olive said, instead of replying directly, "is there still a vacant room in the nurses' quarters?"

Approaching her, arms out, Luana smiled in sympathy, almost in gratitude, and she embraced Olive in a motherly hug, her whole soft body pressed against her, as if to give her warmth. Their foreheads touched, Luana's sweetened with soap, her thick arms enclosing Olive.

"Yes, got one for you," Luana said, and seemed sure that this request for a room meant that what she suspected was true: Olive was ailing.

"Because I'm going to start working nights."

"Sure," the woman said, and hugged her closer, feeling that this was an excuse for the ailment — or was it the guy? — and she did not want to give any details.

Olive moved some of her clothes from Sharkey's closets and drawers on a day of big waves, and as she was putting them in her car he texted her that he was all right — reassuring her, as though she might be worried about him. He did not ask about her.

He never asked. On the high-surf days she drove to Sunset or Waimea, or farther down the road to Alligators or Leftovers or Marijuana's, and found him with her binoculars. It was as though he were not a man at all — certainly not one who'd been jarred by an accident ("I ran into a drunk homeless guy"). No, he was like a rare form of marine life, a sea mammal in the foam, the water dog he claimed to be, slipping down the face of a wave and riding it nearly to where it broke, and instead of crawling to shore, cutting across the lip and paddling and diving beneath the waves until he was out to sea, in the lineup again, preparing to drop in.

At the end of the day he would go home, drink a beer, make himself an omelet, and sit, lit by the sunset, inhaling the last of the light into his body. He was fine. He said so in his occasional messages, telling her he'd had a good day, less like a text to his lover than an announcement to an anxious world, eager for the latest bulletin from Joe Sharkey.

He didn't ask, but she was not well, with a sourness in her gut, fatigue, and lightheadedness. Her being among other women was a comfort, for their sympathy and gentle manner — and most were nurses, trained to be healers. She knew they were scrutinizing her out of concern for her well-being, not out of nosiness — niele, as Luana called it. Luana, in the room next to hers, took to sizing her up and putting a motherly arm around her when, in the evening, they headed to Emergency for the night shift.

Olive felt compelled to say, "You mustn't fuss. I'm really all right, you know."

But her denial made her self-conscious, and Luana's smile seemed an understanding that something was wrong.

"You never eating nothing."

"I eat enough."

That seemed lame too. All the nurses ate together in the hospital cafeteria; it was impossible to hide anything from them, especially from their nurses' watchfulness.

One night, admitting a woman who showed signs of having overdosed

— limp, nauseous, dizzy, with depressed breathing: all the signs; she'd been left by a man who'd hurried away — Olive struggled with the woman, who was heavy, her flesh cool to the touch. She put her on her side in a recovery position and went faint. She staggered, but she was caught in her fall by Luana, who took over, urging Olive to lie down, then sped the woman to the doctor on duty. She soon returned to Olive, who lay doubled up.

"I'm better."

Luana frowned. "I'm thinking for a long time, Ollie — how you know you not *hapai*?"

They used the word all the time at the hospital. That thought had occurred to her, that she might be pregnant, but her periods were often irregular or late, so she'd kept an open mind. And what was this? Only a week or a little more of nausea and fragility. And she related it to the disturbance she felt, provoked by Sharkey's strangeness.

"I don't know."

"Let's we do one test," Luana said, pulling open a drawer and poking at small plastic boxes. "You need to make *shishi*."

They did the test together, Luana manipulating the test tube and the litmus paper while Olive sat watching, wondering, listening to the clatter outside the room, keenly aware of the anxious questions of the injured, the smells of illness and disinfectant.

"You *hapai*," Luana said, and hugged her.

11

Leftovers

Holding her fists at her side, Olive stood in the darkness of the lanai, in a cloud of fragrance from the night-blooming jasmine, watching him through the wide opening of the sliding screens. Sharkey looked caged, squatting under the glare of a floor lamp, digging at the cuticle around a fingernail like a monkey in a grooming ritual, his teeth bared, his hair wild, his tattoos gleaming on his golden skin. He wore only his board shorts — he'd been surfing; crusts of sea salt glinted on his shoulders, salt crystals also dusting his hair and his sticky arms.

As Olive stepped into the light he twisted his head — also a monkey move, swiveling his eyes — and, looking up, he ceased grubbing with his fingers and flashed his teeth at her. In her green nurse's scrubs she was easily seen in the panel of light from the window.

She thought she heard him grunt — or was it a word? — and drew back, a little afraid. She'd been away a week, in silence, and had never run from him before. She did not know what to expect and was so short of breath in her anxiety she couldn't speak — in any case did not know what to say.

He sometimes smiled when he was furious. He was smiling now. She took another slight step backward.

"Pass me that towel, eh?" he muttered.

She slid the screens apart, kicked her slippers off, and walked through, shutting them behind her, and stooped to pick up the rag that lay beyond his reach. Handing it to him, she drew away, bowing involuntarily.

With the rag in his fist he worked the cloth over his sweaty face, clawing his hair at the same time, another ritual she knew. Then he dropped the rag and began examining his toes. Even from a distance — she was about eight feet away — she could see that he was scratched, the cuts showing as pale scores and grooves and reddened skin.

"You've been out?" The words lumped and seemed to catch in her throat.

"Like I said, yeah."

When would that have been?

"Got pinched in the barrel — gas-chamber action."

He made a noise softly, *kek-kek,* that might have been a laugh. He was calm, and so, reassured, she took a seat in the chair near where he squatted.

"Tossed in the foam ball."

He splayed his fingers, showing how they were badly scratched, then he crooked them like monkey paws.

"Motion in the ocean," he said. "And after all that I got planted on the rocks." He gathered himself and hopped upright and stood, grunting again, walking away from her, round-shouldered in his fatigue. "Never mind. A good day. How was yours?"

Now he was lit by the open refrigerator, leaning at the shelves, poking at plastic containers of leftovers — broccoli, pasta sauce, salad, cubes of raw fish.

"I'm hungry."

Either this was all an elaborate show of being cool, or else he hadn't realized she'd been gone for seven nights, and that seemed impossible.

But that was all. He halved an avocado, pried out the pit, filled each half with ahi poke, and gave one to Olive.

"Have a beer."

"Not for me."

"Wine — I think there's some in the fridge door."

"I'll pass."

"You joking?"

"I'm off alcohol."

"You practically killed a bottle yesterday."

She stared at him with such incomprehension he shrugged and went to the table and began eating, swigging beer, while she watched, not touching her avocado. When he was done he yawned, said, "I'm beat," and went to bed.

"I'll put these plates away," Olive said.

Like that, she moved back in with him.

He was up early the next morning, heading to Sunset to surf — she saw him on her way to the hospital: he was sitting on his board, rocking in the swell, small in the water, with the immensity of the ocean behind him shimmering in the clear dawn light that gave the wide surface of the sea the texture of fish scales.

He was alone on the lift of the wave, still there when it passed, and she slowed her car to watch him. She thought of pulling over to see him take a wave, but she knew his skill and it was enough to see him so solitary, rising and falling on the swell, riding his board as always like a horseman on the steep hill of water, waiting to catch a wave and drop in.

And what after all did she see of his life as a surfer — what did anyone see of the figures rocking in the water? Not much, hardly anything, and so what she knew of this passion of his was negligible. His real life — the life he lived in the waves — was unseen and almost unknowable.

No one onshore, few even in the water, saw the surfer with any accuracy. On a day of good waves she often had trouble picking him out of the lineup of seven or eight bodies, some fighting the boil, others aiming their boards through the crest, a few behind it all bobbing and thrashing, levering their boards into position. They might have been dolphins, alike in their sleekness and size, anonymous in the beauty of their movement in the rough water and the whiteness of the wind-blown chop, the grace of their buoyancy.

She surfed but could not call herself a surfer — he had encouraged her to improve, bullied her at times to join him; yet even then she knew she would be too preoccupied to watch him. No one but the surfer knew what the surfer was able to do; the surfer was alone on the wave, the succession of waves, a set of seven typically, and chose one and rode it to shore, becoming an individual at the nearer break. Or wiped out and was lost in the foam, and sometimes — without anyone seeing — the surfer was tumbled over the falls and held down and drowned by the wave he was riding, tossed as though from a bucking bronco and trampled to death in the suds.

People had praised Sharkey on the North Shore, he said — mobbed him, touched his arm for luck; women hugged him, men too, some of the women eager to loop a lei over his head so that they could kiss him, as was customary. He was a speck in the surf, an insect skittering on a great wave's face, but he was for most just a famous name, Joe Sharkey, big-wave rider. His life on the water was hidden. He might, for all of that, have been a fish — sometimes flipping himself free of the sea, twirling across the surface, causing shouts, but most of the time beneath the water, squirming and flashing.

Olive had heard — first from others, then from Sharkey — that his greatest ride had taken place on a high broad marching wave one hundred miles at sea, the wave face eighty or a hundred feet, an immense jawline — witnessed by no one. The jet ski that had towed him out to Cortes Bank had toppled on the far side; the skipper of the boat that had taken him there had been fighting a wave of his own.

"Did you see that?" Sharkey yelled when they found each other, the boat-man and the man riding the jet ski.

Neither had seen him. That he was upright at the end of his ride, on his board, waist-deep in froth, was proof that he had ridden the monster. But between the takeoff at the top, tipping himself across the face of the wave, and his howl of joy at the end of it, standing on his board and skidding through the mass of broken water and pools of foam, he had been hidden.

He was hidden from her now. She had returned to live again in the house without his having remarked on it, as though she'd never left. She needed somehow to get his attention. She knew she had the means. The thing was to tell him her news at the appropriate time.

He was entirely self-absorbed, another effect of his solitude — his hidden passion and achievement as a surfer. But it was the apparent selfishness of sick people too, preoccupied with their ailments. She accepted that, because she saw that though he was alone, he was never lonely. But it worried her that his solitude had intensified since the accident, to the point where he seemed in a stall, repeating himself, seemingly oblivious of time passing, lost and left behind, in a bubble.

Part of his memory had been left behind on the rainy road at Waimea, where he'd killed the man on the bike. He needed reviving, he needed to begin living again, he needed new things to care about — new waves, bigger waves; he needed to care about her. And who was his victim, the nameless corpse on the road, the man he had killed?

She thought that her refusing alcohol might make him wonder. But he didn't ask. He ate, he drank, he slept, he hugged her; and when the surf was up he was in it.

Always disappointed in fine weather when the waves were small — "flat to a foot" — he was becalmed at home. She waited for one of those days, a Sunday when she wasn't working, and bought a bento and some trays of sushi at Foodland and suggested they have a picnic at Three Tables Beach. There they sat on their towels, balancing the trays on their outstretched legs.

"Might see a late whale," Sharkey said, and studied the break at Rubber Duckies. But the swell was so gentle a snorkeler was crossing where days before the waves had been head-high.

Olive found she couldn't face him and say it. She lay flat and embraced him, clasped his head and held it next to hers, put her mouth against his ear.

"Do you love me?"

"Yes."

"Say it."

"I love you."

"How much?"

"More than my mother."

She laughed. "You told me your mum was a pest."

"That's what I mean. She drove me crazy. You make me happy."

"Would you be happy if you knew I was pregnant?"

His hair was hot and damp against her forehead, and she could feel his breath moving through his head, vibrant in his scalp. He didn't speak. He went on breathing, his breath like a process of thought, air seesawing in reflection.

"It's very early," she said into his silence. "I almost wasn't going to tell you. But I've been feeling so awful, and now I know that's related to it. And it's — see — it's not just about me. It's ours, our decision."

Still he said nothing. She held him, the warm breathing man, the sun on them both, the small waves pushing at the shore, their splish-splash, their gulp on the sand. She did not want to say anything more, either to convince him or to talk herself out of it. So she moved away from him and rolled onto her back, feeling pleasantly scorched by the hot sand.

But he threw his arm around her and drew her to him. And now his mouth was against her ear.

"Getting tubed is like being born," he said.

"So you're okay with it?"

"I'm stoked."

"You're always so down on other people's kids."

"This is not other people's kids."

Now she turned to him and held his face and said, "You're happy."

"It makes me feel young."

"You are young."

"When did you find out?"

"That week — when I was away."

"What week? When were you away?"

He seemed to believe that she was teasing him. He had taken such pleasure in the news of the child that she didn't want to break the mood by insisting he was mistaken about her not having been away.

Instead of contradicting him, she said, "I seemed to have morning sickness. I thought it was a bug. One of the nurses made me take a pregnancy test. 'You *hapai*,' she said. I still feel like a dog's dinner sometimes, but it passes."

"Imagine," he said — he was looking past her, smiling at their baby. "People will think I'm his grandfather."

"They'll adore him. They'll know his father is Joe Sharkey."

"Little kids are amazing surfers. I started young. I've seen five-year-olds paddle out and catch a wave."

He was still staring past her head, studying the water, seeing his child on the gentle wave that was bulging toward shore, the sort of wave a child might ride, planted on his board and shrieking with joy.

"Three-year-olds can learn to swim. These great athletes — they always started young. And you know, surfing saved me when I was miserable at school. It's not a sport — it's a life choice."

Olive could feel his body tensed with excitement, the eagerness hardening his muscles. She'd been unprepared for it — she thought it was something she'd have to defend or argue for; but he accepted it, and it was more than acceptance. He had seized the thought, and he was already seeing a surfer, a companion, a friend, in a way that first surprised and pleased her and then alarmed her.

He was gleeful on the way home, nodding, seeing through the front window — what? — the child on a surfboard, a child in his arms, a little hero.

"It's still early," she said, to caution him. "Maybe six weeks. Anything can happen."

"It's going to be fine. You just need to stay healthy."

"I'll stop working nights."

"I don't mean that. You have to eat better. You need to spend more time in the water. You have to be buoyant."

One of his unshakable beliefs was that to be healthy a person needed to be immersed, floating, tossed by waves, twisting beneath them, reliving the ancient memory of our ancestry as sea creatures, recreating that life and evolution by spending part of every day in the water. And in the late afternoon, the sunset blazing in the distance, swimming to shore and flopping in the shore break and scrabbling in the boils of foam and the lacework of bubbles, until finally, streaming with water, crawling onto the sand and creeping up the beach. It was his daily ritual, a celebration of his being a waterman.

"Take some time off. Get into the water."

"I've got some sick days coming to me."

"You need some water," he said. He was still driving. He reached for her leg and squeezed it gently.

But the deftness could only have come from many years of practice. How often in a car with a woman has that gesture served him, she thought — the reach, the squeeze, the click of his tongue on his teeth? A man winking at her had always made her sigh and turn away.

So she was surprised when he kept his attention on her. That night and thereafter she became the embodiment of the child for him. He seemed to treat her with the tender love that he had for the child to come. Holding her, he was holding the baby, and all the fear she'd had in telling him the news vanished. He was a different man, a hopeful one, thinking of someone other than himself. And she was different too, incredibly, soon to be a mother. That gave her joy and a sense of power she had not known before. Already she felt a throb of new vitality; she was strong.

She had not expected him to take such an interest, but he did, he was inquisitive and full of advice, seeming to take possession of the child while the little thing was not yet a bump in her belly. The child, so far, was her nausea, her dizziness, her feeling in the morning that (having drunk no alcohol at all) she had a hangover.

Sharkey had a child's impatience, a need for news, the mildly cranky are-we-there-yet? sigh of frustration. She knew his hatred of waiting, yet with his harping on the fact that the world was overpopulated — "man is an invasive species" — it seemed odd to her that he clung so fiercely to the notion of having a child of his own. Maybe his age was a factor, the realization that he could have an heir, someone to carry on in his name. He was protective of her because the child was within her, and at times he was so single-minded about the baby she had to remind him that she was only in her second month — there were months more. She knew she didn't look pregnant, and were it not for the bouts of nausea and sleeplessness she would have paid no attention.

Yet he talked of little else. He still surfed when conditions were favorable, and always begged her to come with him, something new for him. Or was it that his memory was faulty, that he could not remember that he'd asked and been turned down? She sometimes regretted that she'd broken the news of the baby so soon; but he had to know, because it was his too, and if he had objected, or lectured her, she might have considered a termination. She didn't want to raise a child alone — that she imagined to be a lonely and difficult road, in spite of what girlfriends, being brave, telling her what she was missing, had said to her. But to raise a child with Joe Sharkey — that would be an adventure. His enthusiasm now was a pleasant foretaste of what his involvement would be, like those parents of surfers who stood on the beach during the Triple Crown, screaming at their kids in the lineup, hugging them when they came ashore. Sharkey had always shaken his head at them — "My mother never did that for me" — but now he promised to be one of them, while the child, months from being born, was smaller than a peanut in her womb.

"You're happy," she said, grateful for his mood but still suspicious.

"Totally stoked." His pride in his potency was unmistakable.

"This is good for both of us."

"For the three of us," he said, his hand on her belly.

In the uncertainty, the oddness, the amnesia, the repetition, and the confusion since the accident — *Who are you?* she often thought — this was the first positive sign. It was hopeful, the assurance of a future, a good omen. He had not seemed to realize how badly stalled his life had been by the accident, the death of the cyclist. But he had not uttered the banal sentence "I ran into a drunk homeless guy" since he'd learned of her pregnancy. She had been a witness to his dullness, and (though he had not mentioned anything of his change of mood) this was a relief. He had been lost, going in circles, and at last this was a way forward. Perhaps, she thought, this was the reason people had kids, one after the other: to be assured of a future, for the children, for themselves.

Sharkey was insistent that she exercise. Work at the hospital, no matter how strenuous, was not enough. What she needed was the thrust and uplift of waves, the purification of the sea.

"The sea is *pono*. It makes you right. It will make you strong — both of you."

Already he saw a family when he looked upon her. He still showed signs of damage — of trauma — from the accident, but she was reassured by his support, and she began to think of them as a family too. Sharkey and she embracing, their little swimmer squeezed between them.

Sharkey led the way, taking her for morning swims before work or meeting her at the end of the day at Waimea Bay or Three Tables, always swimming with her. The waves were so small that once through the shore break they were in smooth water, Sharkey stroking beside her, rising and plunging, dolphin-style.

It seemed to work; the exercise helped her sleep, the sleep itself calmed her, and her nausea was eased. She began to believe in him again, in the way she had when they first met, listening to his stories, seeing him triumphant on a wave; and he was a hero to her again, all that a father should be.

"You could try stand-up paddling. We could go out of Hale'iwa in the harbor, where it's really glassy."

"What if I fall?"

"Falling in water is like flying. Or take one of the boogie boards."

She allowed herself to be persuaded to use a boogie board. She took a swim fin for one foot, as was the custom. Sharkey drove along Kam Highway, looking for a likely spot, and passing Waimea he glanced at the waves and said, "You could handle that."

"Not here," she said. "Not this place."

"The waves are clean."

But superstitiously — he was near the spot where he'd killed the cyclist — she said, "Let's go farther down."

He had not noticed the pothole, usually filled with a slop of reddish water, the runoff from the clay of the embankment, the scene of the accident.

Though he passed it most days he never spoke of it; it was as though it had never happened. Now she was on the verge of admitting that it was over, except that he was at times as repetitious as ever in his stories and reminiscences. Only the promise of the baby offered hope: the one bright spot in their lives, something to live for.

"Gotta stay healthy," he was saying — and now she heard the cawing of his mother's voice in his nagging. "Maybe try Lani's, or Alligators."

The surf breaks served as way markers on the road along the irregular shore; no one spoke of a particular tree or house or bridge but always of the name of a break. *I live at V-Land.*

He pulled in at a stony opening near the break at Leftovers, parked in the shade of a dense hedge, and unstrapped the boards from the roof of the car.

"Don't worry — I've got your back."

On the smooth lava boulders near the black rock pools at the shore she slipped the swim fin onto her foot, then followed Sharkey into the water, dropping onto the board and holding herself against it, kicking hard with her fin. Sharkey, plunging under waves, was still heading out when she turned and bumped in on a small wave. Gesturing to the larger break, he was saying something.

"I can't hear you!" she called out.

She paddled in his direction, and she found, as she had discovered on other occasions, that without much effort she was farther from shore than she imagined — was it the riptide or an effect of the wave action that drew her out? Sharkey was nearer now, roaring in the turbulent water, still beckoning.

The shore was now just a strip of yellow sand, the green slope of hill, the mountainside behind it. Olive became afraid, so far from shore, in the lift of waves, her face slapped by sudden chop, her board pushed against her.

She wanted to say, "I'm scared." But Sharkey would have scoffed. Instead she said, "Show me how."

In the moments of this confusion she realized she was being pulled beyond the outer waves of the break.

"Use the wave to get back," he said. "You're trying to swim. Do this."

He crested a wave and hugged his body board and rode, gliding beneath it out of her sight line. Bobbing up thirty feet away, he gestured and shouted.

"Take that one!"

But she mistimed it and floundered behind it, and when she tried to chase it she had to struggle to hold the board, kicking fiercely, wondering whether she was making any progress. As she fought the push and slap of the water a wave broke over her, tipping her sideways, yanking the board out of her hands. She plunged after it, caught its rail, and tucked it under her, trying to steady herself again — and where was Sharkey? Another wave took her and rolled her over, but this time she clung to her board, first awkwardly under it like a turtle on its back, then climbing onto it. And then, looking for Sharkey, she saw that the shore was more distant than before — and, worse, a crosscurrent was taking her sideways toward Waimea. So she kicked harder and clawed the water.

What started as a stitch in her side widened and gripped her in a cramp, preventing her from being able to kick — kicking brought pain, and she was immobilized, hugging the board, trying to get a glimpse of Sharkey. She tried to yell, but simply raising her voice made the pain worse, straining the muscle in her belly, tightening the knots of her cramp.

Then she screamed, helplessly, intensifying the pain, feeling foolish and desperate. It was a new and frightening voice. She thought, *Why did I agree to this?* and mocked his solemnity — *The water is* pono — and tried not to cry.

Then Sharkey appeared, rising out of a nearby wave, not like a man but like a water creature, an agile sea monster, large and unsinkable, his hair plastered to his face, streaming with frothy water. He swung himself across the wave and tumbled next to her, smiling, reaching to steady her board.

"Help me," she said, gasping in a small voice, because it was too painful to shout. Even a deep breath worsened the stomach cramp.

"Let go of your board. Hold on to me."

She flung herself at his shoulders and held tight, and could feel the warmth and strength in the hard sinew of his muscles. His head was down, plowing the water, as he swam and surfed, riding successive waves toward shore, flat on his body board. She was sobbing with relief now, glad he couldn't see her, thinking, *I'm saved.*

But he was slowing, the heavy water was an obstacle, and there were long moments when he seemed lost and weakened by the butting waves. And she felt weak and in pain. Though she wasn't kicking — couldn't kick — she felt the cramp twisting her insides. Only by drawing her legs up and bending her knees was she able to lessen the pain. Her crouching posture impeded his swimming and slowed them, yet they were nearer shore, in smaller waves and in sunshine, Sharkey parting the water and propelling them with out-stretched arms, grunting with the effort — unusual for him.

"You okay now?" he said. "You can probably stand up here."

Slipping from his back, she tore off her swim fin and found her footing in the sand, staggering a little, whimpering with exhaustion, still bent over with the cramp and that obscure pain in her gut.

Behind her, Sharkey said, "Hey, there's blood in the water."

By then she was kneeling on the beach, clutching her belly, howling.

12

Under the Wave at Waimea

All existence is repetition, as regular as the rise and fall of breathing, the tick-tock of waking and sleeping, enclosing the back-and-forth of daily life, the shuttling to work, to home, the rituals at weekends of shopping and cooking, each day, each week an apparent humdrum repeat of the last, especially muffled and unmemorable on this island of brilliant sunshine. Years of this. It is, this existence, a peculiar buoyancy, undisturbed, an economy of effort in a slow spin of vitality — life as rotation.

You might hope for more — for difference, for change, for harmless drama — but you learn that an unchanged life is reassuring, that sameness and placid monotony are safe.

These thoughts were Olive's in her reliable car, going to her usual job, down the same road, on another sunny morning.

And then the interruption, the surprise, the nausea of an obscure complaint that was a sign of life; the news of her pregnancy, the shock of termination, which was worse than unfortunate, which was death.

Slashes of sunlight lit the road under the ironwoods and the palm trees, as on every other morning of her routine, yet this day was different from those days of no surprises, no magic, no windfall, no distracting event, the guarantee of the ordinary.

The miscarriage changed that. That morning, leaving for work, she'd said, "My baby is dead."

Sharkey had stared as though she'd lapsed into another language.

She could not keep herself from sobbing, thinking of what she'd lost: her child, a future, a continuation, a new life — hope, love. Yet strangely, what her training would have a termed a spontaneous abortion was proof of life too, more dramatic than the accumulation of sensations that sometimes swelled to become significant — new experiences, new people, fresh omens, variations in the routine as subtle and welcome as an unexpected smile.

She wept for the child who was gone, she wept for herself, she wept most of all for the man who now seemed unaware of what had happened, the man who had forgotten how to weep.

He said, "Is there a problem?"

She would have said, "The problem is that you're asking that question. Your question is proof of the problem." But she didn't want to risk being misunderstood. "You are the problem" was too brutal, yet it was nearer the truth.

The pregnancy was not a provisional state; it was a child within her, growing bigger each day — not a cluster of cells, fishlike in the water of her womb, but a little person, with a head and arms and feet, with fingers and toes, waiting to be released, to become — she saw this too — a swimmer in the world, a companion, a friend, a joy and a consolation. That was what she saw, that was what she had lost.

And Sharkey, who had been so enthusiastic about the child — the potential surfer, buddy, dude — had lost his fervor, did not seem to remember now that she'd been pregnant. He sank back into his half-smiling delusion in which he believed he was active, the waterman, the gardener, the chicken farmer, the orchid-grower. Yet he hardly left the house.

Thinking back to his rescuing her when she'd panicked in the waves at Leftovers, she now remembered how slow he'd been to see her, how clumsily he'd dug at the water with one hand while holding his boogie board — and she'd clung to him, feeling the struggle in his shoulders, and that tension had added to her fear. She'd sensed that he was weakening, not the Waimea lifeguard she'd known, nor the Sharkey who refused to be towed, who paddled out and dropped in to ride the long faces of waves on big North Shore days. He was slower and uncertain, and why?

In the suddenness of blood at the beach, the scorching pain of the miscarriage — the mess, his bewilderment, her grief — she hadn't given much thought to his insisting that they swim out to this distant wave, farther than Chun's or Alligators or the others. And he had abandoned her there. Nor had she preoccupied herself with his clumsy rescue — his lumbering in the surf. But now it seemed to her that he had contributed to the loss of the baby — and more, that it was another disturbing feature of this recent life of his, a blundering, a vagueness, a forgetting, a step backward, another accident, a repetition in the limbo that was his life now.

It was hard for her to admit that this strong person was weakened, or if not weakened physically, then diminished; that he needed her and that his dependence on her was something he still could not acknowledge.

It was news: that in the seemingly endless repetition of life—the back-and-forth—there was something imperceptible, a slowing, a diminution of vitality, and so the apparent sameness was misleading. He repeated his stories, but at the same time he abbreviated them in the slippage of his memory. His life appeared to be going in circles, but they were narrowing circles.

She saw something moribund in it: in the house, which had acquired a clammy gloom; in Sharkey, who seldom exerted himself—which was why the day at Leftovers had been a disaster. He sat and stewed, and when she returned to him after work every day he would tell her a story she already knew, that he'd told her before.

What was wrong? It was not just his stopped life but also his visible deterioration. Sameness is never sameness when it is so persistent in nature; sameness is decay. It was bad enough that in his world nothing was new, but the truth was that he was growing smaller, his aura dimming, and his world too was shrinking.

On the evening she returned and he began with a fixed smirk (he was holding a joint) to tell her again of the business with the package of *pakalolo* that Moe Kahiko had sent to him, she remembered that he'd first begun this story in the car moments before he'd hit and killed the cyclist.

"I done a bad ting," he said in Moe's dull, droopy voice.

"No," she said, shaking her head. "We can't go on like this."

But Sharkey kept talking.

She leaned at him and said, "Don't. Please park it."

He stopped talking yet kept his facial expression, Moe's frown, exaggerated, foolish, obtuse. It had been a good enough story the first time. Now, like all the others, it was monotony, noise in her ears and eyes. She wanted to scream.

"What's your deal?" he said.

"My deal," she said, and thoughts fluttered in her head, winged things slapping into each other and against her skull, rousing other thoughts, sending them flying, waking them to fury—none would settle, none would roost, all of them squawked for attention or beat their wings behind her eyes. She pressed her head to quiet them.

"You're fretting again," he said, like a boast, a big confident put-down.

"Not fretting."

"What then?"

"Desperate," she said. "Don't you understand? I just lost a baby in the surf at Leftovers while you were pulling me to shore. I'm not blaming you, though the wave seemed a mile away and maybe I started losing it as I paddled out. But you don't remember that—you don't remember anything. I think it was an omen like all the other omens, that nothing in our lives would go right. Nothing has gone right since the day of the accident — it's been one bloody thing after another, nothing has been normal. You were acting strange. I tried to get away. I discovered I was pregnant — you seemed happy about it, and then, wouldn't you know, I lost the baby in all that surf. And my nausea has gone away. I'm sleeping better. I have no cramps. I've recovered my health. I'm seeing things clearly. And" — here her voice broke — "I'm desperate."

Sharkey listened to this without an expression, though it seemed to her that he had a fixed look of mild impatience, as though listening to her speaking was just a question of waiting for her to finish — not objecting to anything she said, because in a short while she would be exhausted and done, delivered of her complaint. Then they could go on, eat something, smoke a joint, go to bed early — and with this in mind he yawned.

Olive was breathing hard; her rant had made her head ring.

Sharkey squinted at her and said, "The accident — what about it?"

"You remember it?"

He stuck his lower lip out, equivocating. She knew that face of his, she knew all his facial expressions, they were often a boy's obstinacy, the reactions of someone who hated to explain. This one meant *I don't understand what you're driving at, but even if I did understand I wouldn't care.* And it maddened her to see this response form on his face.

"That drunk homeless guy."

"It was a man," she said, her voice rising. "You killed him."

An accident, he thought; an obstacle, like many he'd surfed in his life.

Like dropping into a mushy wave at a break he'd never surfed before and finding as he cut left that it was not mushy at all but instead the curved face of a slowly forming barrel, overtopping him until, in seconds, he was in the tube, shacked as though in a cave of blue ice, and seeing only a narrowing lozenge of light at the far end, which was his only salvation as long as he steadied himself in a crouch and maintained his speed, but he did not know for sure whether he would make it out of the barrel upright until he succeeded and burst into the blaze of sun, the barrel breaking, squeezing and closing behind him like snatching hands in a smash of heavy water.

Those waves, so many rides on the sea and on land. He saw that he had surfed through life and that he had trained himself to overcome the opposition of so many people — school and home and the casual assaults of locals. He'd done nothing but surf. Roosevelt High School was a wave, girlfriends were waves, debt was a wave, guilt another wave, sex was a fun wave, his brief marriage a junk wave, his mother one of the trickiest waves, and he'd sometimes wiped out or suffered a hold-down, but he had always made it to shore and gone on surfing. *Me and my stick: there is no other way I know how to live.* Every ride prepared him for the next one, until it seemed the whole of life involved surfing from one wave to another.

That drunk homeless guy on the old bike at Waimea that Olive kept mentioning — he was a wave that Sharkey had ridden to safety, and he was onshore again, contemplating another wave.

Introspection wearied him, like the shudder and rumble of an engine running. He was unused to it, his head heavy with the weight of these reflections, and he was out of words. He lifted his eyes to Olive, yet his eyes said nothing.

But Olive was grimly satisfied. It seemed that he had lapsed into his old indifference, because it helped prove her point.

"Don't you see that since then — since killing that poor man — nothing has gone right?"

He still eyed her, his head at a slight angle, and she knew it meant defiance and doubt: *I don't see what you're seeing, and therefore you're mistaken.*

"Maybe you don't see it," she said, replying to the expression on his face. "I don't blame you. I think it was traumatic for you, killing that man. But I see it and I think I'm losing you. You're suffering some kind of weird hangover, like you've been on an epic bender. You seldom go out, though you say you do. You sit staring at the trees. Half the time you don't feed the animals, and I do it, or I get Moe Kahiko to do it." She thought a moment, breathing hard. "You repeat yourself, the same stories, none of them new — and I mean, I'm sorry, but it's horrible to hear you repeat them."

She kept herself from saying, "And it's a flaming bloody bore," though the words were in her mouth.

"So what?" he said.

"The same stories."

"Everyone does that," he said, and from his sour tone she saw that she'd stung him. He was proud of the way he could hold a room of listeners with his stories — of surfing, of travel, of near escapes, of big waves, unusual people, strange meals, distant coasts. He sat on the bright beach like a Sun King and charmed men and wooed women with his stories. Hearing his stories, Hunter Thompson had said, "You could have been a writer."

"Yes. Everyone does that, but not like you — the same stories, the same days, the same you. When did the accident happen?"

"Can't remember."

"Six weeks ago. It was a Saturday night. I marked it in my daybook." She searched his face for a reaction. "What has happened since?"

He shook his head and blinked — not *I don't know,* but *It doesn't matter.*

"Nothing," she said, answering her own question. "You sit, though you say you're surfing. You don't eat unless I'm cooking and urging you to. And nothing's new, everything's stale, and you know what that means?"

Still, he was unmoved; he examined his fingers, picking at them, his monkey grooming.

"You made me pregnant," she said. "We were hopeful. I took it as a sign. Then I lost the baby. Losing it was the real sign."

He seemed to strain, to take this in. He mumbled, "Blood in the water."

She dropped to her knees and held him, and could not keep herself from tears, though she wasn't crying.

"I remember the blood," he said. "No one forgets blood."

"It was a baby." She said it in a pleading voice, and moaned in sorrow. Then she breathed deeply to clear her head, and when she had her composure back she continued. "It all adds up."

"Some kind of curse," he said, but without emotion — just asking.

"No, no," she said, and gripped his legs and looked up at him in his chair. "It's not witchcraft. It's a shadow hanging over you — and so it's over me too. Something like denial. Don't you feel it?"

He made a face — it wasn't dismissive, it was thoughtful: in some dim recess of his brain he had heard her. Instead of replying, he sighed, long and loud, a tremor of resignation.

"I don't know," he finally said.

To Olive this admission was like a victory: he was no longer indifferent, or certain in his arrogance. She said, "Tell me honestly, how do you feel?"

"You mean about the accident?"

"Yes, killing the man."

"I feel it hasn't happened yet."

This took her by surprise. She said, "I don't get it."

"The collision," he said.

"Hitting the man. Killing him."

"A collision isn't one person hitting another — it's when they both hit at once. A guy on a bike and a man in a car going bang." He said this in a soft explaining tone. Then he frowned, pressing his lips together. He said, "It's like I'm waiting for it to happen."

"But it happened." She thought, *He hasn't processed it, he's still trying to understand it, he can't face it.*

"Did it?" he asked. "Most days I wake up happy, but I might remember a little detail or two. And then I shut it off. I figure someday I will wake up and I won't remember anything. It won't happen." A smile flickered on his lips. "See?"

He was like a small boy in his denial; even his tone of voice was whispered and weak and bewildered, this sunburned and tattooed and muscular man, childlike.

"It was a man," she said. "He died."

He blinked again, a small boy, shrinking in his confusion.

"You ran into him."

"Collision," he said, correcting her. "It was dark."

"I know. A bad night."

"All that rain," he said. "My sore foot on the brake."

He seemed to be simplifying and excusing himself again. She spoke softly: "You killed that man."

This registered as creases at the sides of his eyes, and in his hurt eyes too; the words had pierced him.

"And all that bad luck since then," she said. She wanted to add, *Bad for you, but it's dogging me too, living with your darkness, losing the baby.* So often with him — and often nursing her sicker, more fragile patients — she had two conversations, the one she spoke aloud, the one she suppressed and kept to herself.

He reached for her, took her small clean hand in his big cracked one, with an eye tattooed at the center of his palm. Clumsy consolation, but perhaps he understood her pain.

"You don't know his name," she said, and hearing nothing from him, added, "Do you?"

His "No" was the tissue of a breath.

"Or anything about him. Where he was born. His family, if he had one. How he lived. Where he's buried."

Still he clutched her soft hand in his rough hand against his leg as she sat before him, and she could feel something like thought in the flesh of his palm and his sinewy fingers. It helped that she was not facing him when she said this, that the voice rose from where she sat, muted, like smoke curling to his head while he stared at the branches outside that were lit by the window.

"We need to know."

She spoke with insistence, and that tone, severe for the first time, checked him. He let go of her hand, dropped it, and got up and stretched, standing before her.

"This is so heavy," he said.

"And?" she said, hoping for more.

"Let's talk about it tomorrow."

That was not what she wanted, yet she felt she'd made progress, and in trying to explain to him the impasse — the stalled life, the bad luck (she resisted calling it karma) — she'd clarified it for herself; found the words for it. Explaining it to him was a way of explaining it to herself.

But the next morning he was out of bed as she was just waking.

"Big day," he said.

"I thought we were going to talk."

"Yes. Definitely. But I'm going out first. Surf's up this morning. Dropping this afternoon. Outta here."

With that he was out of the room, heading to the garage to strap the board on his car. And she felt winded — defeated. That was his life, one evasion after another. *I'm not into sitting around, man.* He would never face the fact of what he had done; he would never understand the effect it had had on his life, that it had cast a shadow over it, and he would live the rest of his life in that shadow, his narrowing existence of bad luck and delay and aborted hope. If she stayed with him her own life would be no better.

One of his earliest stories ended with his saying, "So you get on a plane. You have great karma — you're stoked, looking forward to the flight and the vacation. You're totally in tune with your karma. But what you don't know is that the pilot has bad karma. And he crashes the plane."

It had touched her at the time, and she'd smiled. "I never thought of that," she said. Now it seemed like a dire warning.

Olive packed for the second time, filled two suitcases with her clothes, emptied the bedside table of her books, murmuring in his voice "Outta here." She was late for work but put all her things on the lanai, intending to pick them up later. Her last glimpse of them saddened her because the things themselves looked sad: the two old bags, the battered cardboard box, a small deformed valise — she saw her whole life in a compact pile. It seemed a negligible accumulation of clobber, and she recognized herself in their bumps and surface damage. She reminded herself of her age — thirty-eight, still capable of childbearing — and thought, *I'm portable.* Everything she owned in the world could fit in the trunk of her car. She was sad, she was happy, and then she saw herself as though in a movie, a dramatic moment glimpsed from a high camera angle, a valiant woman, moving out to begin again. She wanted to dislike Sharkey, but when she considered him and what had happened, she felt only pity.

Still, goodbye. Outta here. Jolly well done with him.

Seeing Luana in the cafeteria with another woman in scrubs — a doctor, wearing her stethoscope like a badge — she waved, and backed away. But Luana beckoned and introduced the woman.

"This Dr. Agawa. She stay all over!"

Dr. Agawa — Japanese, slim, petite, sweet-faced — turned out to be a surfer, running a clinic in the Solomon Islands. "My clinic was on Santa Isabel, so I'm lucky. Good surf at Papatura."

"Good surf here," Luana said. "Da bess. Big, da waves!"

"I'm locum here for this month," Dr. Agawa said to Olive.

"How are you liking it?"

Before she could answer, Luana said, "Funny case today. Family members bring him in. Got no mojo, they said. Just staring out the window. Not eating."

As though to calm Luana's ebullience, Dr. Agawa lowered her head and said in an earnest whisper, "Give-up-itis — it's a serious condition."

"Give-up-itis is a diagnosis?" Olive said.

"I've seen it in the Solomons. It's been written about. You know, abulia — lack of willpower, someone fading away."

"Sort of suicide?" Luana said.

"No. It's involuntary," Dr. Agawa said. "Voodoo death."

"I adore these rarefied scientific names," Olive said.

"That's what a certain Dr. Cannon called it. He's the fight-or-flight guy."

Luana said, "A Hawaiian woman eats a coconut under the *kapu* system. She realizes she broke the *kapu* and she stops eating. Stops everything. Pretty soon she wen' *make*. Old Hawaii tradition."

"Psychogenic death," Dr. Agawa said.

Olive said, "From breaking a taboo?"

"Or any serious trauma. You know how trauma affects the nerve circuits in the brain. It can cause the anterior cingulate circuit to malfunction — kills motivation. How do you survive in life if you have no motivation? The next phase is apathy. Give-up-itis. It's been studied."

"In the Solomons?"

"All over. Concentration camps. Prisons. Situations of extreme desperation. People give up. Maybe that guy this morning."

"But they don't know they're traumatized?" Olive said.

"I guess they're not really conscious of anything," Dr. Agawa said.

Luana widened her eyes and spoke to Olive. "Awesome, eh?"

That evening she returned to the house before dark so that she could load her things into her car to take them to her room at the hospital, the same one she'd used for her previous escape — but she'd find a better place eventually.

She was thrown by seeing cars in the driveway, a motorcycle she recognized — one of his surfer friends — and the orange-and-white pickup truck of the lifeguard rescue patrol, its warning lights flashing, a jet ski mounted on the trailer.

"He's going to be all right," someone said insistently to her as she mounted the stairs, and the urgency of it made it sound insincere. Men and boys, barefoot in board shorts, crowded the lanai. A man in a long-sleeved lifeguard shirt walked quickly toward her, more to prevent her from entering the house than to console her.

Before she could speak, he said, "He wiped out — a big drop at Waimea — and his board probably hit him. He was way under. He swallowed a lot of water. But look" — he was holding her wrists, steadying her, restraining her, because she was fighting him — "he's going to be fine. We're talking about Joe Sharkey."

She wrenched free of the man and hurried into the house, where he lay on his sofa. He was almost unrecognizable — a different man inked with Sharkey's tattoos, corpse-white, his eyes pink and staring, his hands and feet bluish and badly cut, a blanket slung loose from his body, his hair spiky and wild.

Seeing her, he feebly lifted his hand in a shaka sign, then his hand fell and became a claw.

"Epic wave. Went over the falls," he said, scarcely moving his lips. "Major hold-down." Then he became self-conscious, dropping his voice. "These guys saved my life."

The lifeguard who had followed her into the house stood beside her, as though in protection. Yet she remained watching, horrified by what she had first taken to be a dead man, Sharkey motionless and pale, his face ugly with fear.

"Heavy water," one of the lifeguards said.

"Monster wave," Sharkey said, and, tangled in his own black shadow, as though still under the wave at Waimea, oppressed by his life, he began to cry, like a small boy in a strange land.

PART II

The History of a Hero

1

Haole — The Scar

He was a child, and at last, after the ache and fatigue of a long flight, like a sickness on a smelly plane, everything was new and pure. The difference was a sweetness he tasted in the soft air, the breeze like a pillow against his cheek. It was a sound too, the flutter of leaves, the scrape of palm fronds, the ocean big and loud and continually foaming to the beach, waves flopping and swirling in a monstrous flush and then gone. The cliffs and valleys behind the house were deep green, the house so simple, with wooden boards for walls, and you could leave the door open. He was different too, always in summer clothes and often barefoot — and conspicuous for his color among bigger, darker people who lived beyond the perimeter fence of the fort in the high green island that was his new home — Hawaii.

He was happy, a new person, and his difference had a name; the gardener, Abe, laughed and said, "You a haole."

This was at the Sharkeys' bungalow on Nimitz Circle in the married officers' subdivision of Fort Shafter. They'd been transferred from the Presidio in San Francisco, and before that spells at Fort Bliss and in Germany.

"We were in Germany too," his friend Charlie Miller told him at school when Joe mentioned it. But Germany was a place he did not know; older people described it to him, a foreign country outside the fence of another base. After two years there all he knew of it was the weather — the cold weather especially. Weather and smells, they were the differences in places. Fort Bliss, a few summer months, was hot, with the sting of dust. The Presidio was chilly, with the clamminess of damp grass, but on weekends his father took him down the coast to Half Moon Bay. His father sat and smoked; Joe watched with longing the boys crouched on boards, looking small and fearless and buoyant in the big waves.

"How do they do that?"

"Do what?"

"That."

"Surfers," his father said, exhaling cigarette smoke.

His father was a soldier, and it always seemed as though his mind was on bigger things; and if Joe asked too many questions his father would shout at him.

In Hawaii his mother clung to him, because his father was so often away, in training, on maneuvers, in school, getting ready, he said — for what?

But one day at the beach, with his father seeing surfers offshore, Joe said, "I want to learn how to do that."

"You can do it," his father said. "But first be the best swimmer you can be."

After that they swam together in the pool at the officers' club, and in the waves in the sea at Fort DeRussy.

But when his father was away, his mother held on to him and said, "The ocean is dangerous."

He saw she was right: the waves were high and thick, and they deafened him when they swept into him, submerging him and knocking him over.

He came to see a pattern at home. When his father spent days with him, swimming or trying to teach him tennis, being hearty, he understood that it meant his father would soon be going away. Then he'd be left with his fretful mother, her warnings about swimming and sharks and sunburn. She didn't play tennis and often drank too much and became weepy.

So his father's attention to him made him apprehensive: the outings and ice cream were a prelude to abandonment and to the serious talk before bedtime, calling him by name and saying he'd have to grow up fast.

"Listen, Joe. You'll have to be the man of the house now." His father smelled of cigarettes; his words were smoky and sour. "But don't worry — I'll write letters, and I'll call when I can."

He left but seldom called, and his letters were to Sharkey's mother, who said that his frequent absences were a sign of his importance. "He's an officer. Do you see how the soldiers salute us?"

Soldiers in the road at Fort Shafter, seeing the Colonel's eagle insignia on the bumper, saluted the car.

One day Charlie Miller, his friend at school and on the base, pointed to a stain on his swimming trunks, saying, "I got that in Germany."

"How?"

"Pickle juice."

"I was in Germany," Joe said. "It was cold. Then we went to Texas. Really hot."

"We were at Fort Lee," Charlie said. "Virginia. Fort Lee Officers' Open Mess. That was where I learned to swim, at the FLOOM pool."

While playing a game they talked of their travels, ten-year-olds, men of the world, Germany, Texas, Virginia, San Francisco. Their game was played with a bayonet on the back lawn of Charlie's house. They stood facing each other, and one boy would throw the bayonet like a spear into the ground nearby. If he stabbed it upright the other boy would shift one foot to the point where the bayonet had stuck. And that boy took his turn to throw the bayonet, so that his opponent had to stretch his leg. And the one who could not reach the bayonet with his foot was the winner.

Joe flicked it in the air. "Where did you get this knife?"

"Germany."

It was black, longer than any knife Joe had seen, and sharp, a thing of power. They passed this weapon back and forth. Holding it seemed to add to their talk of travel, to make it important.

One afternoon Joe threw it hard, and two inches of the blade snapped. Charlie picked it up and held the broken tip against the end of the blade.

"It's my father's."

Joe dreaded what Charlie's father would say, and feared being blamed for breaking the bayonet.

"Are you going to tell him?"

"I have to," Charlie said.

He seemed brave, saying that, with a truthfulness that intimidated Joe. They entered the house together, but when Charlie showed his father the broken blade the man merely frowned. He'd been sitting, reading a newspaper. He put the paper down to consider the broken bayonet, then held the bayonet in one hand, the broken tip in the other.

"Nazi," he said, putting the pieces on the low table beside his chair. He pushed the pieces away with the back of his hand and frowned and then raised his newspaper from his lap, shielding his face from the boys.

"He's mad at us," Joe said outside, but Charlie just shrugged.

Joe didn't tell his mother. She would fuss. His father was away again, and he felt that part of his being the man of the house now was to keep such incidents from his mother. She'd be upset, she'd blame him, or Charlie; she would try to make the situation better but only make it worse. She'd go over to Charlie's house, she'd talk too much, and when she got home she'd drink, and cry.

So when she said, "Are you all right?" he said, "Yup."

He did not report on his day, or anything that happened in his life, and if something went wrong he kept it to himself. He might be reprimanded at the main gate for not checking at the guardhouse — for just walking in, and being yelled at by the sentry. He said nothing. He said little of school. He mentioned his friends' names but did not elaborate. Sometimes, after he'd spent a whole afternoon at the pool, he'd say (because his mother insisted), "I was at the rec room."

His secrets were small, but they mattered, because they were his secrets. He wanted to be a better swimmer, a better student, a faster runner. He knew he was unformed, still learning. He refused to offer progress reports. He was ashamed that he was so small and incompetent — not good at anything — but that was a secret too.

His habit of concealment strengthened him. Being truthful was a form of nakedness he could not bear: you were exposed, you were weakened, you'd be ridiculed or scolded. Seeing Charlie Miller explaining to his father exactly what had happened with the bayonet, that truthfulness ended in Charlie's father's sulking and silence. And a greater reason for resisting was that grown-ups were themselves strict keepers of secrets — Joe's father's disappearances and false promises, his mother saying "I'm exhausted" when she was drunk. They lied; he said nothing, yet his silences were not lies but evasions. Someday he would be strong — in his heart he wanted to be a hero, and wished he knew how. But for now he did not want anyone to know him.

One incident, to his shame, could not be kept secret. Long before it happened, his dread of it, and sharpness of his fear, convinced him that he would face it and be harmed. He possessed the accurate premonition of a frightened person, in the way that someone fearful about tipping over a precious teacup on a tray is certain to bobble it and break it.

It was a dog. What moment, what catch or tremor in the past, had imprinted on him a fear of dogs? Maybe a guard dog slavering on a leash and growling, tugging a soldier past the fence of a base somewhere. It was first of all the sound of them, the hoarse bark that gnawed at his throat, the dog's bark that said, *I am coming for you.*

The family's constant moves from base to base meant they never had pets bigger than goldfish. Joe scarcely saw a dog except the ones leaping at him from behind a fence, but he was keenly affected by a bark. The choking growl was like an expression of hunger for human flesh; of anger too, being denied it. His sense was less that a dog was going to bite him but rather, given the insistent bark, the dog working its jaws, that the creature was going to seize him with its teeth and chew him and eat him. The mere sound of a dog made him hold himself so still as to be rigid, and he knew he had no protection other than his skinny hands.

He always looked terrified, because the owners, or the people nearby, said, "He won't hurt you," and when Joe looked tearful and unconvinced, goggling at the thing, the owner would say, often with a hint of satisfaction, "See? He knows you're afraid. He can smell your fear."

He hated them. They sensed his hatred. He had come to love ocean waves and learned to duck under them and bob up behind them. The thump and crush of water, the fetch of wind on it, was like the rhythm of life. Even when he was tumbled in the shore break and his father had to yank him to safety, he held his breath and laughed when it was over. He had no fear of water. He did not mind being alone in the dark — he talked to himself. He climbed to the highest limbs of the trees in his yard and swayed there in the sunshine. He knew how to start a fire. But dogs . . .

They shortened their muscly necks to their shoulders and barked at him from behind fences, leaped at him, making the chain links clatter from the force of their yellow claws and dirty paw pads. They dashed to the limit of their tethers, half throttled by their collars as they reared, standing on their hind legs and threatening him with insistent yelps. Even the ones on leashes that he passed on the sidewalks of the base trotted toward him and sniffed him wickedly, the damp prune-black nose prodding him. Was it his smell of fear, his stiffened fingers, his leaning-away posture? Or that he was new here, a haole boy?

The owners smiled, as though the barks proved their dog's superior instincts, and they seemed to rejoice in the suggestions of the pet's wildness, the sense that the dog was powerful and fearless — a protector, courageous in its vigilance, perhaps displaying a feral anger and ferocity that its owner was too timid to show, the barking dog like the manifestation of a hidden self, another secret of grown-ups. Sharkey sensed there was an angry dog inside every teasing dog owner.

Seeing the tears in his eyes, the terror on his face, his mother tried to shield him.

"What's wrong?" she asked.

"Nothing."

"Are you afraid?"

"No!"

But she always consoled him. And his father took the view that the expression of any fear demanded to be overcome.

"I tell my men," he said, "'Get over it.' I have ARVN guys who are afraid of jumping out of a plane — scared shitless."

Joe stared, knowing what was coming.

"But they jump. I make them jump."

"What if they really don't want to?"

"It's an order. It has to be obeyed. Or we push them out. And the next time it's easier."

"That's different," Sharkey's mother said, coming to his defense, and he hated her for suspecting he was afraid.

"It's fear," his father said, his mouth going square, showing his teeth. "Experience makes fear go away. I have men in operations, Special Forces from the forward firebase, who are practically gibbering. 'I don't want to go!' 'Let's turn back!' 'I'm scared!'"

He reached for Joe's shoulder, got a grip on his shirt. Joe said nothing. He'd heard this before. It was one of his father's stories, a way of defining himself. You couldn't interrupt or he'd howl.

"I grab them like this," and he tightened his grip. "I tell them, 'Consider yourself already dead'"—he smiled, those teeth again—"'and you'll be fine.'"

But of course his father was away when the incident—the inevitable incident—occurred.

It was the sort of hot Hawaii midafternoon when the sun dominating a cloudless sky seemed to burn him small. He'd gotten off the bus at the end of the street and was walking past the house with the dog when, as he expected, and feared, he heard the loud barking. He knew the bark, he knew the dog, the one that could make it to the edge of the lawn on his tether. As on previous days, Joe crossed the street so as not to enrage the dog further, and he waited for the dog to be jerked back on his tether.

But the dog kept coming, making straight for him. He bounded across the street, his tongue thickened and drawn aside by his speed, and he leaped as he approached, knocking Joe to the ground, and began angrily to chew his face, snapping his jaws.

Later Joe wondered why he hadn't screamed for help, why he submitted and said nothing. He guessed that there is a reaction of extreme terror that silences you—this, and the recognition perhaps that there is no hope; that you're done for, so desperate that you're resigned to your fate, to be torn apart by the dog.

In the midst of it, batting at the champing dog, its slaver on his arms, he heard a shrill whistle and a voice shouting a name that sounded like Max, but his terror was so intense by then that he could not react, trapped beneath the dog's jaws. It was not an imagined pain produced by fear but stabbing paws and teeth in a growling mouth tearing at his face.

"I said, get down."

What struck him as frightening was the man's futile voice demanding casually in English that, half crazed in its attack—Joe's face in the dog's mouth—the dog would understand and obey. Yet amazingly the dog grunted and let go.

Whoever had spoken dragged the dog away—Joe could see the man and the dog above him as he lay on the sidewalk, the man twisting the dog's collar, saying, "You all right?"

Gouts of saliva drooped from the gagging dog's jaws.

Joe said, "I think so," because he was alive.

And then, "You Colonel Sharkey's kid?"

"Yes, sir."

"Oh, shit — I'm really sorry."

By then other people who'd heard the commotion, women mostly, had gathered to help, dabbing at Joe's face with hankies and saying with such nervous insistence, "You're going to be just fine, sweetheart," that he felt certain he would not be. They helped Joe to his feet and took him down the street to his house.

His mother shrieked and became a mother Joe had never seen before — wailing, angry, vowing to report the incident, demanding the name of the man with the dog.

"What's his rank!" she screamed.

"Get the boy to Tripler," a calmer voice said, and then he was in the backseat of a car, his mother still shrieking, being driven to the big pink hospital.

Under a bright light, voices above him and all around him, he lay on a table, fingers in his face, stitching him, other faces leaning over him, murmuring to him, words of kindness and concern, while his mother still chattered and sobbed. "You have a brave boy, Mrs. Sharkey." "You're due for a Purple Heart, son." "The dog wasn't on a leash." "The boy will need shots."

His face bandaged, and no school, the back-and-forth to Tripler, ten days of antirabies injections — he felt singled out and special, privileged, an object of interest. Everyone was kind to him, and for those ten days he felt like a soldier who'd been wounded in battle, an intimation of what it meant to be a hero.

A succession of whispers and echoes revealed the stages of the aftermath, each day something new, often in the repetition of his mother talking on the telephone. The dog had not been on a secure leash. The attack had caused physical harm and emotional distress. "Scarring." "Compensation." The base was liable.

Silent, still bandaged, sitting in a too-big leather chair in an attorney's office, he listened to his mother pleading.

"You have an excellent case, Mrs. Sharkey," the man said. "It's up to you whether to settle or sue."

On these car journeys to Tripler and to the attorney's office, Joe became accustomed to soldiers spotting the insignia on the bumper and standing at attention while his mother drove past them as they saluted the car. Seeing them, he touched his face and hoped they could see his bandage.

When his father finally came home, it seemed a satisfaction to him that Joe had endured the attack. Before he hugged him, he touched Joe's face, saying approvingly, "Battle scar." And in the next weeks his father and mother met again with the lawyer, Joe in the leather chair listening, or watching them examine documents, the repeated words, "Settlement and release agreement." Whatever the amount of the settlement, it was enough to allow them to move from their house at Fort Shafter to a bungalow at the edge of Manoa Valley, near Punahou School, which Joe entered that same year, as an eighth grader.

He was now in a world without uniforms, and because the wound took so long to heal and left a thick pinkish purple scar, he was conspicuous, not just a new boy but a new boy with a fresh scar on his left cheek, the stitch punctures clearly visible. The scar and his newness set him apart. He was on the fringe with the marginal boys, the sulkers and rebels, the other newcomers — the *malihini*, the ones who sneaked and smoked and talked about surfing.

2

Special Forces

Long before his mother told him, he knew when his father was about to arrive home from Vietnam. It was a vibration in the house that trembled in his head, like furniture being shoved in the next room, his mother clumsier, bumping through the parlor with a drink in her hand, fussing to make the house orderly, primping in the mirror as though squinting for approval, visiting the hairdresser, and talking fretfully to herself. "We'll have to do something about that stain on the table," or "Those faded slipcovers will have to go," all of it a sorting-out and preparation, as though for the visit of an inspector.

And it did seem as though his father was making the visit to carry out an inspection: to be brought up to date, to make sure the house was in order, to examine Joe's school reports. The knowledge that her husband was coming home made Sharkey's mother nervous — "He won't like that" she'd say, if she saw that Joe's room was messy or that he'd broken something.

Though his schoolwork was good and the Punahou teachers were patient, he was ignored or snubbed by the other students and had yet to make a friend. But he said nothing about that to his mother, who concluded from his good marks on exams that all was well. Nor did she know that he surfed at Magic Island most afternoons, even when he claimed he was swimming at the pool or engaged in school projects. Surfing was another secret, because he loved it, and because he was still learning and did not think he was a good enough surfer to tell anyone.

Each time his father came home he was reminded of the man, how he looked, how he talked, how he'd have to get used to him again. His brutal haircuts, buzzed close to his head, showed his bumpy skull and the white slashes where his scalp had been somehow gouged. And his first words to Joe were usually "You need a haircut."

"I told him, but he wouldn't listen," Joe's mother said in a sorrowful voice.

"And let's see those hands."

His father snatched at his fingers, twisting each one to get a look at the fingernails, usually bitten, to his father's rage — a grunt of disgust as he flung them down.

Joe knew when he was standing next to him that his father was average height and slim, but he carried himself with authority, his steely order-giving voice demanding attention. When he was home he seemed to fill the house, as though his aura, which was both light and shadow, enlarged him. He never laughed. He said little about Vietnam except "There's no war," and to the next obvious question, "It's a pacifying operation, Joe. I'm commanding a unit of advisers," and he paused, and ended the discussion in a tone of muffled secrecy: "Special Forces."

The other reminder — making the man bigger — each time he came home was his father's odor, a tangle of aromas that clung to him, this thickness of odors another enlargement. He smoked, he drank — the burned, stale smell of Lucky Strikes, the smack like a sharpness of sour sugar that was whiskey on his breath. Not a human smell at all, it made him seem oddly edible. And it produced a gagging moment of suffocation when Joe was hugged.

Of the house in Manoa, his father said, "This is how the rest of the population lives." He cocked his head as though looking at a crowd. "Civilians." Of Punahou, he said, "Private school. Never thought we'd be able to afford it on my salary."

"It's got a pool," Joe said. "Better than Radford's."

"Good school. You'll have a great shot at making the academy."

West Point the only ambition — that had always been the measure and the goal. His father, Class of '45, had been posted to Germany, had fought in Korea with distinction, and on the basis of his command in Korea had been selected to lead the first contingent of advisers in Vietnam.

"Maybe we could hit the beach," Joe said that first visit after they moved.

"I'm not on furlough," his father said. "I'm here for briefings."

"I only hope you're safe," his mother said.

"No one's safe in 'Nam. If you want to be safe, you don't run recon patrols into the boonies." To Joe he said, "What language are you studying?"

"French."

"Good. They speak French over there. My men — the ones I'm training, the locals, Vietnamese — they need an interpreter. If we're still there, you won't need an interpreter."

This meant that after Joe graduated from West Point and was an officer, assigned to lead a unit in Vietnam, he'd be able to give orders in French. His father was always certain of the boy's future.

"Are your men tough?" Joe asked, wanting to hear that they were brave soldiers, because it was a way of determining his father's safety.

"Some of my ARVN are good soldiers," his father said, and smiled. "But you know what? When they want to have a whiz they squat on the ground. I say to them, 'Get up! Piss like a man!'"

Joe did not mind that he was hard on him. The Colonel was hard on everyone.

In barking orders, seldom listening, his father took charge. But Joe saw him in his chair — mother cooking, mother cleaning, mother doing laundry — and it seemed that his father did not know how to do anything but give orders. He held himself apart from his family, and Joe guessed held himself apart from his men, the ARVN, he called them, who were not Americans.

He was always an officer at home, and sometimes a father. It seemed he did not know how to be a friend. But he said that fifteen years in the army had taught him that friendships were dangerous.

"You don't take orders out of friendship, because you like your officer," he said. "You take orders because you are required to obey. Your commanding officer is not your friend. It doesn't matter whether you like him or not. He is your superior."

Friendships are fatal to authority, he explained. People break the rules because of friendships. Discipline fails, and lives are lost when rules are broken or orders not obeyed. He said this snapping at Joe, puffing a cigarette, pausing to tap its ash into the saucer under his coffee cup.

"Your friends will let you down — they will fail you," he said. "And they'll expect to be forgiven, and why? Because they're your friends."

Joe said, "Anyway, I don't have any friends. I'm the new boy. They hate me."

"They don't hate you. They don't know you. If anything, they're afraid of you. Don't let them know you — keep them in the dark — and they'll go on being afraid." He touched Joe's scar. "Treat them like that mad dog."

Misled by the scar, his father had the idea that Joe, in the struggle, had fought off the dog's attack and somehow defeated him; the man did not know, or could not understand, that Joe had hugged himself and fallen, going rigid in his terror, submitting to the dog's jaws, overwhelmed and terrified until the owner called the dog off.

"Are your men afraid of you?"

"Yes, sir, damn right! That's why they respect me," he said. "And that's why they obey. What sort of an officer would I be if I gave orders that weren't obeyed?"

He seemed to be exhausted when he was home, sitting in the armchair in the parlor with the shades drawn. He smoked, he drank, he scratched his scalp. He always wore khakis.

Drinking calmed him and sometimes he smiled, his eyes watering, and at those moments he became affectionate, calling his wife "Swee' Pea" — "Come over here, Swee' Pea, and give the Colonel a kiss" — which embarrassed Joe, who would hurry to his room when his mother approached the man in the chair, patting his lap. "Sit here, Swee' Pea."

"I wish I spoke French," he said in a rare instance of regret — probably drunk. "I'm glad you're learning it."

"J'essaye," Joe said. *"Au moins, j'essaye."*

And his father looked closely at him with wet delighted eyes.

"The French made a mess of things," he said, confiding, because he was pleased to hear Joe speaking French. "Now it's our problem."

"How long will you be there?"

"Joey, don't you see? I take orders too." He sipped his drink — it was always bourbon. "I don't know. But even if I did know I wouldn't tell you."

They were no longer on the base, so he couldn't compare his father with other officers anymore. They lived among civilians, and the fathers on this suburban street were home every night. They drove to work each morning and returned at six. But his father's life was the army; he did not live in the house, he visited it, dropping in on his wife and son on short notice, as though in a surprise inspection. His real home was the base in Vietnam. He was a full-time soldier who kept in touch with his family and who brought the tone and command of the army to the little bungalow in Manoa.

"Not a job," he said. "It's a calling. It's a duty. Special Forces."

Mistrustful of friendship, he did not know how to be a friend. And his idea of fatherhood was absolute authority, a giver of orders. But that suited Joe, who obeyed, and he knew that as long as his father commanded him, issuing orders, and Joe carried them out, his father would be appeased and would not ask for more. And the satisfaction for Joe was that because he was an order-taker — "Yes, sir" — his father would never know him, never know his secrets, his worries, his sadness, his weaknesses, his shortcomings; because he was obedient. And his father never asked.

No sooner had his father established a routine in Hawaii for a week or two — "Get a haircut," regular meals, drinking and smoking in the armchair, an evening dinner at the officers' mess at Fort DeRussy — then he was gone, always swiftly, always first thing in the morning, always unexpectedly; and another life resumed, Joe's mother brooding.

So Joe knew that he could not depend on him, and it was just as well his father didn't know him, because he would have been disappointed; he might have raged.

Joe's grades faltered. He tried out for the water polo team and, though he was a good swimmer, didn't make it, because water polo was not just about swimming: it involved thrashing for the ball, and shouting, and a rowdiness he could not muster among strangers. This failure added to his sense of being an outsider — no other boys from Fort Shafter attended Punahou. But there were boys he recognized as misfits like himself — the geeks, the jokers, the surfers.

They had one thing in common, smoking *pakalolo*. Being stoners was their secret and their bond, and it made them a team of outlaws. With this secret they were loyal to each other. Smoking was their shared activity, and as it was always covert, it amounted to a ritual.

The Punahou teachers were proud of the school; they spoke of it with fondness, remarking on its traditions and its heritage. They emphasized how lucky the students were to be studying there and how they had to live up to the reputation of this great institution. "Be true to the Buff 'n Blue!"

All this emotion was bewildering to Sharkey; Punahou was a name, nothing more, and the way the teachers and older students spoke of it mystified him and made them seem silly and sentimental. He was used to students hating school or satirizing it, not praising it. The boys at Radford, most of them military children, were a rough crowd who regarded the teachers as irrational and overbearing — people to avoid or subvert with pranks. But Punahou teachers were at pains to stress their friendship with the students, and any suggestion that a teacher could be friendly with a student made Sharkey suspicious.

"I tell my men I am not your friend — I am your commanding officer," his father, the Colonel, said. This made sense to Sharkey.

A friendly teacher was a worry. What was it they wanted to know? Why were they pretending to care? Their smiles seemed false and their compliments a kind of manipulation.

Sharkey had expected bullying. He'd experienced mild bullying at Radford, name-calling, petty intimidation, occasionally a fight after school in the parking lot. He found none of this at Punahou. Yet there was something else in the air, not threat but a palpable sense of superiority; just the posture of some students, the confident way they walked, the way they spoke or gestured, oppressed him, and the only name for it was snobbery, something new to him and awful, because snobbery was not violent but instead a kind of poisonous lying. It was much worse than bullying — you couldn't fight a snob, you couldn't win.

The scar on Sharkey's face made him conspicuous, a person of interest. To increase speculation and make himself mysterious, he refused to say how he'd gotten it. He did not want anyone to know him.

In his father's stories there was always a mention of Special Forces — never names or numbers of people, or reasons for them to be special, but only a shadowy gathering of faceless men intent on a mission, recon patrols, working in darkness. *Consider yourself already dead.* Sharkey imagined them to be heavily armed, wearing camouflage, prepared to defend themselves and the country, a fighting force united in their common fear of Colonel Sharkey.

The boys at Punahou, the ones who became Joe's friends, were united too — he thought of them as Special Forces. None were outstanding students, none had any other friends, none were on school sports teams; all of them smoked *pakalolo*. And among the smokers and the stoners was a surfer, Harry Ho. It was Harry Ho who showed Joe his first effective moves on a surfboard, his balance, his foot placement, his stance. And Harry introduced Joe to the older surfers at Waikiki, who called themselves the Beach Boys, another group who were like Special Forces.

So the world of Hawaii seemed to be made of different contained groups, who shared interests — not Radford students or Punahou students, but smaller numbers within those larger groups, like packs of dogs, who felt safe with each other and who had secret activities all their own. In the case of Sharkey's Punahou group it was smoking *pakalolo*, a ritual that was all the more attractive for being forbidden.

The headmaster, Dr. Emmett Chock, denounced it at morning assembly after prayers, saying how harmful it was — a drug, unlawful and unhealthy. And side by side, Sharkey and Harry Ho smiled, as the two most committed stoners, both of them surfers, Harry expert, Sharkey improving by the week.

And so Sharkey knew for the first time what it meant to belong to a band of brothers, the Special Forces of a small group of boys whom he could trust to be on his side, who sat together to eat, who kept to themselves during school hours, who were always on the margins, who never mocked each other, though they knew they were geeky and mockable; who seldom had long conversations and yet were in agreement on most things. Their ritual consisted of meeting after school in the far corner of the parking lot, behind the lava-rock wall next to the monkey pod tree, and passing a blunt from hand to hand until it was a small squeezed roach. It was their ritual of defiance that made them happier afterward, buzzed and always laughing.

Huddled that way they felt protected together, and when they saw each other in the playground or the pool they gathered in a cluster, ill-assorted, badly matched — Harry Ho was athletic but small, Walter Opunui wheezed with asthma and panted when he smoked, Alex Louie was skinny and sallow, Willy Miranda wore thick glasses, and Kali Fifita was overweight and slow. They jeered at the school teams; they knew they were viewed with suspicion, if not despised. But they had each other. They recognized their weaknesses, but it was secret knowledge; they did not use it to their advantage, or mention it.

But they saw they had strengths too — Harry the surfer, Joe his friend with the forbidding scar, Opunui always had money, Fifita had access to *pakalolo*. From this mutual protection a close friendship emerged, even a kind of sweetness, and as they smoked murmuring, remembering incidents from school, how Willy found a mistake on a math equation on the blackboard or Harry said to the chaplain after a Hawaiian prayer in Bible studies, "But Akua means spirit too, not only God — can also mean devil, or ghost," or the day the English teacher said, "Where do we find true aloha?" and Sharkey raised his hand: "Only on the shirts." He was scolded in the class but praised for his wit behind the wall near the monkey pod tree.

"You so *kolohe*," Harry said, passing him the butt.

One day in the cafeteria a senior boy attempted to talk to Harry, singling him out, as though to separate him from the group.

Harry said, "Keep walking."

The others were grateful to him for that. They were sensitive to slights. But though they felt weak as individuals and miserable at home, they were strong as a group and liked to think of themselves as a *hui*, a new word for Sharkey, explained by Harry as a little gang.

It was through Harry Ho that Sharkey at last learned how to manage the bewildering Hawaii world, and to move on. In spite of his father's warning, Harry was his friend, but by silent agreement they never spoke the word. It was an understanding. Other than the boys in the *hui*, Harry had no friends at Punahou. But he had many in town; he knew his way around Honolulu, the surf spots especially, and he favored the less popular ones, avoiding Diamond Head and Waikiki and using the breaks off Ala Moana, at Magic Island, where he kept his board chained to a rack. Harry's surfer friends became Sharkey's friends, and though Harry's friends were dropouts and stoners, they were connected.

On one of the early days at Bomboras, the break off Magic Island, a local surfer saw Sharkey paddling into the wave and called out, "Eh, haole — try wait!"

And a boy in the lineup whom Sharkey did not know said, "He's cool. Let him ride." Then loudly, "Take the wave, Joe!"

The boy who defended him was Ashley, one of Harry Ho's friends, and after that no one questioned Sharkey's right to be on the wave. They all became Sharkey's defenders, and in time his surf buddies.

He kept this knowledge from his father, that you managed here by having a friend, who trusted you and defended you and taught you the island ways. Without a friend, you remained on the outside and were excluded, and sometimes tormented. As a friend you became attached to a *hui*, ultimately to an *ohana*, a family, because you were trustworthy and willing to share what you had. And once you were part of an *ohana* no one questioned your right to be on the island.

Sharkey saw that Harry Ho had chosen him from the Punahou *hui* and introduced him to his friends outside the school — surfers, divers, fishermen, watermen generally. Uncle Sunshine was one of the old surfers who called himself a Beach Boy — older than the Colonel, yet age made no difference. He was a friend, he gave Sharkey surfing tips. All that mattered was trust, and Sharkey was happy.

The Colonel had been wrong. As a consequence of having one good friend, Sharkey had many friends. Sharkey found a balance with his friends; he greeted them on arriving at school, which was a fifteen-minute walk from his Manoa house, and they kept together in the playground — the nonjoiners, the stoners, the outsiders. They met after school and smoked, and, laughing — buzzed — Harry and Sharkey walked to Ala Moana and went surfing, no matter the conditions, even if the only wave was a foot-high crumbly mushburger frothing toward the shore. Afterward, under the palms, they smoked some more and studied the sea, which was limitless and stretched to the horizon, to where the late-afternoon sun pooled and became molten, the low clouds like flesh, bulging and blushing as the day waned, and finally crimson, the color bleeding from them, until the last gold blob dropped and a green flash glowed as an afterimage.

"*Eh ka nani,*" Harry said. "Beautiful."

They kept to themselves. They did not think anyone took any notice of them. Sharkey believed himself to be so mediocre he was invisible.

So he was surprised when one day Dr. Chock approached him and said, "You're Joe Sharkey?"

"Yes, sir."

"Empty your pockets."

3

The Mark of the Beast

I t seemed a cruel and sideways question, the headmaster — Dr. Emmett Chock — saying to Sharkey's mother, "I wonder if the young man understands why he's here?"

With his fingers on his cheek, his hand hiding that side of his face, the badly healed scar like the letter C, still livid with teeth marks and stitches, Sharkey had been staring out of the office window. The day glowed with the last spatter of the shower. The morning was now drenched in light, the splashed blossoms on the plumeria tree thickened by the dazzle. Small simple raindrops were enlarged by sunlight to honey-colored syrup. The way they lingered and drooped, as though for him alone, gave him hope.

It took some moments for his sun-dazzled eyes to adjust to the shadowy room. His mother came into focus, looking ill, and the beauty of what he had just seen had the effect of making Dr. Chock doglike, his gray face and coarse hair, his loose jaw chewing in disapproval, exaggerating his underbite. The man poked at the papers on his desk with his yellow nails, then sniffed his fingers.

"Yes, sir, I do," Sharkey said.

Dr. Chock probably wanted him to say more. What was the point? Sharkey knew he was being expelled.

"Maybe he hasn't lived in Hawaii long enough to learn our concept of *pono* — goodness, virtue, righteousness, sense of duty," Dr. Chock chanted, as though Sharkey were deaf or absent. "*Kuleana* means responsibility. Being *pono* is being true."

He knew that: they talked of nothing else at morning assembly; the word was repeated in the state anthem, "Hawai'i Pono'i," they sang most days. Yet that did not keep the older students from smoking *pakalolo*.

Kick me out, just let me go, he thought. But in his solemnity and slowness Dr. Chock seemed determined to make a big deal of it and deliver a lecture. And Sharkey could see that the headmaster was enjoying it, seeing himself as *pono* and Sharkey wicked and untrue, whereas he regarded himself as neither good nor bad but only fourteen and foreign in this place, a haole among locals.

In her humiliation, his mother was afraid, tipsy with confusion, and when Dr. Chock said, "I was hoping your husband would also be here," she got tearful, sounding drunk, saying in a trembling voice, "My dear husband, Colonel Sharkey, is in the army, on a tour of duty, serving his country in Vietnam," as though pleading for sympathy.

"We have many children of servicemen of all kinds," Dr. Chock said, and "army brat" was implied in "all kinds." He tapped his cheek to call attention to the corresponding part of Sharkey's cheek, the waxen flesh of the C-shaped scar and the roulettes of the oversized stitches, as though indicating disobedience.

"That was an accident," Sharkey's mother said. "That was a dog bite."

Blinking at "dog bite," Dr. Chock recovered and said, "And they don't habitually dabble in drugs."

But they did, all the time, everyone did, one corner of the parking lot was a haze of blue smoke after school. The only difference was that they did not get caught. And "dog bite" to Sharkey made him wince at the memory of the hoarse choking bark that gnawed at his throat, the bark saying *I am coming for you.*

"I wonder if he's listening," Dr. Chock said. "If he understands his *kuleana.*"

The way he put it, with a jowl shake, enraged Sharkey, so he said nothing. It was over, he was finished.

"I was hoping it wouldn't come to this," his mother said. "I don't know what to do with him."

"Joe is not the first of our students to be involved in drugs."

Sharkey's mother clasped her handbag tighter on her lap and leaned forward, looking hopeful.

"But the others showed some remorse," Dr. Chock said. "And they were more cooperative because they understood their *kuleana.* They demonstrated *kokua* — help, in the Hawaiian way."

"I know he's sorry. He told me — didn't you, Joey?"

The petals of the plumeria seemed to blink as more honeyed raindrops fell.

"How would I know that?" Dr. Chock said, tapping a fingernail like a claw onto the expulsion form. And before Sharkey's mother could speak, he added, "Sorry is just a word. I am looking for a deed. What I want to hear is real contrition, something *pono.*"

Sharkey's mother canted her head to the side, as though assessing Sharkey's remorse, but she frowned, unable to read him.

"We are *ohana*—family—at this school. If the young man perhaps showed *kokua*—shared more information with his *ohana,* as to the source of the drugs— I might be inclined to a more lenient view."

Now a raindrop from a drooping petal struck a petal on a lower branch, and the tap of one syrupy drop was enough to dislodge it. Sharkey watched the pinkish blossom fall, lighting like a butterfly on the dewy tips of some slender grass blades, making them bend.

"Joey, tell the headmaster what he wants to know."

So this was the reason for the ritual. Dr. Chock was asking Sharkey to snitch on the other stoners, especially his friend Harry Ho, who was a fellow surfer. Everyone had weed, it was easy to find, the headmaster must have known that. But he wanted Sharkey to submit. This wish gave Sharkey strength: he realized that he had power to deny the bossy man what he wanted.

"Are you going to show *kokua*?" Dr. Chock said. "You'd also be helping yourself. And that would be *pono.* In the true Hawaiian way."

Now Sharkey smiled, for the only time that morning, no longer feeling small and cornered, eavesdropping on his fate.

"No, sir."

"He should be punished," his mother said, and recoiled, looking fretful, as though shocked by the words she'd just uttered.

"Are you in military housing?"

"No. We live off base. We—" She began to explain, as though giving a reason, but became flustered again and said, "We're in Manoa."

"You'll have to enroll him at Stevenson Intermediate, or maybe Roosevelt," Dr. Chock said, his jowls registering satisfaction with a shake, and not a smile but a show of bonelike teeth. "Roosevelt's your nearest high school. A private school won't take him, with his record. A public school might be just what he needs."

Even that was not the end of it. Dr. Chock slid papers across the desk and gloated, his mouth open, as Sharkey's mother signed them, and before the session was over she was in tears.

"The boy is *pau* here," Dr. Chock said. "Finished."

Outside the school, before his mother could gather her wits to speak, Sharkey said, "I'm going to catch some waves."

He hurried away from her squawk—she was calling out, "But why?"— escaping down the sloping still-wet sidewalk, in sunshine, to Ala Moana, where, at Magic Island, he kept his board. And there, just off the beach at Bomboras, he surfed until sunset, alone, because everyone else was in school. Sliding on water, leaving no trace, he was stirred to the thought that the surface of the sea was forever unmarked, ageless, mirroring the purity of the sky, and could never be scarred.

They paused outside Roosevelt High School, before the lawns, the bell tower, the entrance, the big, neatly printed sign HOME OF THE ROUGH RIDERS, and under the portrait of a Hawaiian with an upraised shark-tooth club the words E KOMO MAI — WELCOME. The carved sign and gateway made it seem dignified — the equal of Punahou. But inside — the doggy smell of bare feet, of hair stiff with dirt, of unwashed clothes, of disinfectant and cheap perfume — the stink hung like a threat. Three heavy Hawaiian girls, bigger than Sharkey, lingered in a corridor, staring at him, and when his mother asked the way to the office, one of the girls pointed with her face to a doorway.

A woman, announcing herself as a secretary, greeted them from behind a high counter as though they were shopping at an old-fashioned store. A wide gilded cuff, engraved ALOHA, on the secretary's wrist dinged the counter as she shuffled papers. After signing them and handing over Sharkey's transcript, Sharkey's mother fretted and said, "My husband's in the military, serving his country. Is there anything more?"

"You *pau*," the secretary said. "He gonna come with me."

She led him — that smell again — to a small classroom, where the smell was stronger. Interrupted in her lesson, the teacher, a young Japanese woman, grinned in frantic annoyance, and when the secretary gave her Sharkey's papers she tossed them onto her desk and said, "Take a seat — over there."

He sensed like a flare-up of heat the heightened attention, all eyes on him, as he walked to the empty desk and sat; but more than anything he was aware of the size of the students — bigger, darker, slouched and sitting sideways. And when the teacher resumed, turning her back to write on the board, Sharkey felt something hit his arm — the bitten stub of a pencil, like a chewed bone.

"Haole," came a growl from behind him. He knew the word from Punahou — howlie, whitey — but never spoken with such contempt. He heard it again like a harsh echo from another throat. He turned aside; a Hawaiian girl in a red dress pursed her lips as though mimicking a kiss. She was lovely, with yellowish glinting eyes, thick black hair to her shoulders, and a flower behind her ear. When Sharkey smiled, she spat at him, then wiped her chin.

"Four *x*," the teacher was saying, scraping with her chalk, "equals sixteen."

At lunchtime he found an empty table, but three boys pushed him aside and said, "We stay here, haole." The cafeteria looked so crowded, all the other tables occupied, elbows everywhere, Sharkey decided to skip his meal and made his way to the playground. A group of girls sat under a tree, covertly smoking, passing a cigarette butt. Some younger children with wild hair kicked a ball. Sharkey walked to a bench at the far side of the space. He sat in full sunlight and put his head in his hands to avoid the glare.

"You the new kid?"

The sudden voice startled him. A boy stood nearby, and at once Sharkey could see the boy was frightened — the way he stood, slightly bent over, something in his blinking and his pinched face, as though he were preparing to flee.

"Hi. I'm Blaine. I saw you in class this morning. That kid behind you, Wilfred, he's psycho. A real *moke*."

"*Moke*?"

"Big Hawaiian guy. He always gives me side-eye."

Sharkey said, "I'm Joe."

"Wilfred lives in a car at the back of the valley," Blaine said. "Did you just come from the mainland?"

"I got kicked out of Punahou."

"I wanted to go there. My folks didn't have the money." And now Blaine took a deep breath and began backing up.

Four boys, led by Wilfred, were walking slowly toward them, scuffing the gravel. What made them particularly fearsome was that their mouths were full and they were chewing, probably the last of their lunch. Seeing that Blaine was attempting to sidle away, one of the boys pushed him against the fence. Blaine crouched and clutched his stomach, as though to make himself small. Wilfred stepped near him and flicked a finger against Blaine's ear, stinging him.

"What you wen' telling the fucken haole?"

Blaine whimpered and held the ear that Wilfred had flicked.

Wilfred confronted Sharkey, his big belly near Sharkey's face. He was fattish, his T-shirt stained, his shorts dirty, his hair tangled, flecks of food on his lips, and he had a dog odor of dirt. "He wen' say something to you?"

Sharkey said, "I don't know anything."

"He a panty," Wilfred said. The other boys laughed, too loud, their teeth large, their tongues scummy. "You a panty too?"

Blaine fidgeted, still crouched, his hands now near his face, as though expecting a slap.

"You got something for me?" Wilfred said, and now he seemed to be staring at the scar on Sharkey's cheek.

Sharkey was still seated. He calculated that if he got to his feet the boy would take it for defiance, or a challenge. So he continued to sit as Wilfred repeated his question, this time coming close — his odor was so strong it made him bigger and meaner. The boy was still focused on the scar, seeming to question it with his open mouth.

"I guess you're the boss," Sharkey said.

"What? Yeah, me da *luna*," Wilfred said, almost in wonderment. "See this *mahu*?" And he gestured at Blaine, extending his reach to flick Blaine's ear again where it was reddened. "He real futless. See how he make ass? If he don't shape up he's going to get lickings," he said, and pushed him. Then he leaned toward Sharkey. "We da *kanaka ohana*. And know what, haole?"

"What?"

"We hate fucken haoles."

And then Sharkey stood up. He was taller than Wilfred but thin, already at fourteen with the suggestions of a swimmer's physique, his second season on a surfboard, the thickening shoulders, the slender legs. Wilfred stepped back, the four other boys looking watchful. But Sharkey did not advance on them. He went over to Blaine and put his hand on his shoulder. He could see why Blaine was being bullied — he was small and pale and scrawny, and he had a girl's soft unmarked cheeks. He knew from Punahou that the small boys got the worst of it. And out of the corner of his eye he sensed that Wilfred, unsure of him, was hesitating, looking closer.

"How you get that bite mark, brah?"

Sharkey touched the scar on his cheek. "Mark of the beast." Then he leaned and said, "Get up, big guy," and helped the cringing boy to his feet.

Wilfred grunted, and just then, at the moment of confrontation, the school bell rang. A teacher in an aloha shirt called out to them and began loudly to harangue them to go back to class.

The ninth-grade teacher was Miss Matsuda. Wilfred was Wilfred Kalama. Most of his little gang sat at the back of the class — Clarence, Fonoti, Sammy Boy, and Braddah Jay, all Hawaiians or Samoans from nearby Papakolea. The pretty girl in the desk next to Sharkey's, the one who had spat at him, was Vai. Vai's friends were Leena and Nalani. Leena was Samoan. The Chinese and Japanese students left him alone, but all the rest were tormentors — muttering at him in class, jostling him in the corridor, the girls as foul-mouthed as the boys; "Fucken haole" was Leena's refrain, Vai still the spitter, Wilfred the intimidator, threatening Sharkey with lickings in the parking lot after school. The only relief for him was their persecution of Blaine Langford, the skinny boy who sought refuge at the front of the room, nearest the desk of Miss Matsuda.

Sharkey kept his head down, he said nothing in class, the work was easy, nothing new — the math and history he'd already done at Punahou. Roosevelt was chaotic and noisy, but it was harder to be anonymous here, because he was a haole and there were so few at the school. He was jeered at and threatened — the threats sounding crueler when they were mumbled in pidgin. "Pretty soon we gonna have 'kill a haole day.'" His books were scattered, his locker scribbled on with crayon, yet he was not touched. He felt pity for Blaine, who was physically bullied — pushed, elbowed aside, tripped, his ears flicked — and he saw how Blaine suppressed his cries, not wishing to reveal his terror.

Sharkey was stared at for his scar, and it seemed to caution the other boys. It was a mark of distinction, a source of power, all the greater because its history was hidden, though there was something in its ragged stitches and discoloration that suggested violence, and so it served as a deterrent.

"That's quite enough," Miss Matsuda said whenever there was a commotion in the classroom. But she never saw the subtle torments and had no idea of what happened in the corridors or the cafeteria or the playground.

Each afternoon Sharkey walked home rather than risk the bus and more taunts: the length of Nehoa Street and then up the hill and left into Aleo and on to Ferdinand, where his mother waited, to ask, "Nice day at school?" and he said, "Yup," and kept walking to his room, where he changed. "Going surfing." And it was then that he caught the bus or walked to Ala Moana, and at Magic Island he was in the water and free again.

But why? his mother asked in a pleading voice when he hurried away, and even when she didn't say it, the question was in her squint whenever he left. It was something he never asked himself, nor could he give any reasons for running to the beach and plunging into the water, or flopping on his board and paddling into the waves, ducking as they washed over him and thrusting into the next trough until he was bobbing beyond the break.

It was play, it was joy, it was as natural and unexplainable as breathing, a pleasure and a relief to be uplifted in the sea. Never mind surfing; just sitting on his board and rising and falling on the plump belly of a swell, far from shore and the tiny people there, behind him the flat Pacific, empty as far as the smooth true seam of the horizon.

Why did he wish to be buoyant in the mild milky ocean until early evening, when the surface wrinkled in a sea breeze and shone, scaly under the slanting sun — sliding like mad in the barrel of a wave to the last kick-out on the reef, when the lip of the tube collapsed in a boil of foam, then tipping himself into the riptide to head back to the purity of the sea, sometimes a beaky turtle's head staring at him with its side eye, and now and then the gulp and snort of dolphins passing in a pod, and never a human voice?

"I don't know," he told his mother.

"It's dangerous," she said.

And he laughed, because offshore, isolated on his board, away from Wilfred and his gang, he'd never felt safer.

It was only in the third week that he saw Blaine on his way home, the same route, walking fast. He moved as if pursued. Sharkey understood: he also was avoiding the bus, and he fled the school as soon as the bell rang. Sharkey followed him closely but said nothing, simply watched the hurrying boy, his hunched-over gait, his arms working. He turned off at Ventura Street, and after a few steps he called out and a faint barking began from somewhere within a small white frame house of peeling paint, a car with a rusted bumper in the driveway, which was partially hidden by an overhanging bougainvillea.

And perhaps with the confidence of being home, Blaine straightened and looked around and saw Sharkey behind him on the sidewalk, backing away.

"Hey." He opened the low garden gate. "You live around here?"

"Up on Ferdinand," Sharkey said, being vague, so as not to reveal that he had followed him.

"Want to come in?" Blaine looked pathetic; he was pleading.

Sharkey hesitated, but as soon as the front door opened the barking began again, and though Sharkey stepped back the dog leaped on him, first raking his face with his paws, then snapping at his feet, all the while barking in that choking slavering way, his jowls shaking.

"Wags, stop," Blaine said in an admiring rather than a scolding tone, and Sharkey found it odd that this small boy was so confident around the fierce dog, and how he seemed to smile in relief when he saw that Sharkey was helpless, fending off the dog by raising his shoe against him.

"Don't be afraid," Blaine said.

Sharkey was terrified; the dog was trying to bite him, leaping to chew his foot.

"He wants you to pat him," Blaine said. "Don't you, Wags?"

The dog was slavering, barking, snapping at Sharkey's foot. And only then, when the dog got hold of Sharkey's shoe, wetting it with the froth of his saliva, did Blaine grasp his collar and pull him away.

"Bad dog!" This loud shout from the boy whom Sharkey had seen as a whisperer and a whiner. Sharkey was impressed, but he was also still terrified. The dog whimpered and licked Blaine's hand and yapped. "See? He's really friendly when he wants to be. But he could tell you were afraid." This was a reprimand, from the boy who cringed when Wilfred Kalama flicked his ear.

Sharkey said, "I was attacked by a dog. At Fort Shafter. That's why we moved."

"Is that how you got that scar?"

"Yeah," Sharkey said, and traced the livid gouge on his cheek that was like the letter *C*. "I had to get a ton of shots."

"Come on in," Blaine said, almost hearty.

But Sharkey said, "Maybe some other time," and walked away, sorry that he had detoured here and determined to go surfing. He glanced back at the corner of Ferdinand and saw that Blaine was watching him, holding his dog's collar, looking triumphant.

That night he wished he had not said anything about the dog attack at Shafter and instead had spoken to Blaine of surfing, how waves did not faze him. The thump and crush of water, the fetch of waves, were like the rhythm of life. Even when he'd been tumbled in a break as a child and his father had pulled him to safety, he had had no fear of water — he was buoyant, the sea was freedom. He felt cornered on land. Dogs thickened their muscly necks and barked behind fences and leaped, making the chain link clatter.

The dog at Shafter had made straight for him, bounding across the street, his fat tongue drawn aside by his speed, and he had jumped as he approached, pouncing, knocking Sharkey to the grass, and begun greedily to chew at his face, snapping his jaws.

Not a dream, but a memory, and even the dog's name, Max, seemed sinister. Sleep saved him, brimmed around him like the sea, and he was submerged. Sharkey slept soundly, but when he woke each morning and blinked and yawned and remembered that he had to go to school, something like a sickness gripped him, a feeling of woe and weakness that was like a stricture in his throat that made him breathless. On many days his hatred of school was a heaviness, like sorrow. At breakfast his mother said, "Did you sleep all right, Joey?" — an absurd question. He always slept well. It was the waking up that was hard, saddened by the knowledge of what he faced.

If he took the bus, it was the loud rowdy boys teasing the girls and throwing spitballs, sometimes calling out *"Hana batta!"* and flinging snot. Or the chant of "Haole!" So he walked, setting out alone, but often Blaine hurried to join him, as though for protection, looking quite defenseless without his dog.

"You should take your dog to school," Sharkey said. "Set him on Wilfred and those big *mokes*."

"The thing of it is," Blaine said, "he's really a good dog."

And that seemed like a rebuff to Sharkey, as though he'd timidly overreacted.

"Want to come over after school?" Blaine said, and it sounded to Sharkey like a dare.

"I'm busy." He did not want to explain that he was going surfing, because he was still learning, and to speak of surfing so soon after arriving in Hawaii would seem like a boast. But it was a private satisfaction, his secret pleasure, taking refuge on the waves.

Blaine said, "He won't hurt you."

"It's not that," Sharkey said. They both knew it was the dog. They were still walking, Blaine limping slightly. "Did you hurt your foot?" Blaine said nothing but still he walked, dragging his right foot. "Blaine, are you okay?"

The boy stopped and flexed his leg, and then, as Sharkey watched, his head cocked to the side, Blaine took off his shoe and poked at something inside, straightening it, a thickness of wadded paper.

"That looks like money."

"My hiding place. Don't tell anyone."

And Sharkey saw at once that it was Blaine's pitiful strategy to prevent the school bullies from finding his money and taking it.

Soon they were among other students walking toward the school, all marching in silence, then gathering at the playground like spectators assembling for a ceremony of savagery or an execution, something wicked to watch. Sharkey took a deep breath, as he did before paddling into a big wave, knowing he faced another whole day of "fucken haole" and *"malihini"* and "panty." Lately it had been "Elvis," because Elvis Presley had just given a concert at the Honolulu arena. He was menaced by the ugly faces of the boys, and it was worse somehow if a girl happened to see him or hear the taunts. The teachers were either indifferent or didn't see, and some of them quarreled with each other. It sometimes seemed to Sharkey that they depended on the tougher boys to keep the others in order. It was all misery, and the only relief was hurrying away at the last bell.

For some weeks they shunned him, turned their backs on him when he passed them. It should have given him some peace to be left alone, but the isolation made him anxious, and their laughter and whispers were hostile. He did not exist. But he knew they'd resume, jostling him, and they did, making ugly faces, screaming, "Fucken haole!"

At lunch break Sharkey sat alone or with Blaine, eating the sandwich his mother had made for him. He finished quickly and went outside to the playground and sat on the hot cement bench in the far corner that he had found his first day, avoided by the other students because it was hot, in full sunshine. There he watched the other students fooling with each other, and hated them. Blaine sometimes came over — often limping, because of the money in his shoe — and tried to start a conversation, looking to Sharkey for protection.

"Haole!"

They were usually yelling it at Blaine, who was weak, and whimpered, and cowered. Sharkey's scar seemed to make them wary, and he was resigned to the shouts. But out of desperate pride, if one of them snatched at his lunch bag he snatched back, and it was like a challenge. But he also saw that they were poor, and they roamed like a pack because they were hungry.

One of those days on the playground, Wilfred accosted him with his little gang, saying, "Where you panty friend?"

Sharkey nodded slowly but said nothing. There was no way to win against five of them.

"He never tell us where he hiding his money," Wilfred said, as always staring at his scar. "You his fucken haole friend. You know."

Sharkey said, "If I knew, maybe I'd take it off him myself."

They left him alone then, and pestered Blaine, and Sharkey understood that because Blaine was a haole they believed his parents were wealthy, but Sharkey had seen the little house on Ventura Street, the peeling paint and the old car, and his dog had looked starved too. It seemed crueler that they wanted what little money the weedy boy had.

But they continued to follow Blaine and flick his ear, and they encouraged the girls — Vai and Leena — to slap him. Nothing was worse than to be roughed up by a girl. But because of this concentration on Blaine, the taunts, the demands, Sharkey was mostly left alone. And when after a few weeks some other boys came after Sharkey, trying to corner him as he was hurrying through the playground after school, Wilfred stepped in.

"Haole," he said. "You know *kokua*?"

Sharkey frowned at the Punahou word.

"It mean help. Help us get the panty money," Wilfred said. "He hiding it in his stuffs."

Sharkey said, "Why don't you leave him alone?"

That was defiance, but the mention of Blaine made them glance around, and they saw that he was at the far side of the playground. So by the time Wilfred recovered, saying, "Elvis, you want dirty lickings?" and "Where you going, haole?" Sharkey had slipped through the gate in the fence and was hurrying across the school lawn. When he looked back he saw the gang of boys advancing on Blaine, and Blaine — white-faced and small and piteous — lifting his skinny hands and pleading.

But the following day, walking to school, Sharkey saw Blaine on Nehoa Street and waved. Blaine did not wave back, and the next time Sharkey looked, Blaine was nowhere to be seen. He wondered if Blaine had been beaten up, but in class the boy was unmarked, and in the playground he heard Blaine laugh — he had never heard him laugh before, and it was a strange sound, like a sudden snorting honk. No one approached him or spoke to him. Sharkey took this to be a good sign — perhaps they were growing wiser, being *pono*. And he laughed when he remembered the word and the way Dr. Chock had spoken it, popping it on his lips.

Wilfred kept away from Sharkey that day too. The routine of classes, cafeteria, playground, dismissal was relieved by the absence of any aggression. Sharkey remained, as always, alone, and when the last bell rang he hurried across the playground and ducked through the gate in the chain-link fence.

It was when he came to the perimeter of the school grounds that he heard the barking — the choking yap that recalled to him the frantic sound of starvation. He looked back and saw Wilfred with a dog straining ahead of him on a leash, because Wilfred was slow, treading on battered flip-flops, and the dog was eager.

Wilfred's gang was behind him, calling out, their flip-flops slapping the sidewalk — there were too many of them for Sharkey to give them names, but Fonoti and Clarence were visible for their size and their swinging arms. The dog had big shoulders and square jaws and a fat droopy tongue that swung as he trotted. Sharkey saw the dog clearly and was afraid, and wanted to run.

Instead of heading home he turned in the opposite direction, walking fast, to Punahou Street, and then to the overpass across the freeway, to Beretania, where he felt he was losing them. Down Kalakaua and through the maze of streets that led to Ala Moana, his heart beating fast — from running, from fear — he fled.

Crossing the grass to Magic Island, he was startled by the barking again — they must have taken a shortcut, and there seemed more of them now, the dog ahead of them, that gagging bark, those teeth — and Wilfred now calling out, "Haole — you got something for me!"

By then Sharkey had found his board in the stack, pulled his shirt over his head, and kicked off his sneakers, and when the dog was at last released and bounding at him he'd hit the water, the first wave of the shore break, the board under him, and was paddling to where the wave lifted, with froth at its lip. And he rose into it and turned, and at this height he saw the dog foundering, helpless, gagging in the thickened foam. Wilfred was on the beach, his gang behind him, and at the back a pale shadow: Blaine.

They were shouting, probably "Haole!" or worse, but at this distance he couldn't hear it, and anyway it didn't matter, because, buoyant in the mild milky ocean, all he heard was the consolation of the waves.

4

Father Figures

U ncle Sunshine said, "I cannot teach you surf. You can only teach yourself surf. If you stay *akamai* and surf every day, you improve. I can tell
you what you doing wrong, that's all."

"What am I doing wrong?"

"You too much smoking, boy. Try stop."

"So I'll stop."

"It more better if you wen' stop. You need good lungs for swim, for surf,
for paddle out, for win. Kids too much smoking, is more worse."

Uncle Sunshine — his nicknames were Sunny or Feesh, he said "sweem"
not "swim," he said "keeds," he said "ween" — was an old Hawaiian with a
wicked grin and kindly eyes who sat with the other men his age at the rack
of long boards at Waikiki, where Sharkey surfed on some days. Harry had
introduced him and vouched for him, saying *My kupuna.*

"You got one fadda?"

"Yes, sir."

"Where you fadda stay?"

When Sharkey told him that he was in Vietnam and said, "Special Forces
— he's a colonel," Uncle Sunshine softened and said, *"E komo mai,"* patting
his shoulder. "I stay army too — all over the Pacific," and pointed to the sea,
dabbing with his fingers.

He was brown, very lean, his skin wrinkled and slack, with brown bony
legs and weeds of yellow-gray hair. Though he was probably in his fifties, he
could have been any age, and was always boyish and agile on his board. His
boast was that he had surfed with Duke Kahanamoku and that everything he
told Sharkey was the wisdom of wave-riding, passed down from the ancient
Hawaiians.

"Duke, he talk story with me. He say . . ."

The first time Sharkey heard the name, spoken with reverence and awe, he had no idea who the man was, but he learned about him from Harry Ho and realized how lucky he was. Uncle Sunshine pointed him out on the beach, the tall brown man, his neck looped in leis, posing beside his thick board for photographers. He'd won medals swimming in the Olympics, Uncle Sunshine said. He was the living link to the ancient Hawaiian surfers, he had met Jack London, he was the most famous surfer who'd ever lived, and there he was, twenty feet away, in a bathing suit.

"How's eet!" Uncle Sunshine called out.

The towering figure of Duke Kahanamoku loosened, the man smiled and flashed a shaka with his free hand, and it seemed like a blessing. And Sharkey again felt that he was part of a larger group, more important than the school, which now seemed merely an unavoidable interruption in the day, between the parentheses of waking and surfing.

"You have to get to the point where the board stay like part of you body, attach to you feet, and you feel the wave power through the board. You not riding on the board. You and the board one ting, walking on water. That what the great Duke say to me." And saying so, he smiled at the muscular man.

Later, to avoid Uncle Sunshine's scrutiny, Sharkey surfed off Magic Island, paddling from Waikiki through a succession of breaks, and across the Ala Wai Harbor entrance to Bomboras. But the idea had been Uncle Sunshine's: to learn the variations of one break, to master it and know its moods.

"Know what the big man say to me?" Uncle Sunshine said to Sharkey one day. "Duke see you swimming from break to break on your board and say, '*Ilio holo i ka uaua* — he the dog that run in rough water.'"

"He said I'm a dog?"

"Water dog," Uncle Sunshine said. "He say you a monk seal. He see something in you. Some people he say, 'She a surf bunny' or 'He a *malihini*.' But to the big man you a monk seal. I cannot say nothing more better."

Like the smile, like the shaka, another blessing.

Swimming sustained him; he swam in his dreams, buoyant in the world, or braced on his board, sliding through barrels at Bomboras. He could not run in his dreams, or cry out, or hurry, but he could swim, and he swam in the effortless tumbling way of a seal. Even on his worst day at school — the mumbled threats, the spitballs, "I was sitting here, haole!" and the attempted shakedowns in the schoolyard — he was heartened by the thought that as soon as the school bell rang he would be on his way to the beach and the freedom of the sea — the blue limitless ocean.

Water was a promise of pleasure, and the bigger the waves, the more space he had to swim and surf, because only the better surfers attempted them, and no one swam for pleasure in any breakers. His sense of weightlessness in the waves; the propulsion of his stroke, water filling his cupped hands; the solitude that enveloped him, and then upright, alone on his board — all of it gave him happiness and hope and the conviction that nothing else mattered. It was as if in surfing he was carving his name in water, invisibly, joyously. He knew now that all the other surfers felt the same — Harry Ho and Uncle Sunshine and Duke — though they never spoke about it and probably did not have the words to describe it, because really there were no words, only the action mattered, the ritual of it all, which was a ritual of purification.

You couldn't puzzle it out or learn how in books; no logical description fitted it. It was a rush, a feeling, a dance.

Stopping smoking was not hard, except for the first week of brown sweats and food tasting sharper and a slight headache. Waking in the morning without a nicotine hangover was odd, giving him unusual clarity, and within a month the smell of someone else's cigarette smoke was so sour it reinforced his vow. He was able to breathe more deeply, without a whistle in his throat. Feeling stronger in the water, he realized how smoking had impeded him — Uncle Sunshine was right. The odd thing was that while smoking weed had gotten him expelled from Punahou, the only punishment at Roosevelt was a three-day suspension.

Not smoking set him even further apart from the boys at Roosevelt, but he still saw Harry Ho after school and at the beach.

"Your guys always hassling us," Harry said.

"What guys?"

"Roosevelt *mokes*, picking fights at the bus stop with the Punahou kids."

Sharkey laughed, thinking how he was now associated with the tough school, the Roosevelt boys, when he knew he had no status except that of a haole in a school that was mostly Hawaiian and Polynesian — the Samoans and Tongans from Papakolea; the boys like Wilfred and Fonoti, who lived in cars, sleeping in the backseat.

Not smoking had another advantage — no one came up to him now and poked him in the chest with a filthy finger and said, "Geev 'um, haole — one cigarette."

When his father came home and hugged him, Sharkey gasped and held his breath — the man was saturated with smoke-stink, the dead-leaf smell of burned earth, and the sweet-sour tang of whiskey. It was an odor of decay and cold ashes, and like the risen fumes of sickness, his yellow fingers, his stained teeth, his endearments growled in his bad breath.

"Joe, you're getting bigger by the week." His father seemed admiring of him, because his father was smaller and slightly shrunken, exhausted after the long flight, short of breath, grinning like a corpse as he sucked smoke out of a cigarette. He moved more slowly, although always stiff-backed, his head high, pinching the cigarette in his fingers.

"I swim and surf almost every day."

"What about school?"

"It's okay. I do my work."

"If you don't keep your grades up, you'll never get into the academy."

For the Colonel, always, the only aim of a high school education was that it prepared a boy for West Point, and West Point was preparation for the world.

"You gotta be smart."

"I thought exercise was supposed to be important too," Joe said.

Over dinner his mother said, "But every day!"

"When there's no surf I don't go."

The Colonel smoked at the table, between courses and sometimes while he was eating, a forkful of food in his right hand, a cigarette in his left. He was smoking now, and often his manner of smoking indicated that he was thinking, a certain way of inhaling or blowing smoke out of the side of his mouth, like a process of thought. He was taking puffs, reflecting.

"My men — not the ARVN but my Special Forces," he said, "some of them surf. We have landing craft near a place called Danang. Just north of it on a lovely shoreline, China Beach, where we bring up our boats. Some of the men surf there — with boards, or body surfing. It's quite a thing to see."

"I'd like to try it there."

"It's deceptive. The most beautiful places in Vietnam are the most dangerous." He was still smoking. He pushed his plate away and tapped ashes into the remains of his mashed potato and spoke past Joe to the shadows at the back of the dining room. "I don't know where this thing is going."

"I worry," Sharkey's mother said. "Sometimes I'm a wreck."

The Colonel picked a fleck of tobacco off his tongue and spat smoke. "Don't start."

On that visit he was home for a week, busy in meetings most days at Fort Shafter, but one morning he said, "Joe, I want to see you doing it. I want to see your moves."

They drove to Ala Moana Beach Park later that day and walked under the palms across the expanse of lawn to Magic Island, where Sharkey lifted his board from the rack.

"I let them surf for a day or so, because they're chopper pilots — they're great at what they do," the Colonel said, as though finishing an interrupted thought.

At the low grassy bluff on the shore above the break the Colonel stood in uniform, feet apart, watching Sharkey paddle out—and Sharkey took care to paddle efficiently, ducking under the incoming sets until he was sitting on the swell, lifted by the boil, waiting for a good wave.

The Colonel moved to the lip of the bluff, in the attitude of reviewing his troops, his khakis glowing yellow in the afternoon sun, his posture, the angle of his head, his visor yanked down, giving him an interrogating look of severity. Because he was wearing sunglasses, his expression was unreadable —he was motionless, enigmatic, peering out to sea, watched by his son, who was rising and falling on the succession of swells. The Colonel was his posture, standing upright, awaiting an order. That was how all soldiers seemed to Sharkey—like men listening for a command, waiting to be told what to do. But studied by Sharkey on his board from the height of the swell, the Colonel looked small and solitary, isolated on the bluff, in a way Sharkey had never seen him before, not like a soldier but like any other man, fragile, decaying in the failing light.

Sharkey tipped his board to catch an oncoming wave, paddled hard to stay on it, then grabbed the rails and got to his feet and rode it, angling himself so that he remained visible to his father until, as the barrel narrowed, he slipped into the foam and swam near to where his father was standing.

"That took guts," the Colonel said in the car. And when they got home he heard him tell his mother, "He's a brick."

Sharkey had never before heard his father praise him with such force; he loved him for it, and despaired of the stink of tobacco smoke and his yellow-stained fingers.

"You're drown-proof," the Colonel said the morning he left. "You're going to be all right."

A few days later Uncle Sunshine said, "I see you fadda. I checking up on you. I see him and I think, 'Bugga no need Sunny.' Just the way you fadda standing I think, he a soldier for sure. And he proud of you. What he doing up there in Vietnam?"

"I asked him. He said, 'I can't tell you.'"

"That more worse. It mean really important," Uncle Sunshine said. "More dangerous, the operation."

"Helicopters."

"Gnarly," Uncle Sunshine said. "I wish I woulda met him, to talk story."

Uncle Sunshine was more attentive to Sharkey after that, kinder, more concerned, as though taking the Colonel's place. Sharkey detected something fatherly in Uncle Sunshine's tone, a note of firmness that was also a note of protection and encouragement, a gruff sort of love. And some days Uncle Sunshine left the Beach Boys and the surfboard stand at Waikiki to paddle across the breaks to Magic Island and watch Sharkey on the waves.

"Loosen up," Uncle Sunshine said. "The wave not your friend but da kine, companion like. It let you do what you want to do. Don't fight the wave, don't try to beat 'um — ride the bugga."

And no matter how tense a day he'd had at school, how severe a standoff with the other boys — because he was always outnumbered, and sometimes sucker-punched or slapped in the face, "fucken haole," as they grabbed his sandwich and spat on it, and because now Blaine the snitch was on their side — no matter how many taunts he had to endure, the prospect of surfing calmed him and gave him hope. And after he'd had some good rides he felt relaxed, uplifted and alive on the wave, and at the end of the day washed clean.

It helped too that Uncle Sunshine was Hawaiian, that Sharkey had been praised by Duke Kahanamoku, because at Roosevelt Sharkey was bullied for being a haole — singled out and told he didn't belong. "Fucken haole, fucken haole" — it was the chant. "Go back to the mainland, fucken haole. Geev 'um dirty lickings!" He couldn't defy Wilfred's gang of ten or twelve locals or Vai's screeching girls, but the bullying drove him to surf; made him a loner; made him strong in the water. And being accepted by Uncle Sunshine meant everything, because Uncle Sunshine was, as he said, a *kanaka maoli*, "real people, here fo'evah."

When in his stammering way Sharkey attempted to thank him for his kindness, the old man said, "You *ohana*."

His mother fretted; she had nothing to do but sit and wait for the Colonel to send a message or to come home. His messages were few; his visits were not vacations, as he said, but always a result of meetings, planning, crises, urgencies, his needing to explain in person to the command at Fort Shafter the progress he was making.

"If they only knew what my men had to put up with," the Colonel said. He was grim, habitually biting his cigarette, holding it in his teeth, square-mouthed, exhaling around it, squinting through the smoke, his eyes puffy from being stung.

"But the enemy is in the north," his mother said. "And you're in the south."

"Have I told you where I am?" his father said, raising his voice. And in that same sharp tone, "The enemy is everywhere. They have trails, they have caves, they have tunnels. Don't make me tell you this!"

And he smoked to calm himself, sulking in his armchair in the front room, with the shades drawn, sitting upright in his uniform.

"I told my men you're a surfer," he said to Sharkey through blue smoke. "They said it's good training for special ops, night insertions."

And the next morning he was gone. Uncle Sunshine seemed to under-stand when Sharkey's father was away. He was more attentive, he made an effort to watch him, he urged him to surf Waikiki, the breaks at Pops or Queen's, where he could see him more easily. But Magic Island had saved him, and he usually had Bomboras to himself, and he always went home exhausted and happy, and shut himself in his room away from his mother's drunken talk, saying, "Homework" — another escape.

He heard his mother scream one of those evenings, her voice carrying to his room. Looking down the corridor, he saw his mother's back turned to him, a man at the door, in black, a chaplain.

"No, no, please," the man said. "It's not what you think. Your husband's alive, but he's been in an accident. A helicopter — a hard landing. Colonel Sharkey is being flown home. He'll be at Tripler tomorrow."

His mother was clutching her ears and whinnying with such force the chaplain had stepped away. But he kept repeating the message and said, "He's in good hands," and finished by saying, "This must be your son," which silenced his mother for a moment, and then she sorrowed again, an agonized gagging, in a voice Sharkey had never heard from her before.

They found the Colonel behind a curtain at Tripler, yellow-faced, a tube in his nose, another in his arm, mouth open, his lips dry, in hospital pajamas. He was asleep.

"He's got some pretty serious internal injuries, from the force of the crash," the doctor told Sharkey's mother. "But he should be out of the woods in a few weeks."

"We've noticed some improvements," another doctor said the next day. But the Colonel was still asleep, his hands on the sheet, palms up, making him look helpless. "We'll call you if there's a change. Go ahead, talk to him. I'm sure he can hear you."

Sharkey's mother pressed her face to the Colonel's and sobbed. When she was done, Sharkey leaned over and spoke into his father's ear, saying, "I'm getting better. I'm hanging ten," and tearfully, "I love you, Dad."

When the call came, the phone rang in darkness, the sound filling the house in Manoa, and Sharkey knew that a call at that hour of the night had to be bad news. He covered his ears as his mother began to scream.

5

Adrift

I n the first aimless and empty days after the funeral and the burial at a military ceremony at Punchbowl, the National Memorial Cemetery of the Pacific — an honor guard, a speech by the chaplain, a bugler playing taps — Sharkey became aware of a wordless concern, a watchfulness in the boys who had bullied him at school. It was not overt kindness, it was mute and awkward, something oblique, a suspension of hostilities that made Sharkey uneasy — no shouts, no swearing, no jostling, no physical contact at all. The boys whispered indistinctly among themselves, they made room for Sharkey, they were subdued and clumsily gentle, as though attempting to ease his mind, vividly expressed when the Samoan girl Vai, eyes averted, offered him a fragrant gardenia, pinching it in her dirty fingers. And Sharkey understood that, though he said nothing, his silence was taken to be grief, and there was honor and power in grieving. They felt sorry for him, but they were afraid too, because in his grief Sharkey was like an angel of death.

Sorrowing weakened him; he felt his body slacken as his energy drained away. He wasn't strong enough to surf, and anyway his mother pleaded for him to stay with her, seeming to believe that she was in danger of losing him too. She clung to him, and he could feel her flesh tremble from the way she gripped him, somehow the sobs clutching at him in the tightening of her hand on her arm.

He had hated to go to school before, but now school was a relief — a break from his mother's despair ("What am I going to do without you?" she wailed) — a consolation too because he welcomed the sympathy of the boys. He had no enemies now. He'd been wounded by his father's death — no one wished to hurt him anymore. And the boys he had regarded as dogs and persecutors he now saw as wounded themselves; they understood death as loss and failure. They lived lives of rejection. They could have been cruel — he was more helpless than ever — but they were kind, they were protectors, and solicitous, seeming to feel a kinship in his misery.

The big ugly boy Wilfred, with the wild hair and the decaying teeth and stinking clothes — the boy who had tried to frighten him with his slavering dog, and who once had slapped him in the cafeteria, saying, "You sitting in my chair, fucken haole" — this tough boy approached him in the playground, his little gang silent behind him.

Wilfred put out his hand. "Dis for you, braddah."

It was a plump well-made *pakalolo* blunt, smooth and dusty from being handled, an offering.

"Make you feel more better. Take away the badness."

The gift alone was a help; the fact that Wilfred was being friendly eased Sharkey's mind, and the weed itself, which he smoked behind his house on the bench under the avocado tree, was all he needed to spend the night with his mother, who held a framed photograph of the Colonel in her hands and sobbed — a long night, but the weed lightened his mood, made him patient, took away the pain, and helped the time pass.

"How's it?" Wilfred asked the next day.

Sharkey said, "It was good stuff. Like medicine."

"Geev 'um," Wilfred said to Fonoti, and another firm, fat, well-wrapped joint was handed over, palmed to Sharkey.

"Anything for you, brah."

Wilfred and the others seemed relieved that they were able to help Sharkey — more than relieved, they took pleasure in supplying him with *pakalolo*. And the boys who'd made his life at school miserable now seemed like rescuers. So, he reasoned, maybe they were maddened by strangeness and wealth and the sight of happiness, but they understood misery and loss and death, and now Sharkey was one of them, in pain.

He sucked in the smoke, shut down his breathing, and held it in his lungs, where it glittered in his blood, bubbled to his head, to his muscles, and he was uplifted and calmed — as though he'd just heard something unusual, to make him laugh and ease his mind, news he'd just forgotten, but good news that tickled him. And the odor too was a tang he came to savor, like the fragrance of green grass smoldering in a great thatched heap, slowly cooking, never bursting into flames, the smoke he could taste, smoke he could swallow, smoke he could eat, that filled his body with a burr of warm light, glowing in his eyes, taking the pain away and somehow inflating him, summoning the image of his father and inspiring forgiveness.

The joints that Wilfred gave him were thick enough that he could smoke half after school and prepare himself for consoling his mother, and in the morning, before school, he smoked the other half, improving his mood so that he could face the other boys, and in this frame of mind he was confident enough to ask Wilfred for another joint. Wilfred always shook his hand —that complex local handshake, hooking thumbs—and directed someone in his little gang, the *kanaka ohana,* to comply.

The *pakalolo* was welcome. It gave Sharkey the sort of lift he needed, for the kindness of the boys made him conspicuous, and their attention oppressed him in ways he hadn't expected. Their forced good humor directed at him demanded a response. For "How's it?" or "How you doin', brah?" he had to say he was doing well, getting over it, though in his silent and sober moments he knew he would never get over his father's death, and even in those times when it briefly left his mind his mother might be near him, tearful, to remind him. Nothing and no one could fill the empty space where his father had been.

He had known what it was like to be bullied — the continual skirmishing, the need to look over his shoulder, the unexpected elbow or insult. What he was unprepared for was the weight of scrutiny in other people's pity, their need to be reassured, as though they were the ones suffering and had to be bucked up. It took energy to endure being pitied, he had to be alert, and prompt, like someone who's expected to offer elaborate thanks for a gift and might be in danger of offending the giver, to the point where such attention could seem like more than a burden, the gift an expression of hostility.

The boys were simple; they needed their kindness to be noticed, their generosity to be acknowledged, because Sharkey had been their victim and now, led by Wilfred, they were making him their friend in a sequence of encumbering gestures.

One hot afternoon after school Wilfred said, "Come," and Sharkey followed him down the hill and through Papakolea, a street of bungalows, and through side streets lined by shacks. When he hesitated and looked behind him he saw Vai from school with one of her friends, a smaller girl he recognized from the class.

Vai pushed the girl toward Sharkey. "Dis Nalani."

The girl smiled and fought off Vai's hand.

Ahead of them, Wilfred had paused near a white van parked at a slant just off the road. "Get in, brah," Wilfred said to Sharkey, yanking a side door and handing Sharkey the joint he'd been smoking. "You need dis."

Sharkey climbed in, but before Wilfred shut the door, the girl Nalani shouldered past him, and then they were sitting on a torn mattress in the stink and heat of the van, the only light the glare from the sun burning from the pinholes of rust on the sides and the roof.

In a shy croaky voice Nalani said, "You want to play with me?"

Sharkey puffed and held the smoke in his throat for as long as he could while considering what to say, but the girl was touching him, seeming to know just what to do, as though she'd been with him before, and when his body had a reply, she laughed a little, a giggle of satisfaction that was muffled when she tugged down his shorts and gripped him with her hard hand, and then in the semidarkness, the heat of her mouth on him, the pressure of her lips, and the tickle of her encircling tongue, as he lay back dazed until, gulping, she was done.

That too was an embrace, an act of compassion, another gift, his first, and it became something he wanted, though he needed to smoke *pakalolo* to get himself through it. He sometimes wondered whether he would have been better off alone — no sympathy, no pity, and away from the agony of his mother. He kept a joint handy and burned it whenever the pain returned, because the sadness he felt was physical — an ache where he imagined his soul to be, at the core of his being.

And the remedy that surfing had always been — the relief of being on the water, tumbled by a great purifying wave — the remedy of surf was replaced by smoke. He felt a sense of panic, of the sort you might experience by losing your wallet or keys, when he patted his pocket and realized he had no more *pakalolo*, and was alarmed to ponder how he'd manage to get through the rest of the day.

This need became clear in this anxious period of crisis — he understood his father's chain smoking and whiskey breath, his mother's drinking — she did not disguise it, she kept saying, "I need a drink," she no longer hid her bottle among the sofa cushions; and he understood Wilfred and the others — they were worried and weak, they made no pretense with him of being tough, they had nothing to fear from him, nor he from them. Blaine, the pale boy who'd betrayed him, kept his distance — he lingered, dull and un-comprehending, but Sharkey understood him now too: he was someone who was happier and less complicated than he'd guessed, and Blaine profited from Wilfred's new mellow mood, his easing up on everyone in general. And Wilfred seemed content in the knowledge that he had the power to ease Sharkey's pain, giving him *pakalolo* packed in matchboxes or sealed in plastic bags or rolled in joints, blunts as fat as a finger.

The sharp aroma and smoke-smell of weed Sharkey now associated with optimism and gratitude, a deep gulp of it the prelude to laughter and forgetfulness. It took away his appetite, it gave him time to think, and his thoughts were always incoherently pleasant. If any shadow loomed, if that pain stabbed his soul, he lit up again, and the pain was gone, the world was bearable, his mother was not a bore, and even school made sense: you went there to meet your friends, you picked up weed and smoked it afterward, and then the day was gone, up in smoke.

He was so dreamy when he was buzzed that his mother did not question his mood; whiskey made her abrupt and irrational, but if he was patient, he tolerated her, saying nothing, and kept her company, she merely sat and sipped and smacked her lips, and was soon asleep in her chair, her head twisted sideways on one shoulder. Then he'd help her to bed, and she was usually still asleep when he set out for school, ducking behind a hedge on the way to smoke the remainder of his joint.

Not surfing, not even swimming, he saw how close he'd come to resembling the other boys. After school the only urgency was to get high — no sports, nothing but idle talk under the trees, and then they went back to their houses, or the backseats of the junked cars, and he walked home and sat in the hot shadow of the parlor, waiting with his mother for the day to end. And before bed and in the morning he saw a new face in the mirror.

How much time had passed since his father died he could not say, but he could estimate it by examining his face, how pale it was from being out of the sun, the sunken eyes and hollow cheeks, his lank shoulder-length hair that had lost the sunburned highlights, the purple teeth marks on his neck — Nalani's love bite. They still met in the van in Papakolea, she still said, "You want to play with me?" He was a pale skinny stoner like the others except that they were dark. He was as dirty as they were now; his mother had stopped doing the laundry, she rarely cooked, she was usually too drunk to notice what he'd become, and most days he got takeout at Zippy's.

He mocked himself for looking like the boys at school, but he did not feel so bad when he saw that his mother too was rumpled and neglected and either drunk or else pickled and sleepy. Drinking made her cranky, and when she fell — stumbled because she was drunk — and injured her hip, only more drinking eased her pain. She sat in a wheelchair instead of the armchair and waited for Sharkey to push her from room to room. The doctors found nothing more serious than a bruise on her hip, but she claimed they were mistaken.

"I have internal injuries, like Dad," she said when she was drinking, and using the Colonel as an example, she threatened to die.

She never guzzled whiskey. She drank half a cupful first thing in the morning — seeming to assuage herself by using her old coffee cup, as though drinking whiskey from a coffee cup represented virtue. Then to maintain the buzz she sipped through the day, tipping the bottle into her cup with exaggerated care. Drink made her ponderous and cautious, as if in her deliberate gestures she wished to prove that she was unaffected, as judicious as ever. But her slow hands and her halting head shakes proved she was drunk — saturated, deaf, unable to stand up, irrational when she was challenged by the simplest question.

In that state she had no idea that Sharkey was high, though now and then when he smoked, finishing a roach, she made a face. "What's that smell?"

Mother and son, each slumped in a chair in the hot shadows of a Honolulu bungalow on a late afternoon, the blinds half drawn, the sun slanting into the valley and burning on the back wall. Sharkey was soothed by the flutter of his mother's light snores. She might wake up and say, "Tell me something," or "When's Dad coming home?" or "Where have you been?" and fall back to sleep.

It was only the drunks on the street who fell down and swore and flailed their arms; his mother was a genteel indoor drunk, sleepy when she was not drinking. Perhaps the whole reason for her drinking, for anyone's drinking, was to sink their worries and be stupefied enough to sleep.

Sharkey did not smoke *pakalolo* to sleep; he smoked to be bright, to take away the dull ache of his anxiety, and to pass the time; he smoked to be a friend, he smoked to be himself — he did not like the person he was when he didn't smoke. And always when he smoked it was as though he was in the water, buoyant but adrift.

Smoking cost money, and *pakalolo* was itself a form of currency that he used to lure Nalani to his house, sneaking her past his dozing mother to his room, where they sat cross-legged on his bed, passing a joint back and forth until, laughing softly, they kissed, and then he held her head, his hands against her ears, and lowered it into his lap, saying, "Don't stop, don't stop."

He handed over fives and tens to Wilfred now, money that he twitched from his mother's purse. But one day there was none in the purse, and his mother was too sleepy to give him any, so he had to say to Wilfred, "I'm tapped out, brah."

"I gotta pay my guy."

"Got no money, brah."

Wilfred thought a moment, in reflection probing his nostril with his finger, then said, "You got one board, braddah."

The board he had not used for how many months? He knew he was too out of shape to swim into a big swell or manage heavy surf, much less to ride a wave, which made the board seem superfluous. But he felt sentimental — it was a link to a life he had not wished to abandon.

Yet he said, "How much for my board?" and at the same time thought, *I can always buy another one.*

"Maybe good for fifty bucks."

So he agreed to sell his surfboard for a stash of *pakalolo,* and after school, when he trooped with Wilfred and the others to Ala Moana and Magic Island, he was reminded of how this had been a regular after-school route, and it seemed that it was someone else's habit, the boy he had been, brisk and efficient, almost unrecognizable now. He was surprised and relieved to find his board on the rack as he had left it, crusted with dirt-flecked sea salt and old wax from being unused, the visible neglect shaming him and making it easier to abandon.

"Dis one good stick," Wilfred said. "Dis been shaped more better." And he ran his thick fingers over the board, brushing the blunt rails clean. "Put some sex wax on dis and it fly."

Wilfred lifted it from the rack and, holding it in both hands, grunted in admiration.

"I used to catch waves," he said. "In Wai'anae — Yokohama Bay. Pray for Sex Beach. My calabash cousin Clay place."

"Put the board down." The voice was gruff and assertive. "Put it down and step away from the rack, boy."

It was Uncle Sunshine, striding barefoot across the grass.

Startled by the man's command and his fierce posture — head down, elbows out — the boys backed up and Wilfred jammed the board into the rack.

"Anyone like beef, I take you on — otherwise get out of here," Uncle Sunshine said. And as he watched the boys sidling away, he called out, "Not you, keed" — gesturing to Sharkey — "you stay here. I got one bone to pick with you." Sharkey hung his head as Uncle Sunshine walked past him, calling out to the others, "Git!"

Then they were alone, Sharkey and Uncle Sunshine, and Sharkey felt woeful, worse than he ever had when faced with a reprimand by the Colonel or his angry mother. They stood half turned away, not facing each other, in the harsh midafternoon sun, under the tall slender palm trees. In what was a ragged thought, not fully formed in words, Sharkey was ashamed in the beauty of that setting — the palms, the ribbed sea, the sun — the sun most of all, making him feel futile and breathless. Nothing could be hidden here — he was naked in this pitiless light.

He found refuge and distraction in considering the incoming waves, how they rose and fell, unrelenting, traveling toward him from the sea, always at the same speed, a kind of consolation.

"You think I *huhu*," Uncle Sunshine was saying. "But no. I real disappointed." He breathed through his nose, snorting for emphasis. It embarrassed Sharkey for being the reason Uncle Sunshine was forced to make this awkward speech, for which he didn't have the words.

"I'm sorry," Sharkey said, hoping to end it.

"Don't say sorry. Don't say nothing. Don't make ass. Fricken *do* something, keed. You look terrible. You got red eyes, you got fish-belly skin. You smoking, and what I tell you? Don't smoke. Smokers don't surf."

Sharkey put his hands to his face as though to hide it, clawing at his cheeks.

"What you father wen' say?"

"My father died," Sharkey said.

Uncle Sunshine went silent, seemed to stop breathing, and was still for a long moment. He then put his hand on Sharkey's shoulder.

"You father no wen' *make*," he said, and with his free hand he pointed to the sky. "He up there looking at you. He inside you and all around. He lillybit disappointed, like me. But he know bym-bye you can get back on your board."

"I want to," Sharkey said, but he felt puny and pale and insincere and did not see any way he could surf. He was not rescued by this man — he'd been ambushed. He wished he'd sold his board, he wanted to get stoned with Wilfred and the others, he wanted to meet Nalani in the van or else sneak her past his drunken mother into his room; he wanted a smoke.

But Uncle Sunshine still had a grip on his shoulder. He said, "Take a look at those boys. I know boys like that. I know they get you *pakalolo,* and maybe other drugs like speed or *batu.* But what I want you to do is look at them good, look at their faces, look at their rotten teeth and bad skin and fatness. You buy drugs from people who look like that, you guarantee end up looking just like them."

Sharkey was still considering the pace of the incoming waves, the slosh and drop and regularity of them. But he had heard.

"So you want to look like that?"

Sharkey reached for his board and leaned on it.

"Not now," Uncle Sunshine said, and slotted the board into the rack, then walked with Sharkey to the shore and led him into the water, going deeper, steadying him while a wave broke over him, and making him stagger with the force of its collapse, dousing his head.

6

Rehearsals

After that sudden spell in the water, which was less a baptism than a near drowning, Uncle Sunshine dragged Sharkey to the sand and wouldn't let him go near the water. "You out of shape. You will drown. You will shame youself. You will shame me," the man said. He was spidery, with slick lizardy skin and squinting eyes, his fingers and toes pickled from constant soaking in seawater. An old man, but he was tougher than Sharkey, a new side of him just revealed — a benign bully, an intimidator to Wilfred and the others.

He saw what the man was made of, the inside of the man, like the inside of Hawaii: no sweetness, but the sinew and survival skills of an islander; and suspicion. He understood sharply the obvious truth, that people have two sides, that the islands just beneath the shaggy green surface were not earth but black rock, that the inner life of Hawaii was molten lava.

"What am I supposed to do?"

"Stay away from those more worse so-called friends . . ."

It was what the Colonel would have said.

". . . and stay away from the surf."

This was at the Beach Boys' surf stand at Waikiki, after dark on a school night. And behind those words he heard the big surf crashing in the distance like something solid moving downhill, a slow and interminable avalanche.

Uncle Sunshine said, "Me, I'm brutal," and made him run from one end of the beach to the other, Sharkey slamming his feet on the sand, to build his stamina, to rid him of his urge to smoke. "You gotta replace one ting with anodda." Uncle Sunshine supervised Sharkey doing push-ups; he ordered him to carve a skateboard up and down the Ala Moana Beach walkway, riding the concrete as if it were a wave, in surf simulation, ducking under the hedges as if getting tubed. He exhausted him, and still he said,

"No surfing until you in shape." The training was indistinguishable from punishment.

Wilfred and his boys at school kept away. Nalani said, "You no like for dating me no more" — sucking his dick in a van was dating? — all of them seeing a new Sharkey over the next weeks, not the pale stoner who'd become their friend but a dark and dismissive and more muscular Sharkey, once again remote, another unreadable haole, but someone they left alone, because he seemed like a stranger again. And there were always other boys to bully.

So Sharkey had a new routine — away from home and his mother, away from school and the other boys — a renewed solitude and a mission.

Uncle Sunshine said, "I see what Duke seen — something in you. You can be good. You can be more better than good. You can be a winner — not to beat the other surfers but compete against youself, to get more better with each wave. To be you best. Who is your competition, your enemy? It is youself. Always against youself."

In the time since he'd first met Uncle Sunshine he'd grown. Nearly sixteen, he was taller, stronger, better able to read a wave. The training on land had toughened him and made him impatient to get back into the water, but Uncle Sunshine said that only when he appreciated what a privilege it was to ride a wave would he be allowed to surf.

Submit, the man was saying.

"You need to be worthy," he said. "You need to be *pono.*"

That word again, but now it had a meaning, because it was spoken by someone who was himself *pono.*

"Those boys from Roosevelt — those girls," he said. "No respeck nothing. They drowning and they don't know it."

Sharkey now saw that he knew very little. He had taken his natural ability for granted and it had made him overconfident. He assumed that he could smoke weed and that he would eventually find his way back onto the board. He had not foreseen how hard it would be, how he would have to prove himself to Uncle Sunshine, who was more severe than any teacher at Roosevelt.

"I not you friend," the man said, unblinking in his lizard look. "I'm you teacher. I'm too old to be you friend. I know more than you. You need to respeck me, to obey, to do what I say. I you *kupuna.*"

He was fierce — where had it come from? The jovial teasing Beach Boy had become a tyrant. He was gentle with everyone else, telling stories under the palms, giving surf lessons, renting boogie boards to tourists, talking about his friendship with Duke, and his *ohana,* and his memory of Pearl Harbor — describing that Sunday morning, delivering newspapers, seeing the planes, hearing the explosions, running for cover. Strumming his ukulele, he was the very image of the jolly carefree Hawaiian.

But there was someone else inside him. The inner Uncle Sunshine was a warrior, with no sense of humor and no patience. With Sharkey he was unforgiving, demanding that he exercise — run laps on the sand, do push-ups, and help with chores, carry boards to the tourists, wash them and rack them. And when at last, after demanding that he recite a Hawaiian prayer, he let Sharkey back into the water, he refused him a surfboard. "Swim into the waves, body-surf, practice breath control. Board is *kapu*. No board until I say so." And Sharkey ran and swam until he was exhausted, until his throat burned and his arms ached and he found himself half weeping with fatigue.

"I will turn you into a water dog," Uncle Sunshine said. "First you need practice. Rehearsing."

This convergence — the old surfer and the boy — was the most important episode in his life; it was the making of him, though he did not tell anyone about it at the time, not the boys at school, not his mother. It was a solemn initiation, too complex to explain. "My father died. I met a guy who became a kind of father figure," he later said. "He got me off drugs." He did not say that Uncle Sunshine examined every aspect of his behavior: his swimming, his surfing, his schoolwork, his dealings with everyone on the beach. "Father figure" didn't explain him. The man was his mentor, his teacher, his *kupuna*, his tormentor, his scold. Sometimes Sharkey hated him, was afraid of him — feared most of all displeasing him, always having to be at his best. But he also knew that if he had not met him his life would have been quite different — he would have been a surfer, yes, but a different one, without Uncle Sunshine's voice in his head, guiding him.

Most frustrating of all was Uncle Sunshine saying, "I know what you can do. I know more better than you. You have one big future."

And Sharkey knew that as yet he had done nothing, and nothing in the future was apparent to him.

"You will be a water dog. You will ride monster waves at Waimea."

At last the day came when Uncle Sunshine said, "Today you surf," and handed him a board.

Head-high waves tumbled in looping rollers toward Magic Island from the distant ocean, where the sun flashed from behind a cloud and blinded him on the way out. "Find you feet," Uncle Sunshine had said, and walked away to deal with the tourists and his friends. "I see you bym-bye." He turned his back on Sharkey and swam across the Ala Wai Harbor entrance to his stand on the beach at Waikiki.

Released to surf, to plunge into the incoming waves, flat on his board, paddling out, Sharkey was liberated from land, from the plodding and the push-ups, the hot hard earth and the sour trampled grass. He was weightless in the water, slipping under the faces of the waves, and he paddled with such gusto that he forgot he'd intended to surf and instead rode past the surf zone to the bluer ocean and bellying swells, the widening water that gave the illusion of being a dome of liquid that lifted him to show him how far he was from shore, and then dropped him into a trough where he was lost, seeing nothing but the sloping walls of the swell.

He was in his element, a waterman, dwarfed by the ocean and buoyant, splashing onward into the golden path the low sun had fretted on the surface of the water. An overwhelming sense of freedom enlarged him, as though he had been launched into the air, was experiencing flight, with no prospect of falling, only soaring toward the flat seam ahead where the sky met the sea.

On that first day, his reentry to the water, he was possessed by the thought that the farther he swam, the more he would change, of the transforming effects of the sea, its health-giving properties, its mothering power to strengthen and purify him. Stepping on earth stunned and aged him, but surfing was a cleansing and the slap of waves a blessing. He fought the urge to turn back to shore.

An hour of this, or more — no one visible on the beach, or on the protrusion of Magic Island — until he was a speck on the ocean, stroking toward the shipping lanes and black freighters piled three layers high with orange containers.

Then he slipped sideways on his board and rode the swells for a mile into the surf zone and the break at Bomboras and swam onto the back of a wave, staying with it until it rose under him and he was teetering on the boil. He scrambled up now, steadying the board, then got to his feet and sped slantwise down the face, braced upright, surfing again, whooping with joy, reborn.

He surfed until the sky was sunless and purple and a smudge like a dust haze gathered low in the sky, and darkness fell. He reluctantly swam ashore, feeling clumsy, his board heavy, stepping over the rocks to the clay at the base of the cliff, stumbling a little.

The first of many days.

His mother seemed to realize that he was steadier now, sober, more careful in the way he dressed, tidier too — and perhaps this was what created a distance and a sobriety in her. After so long alone, stubborn and inert in her chair, drinking to face the day, drinking to get through the day, drinking so that she could sleep, she stirred from the house, accepted the invitations of some officers' wives she'd known at Fort Shafter, and went to parties. "Just for grins," she said, so as not to seem as though such outings mattered in the least.

Within weeks she was being escorted.

"Imagine, Joe," she said. "What a hoot. I'm dating."

He hated the teasing way his mother spoke the word, he was embarrassed by the girlish way she used it, as Nalani had; and whatever it meant, he did not want to know. She no longer drove herself, and Sharkey was glad of that — she'd never been a good driver, and her drinking made her dangerous. So Sharkey was relieved that she was escorted, reassured that she had some sort of masculine friendship, and bewildered by her happiness — seeing these men brought her a kind of joy and protection that he had never been able to provide. He wondered if at heart he did not want to make her happy but instead contrived to upset her, or to take revenge by sneaking Nalani to his room. She seemed to know this, sometimes muttering, "Why do you do this to me?" but never specifying.

He missed the Colonel, who had occupied the roles he was not able to fill — father, husband, friend, support, fellow drinker, lover. But the Colonel was gone.

The men dating her were her age or older, nearly all of them military, he could tell; even when they wore an aloha shirt, they were stiff-backed, heads up, the shirts tucked in, and she showed an intuitive sense of rank in choosing to see only senior officers. They picked her up, usually in the early evening, not long after Sharkey got home from surfing or school, and they dropped her off before eleven, both of them a bit tipsy, whispering, giggling, but the men didn't linger, except to exchange a few words with Sharkey, the usual greeting: "And this must be Joe!"

They were kind to him and always complimentary, excessively so at times. Maybe it was their way of proving to Sharkey's mother what good men they were, what good husbands and stepfathers they might be, as though rehearsing to be his father. Used to military housing, they always remarked on the bungalow, its garden, its seclusion on the leafy street. Did they know how much money his mother had? Probably. There were no secrets at the base, and the Sharkey family was the subject of whispers — the dog attack, the disgrace of the dog's owner, the financial settlement, the move to Manoa, the Colonel's death, and the scrutiny of Sharkey's mother, the sightings of her at parties.

The uncertainties of army life, the enigmas of command, made gossip inevitable, especially among those left behind, the wives and children; the whispers were a response to the army's code of silence. Sharkey was ashamed to think that his mother, who was in her midforties, might be talked about as a partygoer, a dater, and a drinker — ashamed for the Colonel's sake. He saw his mother in a new way, as a woman vain about her looks, her body concealed beneath her carefully chosen dress, her heavily made-up face, someone's date.

"This is Major Crandall," his mother said one day when Sharkey arrived home from the beach. It was around seven, dark, his mother in a party dress and pearls.

"Hi," Sharkey said, averting his eyes and trying to get past the man.

"Your mom tells me you're a surfer."

"Yeah, I've been doing it for a while."

"Yes, sir," his mother corrected. "Remember who you're talking to."

He thought, *I am talking to a man who is taking my mother on a date, to a party or a bar or the officers' club, to get drunk, and I don't want to know more than that.*

The man, Major Crandall, said, "I'm from San Diego. I've done a little surfing. 'Hang ten.' That's what we always said."

That was another thing — their way of relating to Sharkey was competitive and patronizing. They would talk about the amazing things they'd done, surfing or swimming; and some said, "I knew your father well — he was a good soldier," as though they were competing with Sharkey, claiming to know the Colonel better than the son did. "We were in some tight situations together — firefights and insertions. I wish I could give you details but no can do — they were black ops."

"Maybe we could catch some waves together," Major Crandall said.

And Sharkey smiled at the presumption, because he surfed either with Uncle Sunshine or alone, and it was never a question of "catching a few waves" but rather of thrashing for hours with an intensity that was both visceral and spiritual — not a recreation, it was a life choice, a commitment. Nothing else mattered.

But Sharkey said, "Yes, sir. Sounds good," because his mother wore her anxious expression, pleading eyes, looking fragile.

How odd and disconcerting it was for him to be at home, to meet the men, to watch them take his mother out, to see her so eager and grateful, calling out as she left, "There's some chicken salad in the fridge." The men were uneasy with him; they knew they needed to be respectful, to have his blessing more than his acknowledgment. It was so strange to see them take her by the hand or steer her with her elbow. Strangers touching his mother, taking possession — but more than that he did not want to know — could not bear to imagine. It was important to him that they made her happy, and though he felt she was betraying the Colonel, whose death was such a painful memory to him, her seeing them gave him some peace; it was a relief from the weepy evenings when she was drunk and drawled, "You never listen to me," or "Say something."

This dating by his mother, seeing her wooed and catered to, distanced him from her, matured him and made him worldly. His mother became secretive and silly, evasive when he asked where she was going, for how long, who else would be there? They were not his questions; they were the questions the Colonel would have asked. But she didn't answer, except to say, "I'll be fine, darling."

He sat up in his father's chair, a saddening whiff of long-ago cigarette smoke still clinging to it, waiting for her to come home, and in that time did his homework. When there was a clatter at the door of a certain kind, a fumbling, a clumsiness, he knew she would be drunk, and the red-faced men would be sheepish and ingratiating — "Joe, I'd like to get to know you a whole lot better."

He remembered Uncle Sunshine, sounding like the Colonel, saying, *I'm too old to be you friend. I know more than you. I not you friend.*

So Sharkey found himself humoring the men — what did they want? — and regretting that he was not more protective of his mother. At the same time he became more passionate about surfing, to be away from home, to remove himself from his mother's evasions.

One of the men, another officer, suggested they go out to eat together, the three of them. This was Captain Van Buskirk, who showed up in uniform, to be greeted by Sharkey in shorts and flip-flops and a T-shirt. He could see that the soldier was dismayed, blinking at him with a barely perceptible tightening of his mouth.

"Dickie!" his mother called out when she saw him, and turned to allow him to kiss her cheek. Then: "Joe — you can't go like that."

"We don't have to go to Fort DeRussy," the captain said. "We can go to the Moana Surfrider."

Sharkey said, "It's all right. I'm cool. I'll stay home."

"I'd rather you joined us," the captain said. "That's an order, son," and he laughed.

But riding to Waikiki, seated in the backseat of the captain's car, Sharkey felt all the old ambiguity and confusion — his mother on a date, the man looking at him in the rearview mirror and sizing him up.

"Table for three?" the hostess asked. She wore a frilly blouse, a flower behind her ear, her hair drawn back like his mother's.

"Near the beach. Edge of the lanai," the captain said.

"Mai-tais at sunset," Sharkey's mother said. "Maybe we'll see a green flash."

But when they looked across the beach they saw a Hawaiian man in board shorts staring at them, a lei around his neck, and he too had a flower behind his ear. He walked toward the rail of the lanai.

"Aloha." He was smiling. "How's it?"

Uncle Sunshine, a softly smiling Uncle Sun, in a clean shirt — laughing, but respectful and a little subdued.

"I know this *keiki*," he said.

Sharkey had wanted to keep Uncle Sunshine his secret, his other life, his real life — the tough *kupuna* teaching him moves on the board and insisting on his being in shape, guiding him, and counseling him in his dealings with the boys at school.

"He da kine — *kolohe*," Uncle Sun said with a giggle.

It was a different Uncle Sunshine — a little silly, submissive, speaking in a broader comical pidgin, standing with his bony knees together, his dark sinewy arms folded, playing the role of a genial Beach Boy. Sharkey's secret was safe.

"You know *kolohe* — mischeevious," Uncle Sun explained.

"I hope you keep him out of trouble," Sharkey's mother said.

"He keep *me* out of trouble," Uncle Sun said, saying *tchrubble*. "We talk story. We —"

Captain Van Buskirk said sharply, "You'll have to give us some space. We haven't ordered yet."

And then Uncle Sun did an extraordinary thing — he apologized.

"Sorry, sir," he said, and he saluted, saying, as he turned to walk away, "Me, I was military."

"Thank you for your service."

But it was too late — the captain had lost him, and the captain had failed Sharkey. What was apparent was that Uncle Sunshine had behaved like a colorful Hawaiian, goofy and a bit bumbling and inarticulate, and Sharkey held the captain responsible. So he would never know what Sharkey knew, that Uncle Sun was a brave big-wave surfer, a great teacher, a fierce soul, and a decorated veteran of battles in the Solomon Islands.

"He sweet on you mother," Uncle Sun said the next time they met at Magic Island.

"How do you know?"

"My *mana'o*. The way he sitting, how he stay. His feets. His hands. His eyes."

But when Sharkey asked about the captain, his mother said, "I'm not dating him anymore."

"He's not interested?"

"He's too interested. He's talking about marriage. I don't want that."

Sharkey's hesitation was like a question, a querying silence.

"Because I have you," his mother said.

7

Wipeout

The winter swells had arrived, big days in January, peaking at twenty-five feet on the North Shore, and that was a Hawaiian measure, of the back of the wave — the face was close to forty, great blue claws of water closing over tiny defiant surfers. In some places on the coast, at Lani's and Chun's, random waves washed over Kamehameha Highway, sluicing it with foaming seawater that drained into the grassy verge on the far side, leaving a surface of sand and broken seashells and twists of brown seaweed, like a warning that the ocean would overwhelm and claim the whole road one day.

The previous year, lying on the beach with his eyes closed, Sharkey had felt the power of the surf, the slumping sound of it rocking his body, but with a brief pause, and then another slump, like rocks pounding into a ravine in a toppling sequence, one boom burying another and becoming a brief hush, a sudden intake of breath, and sitting up, Sharkey had seen the surfers like flotsam, bobbing in the subsiding swirl of the boil.

In town, at Magic Island and Waikiki and Diamond Head, the surf had dropped — "flat to a foot," as Uncle Sunshine put it. But he encouraged Sharkey to look at Waimea Bay and Pipeline, to have an idea of what big surf looked like.

"I've seen it before. Last year."

"Dis week is more epic. Big, da wave."

"Should I bring my board?"

"Yah. But be *akamai*. Dis weekend insane."

"I wish you could come with me, Uncle."

"More better if you go alone." The old man studied him for a moment. "You gotta get used to stay alone if you wen' take this more serious."

Alone, Sharkey thought — *I'm alone at school, I'm alone at home, I'm alone here with Uncle Sun.* I not you friend . . . I you *kupuna. I am obviously alone, an obvious haole, with the sun beating down on me, squeezing me small.*

"Okay," he said.

Still, he did not feel that he was ready; he wished for company for the forty-mile ride to the North Shore, someone to talk to on the beach, a bit of encouragement perhaps, from a friend he had not seen for a while — Harry Ho. So after school he walked down the road to Punahou School and waited at the gate of the driveway for the bell to signal the end of the Punahou day.

When the bell rang and the students began to fill the driveway, he had a pang — they were so well dressed, so confident and clean, laughing, yet so orderly, so different from the after-school mob at Roosevelt. They wore shoes and socks. They carried book bags and briefcases. There was a seriousness about them, and even in their laughter a restraint and politeness. Their bags bulging with books, they were going home to study some more.

Harry was among them. Seeing Sharkey, he walked quickly toward him, and they smacked hands.

"Surf's up big on the North Shore."

"Yeah?" Harry weighed his sagging book bag by its strap.

"Come on — tomorrow!"

"And skip school?"

"Why not?"

Harry looked shocked, and then smiled. "Cannot. Maybe check out the waves this weekend."

"It'll drop by then."

"Joe," Harry said, and shrugged, holding his book bag, looking helpless, with no reply, and finally said, "I don't know."

But he knew; he had given his answer. He was a student in a high-pressure school, he took his studies seriously, he was aiming to go to college on the mainland, and though he was a passionate surfer he was purposeful — his schoolwork came first. For Sharkey, studies were no use, they taught him nothing he could apply to surfing. And the school was a battleground. What he learned at Roosevelt was the usefulness of being oblique, of never meeting a person's gaze, all the Hawaiian evasions, making deference look like humility, not taking sides in negotiation, remembering he was a haole — a minority that was routinely picked on — and all the other public-school persecutions, unknown at Punahou.

He had earned a reputation as a geek and a loner, just another fucking haole. He was generally left alone, but he knew his place was on the margin, eating in the cafeteria alone, keeping to himself on the playground, vanishing as soon as the last bell sounded, and then off to the beach to surf. His scar had given him status, the death of his father had bestowed a measure of concern and protection, but really he didn't matter anymore, not even as someone to be bullied, and these days Nalani had a new boyfriend. Sharkey did just enough work to get by and in that way remained inconspicuous, knowing it would be much worse for him if, like Blaine, he was teased for getting high marks.

But his dreams were lit with the turbulence of breaking waves — no longer unreadable in their turbulence but distinct in their changing forms, rising, cresting, tubing, far from chaotic, showing rideable contours. His dreams proved to him that his ambitions were huge, perhaps too great to reveal to anyone. Better surfers, or nonsurfers, would mock, they would laugh, they'd say, "How?" or "You're dreaming" — and it was true, he *was* dreaming. His mother pressed him for his plans. And consumed by plans, he said, "I have no plans."

She said, "Because you have no ambition."

How wrong she was; yet he would never have been able to explain what he felt. He was now sixteen years old. To say, "I'm going to be a big-wave surfer" was preposterous, something like saying, "I'm going to write a book."

"So what will you do about money?" he imagined her saying.

"I'll go on the tour. Prize money," was the reply he did not dare to make. "Maybe get some endorsements."

His mother had a peculiar mocking laugh, like a parrot squawk, which she would have used on him, hearing that, her mouth wide open, the roots of her teeth exposed.

Uncle Sunshine did not mock. He had faith in Sharkey's ability, but such faith was oppressive too — it was also a burden, it came with high expectations. What was the answer? To dream, to harbor his secrets and keep them pure; to avoid revealing anything of his yearnings or his self-belief. The Colonel had been right: No friends. Keep to yourself. Trust no one. Find your own way down the face of the wave.

Harry Ho called him. Harry always felt he owed Sharkey a favor, because way back when Dr. Emmett Chock had asked him to name the Punahou boys involved in drugs — the group of stoners that smoked after school — Sharkey had shrugged and said nothing, refusing to cooperate, hardly acknowledging the question. And for his refusal he had been expelled, condemned to Roosevelt High School and the gangs and "fucken haole."

"I could ask for the day off," Harry said. "Something like compassionate leave. Say it's a family matter. And it's kind of true. You're like *ohana*."

It sounded to Sharkey like pity, or an obligation. Sharkey hated hearing it. Harry had plans to surf and was competent, but always put his schoolwork ahead of surfing, and that meant he would never be a great surfer — he was not wholehearted, he'd be a weekend surfer like his father, who was a dentist.

"I changed my mind," Sharkey said. "I'm not going."

"Really?" Harry was silent a moment, then said brightly, "Okay. Keep in touch."

Harry's tone had changed. He was relieved; he had not wanted to take a day off. Sharkey had spared him—not as a favor; he had decided that he didn't want to surf with him, he needed to be alone, to concentrate, to make his mistakes without witnesses, or friends, or antagonists.

He skipped school; he borrowed his mother's car. Driving along the freeway past the exit sign, FORT SHAFTER, he mourned his father and at the same time was rueful, knowing that being a mediocre student, not aspiring to the academy—he'd never get in anyway—he would have disappointed the man, who had had hopes of Sharkey being a soldier.

Then he was glad that he had passed the Fort Shafter exit and the off-ramp to Tripler and was heading north, detouring through Waihawa and the pineapple fields and, on the crest of the hill, the cane fields sloping to the shore, to the left the chimney of the sugar mill at Waialua, a plume of smoke borne seaward on the trade winds, and the sight of the sea beaten to foam at Hale'iwa, and the ocean thickened as far as he could see, to Waimea and beyond, to the mass of clouds over Kauai. As the surf report had promised, a big day.

Getting out of his car at the parking lot at Sunset, he heard the loud rollers booming on the shore, and it was like a welcome. He unslung his board from the pads strapped on the roof and carried it on his head to the beach, where a crowd of people watched surfers taking the waves. But their voices were smothered by the waves tipping forward into a noisy boil and riding to the sand with a continuous rub and hush, the ocean brimming against the beach.

There Sharkey sat, marveling at the small figures breaking out of the froth at the top of the waves and scrambling to their feet and making white trails in the blue as they raced sideways down the face of the wave, some of them to be swallowed, enclosed in the foam, others outracing it, braced upright as the wave diminished. At intervals between sets the sea flattened so completely it was a great blue puddle dotted with bodies, bobbing there like survivors of a sinking—and then the sets began rising again and the bodies were tossed into their troughs, and soon surfers standing on boards exploded through the foamy brow of the waves and raced down their slopes.

Sharkey studied the posture of the surfers, the way they steered and cut back and slowed, dismounting to paddle through the waves again to ride another. They were all movement, and buoyant, a breed of aquatic creatures, and the best of them rode through foam to the clearer curve of the wave, exulting as they flew toward the beach. One agile surfer in a red wetsuit — a woman, he could see — seemed more resourceful in her bounce than the others, and slimmer — a human sliver — confident on her board in ride after ride, back and forth on the waves, until at last she rode in, nearer the beach, steering her board through a low moving shelf of foaming water that carried her all the way to the sand. And he saw that she was young, a girl, about his own age, yet at a distance, when she'd been on a wave, he'd taken her to be much older and majestic.

She was a sprite. She lifted her board and hugged it to her side and, head down, gasping, walked past him, treading the soft sand. She could have been his sister.

That was when he fixed the collar of his leash to his ankle and aimed his board at an incoming wave and flopped on it, paddling, nosing his board out through the low shore break. He drove his hands down hard, propelling himself forward with energy, yet he was anxious — the first time on this wave; he could feel it in his throat like the onset of nausea.

That's good, Uncle Sunshine had said of the feeling of uncertainty.

Good? The sense of unswallowed anxiety that was a sort of disgust that wouldn't leave him.

It make you more careful, the man said. *You always find what you afraid of. Or it find you.*

But Sharkey thought mainly of the teenager in the red wetsuit who had appeared at the top of the big wave and clambered to her feet on her board and then had stood and ridden in a confident crouch, slipping through the barrel as it narrowed and standing straighter as the wave thinned and chucked her onward, all the way to the shallows, where she stepped off her board and pirouetted onto the sand.

She was his inspiration as he paddled out, thinking, *If she can do it . . .*

Duck-diving under the incoming waves, he could feel their strength, the moving water not like water at all but like muscle — and though he knew he always surfed well at Magic Island and had confidence there, the surf break here at Pipeline was different altogether, a peculiar lift and push, a density that was new to him; and the sense too that a shallow reef lay under him, the solid ledge that formed the wave and was a blur of darkness beneath him.

When he got to the lineup he followed protocol and kept away from the other surfers, as Uncle Sunshine had told him. "You have no rivals," the man said, "no enemies. You only compete against youself."

He watched the other surfers study the incoming waves, each successive wave in a set rising higher and revealing as it rolled a bulge of blue water like an offering. And so the surfers judged its speed and maneuvered for the best position to gain a place in the lineup, paddling hard to push through the inward-curving face.

The swell heaved Sharkey up to the height of a housetop, and he sat, as though on the roof peak, and saw the other surfers, one by one, vanish over the edge and become lost in the boil before it. What alarmed him was the way a surfer looked as, wiping out, he flipped above the top of a wave, his leash tangled, twisting down, his board tumbling after him, and both then buried beneath the smothering froth of swirling water.

When all the other surfers had taken a wave and he was alone on the swell, Sharkey steeled himself and, positioning his board on a rising wave, paddled like mad to stay with it and overtop it. And what he saw astonished him, for as the wave rose the base of it fell away, forty feet or more of its gleaming curve, and as he scrambled to his feet to ride it he slipped and fell forward, and the wave closed over him, an indifferent feature of the sea, vast and implacable, pressing him and overwhelming him and taking him down, burying him — not in fury, not a god or a giant but a dumb sudden stunning bigness that bulked above him and just as suddenly collapsed. Seconds of its colossal wash before another, heavier wave swept over him, past a shaft of sunlight, tumbling him into suffocating darkness, burying him again.

Bubbles rattled in his ears, his leash tugged at his ankle, he fought the surge — the thick sweep of water — and was dragged down until he reached and slipped the leash over his foot. His board banged across his body and then he was on his back, staring at the sun, the shore break licking at him.

He knew he was bruised from the thump of his board and being pushed against the rocks, but more than anything he was embarrassed — afraid that he'd been seen. He crawled up the beach on all fours, his knees bleeding, and his arm was sliced — probably by the fin of his board. Before he located his board and dropped to the sand, he looked around. No one had seen him, or if they had, they were as indifferent to him as the wave that had crushed him.

No — the girl in the red wetsuit sat with her knees together behind him on the beach. She must have seen it all, his wipeout, his struggle, his creeping up the beach. He waved to her, and with a simple flick of her hand she waved back, then averted her eyes — so bold on the waves, so shy on the beach. And perhaps feeling conspicuous, she picked up her board and walked away, treading the sand in a stately way like the strut of a shorebird.

Uncle Sunshine's voice was in his head — a stern command to go again, to take another wave. This he did, not at Pipeline but down the beach at Off the Wall, where the waves were breaking left and were smaller. Purely to make a point, for his morale, so that he could tell Uncle Sunshine he hadn't been defeated, he paddled out and rode a wave halfway in, and then another.

But the wipeout had exhausted him, and back in his car, shivering, frightened at the memory of what he took to be a near drowning, he put his face
in his hands and sobbed for a moment, his whole body convulsing. Breathing deeply, he recovered, sighing, and reversing the car saw himself in the
rearview mirror. He was amazed at his tears, that his eyes and cheeks were
dirtied by his fingers — a face of suffering and triumph — and that he felt
such relief.

8

Welcome to the Wave

Before that first big wave of his life, his wipeout, the hold-down, his near drowning, it had never occurred to Sharkey that he might fail. Was it Uncle Sunshine's belief in him that made him reckless? Perhaps the man, being a *kupuna,* had challenged him, knowing the risks, so that he would take the wave and taste fear. *You always find what you afraid of.* Sharkey had not imagined being swung so high on a wave — balanced on its brow, suspended over the great vertical swoop of its face, looking down at the glittering plow of moving water and, losing his footing on the board, feeling terror, as though he were being thrown into its blade.

And that was only the beginning of the ordeal. The worst of it had come moments later, when, suffocated by successive waves, he had lost all sense of up and down in the wash. Though he'd gotten the leash off his ankle, he was not saved by quick thinking. What followed had been the result of the churning of the shore break, which had tossed him forward like a splinter of driftwood. He'd been lucky.

Seen from the beach, the distant sets had seemed smaller and rideable, not the canyon walls and sweeping ravines he encountered when he paddled out. Nothing at Magic Island, where the winter swell was less than head-high, had prepared him for this. Not even Uncle Sunshine's casual warning had helped.

"I think maybe you wen' wipe out," he'd said, seeing Sharkey's gashed arm afterward, the bruised flesh of his knees.

"Yes, sir."

"That's good. Only two kine surfer, da kine wen' wipe out already and da kine gonna wipe out bym-bye."

"It freaked me out."

Uncle Sunshine laughed. "Yah! If you say something different I call you a bull liar. Was a big wave?"

"Da kine," Sharkey said.

He saw it again, fierce-faced, a monster, the smooth incurve below him, lengthening, fattening, defying him with an abyss — his feet slipping from his sliding board, falling into the slope of water and being sucked into darkness.

"Was epic yesterday," Uncle Sunshine said.

And Sharkey remembered his face in the rearview mirror, streaked with tears, contorted by what he had just suffered; yet in that ugliness he was triumphant — he was alive. He had no way of explaining this feeling, but Uncle Sunshine seemed to guess it.

"Was one good lesson for you."

Perhaps the experience of fear still lingered on his face, imprinted as a reflex of memory, a twitch of muscles that he overcorrected with a set of his jaw, making the afterimage of his fear more emphatic.

"You never forget 'um."

Nothing could undo that shock, was what Uncle Sunshine was saying, but the failure made Sharkey strong, as no success would ever do. Something had died in him that day of the wipeout — youth and stupidity, maybe. He was older now, and for the first time — in the wipeout, the recovery, his tears, his sobs — he saw what bravery was: not recklessness but facing fear.

"I'm surfing today," he said.

"Not here," Uncle Sunshine said. "You gotta go back to the North Shore. Catch some big waves. They more less than yesterday, but they still big."

"I don't have a car. My mother's using it."

"Take the fricken bus like everybody else. Like normal people." Uncle Sunshine grasped him by the shoulders. "You wen' learn nothing more here on these manini waves. Go up to the country — you ready now."

"You sure I'm ready?"

"I think." Uncle Sunshine was nodding. "You got scared shitless, so yah, I think you ready."

Then Uncle Sunshine put his face close to Sharkey's, nose to nose, and breathed the ritual *ha,* and it was like a blessing and a sacred sendoff.

Sharkey stood out with his shorter board at the bus stop on Ala Moana, and the bus driver smiled at him in exasperation — crazy haole — and told him to sit in the back.

More than an hour along back roads to Pearl City and Kam Highway to Wahiawa; through the pineapple fields and the long descent to Hale'iwa and the North Shore, to Waimea Bay, where he got off. And ever since the bluff above the pineapple fields he had studied the white ribs of surf and tried to read them, and hoped they were smaller than yesterday.

He was relieved to see that the surf had dropped, though some sets were ten or twelve feet. He carried his board down the beach, fixed his leash, and paddled out to the lineup, where surfers were bobbing on boards — locals, he saw when he drew closer.

"How's it?" he called out.

No one replied, no one greeted him. All were watching the incoming sets. Sharkey paddled away from the others, so as not to intrude, to show respect; and when in turn they took the well-formed waves and vanished beneath them, Sharkey braced himself and straightened his board and positioned himself to thrust himself over the top — "charge it," as Uncle Sunshine said.

His legs trembled as he found his footing and they were still unsteady as he rode the wave, breaking right, away from the rocks, at the inside spot they called Pinballs, on the slant of the slipping, diminishing wave to the middle of the bay. Timing his fall, he dismounted and snatched his board and ducked into an oncoming wave and paddled back to the lineup, and rode again, this time with steadier legs.

When he was done — ten rides, two wipeouts — he found his small pile of belongings — his T-shirt, his flip-flops — and took a shower at the changing room and walked to the bus stop with his board. Within minutes a pickup truck stopped, the driver gesturing for him to put his board in the back.

"Was more bigger yesterday," the man said as he drove away.

"I caught some at Pipeline."

"Ass good. Was big."

They rode for a while, the radio playing indistinctly, a whisper vibrating in the glow of the dashboard. The cab of the pickup smelled of wet dog fur and greasy rags.

"You got a name, brah?"

"Joe Sharkey."

"Sharkey." The man lifted his head, looking pleased and smiling, and he revealed himself as a boy, not much older than Sharkey, but Hawaiian, with a mass of thick curls and a dark complexion and a blunted nose. "Thass a good name — Sharkey. Maybe a shark your *aumakua*."

"What's yours?"

"My *aumakua* is a monk seal."

"Your name?"

"Eddie Aikau."

He spoke his full name with unusual clarity, like an announcement, and nothing after that, a pause, as though waiting to be recognized — an odd and unexpected formality in the smelly cab of the old pickup truck, passing through Hale'iwa.

In the extended silence the smell was stronger. Sharkey's perception heightened, but his alertness gave him only the doggy odor and the rattle of the loose door latch. After the eager greeting — *Thass a good name* — he was a stranger again, though the young man was still smiling.

He finally said, "I wen' ween the Pipe last year" — not as a boast but stating a fact.

Sharkey jerked to attention and faced him. "Really? No kidding? That's fantastic — oh, man."

And now Eddie Aikau became quiet, gripping the wheel, nodding a little, his mop of hair exaggerating the subtle motion of his head. His expression was a mixture of modesty and pride, pleasure showing in his eyes, his lips pressed together in satisfaction. He had said enough; he was a listener now, he looked receptive — it was Sharkey's turn.

"How did you do it?" Sharkey asked, but did not wait for an answer. "That's incredible. Who did you beat? How do you train?"

And he went on gabbling as Eddie Aikau tried not to smile. What excited Sharkey was that he was looking at someone roughly his own age — his own size, though obviously stronger in the shoulders, a boy like him, someone who excelled at the only activity in the world Sharkey cared about — not his equal but superior in skill, a winner, the boy he wanted to be.

Sharkey was still talking, but only to fill the silence and to disguise the eager gaze of his admiration.

"I go out every day," Eddie said softly. "Even if no got waves I paddle to Hale'iwa, five, six miles. If got waves, I surf all day."

"That's it?"

"I don't do nothing else. Surfing is life, brah."

"Yeah."

"One thing more you need" — and here he tapped his chest.

"Heart," Sharkey said.

"Heart, yeah. But other ting. *Mana'o.*"

Uncle Sunshine had used the word, but Sharkey had been too shy to ask the old man its meaning. Yet with this easygoing boy he said, "What is that?"

"*Mana'o* something inside you tell you what's right or wrong," he said, the fingers of his free hand resting on his chest.

"Gut feeling," Sharkey said.

"Eh," Eddie said in acknowledgment. Then, farther down the road, "Gas, grass, or ass — no one rides for free," and Sharkey gave him a dollar.

Years later, reliving this experience, describing the ride to people, Sharkey said that it was more of his luck—pure chance—two surfers at the beginning of their careers, riding in the old pickup truck after a big day at the beach. Two young warriors, heroism ahead of them.

The moment was made magical by the passage of time—taking on a glow, a piece of personal history enlarged and given glamour in retrospect, another life-changing encounter, a memory that moved him whenever he remembered it and described it to the people who asked, "What was your first big wave?"

"It was a boy like me in an old truck, who gave me a lift on the road."

He did not mention wiping out on the monster wave, being gashed by the fin of his board and lacerated on the rocks of the reef, or being choked by the second wave hold-down, or, back in his car afterward, sobbing, his face splashed with tears, amazed and frightened by his own whinnying and the sight of his pitiful face in the mirror. None of that.

He spoke of being dumped by a huge wave, and then, undaunted, paddling out and surfing until he'd gotten six good rides, returning the following day to surf again, and finally standing at the bus stop at sundown with his board, and the pickup truck slowing down—no other vehicle on the lonely road, and only one streetlight illuminating the encounter, the two boys meeting for the first time, the haole and the Hawaiian, and riding into the record books.

". . . and he said, 'I'm Eddie Aikau,' and we drove away together."

So much had happened since, and he'd told the story so many times, that Sharkey could not say for sure whether Eddie had dropped him in Hale'iwa or driven into town; whether they'd stopped for a beer or shared a joint; whether they'd met the next day or weeks later. Had Eddie said, "Sharkey—that's a good name" that night, or had it been later, another day, less dramatic, just a casual remark?

Sharkey could not say. The fact was that he'd met Eddie and they'd become friends. Eddie had encouraged him, dared him, to take bigger and bigger waves, recklessly, because big waves were all that mattered, not the dances and cutbacks and hotdogging on average surf; you made your reputation on the rides through barrels and long steep drops on monster waves.

But when Sharkey looked back on his life he did not see failure or disorder or the tearful face in the rearview mirror. Nor doubt, hesitation, or retreat; he saw only conviction, a strengthening of resolve, a kind of nobility as he faced one wave after another, each one bigger than the last, the story of his struggle simplified in the telling, so much so that it sometimes seemed he could not say for sure who he was, or where he'd been, or how he'd gotten to win the Triple Crown.

And years later, after Eddie was lost at sea, paddling away from the overturned canoe *Hōkūleʻa,* to seek help, a memorial service was held and Shar-key was not asked to speak. At the time of his disappearance in the darkness and the wicked waves off the Big Island, Eddie was a devout and energetic Hawaiian, risking his life for his fellow crew members on the canoe, and Sharkey was pursuing his ambition to triumph in big-wave surfing.

"I was somewhere else, on a wave far away," Sharkey said at the time of the Eddie Aikau memorial — the paddle-out, the casting of flowers in the enormous circle of surfers on their boards, slapping the water in honor of their friend.

Was it true that he was elsewhere? He could not remember. What mat-tered was that as a boy he'd met Eddie, a boy like him.

Big influence, he would say later of Eddie, after Eddie disappeared in the sea and there was no one around to dispute it. He conveyed the impression, one that a nonsurfer would understand, that Eddie had taught him how to move on the big waves, the secrets of Hawaiian wave-riding, consecrating himself to the surf. And for years, in the anecdotal way of North Shore surf-ers, he was associated with Eddie and won the contest that was held in his name at Waimea, saying in his acceptance speech, "I knew this great soul" — and the story of their meeting on the road, in the golden dusk, two boys headed for fame. "Destiny."

What he did not say — the simple truth — was that he had always surfed alone. Going out every day, exhausting himself, surfing until nightfall and often in the dark, bobbing in the water, he learned the behavior of waves, their mood and curvature, how they lifted and curled, the ways in which a certain bellying just beforehand suggested slippage and speed. He learned to predict from the swell what a wave would do, by studying a break, reading it thoroughly, the inner life of its push, as if each length of wave were a line of poetry, each set a stanza, with its internal rhythm, so that he could insert himself into it — not waiting for the wave to accommodate him but some-thing deeper, meeting it on his terms, finding harmony, becoming the wave.

Friendship with other surfers helped. The early advice of Uncle Sun-shine had given him discipline, but while he insisted that all surfers felt a kinship and learned from each other and were mutually supportive, always spoken of as the North Shore *hui* — "da braddahs" — they were solitary on their wave and often resented each other, and had taught themselves to surf and become better through repetition, surfing every day, taking the biggest waves, because those were the waves that demanded the most agility and strength, the most nerve.

These young men, he knew — but didn't say — pretended to be a tight group, and celebrated and drank beer together and preened for the girls. But they were alone — alone in the sea, alone in their lives, like the sea creatures around them, slipping through the ocean, the turtles and seals, the schools of fish and pods of whales you'd mistake for companions, not realizing that they always swam alone.

What mattered most in Hawaii was his being left alone — not embraced but allowed to be himself, as long as he was respectful. From his earliest days in the islands he was aware that he was a haole among locals, and, conspicuous, likely to be persecuted for his difference, or at least teased, and perhaps rejected. The rules were unspoken and arbitrary. He never knew whether he would be challenged by surfers in a lineup or threatened with a fistfight on the beach or simply yelled at — "Get off dis wave, haole!" So he learned to be circumspect, he took nothing for granted, he practiced humility, and this observance of protocol was as important as obeying the mood of the wave itself. After that, as an obvious haole, he needed to succeed on the wave, ride it well and repeat it, because he was watched.

The day that stayed in his mind as the turning point was not the one on which he met Eddie, or the one on which he rode his first big wave, or any day of sage advice from Uncle Sunshine — who was in any case confined to Waikiki with the other Beach Boys, seldom venturing to the North Shore. It was another day, of a random encounter which, looking back on it, seemed like a tribal rite.

The biggest waves at Pipeline broke to the right. Sharkey wanted to ride them but knew from whispers that local surfers kept everyone else away, as though observing an ancient taboo. Being forbidden from that portion of the Pipe meant that he might never learn the skills to ride it and prove himself — which was, all along, the whole purpose of the taboo, an expression of privilege and belonging and exclusion.

It had to have been months after getting to know Eddie Aikau, because he had his own car now, his board on the roof rack, and he routinely skipped school whenever the forecast promised big surf on the North Shore — a beautiful day, to hell with school, a sense of being a runaway as well as a trespasser. He lingered on the beach, watching the sets rise, and then dared himself to paddle out, to take a chance against the cluster of surfers astride their boards in the lineup, becoming more alert as he got closer to them. He heard their low barks over the gulp and dump of breaking waves.

Then, "Eh! Haole!" from one dark tattooed boy sitting on his board.

The others glanced at him, their heads jammed into their shoulders; they were neckless under their wet hair, and dangerous — water dogs.

"Get the fuck off my wave, haole!"

Sharkey prepared to paddle away — looked for a dip in an oncoming wave and began to work his way toward it. He had seen fights in the water, he had heard stories of outsiders being knocked from their boards and the boards themselves smashed. He lay flat and moved fast, and there came another shout.

"Joe Sharkey!"

At first he mistook it for hostility, it was so shrill. But he saw that the boy shouting it was Eddie — the wild hair, the knobby nose and big doglike jaw. He was beckoning Sharkey to the wave and in the same gesture calming the pack of other boys, who backed off.

So Sharkey was welcomed to the wave and allowed to surf it, and later, on the beach, Eddie said to the others, "Sharkey — he's *ohana.*"

9

Competition

They were amphibious savages, they were sea creatures, wild mongrels and water dogs, their wide shoulders and thick necks were burned black from surfing all day; they were tattooed, they had no interest in anything on land — they looked awkward onshore, walked haltingly, bowlegged, bare-foot on sand and pebbles, and were smaller than they seemed when they were standing on a wave. Anytime the surf was up they set off in the morning, and if it remained high they stayed in the water all day, perhaps resting on the beach, flopped like monk seals, and still taking waves after sunset in the gray sea that in places looked like hammered iron.

On land they were paler, their skin sodden, their hands bluish and pick-led from the whole day in the water. The boards that had been so buoyant were big and hard to grip, banging against their bodies or buffeted by the wind gusts, sometimes scraping the stony ground, thick awkward things that had been so light and swift on the water.

They lived to surf, chasing each other like puppies through the incoming waves to the outer break. Sharkey, part of the *ohana* now (as they put it) — but it seemed more like a pack of dogs — followed them, paddled behind them, bobbed with them, took the waves that no one wanted, and always, as the younger brother, was the last one to ride to the beach. It was a form of respect, this hanging back, but his watchfulness helped him improve his technique. Uncle Sunshine had said, *Find the rhythm to mount the wave and learn to ride it.* But Eddie and the *hui* had devised different ways of taking the wave, timing each move onto the board and charging — "hard charge, Hawaiian kine," Eddie said — and since the right speed was essential — the speed of the board had to match or slightly exceed the speed of the wave

— being a strong paddler was essential. Balance could not be taught, but a way of kneeling and standing could be imitated.

After that, only repetition mattered, and even at twilight, just before the green flash, when he was tired, Sharkey's form was good enough to allow him to ride his board all the way to the beach, striding off it onto the sand in a dance step he perfected. He might be exhausted then, not realizing how tired he was until he began walking on the beach, stumbling up the sand of the steep eroded part of the foreshore, now and then overcome and dropping to his knees. And it was odd, that tottering on land, because his swimming had been effortless. You didn't know how tired you were until you came ashore.

The frolicking of the *hui* — Eddie and his friends — was a game that grew to a form of competition. They dared each other to take a wave, they teased, they chased each other across the swells and in their moves attempted to be singular. Sharkey tried to keep up with them, and though they were more experienced and stronger, they sometimes acknowledged his effort.

"You da weenah," one of them called out at the end of one surfing day — a day on which Sharkey was aware of his easy balance on the board, and, relaxed, able to ride more easily, his confidence making him supple, with a greater control.

The satisfying part was that Sharkey had been unaware that he'd been competing — and his instinct was that competing went against everything Uncle Sunshine had taught him. But the others had noticed his improvement.

They surfed Waimea and Sunset, Chun's and Leftovers; but the best, the most symmetrical barrel was at Banzai Pipeline. Eddie said, "If you can ride here, you can ride anywhere." So Sharkey concentrated his effort on the Pipe, where he'd once painfully wiped out, to master the wave and course through the barrel, kicking out before the reef.

On these weekdays of his playing hooky the beach was usually empty, so he was surprised to see a gathering of workmen one morning putting up a white canopy and a staging for seats — men with tools assembling and bolting pipes, tightening the guy ropes of the tentlike shelter, which gave to the beach a gaudy air of clutter, circuslike, the setting up of an encampment.

"If the surf stays up, we got a contest," Eddie said, and named the sponsor. "Are you in it?"

Eddie shrugged and tossed his hair. "Just like every other day out here except some people they wen' try judge us — give us points. But you gotta sign up."

Before the day was over, Eddie took Sharkey to the tent where the organizers sat and introduced him, vouching for him.

"Dis my braddah Joe Sharkey—he a shark, like his name. Try put him down."

Among the Hawaiians watching, Sharkey still felt like a skinny white kid. He laughed nervously as he signed, paid his fee for competing, filled out the forms. Walking away, he realized that though he had laughed a little, he had not said a word.

When he arrived home that night—past eight o'clock, because of traffic—Sharkey's mother was waiting, looking stern, something on her mind, the muddled severity she often displayed when she was drunk.

"Sit down, Joe, please," she said, sounding sober. But he knew her tipsy tone. She spoke more daintily and slowly when she was very drunk.

She had an envelope on her lap, her splayed fingers pressing it flat. As she spoke she lifted it and picked the flap open, her head wobbling as though with effort. She drew out a folded sheet of paper and opened it in a stagy way. Drinking turned her into a ham actress.

"'Dear Mrs. Sharkey,'" she read, with an exaggerated fluting of concern. "'It has come to my notice that your son Joseph has been absent from school since classes resumed after the Christmas break. As it is now January twenty-fifth and his absence continues, I must request that you meet for a conference in my office.'"

And then she fluttered the letter like a hankie and said, with emphasis on each word, "Where have you been?" Belching slightly, a burp that jogged her head, she rapped on the arm of her chair, disturbing a pair of white gloves folded there.

Sharkey wanted to say, "Where have *you* been?" but he knew: she'd been dating Major Crandall once again—she'd disposed of Captain Van Buskirk. And it had been a great convenience to him that she'd been preoccupied, out early in the evening, home after midnight, asleep when he set off for the North Shore. He did not want any details; the very sight of the men his mother dated made him squirm.

"Did you hear me?"

She was dressed to go out, in a costume that was so odd in the heat, a green silk dress with a lacy collar, frilly sleeves, the white gloves on the arm of her chair, black heels. She was white-faced—masked with powder—and had a pillbox hat on the side table, where her empty glass sat, its rim smeared with lipstick. She selected a cigarette from a tray near the glass, twiddled it in her fingers, and poked it between her lips.

"I've been training."

She twitched at the unexpected word, as though he had flicked her face with his insolent finger, and she snatched the cigarette from her mouth.

"Training — for what?"

"Surf meet."

"What do you know about surfing?"

"A few things."

She nodded at this disapprovingly. "Ronald said it's dangerous."

Ronald was Captain Crandall, who said he'd surfed in San Diego. His mother quoting him as an authority angered Sharkey, but he decided not to reveal his anger, nor to give anything away.

Although his mother was alone in her chair, it seemed he was facing two people, both of them hostile witnesses.

"Maybe it's dangerous for Ronald."

She snorted and clumsily lit the cigarette, snapping her lighter. "And not for you" — blowing smoke at him.

"It's a challenge, I guess."

"And this surf meet," she said in a mocking singsong, "I suppose you think you're going to win."

"I don't know. That's why I signed up. To see if I'm ready."

Because his mother was smoking a cigarette, tapping it in the ashtray, sometimes blowing and sometimes chewing the smoke, Sharkey had a better idea of her mood. The way the smoke left her lips told him she was agitated and confused, and now and then puffing and inhaling instead of replying, as she did now.

"Dad always said, 'Big risk, big reward.'"

"And look where it got him," she said, expelling smoke.

"Dad was a hero," Sharkey said, the first time he'd raised his voice, though his voice broke in grief.

"What about me? I'm a widow. He left me to look after you." She seemed to fortify herself, puffing again. "And you're such a disappointment."

Sharkey was not dismayed. He smiled at her for rejecting him, because it freed him from her. How much worse it would have been if she'd clung to him. She'd spent more than two years since the Colonel's death seeing men — army officers — apparently enjoying herself. Sharkey wasn't fooled by their bonhomie. They knew she was wealthy, they were looking to replace the Colonel — or even if that wasn't their plan, they were romancing his mother, another sort of competition. He was glad she was preoccupied; he was happy when she left, happy when he came home to an empty house to find her note: *Gone out — won't be late*. But she always was late. So what? It left him in peace. He enjoyed the solitude of the house after exhausting himself surfing. Alone, he reflected on the joy of being on his own wave.

"I know I'm a disappointment to you."

She exhaled smoke through her lipstick-stained teeth — a blue plume of satisfaction — then nodded, puffing again, a sort of mute agreement.

"But I'm not a disappointment to myself," he said. "I like what I'm doing. I'm learning."

"Skipping school," she said. "Your marks are terrible. I have no idea who your friends are. I get this letter" — she slapped it on her thigh, where it had lain all this time.

"I'm happy. I'm doing what I want to do."

"You have no ambition!" she said, and mashed out her cigarette in the ashtray.

He laughed a little — angering her more — because she was wrong. He would never be able to explain it to her, so why try?

She asked, the day of the surf meet, where it would be held; and when he told her, "North Shore — Pipeline," she said she probably would not be there. But after Sharkey arrived and signed in and got his number, he saw her a little way down the beach, incongruous at Sunset Beach in city clothes — his mother in a dress, and beside her, holding her hand, Ronald, in an aloha shirt and slacks, the captain in civvies.

They looked out of place and awkward, the wrong shoes, the wrong clothes, his mother in a pillbox hat, Ronald looking military in his posture, his shirt tucked in, his shoes shined, signaling to him with a thumbs-up.

Sharkey kept his distance, annoyed that they had come, distracting him, calling attention to themselves. He wandered beyond the spectators and the canopy and crouched beside his board, waiting for his name to be called.

In the sequence of six heats, Sharkey's number was last. He sat alone, watching the others — Eddie in the first heat, the others he knew before him — and saw them trying to outdo each other. Eddie's persuasive advice had always been, "Stay mellow, brah," but he was jamming his board, swiveling on his wave, slicing through the barrel with his arms out, emerging in a squat stance before racing, until he reversed and vaulted over the wave, and at last slowed to step off in shallow water, looking joyous.

The others seemed to take cues from Eddie, echoing his moves, going him one better with repeated cutbacks, and there were cheers for them from the clusters of spectators seated on the sand. Sharkey's mother and Ronald stood at the back of the beach, under the palm trees, near the judges' canopy, frowning at the sea.

When Sharkey's name and number were called, there was a shout from Eddie, but no cheer of recognition as there had been for the others. Sharkey paddled out, aware that he was being scrutinized as a stranger, one of the two haoles at the meet, and when he swam to the wave he did not know any of the three surfers who'd gotten there before him. They sat on their boards, waist deep in water, not acknowledging him — and he saw dogs again, teeth and jaws and narrowed eyes, necks shortened in threat. They bobbed together, riding the swell, Sharkey at the edge of the lineup.

No one onshore could have seen them clearly enough to understand the mood of rivalry or heard their snorting at him; but it didn't matter. What mattered was waiting for a wave and choosing the right one before the horn blared and he was out of time.

So he paddled hard on the first good wave, and because he was last in the lineup, away from the others, he was at an advantage. He danced around the trim line, pierced the lip, and, charging, found his feet, cut right and rode through the barrel, at one point high on the foam ball, and when he emerged at the far end of it, kicking out as he'd seen Eddie do, he heard a cheer — and the raised voices lifted him. He turned to see the crowd on the beach, a wall of bodies, eager faces watching him.

"You done good," Eddie said, generous as always, meeting him at the shore.

"You done better."

"I know dis wave. I stay lifeguard here, brah."

More heats, more noise. Sharkey surfed three more times but did not feel he'd improved on his first ride — the thrill of it, the howl from the beach that was like a welcome to him as he'd shot out of the barrel.

He sat with Eddie and the *hui,* the pack of water dogs, while the results were tallied. The winner's name was announced with the points he'd gotten — a boy he didn't know; and then Eddie, the second prize, and Kanoa, who was in the *hui.* He was not surprised that he hadn't won, nor did he feel that he'd lost. The boys in his heat came over to congratulate Eddie: they were not really dogs — they said "Aloha" to Sharkey. What struck him, sitting there on a beach — the winners garlanded with leis — was that he was among brothers.

Then he remembered his mother. He looked at where she'd been standing with Ronald, but they were not there, nor anywhere on the beach.

The house was empty when he got home. But he was elated, pleased with his rides — he'd done the best he could, and knew he could do better with practice, if he devoted every day to it. It was a competition but it was also a ritual, a game, a rite of passage, a celebration of brotherhood.

His mother was late and, being late, seemed to be making a point, asserting herself — slightly tipsy, severe in her silence. She peeled off her gloves and unpinned her hat.

Sharkey lay stretched out on the sofa, heavy from the fatigue of the day. Standing over him, rocking slightly, his mother smacked her lips.

"I sincerely hope you've done your homework."

She was not tipsy, she was sozzled, and he felt sorry and embarrassed for her as he always did when he saw that she was being unreasonable, and was glad there was no witness to her foolishness.

"I didn't go to school today. You know where I was."

She sat down in her usual armchair and kicked off her high-heeled shoes and stared at him, nodding, as though bringing him into focus.

"We went all the way out there," she began, "Ronald and I." She was still nodding, like someone dropping off to sleep, and did not speak again for a while. Time passed slowly when you were drunk; even Sharkey knew that. "For nothing."

He snorted, refusing to acknowledge what she said with a reply.

"You lost." With a little giggle of satisfaction, as though she had won, she fixed her gaze on him. And he saw with pity and disgust that her upper lip was chafed, some of it due to smeared lipstick but mostly it was rubbed and reddened. And he was reminded that Ronald had a mustache.

After that, nothing that she said with this mouth, with this face, mattered to him. She was someone he didn't want to know. And, predictably, when he said nothing, she became remorseful, another stage in her drunkenness, and began to cry.

He left her whimpering in her chair and went to bed and surfed in his sleep. In the morning, leaving the house before his mother awoke, he strapped his board to his roof rack and drove to the North Shore, vowing that he would drop out of school. It wasn't complicated — it was legal, he was within his rights to quit. He was over sixteen, half his class had quit, all the bullies were gone, one was in jail, Nalani was pregnant, another girl was married. His classmates had grown up fast, but seldom followed through on any plan. They abandoned whatever ambition they had and stayed home, and their families enclosed them, protecting them, sheltering them, helping them raise their kids.

Not Sharkey. His mother said, "Your father would be devastated."

Sharkey thought, *If only he could see you.*

"What will you do now?"

"I don't know."

He did not know what he would do — true. But he knew what he wanted and felt it thumping inside him, more strongly now because he was facing his mother. *You lost.* Another spur, another goad, a challenge.

She had shown him her hand. She would never have a claim to his victories. *I don't know if it will happen,* he thought, *but I know what I want. I want to surf, I want to win.*

10

A Rescue

Later, when he was much older, dominating the tour, he'd see a barefoot boy of sixteen or so, deeply tanned, the glow of sunshine on him, golden salt-crusted shoulders, thin legs, wild blond hair like crushed feathers, his underlip thrust out in defiance, in a torn T-shirt and faded shorts, a big board under his arm, and he'd feel a pang for this fallen angel. He wanted to say to the boy, "Don't listen to your mother — keep doing what you're doing," but the boy wouldn't listen and didn't care and would of course do whatever he wanted to do. He also wanted to say to someone — anyone — "I see myself in that boy."

But there was no one to tell, no one who would understand. He was alone with the thought. The boy, that gangly twitching amphibian, half civilized, a fanatic, jumpy with ambition, didn't know what was going to happen to him; his whole life ahead of him, he only knew that he had a passion to be on a wave. He was alone too, and happier that way, with fantasies of glory in his head.

Whenever his mother was nearby Sharkey would chant in his mind, *With you I'm more alone than when I'm on my own.* A single mother, he saw, was like a bossy older sister, and she distrusted him, she hovered, and inflicted the worst sort of intrusion: she said no, and then she was gone, out of the house, on a date. His wish to be alone she took to be inspired by his streak of cruelty.

The Colonel had believed in him, and that belief had made Sharkey confident. The Colonel had also had a sense of proportion — some things mattered, others not so much. He had seen men die in battle; next to that, what else was worth lamenting? Being under attack in a firebase mattered more than cutting your thumb on a tuna-fish can or even crashing your car. Losing meant more than winning, but putting forth your whole effort mattered most. Were you shit scared? "Consider yourself already dead" and take the leap, no retreat.

To his mother, everything mattered equally. "A strange thing happened today," Sharkey had once said to her, preparing to tell her how a pretty Chinese girl in his class, seeing him alone in the school playground, had come up to him holding two cans of soda. She was small, slender, kitten-faced, chinless, and she crouched obliquely with a little bow. "This one for you." It was a day when, reverting to their bullying, Wilfred and his friends had been brutal to him. "Fucken haole!" And the girl, Mee Ling, was an angel.

His mother said, "Wait" — staring, she wasn't listening, she rummaged for a pair of tweezers and plucked a hair from between his brows. "You can't go around like that." When that was done, she said, "What were you going to tell me?"

"Nothing."

For those who believed that everything mattered, nothing mattered. They lived in a smothering clutter of concern and were never happy.

"Look at the time. I have to put on my face." She dressed for men, for other people.

When she was gone, he was glad; his confidence returned, he was himself again.

Uncle Sunshine's motto was *There's always another wave*. Sharkey's mother sometimes alluded to the loss, because it was the only time she'd seen him surf. She did not know that he'd begun to win — not contests, but the daily rough-and-tumble in the waves at Sunset and Waimea. In the tribal rites of surfing, the young surfers were merciless in their quest to be warriors. Other surfers knew better than anyone who the up-and-coming surfers were — Sharkey could see that he was gaining respect, because they matched themselves against him. It was better that his mother didn't know, better that he was detached from her, detached from school.

He dated the onset of his adulthood from this period. His mother was preoccupied with her boyfriend. Sharkey dropped the pretense that he went to school every day; his many absences meant that there was no going back, no way of catching up with schoolwork, as in the dream he often had of being naked and unprepared and late for class. He quit entirely, saying so in a short scribbled note of farewell, ridding himself of the uncertainty and the sense of failure, leaving behind the skirmishes in the playground and the exasperation of teachers, though he wondered what would become of Mee Ling, who had risked the taunts of the class by offering him a can of soda.

He said to his mother, "I'm quitting school," and when she howled he left the house and went surfing. His decision to quit gave him a great day on the water. His mother was calmer when he got home, exhausted by her hysteria.

"What will you do?"

"Maybe be a lifeguard."

Eddie Aikau had vouched for him — Eddie had quit his part-time job at the cannery and was now a full-time lifeguard at Sunset. Sharkey passed the test and earned a Red Cross certificate, and was assigned to Aliʻi Beach in Haleʻiwa. His mother was bewildered that he had gotten a job so quickly, that he had responsibility and a uniform and a salary — amazed that he knew people who helped him. Becoming a lifeguard on the North Shore was another rite of passage for lucky surfers — more like being a member of an exclusive club or a secret society than a city job, and with greater status. But it was not his ultimate aim, only a strategy to stay near the water.

The lifeguard chair was a throne, upraised, eight feet in the air, under a red canopy. He sat, his legs out straight, in the shadow of the canopy, wearing sunglasses, not emerging except to warn the tourists — Japanese girls in floppy hats and summer dresses — of the surf on big days. Using a megaphone, which gave him an older voice that crackled with authority, he called out, "Keep away from the shore break. You can be knocked down and swept out."

And now and then a Japanese tourist, a girl usually, perhaps not hearing or not understanding — or heedless — was knocked over by the push of a wave and slipped and was dragged away by its outgoing wash, and Sharkey leaped from his tower, carrying a float and a coil of rope. He dashed down the beach and dived for her, encircling her with his arm across her chest so that she lay on her back against his hip, and brought her to shore.

The first time it happened, it set off a series of events that changed him. A Japanese girl in a yellow dress was swept out. He swam for her. He stayed with her and she clung to him, sobbing, Sharkey whispering to calm her while her friends fretted at a distance. And feeling the softness of her flesh, the tremor of her helplessness, Sharkey was aroused. He had not touched a girl since the last time with Nalani, and had longed to. But Nalani had a new baby and all the desirable girls had boyfriends.

Soaked, moaning in fear, her thin dress clinging to her slender body and the outline of the seams of her underwear, her hair tangled and her face crumpled in terror, the rescued girl at Aliʻi Beach looked naked and powerless, and, sobbing on the hot sand, with Sharkey kneeling over her, she seemed sacrificial.

When she recovered and dried her face and sat up, she seemed ashamed of what she'd done — touching him, holding him in the water. She hid her face, and then ran to her friends and was gone.

But that experience, the drama of rescue, grasping the girl's body and hugging it, gave him the choking sensation, the wordless clumsy groping he came to know as desire, and he wanted more.

"I heard you wen' done a rescue," Eddie said later in the week, at their Friday *pau hana*—beers on the beach. "That's good. That goes on your record. That's big points for you." And peered closely at Sharkey. "You no look happy, brah."

"She made me horny," Sharkey said.

Eddie laughed at the unexpected word.

They were sitting cross-legged in a circle, Sharkey, Eddie, and four other lifeguards, at the far end of the beach at Waimea, where they met every Friday at sundown to see the green flash, to drink beer, to smoke *pakalolo,* to talk story—seldom stories about being a lifeguard, usually about the surf: was it rising, was it dropping, was a new swell expected?

Sharkey enjoyed the ritual, feeling that he belonged to this little band of watermen. School had not worked, his mother didn't know him; in town he was reminded of his failures. Here on the North Shore, among his fellow lifeguards, he was among friends. His was a job that came with distinction and authority; the lifeguard commanded the beach, he was obeyed, he sat upraised in the open, and whenever he made a rescue it was a spectacle.

He was the only haole among the lifeguards; as Eddie's protégé he was respected. Eddie often told the story of how they'd met that evening on the road to Hale'iwa and how in that meeting they'd felt a bond. Eddie made the meeting sound momentous. He did not remember saying, "Gas, grass, or ass —no one rides for free," and Sharkey giving him a dollar.

At the perimeter of the circle of boys in yellow lifeguard T-shirts and red shorts, some girls had begun to gather and kneel, more numerous on Fridays because the weekend loomed. Like an extension of the boys' tribal rite, the girls sat a little distance apart, pretending to be uninterested but often glancing over at the lifeguards. Sharkey resisted staring at them, fearing that he might choose the wrong one. He knew from Roosevelt High School that though the girls kept to themselves, whispering, and allowed themselves to be teased by the boys, each girl had a lover among the boys. It was only after dark that they met and paired off, and it was dangerous to presume and flirt, since every girl was spoken for.

"Hear that?" Eddie said. "Haole boy wen' rescue one Japanee wahine and he come horny."

"She had no muscles," Sharkey said. "She was so soft, her flesh like something I could eat. And she was all wet, her clothes sticking to her."

"Ha! You see surf bunnies with plenny papaya in little bikinis all day long and you get horny when you see one Japanee wahine in a wet dress."

Sharkey laughed and tried to deny it, but it was true, just as he said. The dress alone made her sexy: a wet one on a soft little body filled him with desire.

"Thass crazy," one of the other boys said.

Sharkey said, "I can't explain it."

"Is a mystery," Eddie said.

He had gotten to his knees. He wagged his head to see across the patch of sand, where the girls had gathered beneath the feathery overhang of an ironwood bough.

"Eh — Rhonda," he said, leaning, then putting his fingers to his lips and whistling.

A small figure emerged from the shadow of the tree, the glow of her white shorts making her visible.

Sensing a moment that might involve him, Sharkey said, "I'm heading into town. Friday traffic," and jammed his beer bottle into the sand.

"Not yet, haole."

Now the girl was beside Eddie, and as though in a gesture of respect she dropped to her knees, looking like a child beside him, with a soft smile and a face like a seal pup's.

"Rhonda — dis haole Joe Sharkey."

Sharkey awkwardly got to his feet but could not think of anything to say, not even "Hi." He felt so conspicuous among the other boys.

"Go wid him."

"Aloha," Sharkey said, swallowing hard, and walked across the sand to the parking lot where he'd left his car, glad for the darkness that closed over him. He was careful not to look back, but when he got to his car, the girl was behind him. She slipped into the backseat, leaving the door open.

Sharkey got into the driver's seat and gripped the steering wheel.

"What are you doing back there?" he said.

"Taking my clothes off." Her first words, a squeaky island voice, singsong, baby talk.

"Why?" he said, and did not recognize his thick throaty voice.

"Come here and find out."

He was trembling as he sat beside her, taking care to close the door so that it hardly made a sound. As he began to hug her, leaning to kiss her, she took a wad of gum out of her mouth and flicked it through the window.

"What are you doing?"

"I don't want it," she said, her breath thick with the sweetness of bubble gum.

"What do you want?"

"I want you in my mouth."

The spoken words worked on him with more force than if she had caressed him, and she said them again in a hot urgent whisper. Then her little hands were snatching at his shorts and her head was nuzzling his lap, until he lay back and rested his hands on her bobbing head, her warm hair in his fingers.

Like the first time he'd surfed a barrel, shooting to the end as the wave closed over him, flinging himself into the sunlight, this was explosive, a relief, filling him with joy and promising more — promising happiness.

The Colonel had warned him, his mother had warned him, and now he knew why. Desire was dangerous to them; they knew they'd lose him to it and never learn his secret.

Rhonda sat up and sighed, shrugged her breasts back into her torn T-shirt and at the same time passed a fingertip across a gleaming snail trail on her cheek, drew it to her lips, and licked it. Then she let out what Sharkey heard as a giggle of wickedness and complicity, but it was only a shy girl's laughter.

"I want more," he said into her hair.

"Me too." Her mouth warmed his ear.

"I have to go now, Rhonda."

"I see you tomorrow, Joe."

"You know me?"

"Everybody see Joe Sharkey, but you nevah pay no attention."

So he was known, he was desired, he had friends, and now, just like that, a lover. He was not a conqueror. He was an initiate — he'd been admitted to a mystery and saw inside the rosy recesses of it, red as the flesh in a mouth. He understood now what was allowed, and knew the wonderful truth: his innocence of girls had been ignorance — what he wanted, they wanted too. That was the solemn secret. No wonder they smiled, no wonder Rhonda wanted more.

Not experience delivering him to maturity — sexual desire made him a child again, a happy boy, free to do as he wished. And now he knew that the girls weren't afraid. They were like him, his equals. It was play, it was joy, it was the childhood he thought he'd missed, to be lived again.

11

Surf Bunnies

They wagged their *okoles* and fluttered their fingers and did mocking hula on the beach near the lifeguard stand and called out "Joe" to him. They watched him surf and met him as he came ashore. They brought him bowls of poke and rice or Spam musubi as presents and watched him eat under the palm trees. They challenged him to take smaller waves and sometimes surfed beside him with more grace than he could muster. They were not strong and so they needed to be more agile, they were light on their boards, they were gleaming mermaids in the water, they knew their limits and so stayed out of the monster surf and rode like nymphs on the waves they chose — surf bunnies.

Unexpectedly, they were his friends. He did not have to pretend to love them, yet he desired them. It was a relief to him that he did not need to woo them or contrive a reason for meeting them secretly — and when it happened, which was after work, most days, they were as eager as he was, and more straightforward.

Snatching his hand, one said, "I stay *hanawai*."

He pushed her hand aside and hugged her.

"My period."

"Want to forget about it?"

"Plenny other ways." And she laughed softly, groping him as he had just groped her and shoving his hand onto her *okole*.

Most of the time it was hurried, a swift grappling and then a convulsive gasp, and when it was over, giggles. They knotted her pareu, lit a joint, and talked about the surf. No memory of what had just happened — it was mutual relief, a frantic hug.

This was the life he craved. It did not matter whether he excelled at riding the wave — he was relaxed, surfing when he was off-duty or on his free days; he found a rhythm in his climb into the wave, a way of appraising it, jamming his board onto it, and planting himself on it, so that the wave and the board were one. And why so smooth? Because he was happy.

This was play, sex was play, lifeguarding was friendship — a team, and that involved play too. None of it was work. He was paid enough that he never had to ask his mother for money. That he was independent confused her, thwarted her in her hovering, since his accepting money from her had held them together, and now he didn't need her.

"I can give you more," she said.

"I don't need more. I don't need any."

Girls had money and sleek bodies, girls had cars, girls had rooms where he could crash, girls had parents who encouraged him. He surfed with Rhonda's father, Kawika, who said, "You got a job. You got respeck."

The pink C-shaped scar on Sharkey's face set him apart, it masked him, it gave the illusion that he was less a haole than the others — someone with a story, a secret, an altered face, the scar a distinction like a badge of honor, as though he'd been injured in battle, more proof that he might be a hero.

From the loneliness of lingering on a swell, waiting for a wave to ride, he became aware that he was being watched, that someone — probably a girl — saw what he was doing and understood the difficulty; and the very fact that he knew someone was watching him — someone onshore to surf to, an appreciative spectator — helped him put forth his best effort. So he rode the wave to the girl on the beach and that night lay in her arms.

It was so simple, this notion that there was someone watching him, someone who desired him — more than one, perhaps many: this attention drove him to perform, the play became serious, and he was reminded of how he wanted to win and had a reason for winning, not for money but to impress a girl, to possess her for a night, or more.

He saw that the other surfers had the same idea, competed against each other to be noticed — less warriors battling for a trophy than a pack of poi dogs nipping each other and lolloping for a favor. Sharkey usually came second or third. He was complimented — so young, smaller than most of them, a haole, but distinguished with a scar.

One day he won at a surf meet at Sunset. He was crowned with a lei, a ring of flowers on his head. The prize was a new surfboard and a ticket to Tahiti, and a girl that night murmured to him, "Watch me, watch me, watch me — what I do to you."

The neglected aspect of his growing up, what was missing in his childhood, was a girlfriend; and now, with money, he slipped out of his mother's grasp and eluded her control. He had lovers.

"Them Tahiti wahine better be careful."

"I'll come back to you," he said.

"Maybe I no stay here. Maybe I no wait."

He was now used to their playful defiance — it made them whole and equal and more desirable.

Tahiti was his first trip away from Hawaii, on his own, away from his mother — she saw him off, looking sad. He arrived in Papeete, set against old mountainous volcanoes, overgrown and thickened in rainwashed green, steeper than the *pali* of Oʻahu. But the town itself was much smaller than he'd expected, no tall buildings, a human scale. The plane had circled and come in low across the reefs, Sharkey scanning the breaks for surf spots, his face pressed against the window.

"New board," said the taxi driver, Hawaiian in his big brown bulk but with a French accent.

"A prize."

"You win this board?"

"Oui, mon ami."

"Vous êtes un grand champion."

"That's me!"

He was someone else, someone exceptional; no one knew him here. He was happy in the freedom of being able to say anything he wished about himself, and still remembered a little French from Roosevelt. He discovered the first day in Tahiti the transformation of travel, liberated in a far-off place.

This is all mine, he thought. He possessed the island with all his senses. The town smelled of sea-rotten wood and old rope and decaying fish, and the women were lovely in their bright pareus, knotted at their breasts, walking beneath the arcades of the shop houses in a stamping, assertive way, as though to show they weren't owned by the French. Food smells, the blatting of motorbikes, and a strange and fragrant cigarette smoke — all new. Another odor he could not identify, from great woven baskets and burlap sacks — blackened husks. He saw it was the sourness of broken coconuts. "Copra, m'sieur."

The taxi driver found him again, calling out, "Champion!"

He strapped Sharkey's board on pads on the roof of his purple Renault Dauphine and drove him along the coast, Sharkey in the backseat, a pretty woman in the front; he was fascinated by the simple knot of her pareu at the back of her neck, which he mentally untied.

"What country?" she asked.

"Hawaii."

The word cheered her; she relaxed, as though he'd announced himself as a relative. And then she was narrating, "Maraa . . . Papara," indicating the surf beyond the reef, and farther on Sharkey saw a wave rising on an outer reef and no one surfing it.

"Stop," he said, but already the taxi had begun to slow down.

"Teahupoʻo," the driver said, and got out with the girl, who helped unload the board. Her hair was thick; she had a flower on her ear; her face was sculpted, thin-lipped, a pretty chin. A slender neck; the pareu still neatly in place, with a simple knot.

The guesthouse was near the beach. He paid extra to stay in the thatch-roofed cottage on the grounds, like a dollhouse. He propped his surfboard outside and threw himself on the bed, taking a deep breath of the fragrance from the open window — fragrant even in the musty room, the bedposts damp and salty with sea air. He felt freedom in the fragrance of every new aroma.

And then a knock. "Yes?"

It was the driver, looking shy, trying to form a sentence.

"Ma soeur — elle veut être ton amie."

He understood "sister," he understood "friend."

That was all he needed to know. He saw the girl from the taxi waiting on the beach the next day, in the late afternoon, as he rode in the last of what he imagined would be the good waves. The surf had been dropping since lunchtime. But he'd been alone on the break, and he had the renewed sense that it was all his, this day was his, the beach was his, and the girl on it, bare-foot in the red-and-yellow pareu — different from yesterday's — fluttering as she walked back and forth, something in her hand. When he came closer he saw it was a rusty machete.

"Now I kill you," she said, swiping with the blade, looking reckless, her eyes flashing.

"Wait," he said, quickly putting his board down.

She screeched, laughing, and ran on skinny legs to where the grassy bank had been eaten away by the sea, forming a ledge, undercut by the tide.

"Votre tête," she said, falling on her knees and selecting a coconut from a pile of green coconuts. Holding it at arm's length, she slashed at it in oblique strokes, narrowing its end with quick chops to open a hole.

Sharkey had been frightened by the sight of the knife. Now, as she handed him the coconut, he felt only joy. The taste of the cool coconut water brought a sweetness to his soul.

Meanwhile the girl had sat down on the grass, cross-legged, and placed a smaller coconut in her lap.

"Can I have this one?"

"Take," she said, and opened her legs.

The coconut lay between her legs, on her silken wrap. Sharkey reached but could not grasp the coconut without disturbing the cloth or grazing her thighs with his fingers. She sat back, resting on her arms, and widened her legs more as he leaned and looked into her eyes and slowly grasped the coconut, his knuckles bumping the warmth of her inner thighs. But he merely held it, he did not lift it, he sensed her body bumping it. When he tried to lift it she brought her legs together and clasped it.

"You like to taste that?"

His mouth went dry. He licked the sea salt from his lips, the sweetness of the coconut she'd cut for him. But now they were alone in the shadow of the palms, half hidden by the bushes of big leaves that grew just behind them.

He nodded, and fearing that she had not seen him clearly enough, he spoke. "Yes — yes."

"*J'aime,*" she said, reaching for his hair and clawing it slowly, "*vos cheveux d'or.*"

He made an attempt to pick up the coconut, but when he did she closed her legs on it again, and on his hands, and she laughed softly. Her thighs were warm against his hands as she laughed again, teasingly. She was staring past him at the setting sun — her cat eyes gilded by it — and the sun sank, too slowly he thought. When they were in darkness she put her face near his — did not kiss him but inhaled deeply, against his nose.

"Where?' he said. "When?"

"*Ici,*" she said. She flung the coconut aside and pushed his head into her lap, clasping it as she had clasped the coconut, and whispered, "*Maintenant.*"

Her name was Fillette, she told him after they'd made love and were lying half asleep on the grass. And that became the pattern of their days — she greeted him in the morning and then was gone — "*J'aide ma mère dans le jardin*" — his school French was a help, but there was much she said that he did not understand. "Garden" meant gathering coconuts and bananas. He surfed all day, she met him at sundown in the bower beneath the palms, and when his week was over she was laughing, he was tearful.

Before her brother drove him to the airport, Sharkey said, "I'll come back."

"*Je serai une vieille femme alors.*" And she laughed again.

"Fillette she say, she be old woman then," her brother said, settling behind the wheel.

At home, in the circle of lifeguards after work, he told his story to the others, who listened intently. He was the adventurer, with the power of the sexy tale of the Tahitian girl at the break at Teahupo'o.

Then Eddie said, "What about the waves?"

"Awesome."

He described the configuration of the break, how solitary it was, the good days, his rides, how the girl had said that in winter it was huge. But his mind was not on the waves, because all he could think of was the expression she'd taught him, which he was too shy to share with these boys, words he had not learned at school: *"Goûtez-moi"* — taste me.

The surf subsided in early spring and the ocean flattened, shimmered as a lake of blue — more swimmers, easier rescues, later sunsets, and still the girls lingered by the lifeguard chair, calling to him, teasing him.

"Haole boy!" But it was affectionate, flirtatious.

To avoid the long drive from town he rented a room in a house near Rocky Point, surfed at Velzyland on his days off, and sneaked girls into the room for . . . what? To him it was never more than play, and for the girls too; blameless, joyous, brief.

He was with a girl on the late afternoon his mother stopped by the beach. His mother was with a man he'd never seen before.

"Puamana, this is my mother."

"Glad to meet you," his mother said. And to the man, "This is my son, Joe."

"Jamie Kunzler," the man said. "I was in your father's outfit in 'Nam, running recon patrols."

"Jamie wants to talk to you about school," his mother said.

"I'm done with school," Sharkey said.

"You'll be in good shape with a high school diploma."

"I'm in good shape without one."

"Can't enlist without one," the man said. "But if you get one and join up, the army will look after you. Put you through college on the GI Bill. That's pretty much a free ride."

His mother stared, saying *Answer that* with her severe gaze.

Sharkey said, "The Colonel — my dad — said we were just helping out in Vietnam. Advisers. Recon. But now there's all kinds of fighting. He didn't see that. A lot of guys are getting killed, and lots of injured men are at Tripler. I don't want to go."

"You don't want to help your country."

"Ever ask yourself, 'Why are we dying there?'" Sharkey said. Then he smiled. "My dad said they got waves."

The man winced, and what angered Sharkey was that his mother was on the man's side — a new man, a new date — and not on his.

"Think of your future," she said. "What will you do?"

Sharkey was holding his board, standing near Puamana. Now he put his arm around her waist and drew her to him, and he faced his mother, who had edged away from Jamie Kunzler, who stood, hands behind his back, at ease.

"This," Sharkey said.

12

The Year of the Rat

The distant boy appeared climbing onto his outthrust board at the lip of the wave at Pipeline just before sunset — half the western sky glowing dusty pink, the light whittling his body small. He crouched on the board and dropped in and cut left, scissoring the face of the wave.

Sharkey watched with pleasure as though seeing his younger self rejoicing and riding, the small brown buoyant boy in the hollow of the water, racing left, jamming the board down in a well-timed bottom turn and carving upward as he climbed to the foaming lip again and spun, sweeping the board across the curling wave, just escaping the collapse of the overhang in a cutback that took him into the sliding trough. There he attempted to carve upward, and swiveling, he toppled, holding his head. Lost in the froth and boil of broken water, he appeared again, chased by his board, tumbled in the shore break.

"He's not bad," Sharkey said.

His new surf buddy, Skippy Lehua, said, "Wahine."

Sharkey laughed, walking down the beach and seeing the small breasts in the wet shirt, the pretty mouth, the too-big board shorts.

"Surf bunny," Skippy said.

But before Sharkey got to her she'd hurried up the beach to her pile of clothes and changed into her dry T-shirt. She was Chinese, small, deeply tanned, her black hair cut short, strands of it burned reddish by the sun.

"You almost wiped out on the reef," Sharkey said.

"I never wipe out. I seen the reef. I bailed." She looked him up and down; she hadn't stopped frowning. "You worry I do a face-plant?"

"I've done plenty there," he said. "How do you think I got this nose?"

"Normal haole nose," she said.

But his talk was simply to detain her while he studied her. Close up he could see she was older than she'd seemed at a distance, a young woman rather than a girl, with slender arms and legs, her shoulders just a little muscular for someone her size, her face catlike and compact, her short hair still plastered to her scalp like a skullcap. She was small and so slim, no wonder he'd taken her for a boy.

Her sweet face and delicate features were in contrast to her tight muscles, flexing now as she rocked on her heels and grasped the leash of her board with her bare toes, passing it with her foot to her hand.

"Monkey," he said.

She laughed — lovely teeth. "My father, he calls me that."

"I want to meet your dad," he said suddenly, and he was not sure why.

She tilted her head at the unexpected remark and scowled. Lit by the setting sun, one eye was tightly shut against the glare.

"You know me?"

"Not yet," he said. "But you're just in time."

"For what?"

"*Pakalolo.* Beer. Grinds. Whatever."

"You don't want to meet my dad," she said. "You a bad influence."

But she sat on the sand with him while he lit a joint and sucked on it and held the smoke in his lungs, gasping a little.

She said, "That fat one cost you, what? Ten bucks?"

"Five," he grunted, still trying to hold the smoke in.

"So instead of I try smoke it, give me five instead."

He hooted at her impudence, then fished in the pocket of his shorts, found his ragged wallet, and handed her a wet five-dollar bill.

"I was joking. I don't want your money. I got one job."

"Where you working?"

"Sunset Grille, waiting tables."

He pinched the joint and slipped the roach into his shirt pocket. "What about a beer?"

"I never drink. Anyway, you don't want to see it. I come all red in the face, can hardly breathe. You know *pakay* — bad drinkers."

"So what do you do for fun?"

"Family." She slapped the board. "And this."

"You need to bend your knees more. And lean into the nose of the board. And keep your feet farther apart." He turned to face the surf. "Too much west in the wave. It's closing out at the corners. You need to compensate."

"The big expert," she said.

He laughed at her defiance, but he was struck by the smoothness of her skin, her hairless arms sparkling with salt crystals, her tiny wrists, her lovely neck. He said, "No. But I know a few moves."

Now he touched her hand with his pale water-soaked finger and traced her salty forearm to the crook of her elbow and up her brown biceps, and as he did he sensed her stiffening, her shoulders rising, her mouth going grim.

"Not that either," she said.

He pulled his hand away as if he'd been scalded. He was thrown, her flat voice like a reprimand, the worse because she was so small yet so severe, as though with that touch he'd violated her. And what? Just a friendly poke on her arm.

"I wasn't suggesting anything."

She shrugged. "I don't like people touch me."

"I'm Joe," he said.

"I know. Sharkey. I seen you shredding Rocky Rights." She faced him, squinting when the last of the sun caught her gaze. "I'm May."

She picked up her board, struggled to keep it under her arm, and muttered something he took to be sarcastic as she walked up the slope of the beach.

"Girl Scout." It was Skippy, approaching him with a can of beer in his fist.

"What's wrong with Girl Scouts?"

"No action."

"You know, that might be cool — the best thing in the world for me," Sharkey said. "Not a contest."

It wearied him to think of the jokey negotiating. Worse, it shamed him to think of how easily he'd had sex with girls he'd met casually on the beach, whose names he never knew — and one in particular, a pale Japanese tourist who'd murmured, "Hurry, mister!" because she had a bus to catch. He was aware that since he had won the Pipeline Masters the previous year girls sought him out, and not only for his glory. He always had *pakalolo,* he had money for beer, he had a car, and one of his sponsors was a sportswear company: he had surf gear, he had free stuff. In return for sex the girl would get a rash guard or a board leash.

May did not want anything, nor did she want to be touched. And she had a job. She was a rare bunny.

"I seen her," Skippy said. "All the guys wen' try her. She so straight, brah. You get less."

"I don't care if I get less."

"You get more less."

"Maybe I don't want much."

"Everybody want something," Skippy said, almost pleading.

"Just a friend," Sharkey said.

The simplicity of a friend, the purity of it, the relief—wanting nothing from her but companionship. She had promise as a surfer, and he would help her any way he could. She'd been cautious with him on the beach, but she'd been daring, at moments reckless on the wave, her moves exceeding her control. She was not strong, but she was sturdy and small, with a low center of gravity. He'd started that way—independent, a bit defiant, hard to convince, determined, untrusting. He too had hated to be touched.

She did not show up the next day. Sharkey waited on the beach, assessing the young surfers on the head-high waves. Skippy walked toward him, swigging beer. He finished it and crushed the can in his hand, squeezing it flat.

"You looking for the surf bunny?" he finally said.

Sharkey was always astonished by how keen-eyed and shrewd an apparently illiterate local surfer could be—louts, as he'd heard them described by haoles from town. But with animal cunning and a kind of hunger they could read your mind.

"Da *tita*," Sharkey said.

That was what she was, a sister. That was the ideal. And he thought, *Maybe that was why I said, "I want to meet your father," perhaps in a fit of prescience, of a yearning to see a whole family, to join them as a brother and a son.*

He found her later at Sunset Grille, not the small dripping surf bunny anymore but taller—her sandals had thick heels, and her purple head wrap gave her a few more inches, with a shapeless untucked blue blouse with loose sleeves, and a skirt—the one piece of women's clothing that was so rare on the North Shore, so feminine, more teasing than a bikini, sexier than shorts. He was noting that distinction for the first time, seeing how it mattered. In a place where most young women were half naked, clothes were provocative.

She was standing at a table of four people, taking their order, scribbling on a pad. He heard her say brightly, "I'll bring you your drinks right away."

As she passed his table, Sharkey said, "What about my drinks?"

"You," she said, and kept walking. "No make ass."

But after she'd served the four people their drinks, she walked over to Sharkey, saying, "What can I do for you, mister?"

"Go surfing with me tomorrow."

"What about a drink?"

"No drink, no grinds."

"You come all the way from Rocky Point to ask me that?"

"How you know I stay Rocky Point?"

"You're Joe Sharkey," she said.

"Yes, I came all the way from Rocky Point to ask you that."

She folded her arms, the pad in one hand, her pen in the other. Her expression gave nothing away. She might have been tasting something — that same evaluating look.

"I stay town," she said. "I drive home after work."

"Really? You don't live up here?"

"I stay with my *ohana*," she said. "Kapahulu side."

The word *ohana* was so complete and all-encompassing, with a reassuring softness and density. "Family" didn't do it justice. It put him in mind of a warm nest.

He was about to speak when there was a cry from across the room. "May!"

Another waiter — a man in an aloha shirt — was gesturing to her with a cocktail shaker.

"See you at Lani's," she said. "Pipe's going to be too gnarly for me."

He was early, eager to see her, pleased when she showed up, walking gingerly, toes raised, off the side of the road where the shoulder was rocky, hard on her tender soles. She seemed nonchalant, but when she said, "Aloha," that touched his heart.

"Come more big out there," she said, looking past him, speaking with respect for the wave.

"Himalayas," he said of the offshore wave, rising and curling. "Someday you'll be riding it. Just not today."

They were watching a surfer charging the wave and dropping into a bomb, carving under the collapsing lip and soon smothered.

"The left bowl has a mean pinch. You need speed," he said. "And there's a heavy rip out there."

Another wave rose before the swimming surfer and he dived into the steep slope of its face and vanished as the wave slid toward the smaller shore break, finally crashing, the whole ridge of water disappearing into its own frenzy of froth.

"Someday," May said.

"Before we go, put your board on the beach. I want to look at your posture."

May set her board down carefully, burying the fin in the soft sand.

"Show me how you stand normally."

She stepped onto the board and stood, flexing, crouching a little, lifting her arms.

"Move those feet apart, put your right foot forward. When you get on a wave, try to remember where they are."

"I try."

"I think you should have a bigger board."

"Can barely lift this one."

"I've got one for you."

He'd brought four boards, different sizes, but all of them longer than May's board and several of them wider. She stepped on each of them in turn, and finally settled on a wide Willis board that Sharkey carried to the water's edge for her.

And then she was in the shore break, flopped on the board, paddling into the surf and duck-diving under a wave, reappearing behind it, seated on the board, rocking in the lacework of swirling bubbles, rising and falling, waiting for a ride. Sharkey watched her climb onto the board with a nimble swiftness that impressed him and steer it left until the wave subsided and slowed and she toppled, calling out a word — a squawk — he understood as triumph.

She did not swim in, as he expected; she paddled out again and surfed three more waves until, exhausted, she rode the big board to the beach and leaped off it with a dance step, and pulled the nose of the board onto the sand but no farther, such was its weight.

Sharkey snatched it from the slop of a wave and carried it up the beach.

"I didn't know," she began, "with a bigger board," and gasped for breath.

"The right board can make a big difference."

"But it more heavy!"

"I'll be your board carrier," Sharkey said.

"Every day?" she said, jeering at him.

He faced her solemnly. "Whenever you want. You ask and I'm there. Okay, sister?"

"Braddah," she said, smiling, and dropped to the sand beside him, breathing hard.

Brother, sister — she was the family he desired and needed. He did not want a follower, a pet, a student, someone who was not an equal. He did not need power over her, he wanted a friend, someone like her. How was it possible to be a mediocre surfer and be so confident?

"I'm tired," she said.

"Let's get a burger."

"Gotta go back home," she said.

"All the way to town."

"To my *ohana*," she said. "They expecting me. You keep this board, yah?"

Then she turned and at her car took out a gallon jug of water and emptied it over herself to wash the salt from her body, wrapped herself in a towel, and drove away without a backward glance, without another word.

And that night at home Sharkey summoned her pretty face and brown shoulders and sunburned lips and replayed her words, the pidgin in her speech, *I stay town* and *my ohana* and *no make ass* and *come more big*. And he tried to elaborate, listing in his mind what he knew about her — her wait-ressing at Sunset Grille, her commuting from town and her family to the North Shore, to work, to surf; her refusal to drink or smoke, her dislike of being touched, the fond mention of her father. And the ultimate puzzle, that she seemed to have no other friends. But she had a family, in that nest that he imagined — that refuge, that consolation. When he had first seen her, alone on the wave, he had been surprised that there was no one on the beach to cheer her — no surf buddies, no one watching except him. But she had an *ohana* waiting in town. He imagined her entering her house, the *ohana* greeting her. She didn't need friends.

She was still like a stranger — he hardly knew her. But that was a goad. He wanted urgently to see her again.

After that, they met whenever she was free to surf and the surf was up. He did not want to see her at the restaurant where she worked, nor want her to wait on him. Some nights he lingered in the parking lot, and when she fin-ished work he said, "Tomorrow?" and named a break, and usually she said, "Cool," and got into her car and headed to town, while he stood, smiling, her taillights vanishing in the night. Such a long drive for her to see them made her family seem so powerful, so whole, enclosing her as he drove back to his house. And his house, once such a consolation as a refuge from his mother, seemed empty now, cavernous and shadowy.

He suggested adjustments to May's technique, which she listened to, al-ways frowning, as though evaluating them. She was a strong swimmer for her size. But though she might eventually learn to surf a big wave, she'd al-ways have trouble paddling into it.

He did not tell her that. Yet she knew. When he said, "You remind me of myself," she replied, "I stay small. I never catch big waves."

"Do you want to?"

"I just want to surf, anything I can. Get more better. That's for why I come here and don't surf town."

"A wise man once said, 'The best surfer is the one having the most fun.'"

"Ass right."

"You live near Waikiki?"

"Kapahulu side."

"Tell me about your family."

She made one of her feline faces, drawing back, then smiled and shrugged, looking baffled and finally amused, as though at a private joke, too compli-cated to share.

"Chinese kine," she said. "My family everything to me. And they geeve" — she hesitated — "they geeve me everything."

The statement left Sharkey wordless and envious, needing her more than ever, feeling something like love for her — desire, anyway, a wish to have her by his side. In that way he saw her family arrayed with him, as in the Hawaiian way he became part of the *ohana*. In a wrinkle of anxiety in his mind he suspected what she would say next.

"What about your *ohana*?" she said.

"I don't have one," Sharkey said. "My father died when I was a kid. My mother's busy."

"Cousins?"

"No one," Sharkey said. "Just you."

He began to reach, to take her hand, to hug her, to reassure himself and her. But in a reflex of hesitation he fought the throb of urgency, suspecting that she would draw back, stiffen a little, and be spooked.

And he smiled at his restraint, because he'd always been so reckless. Perhaps May was the proof that he could be chivalrous and unselfish; that he would know her better by respecting her, that winning her trust was everything. He admired her for being self-possessed, with a spirit that made her resolute. She was not a great surfer, she might never be, but she had mastered the mental challenge of surfing. She had the strength of mind to ride a wave, which was the ability to stay clear-sighted and in control. She would always be a happy surfer.

She had mastered herself, through willpower, fending off men. And when she told him how they'd pawed her and pinched her, Sharkey recognized his old obnoxious presumption with women. It was the support of May's family that had given her confidence, the big Chinese *ohana* in town, which was more like a nation than a family. Thinking of them, he often had a glimpse of his house in Manoa, his coming home after school. His widowed mother smoking a cigarette, her drink on a side table, waiting for a man to take her to dinner. "I won't be late," she'd always say, and she was always late.

"They worry about me," May said. "But I know they proud for me too, because I don't ask them for anything. Only for aloha."

Sharkey did not say what was he was thinking: *I have no family, and even when I did have the Colonel and my mother, I did not have that kind of love.* The power of this family behind May was something he had never known, and drew him to her, and it made her marvelous. After a few weeks of surfing with her and carrying her board and watching her drive away, she was still resolute, self-possessed, wholly herself — a rarity in his experience. Always eager to see her, bewitched by her body and her beautiful face and her resourcefulness on her board, he wondered if he was falling in love.

He'd always thought how women assessed him, and other men, with the woman's question "Is he the one meant for me?" Because he'd always felt, even in the recklessness of the North Shore, that the women wanted more, wanted a partner, or a baby — for them the sex was the beginning of everything. For Sharkey, for most men he knew, it was something accomplished, a done deed, of always going home alone, sex as something final, a kind of cure.

But he began to think, *Maybe she's the one meant for me* — his future — and he loved her for resisting him. Her resistance was like an element in their courtship.

Still, they surfed, he sometimes met her at work, and he saw her off as she headed back to town many evenings. In his mind, she was driving into the unknown, and so one day at the beginning of February he asked again about her family.

"Maybe you get a chance to see them," she said as she poured a gallon jug of fresh water over her head and let it splash over her body as she shook herself and tossed her hair.

"I'd love to."

"Maybe New Year's."

"It's over," he said. "That was a month ago."

"Chinese New Year," she said, blinking water out of her eyes. "The Year of the Rat. I'm taking the week off from work. Staying in town — no surfing."

"Party time?"

"Family time," she said, and the suggestion of intimacy gave him a pang. "Family dinner. Wong *ohana*."

"I envy you."

She stood straight, hands on hips, still dripping. Her eyes were on him, but she was not looking at him; the eyes were unfocused, gleaming with the fluidity of intense thought — a calculating gaze that was like blindness, droplets from the water jug glinting on her long lashes.

"I never invite anyone before," she said, and licked some drops from her lips, and shrugged. "Okay."

Sharkey was grateful and relieved and expectant. In all that time, the month or more of giving May his full attention, of avoiding his old girlfriends and his surfer buddies, he had dropped out of his circle of friends — had chosen to surf with May at breaks where he was sure he would not see them. But he was happy in his concentration. It was how he imagined an old-fashioned love affair, his spending time with her, carrying her board, wooing her in his way. And this adjustment, resisting himself, he was impressed by her example — the way she had fended off all other men. It had strengthened him but also isolated him, in the way love does, by his need for her, that nothing else mattered and no one would understand. It was a rare thing for him — he could not remember a time when he'd felt so insecure.

And that other fact, that keeping her distance as she became more important to him, the knowledge that he had no one else.

He saw that what he was living through was nothing that he'd known before, not his picking a woman, singling her out, and snatching her — the woman flirting or waiting to be chosen. This was a dance, during which he and the woman circled each other, whispering, interacting, assessing, not touching but existing in a vague companionship and surfing together, the basis of a future. May did not flirt, she did not confide, and so she had power.

That May had a whole family magnified her, made her seem decent and protected, a world away from the North Shore anarchy of Sharkey's recent years.

She was gone for almost a week. He suffered this absence and discovered the helplessness of a lover, in thrall to a Chinese fox-witch. And then she called.

"Meet us at the restaurant," she'd said. "It's more better we don't show up together. My father so strict. He trusts me, but he don't trust anyone else."

So Sharkey drove to town, murmuring *so shtrick*, forty miles in his peeling VW bug, to the restaurant she'd named, Hee Hing's on Kapahulu. Self-conscious about the condition of his car — the dents, the rusty roof rack, his sponsors' bumper stickers — he parked a little distance down the street under a kukui nut tree. He walked to the restaurant on the hot cement sidewalk, the sun bearing down on him and slowing him as he squinted in the glare, hating the side streets of bungalows and small shops, the whole neighborhood paved over.

Going into Honolulu meant a change of climate, of landscape, from the North Shore shacks to the suburban streets and high-rises, the crush of people and cars. It was hotter here, leeward, under the mountains, without a breeze, a different place, and reminded him of his school days, hurrying down the back streets of Makiki in the afternoon sun to the safety of Magic Island to surf.

The dining room of Hee Hing's was visible in the big rectangle of window under its red sign, on the second floor of a newish square-jawed building, a staircase at the side. Sharkey climbed two flights and went through the foyer where people were waiting for tables.

"Wong party," he said when a spiky-haired Chinese man in a red shirt stepped forward to block him.

"Got plenny Wong. Which Wong?"

"No idea, man."

The man impatiently waved him into the loud room, where thirty or more large round tables were ringed with diners and piled high with platters of food. Sharkey stepped into a density of heat and noise, the clatter of plates, the screech of talk, and, added to the din, three television sets set on high shelves against the walls. Simultaneous snow scenes were being televised — a brilliant whiteness of steep slopes, skiers carving their way downhill, speeding through sunshine, throwing up snow as they turned. But the sound was inaudible in the racket of the restaurant.

Making his way through the tables, among the odor of frying fat and soy sauce and scorched meat, Sharkey began to perspire in the stifling room, his shirt sticking to his body. All the tables were occupied, and he smiled to see that all the diners were Chinese, reaching with chopsticks at the platters and chewing and yelling. He looked for another haole and saw an old mustached man at a corner table, who signaled to him with a shaka, as though to a friend.

Searching the room, he saw May at a far table, gesturing — she had obviously seen him first. He hardly recognized her in her dress, ankle-length and silken and crimson. As at her job at Sunset Grille, she was more alluring, sexier, in this dress than in her skimpy bikini. Her hair was combed and styled, molded to her head like a black cap, a creamy plumeria blossom fixed at her ear. She waved him near, but when Sharkey got to the table she avoided touching him and stepped toward an old man and hugged him.

"Dad, this is my friend Joe I was telling you about."

The old man was about to put something into his mouth. He glanced upward and winced a little at Sharkey, then nodded, peeled the thing he held in his hand, and nibbled at it. It was a severed chicken foot. He went on nibbling as May stepped away from him and pulled out a chair for Sharkey.

"Chicken feet — cool," Sharkey said.

"Phoenix claw," a fattish young man said in a scolding tone, his head tilted, his mouth twisted, gnawing one of his own. He was pale and jowly, with a clammy face, in a flower-patterned shirt.

"My brother Winston," May said, but the man looked away and kept eating. "And this is my mother."

The older woman said something, but Sharkey could not hear it over the racket. She fluttered the fingers of one hand, and with one finger of her other hand was encircling a bowl of poi, gathering a purplish clot of goo on her finger. She poked it into her mouth and wiped it on her tongue.

"Dis so *ono*!" she shrieked — he heard that — and dipped her finger into the bowl again.

As he sat and scanned the table, he saw two other women, one in a hairnet and green scrubs, the other in a stained sweatshirt, with wild hair. They were dabbing at the platters with chopsticks as Sharkey said, "Aloha."

"My sisters," May said, and tapped the arm of the woman in scrubs. "Winnie, say hello."

"I'm on call," the woman said, tugging at her green shirt.

"I'm Wallis," the wild-haired woman said. "Did Wendy tell you I'm the *lolo* sister?"

Leaning closer so that he could be heard, Sharkey said, "Wendy?"

"That's me," May said. "I got sick of the rhyming names — Winston Wong, Wendy Wong — so I decided to call myself May."

"It means beautiful in Chinese," Wallis said, and ran her fingers through her hair. "My problem is I got no *kala*. No money. My life *kapakahi*. Wendy beautiful, Wendy got plenny money, Wendy got haole boyfriend."

"Joe's not my boyfriend. He's my surf instructor. And I got money because I got a job, Wally."

"I want to go to the Olympics," Wallis said, looking up at the TV set. "See some real snow."

And Sharkey realized that it was the Olympics being televised, the skiers still speeding down the snowy slopes. As he watched, one of the skiers fell and skidded and spun into a net fence.

"He done a *huli!*" Wallis said.

May was still introducing Sharkey to the others at the table: a solemn Chinese man — "My brother-in-law, Kenton, Winnie's husband" — and four small children — "Nieces and nephews" — whose names were lost in the noise.

One of the small girls was kneeling on a chair with a boy standing next to her, both of them giggling and taking turns as they jammed handfuls of rice into a drinking glass half filled with water, while another boy lay on the floor kicking the legs of Sharkey's chair.

"Winston was Chinese Man of the Year," May said, "at the Tien Tao Ming Society." And Winston heard — he nodded — but went on tonging food with his chopsticks. "Like she says, Winnie's a nurse, but she's super-important at Queen's. If someone is, like, having a spasm, they'll call her. See that little box? It's her beeper. She'll get beeped and she'll have to go."

"Pager," Winnie said, patting it.

"These children," Sharkey said, his chair jogged with the boy's kicks.

"Two are Winston's, the other two Winnie's," May said. "This is Galen," of the boy thrashing on the floor among scraps of food.

Seeing the boy on the floor, the old woman said, "Oh, da cute!"

"You try the pig?" Wallis said to Sharkey, tapping her chopsticks on the platter of dark shredded kalua pig. "They *imu* it round the back. Hee Hing famous for it."

Before Sharkey could respond, Winston said to his mother, "I told that fricken haole guy he never join the *hui*. Hell with him. He never bring no *omiyage* for present."

"Because of that wahine," the old woman said. "She big trouble."

"Plus plenny *niele*," Winston said. "Never keep her nose out of other people business. She part Hawaiian, and the other part maybe Portugee."

"I came back from the war," May's father said, still nibbling a chicken foot reflectively, and gesturing with it as he spoke. "I thought maybe I join the Elks Club. But my *pakay* friends say, 'Don't do it, Wallace.' I say" — he chewed and swallowed and now had the whole table's attention — "I say, 'I give it a try.' But was no good. The Elks then was too much haole and some Portugees. Exclusive kine."

May said, "But they never let any wahine join up."

"No wahine in the Tien Tao Ming," Winston said. "That's why it same like a secret society."

"What's the Tien Tao Ming?" Sharkey asked, intending to be polite.

But when Winston did not reply, May said, "Like a club. Chinese kine."

"You got one job, mister?" May's mother asked.

"Joe's a surfer," May said.

"That one job?" The old woman smiled at the thought.

Sharkey's shoulders moved with the kicks against his chair. He said, "I got some sponsors, a few endorsements. I'm competing on the tour."

"Where you go?" Wallis asked, and she too was moving, beating her feet on the floor, her knees jogging up and down.

"Wherever there are waves," Sharkey said, and realized that May had slipped to the other side of the table, where she sat between her father and Winston.

"The bitter melon," Winnie said. "So *ono*. I eat it fast before they beep me!" She spooned some into Sharkey's bowl.

"Eh, stop it, kids," Wallis said to the two who were still filling water glasses with handfuls of rice.

"I can discipline my own *keiki*," Winnie said, and pushed the glasses to the center of the table. She scowled at the children. "Don't waste food."

"They so *kolohe!*" May called out. "Oh, da pretty."

At that, the children darted under the table — Sharkey felt them bumping his feet. He looked to May for relief, but she was hugging her father, nuzzling his neck.

Wallis said, "Wendy was a late baby. Kind of a caboose. My mother *hapai* when she was late-forty-something. Eh, Ma?"

Hearing her name, the old woman looked up and seemed to see Sharkey for the first time. "You from mainland?"

"I came here when I was little. My dad was military."

The word seemed to cast a blight upon the table, killing conversation, and no one had a response.

"He died," Sharkey said.

And that was worse, a darkening that was palpable. May's mother frowned, Wallis grasped her hair and gagged a little, Winnie looked for refuge in her pager, studying its green light. But it was not a silence, only a pause that was filled by the howl and racket of the restaurant. They looked at the television sets, where a dark figure speeding down a ski jump took flight.

Winston solemnly unfastened the flap of his briefcase and brought out large squares of red paper stamped with gold Chinese characters. He handed one to the old man and said, "Long life, Pop."

May's father plucked a chewed chicken foot out of his mouth. He said, "No. It say, 'Good Fortune.'"

"Same thing to me," Winston said.

"Chinese Man of the Year," May said, and Sharkey could not tell whether she was mocking her brother or praising him. But he didn't respond, he was still handing his father lengths of gold-printed red paper.

"This one is 'Fa' — Make money," he said. "This one 'Double Happiness.'"

One of May's arms was around her father, the other around her brother's shoulder. "This my double happiness," she said. "My *ohana*."

"He no like bitter melon," May's mother said.

Sharkey looked at his bowl, green blobs afloat in their own viscous juice, where Winnie had dropped them.

"These *fun* noodles," the mother said. And tapping the rim of dishes at the center of the table, she said, "Teriyaki chicken. Lomi salmon. That macaroni. Potstickers. Plenty poi. No more chicken feet left!"

"I'm good with this," Sharkey said, and prodded the goop in his bowl.

May said, "Joe was a lifeguard at Ali'i — Waimea too. Monster waves there keep him busy."

"What kine money they make?" Winnie asked, still staring at her beeper.

Winston sniffed and said, "That fricken haole guy was so bummed out when I told him we don't need him, or his wahine. He so ignorant of the culture rules. Take your money somewhere else, I said."

Wallis said, "Eh. You could be one yakuza gangsta man with all them tattoos."

"You have any children?" Sharkey replied, folding his arms, trying to minimize his visible ink.

"Got a poi dog. Real ugly mutt," Wallis said. "That's my baby." Then she poked Sharkey's arm and said, "Eh, you a good conversationalist."

Sharkey could not think of a reply. He saw that May had found a baby and was holding it, making noises at it. Embracing her father, hugging Winston, bouncing the baby on her lap, she was in her element. "Brandon!" she cried to the baby's face. "You have one luau next month! Say aloha to Uncle Joe!" She was more content than he'd seen her — happier than when she'd surfed a big wave. She was not a surf bunny; she was the obedient daughter of a stern unsmiling man, a member of a family, a tight fit in an *ohana*.

"Get one *keiki* for yourself!" Wallis said to May, pinching the baby's cheek — too hard; the baby began to bawl.

The family: how Hawaiian they were, Sharkey thought — more Hawaiian than they perhaps knew, and they might have objected if he'd mentioned it, since they presented themselves as having so much Chinese pride.

"Be right back," he said, to get away from the crying baby, and stumbled through the packed restaurant to go to the lanai to smoke a joint. Other men were there, smoking cigarettes.

One of the men said through his teeth, *"Gong hei fat choy."*

"Far out, man," Sharkey said, swallowing smoke, squinting in the glare of the afternoon sun. He turned and put his forehead against the glass of the restaurant window and, searching the room, at last found the Wong table.

At Roosevelt he had been the bullied haole, yet he'd had a vague sense of attachment, doing battle and sometimes winning. But at this meal, with this family, in this restaurant of Chinese families yelling and eating, he had never felt so alien. The mention of surfing evoked nothing but murmurs of disapproval. May seemed unable to defend Sharkey to her family, but worse, Sharkey was incapable of defending himself.

A family somehow fitted together, unlike the Colonel and his mother and him, not a family but strange pairings for him, first with his father, then with his mother, all of them discontented, a bad fit. The Wongs were exuberant, and May was one of them, with a role as respectful daughter, adoring her father, humoring her mother, admiring her brother and sisters. She fooled with the children, whom Sharkey saw as annoying. But he was an outsider, he was not entitled to an opinion, and anyway even the pesky children belonged to the family. These brats had membership. He smiled, remembering how he'd seen May as a sister, and hoped he might be brotherly until she allowed him more access. He'd liked their abstinence, no hugs, once or twice a chaste kiss on her cool lips. He was glad it had gone no further: her keeping him away had freed him. There was nothing to explain, nothing to apologize for. He was a stranger.

Buzzed from the *pakalolo*, he peered at May's father and imagined saying to him, "You have nothing to fear from me. I want nothing from you. I am May's friend, that's all — and hardly a friend. Just a haole who surfs with her."

When he returned to the table, the old man was holding a red restaurant menu and peering through wire-rimmed glasses. "It say here the rat is *aka-*

mai. Very clever. Save things—save money, and maybe a little cheap with money too. Have lots of children."

"*Iole* we call rats when I live on Big Island—some *iole nui* come so big," Mrs. Wong said. "Trouble with rats is too many *keiki.*"

Then Wallis turned from the snow scene on the television screen, hitched herself in her chair. "*Lai see!*" she said, and the children shrieked.

"Money," May said.

The old man was shuffling a thickness of red envelopes. He tapped them on the table to straighten them and worked them with his thumbs.

"There goes my pager," Winnie said. She stood up, brushed crumbs from her scrubs, and said, "Mummy's got to go to work." And to the solemn man, "Kenny, get them in line."

Kenton pushed the children toward to the old man, the children falling silent, a faint expression of hunger on their faces, which were smeared with food. One by one they crept near the old man, who handed each one a red envelope. Clasping the envelopes in sticky fingers, rewarded, they dropped to the floor and fought for space between the chairs while the others re-sumed eating.

"When you was born?" Mr. Wong suddenly asked Sharkey.

"Forty-eight," Sharkey said.

The old man picked up the menu again and ran his finger down the back of it and exclaimed, whipping off his glasses. "Was a rat year too!"

"I born fifty-one," May said. "Rabbit year."

"You're a bunny," Sharkey said. "I knew that."

"Let's see," the old man said, tapping a yellow fingernail on the menu. Then he grunted. "It say here that rabbit and rat not compatible."

"Yo, heinous!" Sharkey said, and laughed, and wondered if anyone would notice he was stoned. "What a shame."

Winston said, "Maybe a blessing."

Slightly dazed from smoking the joint, Sharkey remembered a fragment of what he had planned to say to the old man. He turned to Winston and spread his arms for drama and said, "You have nothing to fear from me, man."

The *pakalolo* had deafened him, and he could not tell whether Winston, or anyone, had heard. No one reacted, though he'd meant it as a thunderous statement.

May was seated next to her brother, and Sharkey saw that they were hold-ing hands.

"Or you, Bunny," Sharkey said, and felt the need for more smoke. "I'm going outside. Don't wait for me."

13

Naming a Wave

A notion that made Sharkey laugh was to name a place, any place on earth — Paraguay, Albania, Baluchistan — and the Hawaiian surfer, innocent on his tiny islands far from the world, looked hopeful and asked, "Got waves there?" But Sharkey could be innocent too, and that was how he heard there was a wave at Christmas Island. He was certain that it hadn't been ridden, at least not by anyone on the tour, because the wave had no name.

The mention had been casual, not the explosive blurt of a surfer with news of a big swell but offhand, from a fisherman he met, who'd flown down from Honolulu, the only route to Christmas Island, seeking bonefish in the flats of the lagoon.

"At the harbor mouth of the atoll, pretty awesome — rocked my boat."

"So you could surf it into the lagoon?"

"I guess."

Sharkey was reassured by this vagueness: a surfer would have known for sure. Sharkey wanted to know. The island now seemed virginal for its unnamed wave, a blue plow blade sliding in from the sea.

It was the spring of his biggest achievement so far, as the youngest winner of the Pipeline Masters. He used his prize money to buy a ticket. He zipped his board into its padded bag, triumphant in his second trip away from Hawaii, to surf the wave and maybe to name it. And at the end of the three-hour flight he pressed his face to the window as the plane banked for its descent. The island was shaped like a bulky magnifying glass, with a thick crusted coral handle, the lagoon serving as the lens, glacial milky blue, a smooth vitreous pool of magic in contrast to the dark ocean around it, frothy and windblown. In the distance, at the break in the reef, a rolling wave lifted, white-maned, and — he was still squinting — no one on it.

As for the rest, the island was narrow beaches and coconut palms, some smudges of villages, a perimeter road without vehicles, no large buildings, a place outside time but with a landing strip much wider and longer than he'd expected.

Off the plane, onto the glare of the tarmac, the passengers awaited their luggage — mostly older men, some of them islanders in white shirts and long pants, and a contingent of fishermen in khaki shorts traveling together. The luggage yanked from the plane was piled in the sunshine to be claimed. A woman standing apart, a brown Madonna in a billowy green long-sleeved dress that reached to her ankles, holding a baby, was trying to get the attention of one of the porters, who was intent on retrieving a duffel bag for a fisherman.

Sharkey caught her eye. But a man in an aloha shirt stepped between them. "Can I help you?"

"That box" — she gestured with the baby — "it mine."

Sharkey watched as the man seized the heavily taped cardboard box.

"It my toaster."

"And there's your bread," the man said with a grim smile — a large carton labeled as forty loaves of white bread from a Honolulu bakery. *Fresh-Baked, Home-Sliced. The Taste of the Isles.*

Then the man turned to Sharkey and said, "Congratulations."

Sharkey smiled to cover his confusion.

"I saw you at the Pipe," the man said. "You killed it. Gerry didn't do too bad either."

"Thanks."

"You guys have youth on your side."

Saying that, the man sounded rueful. He wore flip-flops, board shorts, his feet dirty, his nose burned, but he had the broad shoulders and slim sinewy legs of a surfer, and though his hair was wild it was thick and sun-scorched, and when he extended his hard-knuckled fingers — showing a pale, peeling, almost amphibious paw — Sharkey knew he was a waterman.

He shook hands, the complex Masonic grip of North Shore surfers, but resented being compared with Gerry Lopez, whom he felt he'd outscored on the day.

"Doc Bowers," the man said.

"I know why you're here," Sharkey said.

The doubting way the man cocked his head and smiled reminded Sharkey of how the older surfers had always regarded him until he'd proved himself at the Pipeline. The old have a special smile they use on the young, and it is the more pitying and patronizing when nothing more is said.

So Sharkey said, "This your first time here?"

"They only started regular flights here a year ago," the man said, and when Sharkey didn't ask why, he added, "I've been looking at the weather. When there's a big southerly swell, like now, that wave's insane."

He hated hearing the man's enthusiasm and seeing his gusto in the tightening gulp of his throat, because it was how he too felt, and any discovery shared was a discovery diminished. He thought of himself as a loner, and he felt mocked and subverted, as when he believed he had an original thought or impulse and he came across someone else who had the same one.

Wanting always to be first, he felt undermined by everything the man was telling him, especially "Maybe we could ride it together."

That the man had not given the break a name gave Sharkey hope.

"First I need to find a place to stay," he said.

"I know some people."

Sharkey resented that too. The man was way ahead of him; Sharkey had no names.

"Please identify your bags," a man in a gray uniform said to them.

They indicated their boards in the big padded sleeves, and their duffels — Sharkey noticed that the man had brought some boxes of food, but did not remark on it, or anything more; he felt already the man knew too much.

"I guess we're the only two freaks here," Doc said.

Outside the small airport building, which was no more than a shed, onlookers stood behind a fence, their fingers hooked on the mesh. One ragged islander in a misshapen bush hat held a square of cardboard, crudely printed BOWERS.

"That's my man," Doc said, and waved.

The man touched his hat, greeting Doc, then introduced him to an older man in a white gown next to him. "This is our fadda priest" — Doc shook the man's hand — "and this our dive master Tofinga" — another handshake — "and my friend Tawita."

Excluded from the familiarity and friendliness, Sharkey said, "There's a hotel here, right?"

"Captain Cook," the priest said.

"Also known as Main Camp," Doc said. "Or you can join me in the village."

"I'm okay," Sharkey said. He hoisted his board bag and jammed it under his arm, and when one of the islanders, stepping forward, said, "Taxi?" Sharkey handed him his duffel and tried to push past the waiting men.

"If I can help," the priest said, reaching and touching his arm.

"I'll be fine," Sharkey said. Again he resented being crowded and imposed upon, when all he wanted was to ride the wave alone. He wished to separate himself from these people, to be away and on his own.

He found the hotel, and a room smelling of its painted cinder blocks; he rented a pickup truck, and he set off the next morning to drive to the far corner of the island, to find his own way of getting to the wave.

There was only one road, dead flat, paved for a few miles, then rutted coral and loose stones and packed sand, and after twenty minutes he slowed to a halt and got out to determine what progress he'd made by taking a look at the lagoon. He walked in the direction of the water through the head-high saltbush scrub, big-winged birds flying up from where his elbows bumped the branches, and he smelled the sour sun-dried seaweed and the sting of salt before he stepped onto crystalline boulders of coral and beheld the great gleaming lagoon. More beaky birds took flight at his appearance on the stony shore. He saw that he was less than halfway to the far side of the lagoon.

Turning his back to the lagoon, he hurried to his pickup truck and in his hurry became lost in the hot air and speckled shadow trapped beneath the low canopy of thorny bush and twisted scrub that stank of marine decay, dead fish and dried barnacles. The broken coral at his feet looked like bleached and shattered bones. What had seemed like the path he'd taken was a rut of packed-down coral dust like a game trail. He saw movement ahead — the fidget of a feral cat, another panicked bird, and the sunlight burning through the meager dusty leaves.

He could not climb the spindly stalks to see where he was; the thorns tore at his arms and he was mocked again — a hundred feet into this vegetation and, ducking and thrashing, he saw no way out, no access to the road and his truck. He ran and stumbled, then sat and, short of breath, wondered whether he was impatient or afraid. Perspiration smeared the blood on his arms. He heard a squawk and called out, as though in reply; but it was a bird.

And then at the height of his panic, flushing another bird — roosting frigate bird — and scarcely able to breathe, he saw the red of his truck through the bush and credited that 'iwa bird with saving him, the bird an omen, directing him. He sat in the truck, simply breathing, hot with anxiety, glad to be alone with his shame at having become so easily lost.

Back on the road, he resolved to stay with his truck and followed the road for several miles, until he came to a grove of coconut palms. The rows and ranks of palms reassured him with their symmetry and their abandonment — they had been set there by a human hand, but it seemed the humans had fled, leaving the place to him.

There were no people anywhere here; the road was overgrown with weeds, and the only vehicle he saw was a wreck, resting on its axles, its front end sunk in sand. Farther on he found a deserted village — empty roofless huts of what had been a coconut plantation — and a barrier of mangroves, their exposed roots opening onto a view of the lagoon. He considered looking for the wave, but seeing that the sun was setting, he feared becoming lost again. He pitched his tent, and in the gathering dusk the mosquitoes and blowflies began to bite. He lit his camp stove, boiled some water for noodles, then crawled into his tent and zipped it against the insects and lay listening to the chatter and whine of night creatures and tried to sleep, insisting to himself that the day had not been a failure.

This neck of the atoll, which had once been wild and then planted with palms, was wild once more. The night air was like black silk, the crescent moon was bleached and pitted and coralline too, and at last he forgave himself and gave thanks for the darkness, the muffled bird squawks, the distant lap of waves against the mangrove knees. The earthen odor, of decaying palm fronds and blackening coconuts and the tang of dead fish — all this, hidden in the thickness of brush and scrub, caused him to rejoice in being alone on this empty spit of coral.

In the morning, hot at seven, under a cloudless sky, he fired up his stove again and made tea, ate one of the energy bars he'd brought from Hawaii, and, leaving his board and his truck, set out to find the wave. This time he noted carefully the way to the edge of the lagoon. He walked slowly, memorizing the path, and when he came to the pocket beach in the slot between the mangroves he saw the low promontory that was one pincer tip of the atoll — a density of palms on tumbled coral — and the white lip in the water that was probably the wave. It was so distant he could not determine its height, though its face was good-sized, and in the glassy conditions it slid from the sea between the pincers of coral that formed the mouth of the atoll before breaking where the water was smooth, another one lifting behind it, and more, a set of six. He saw himself crouched on the leading wave, jamming his board into the blue tube, making a dramatic entrance, riding into the lagoon.

Beyond the sliding wave and the pale blue water, on the far shore, was a small scattered village, low buildings of rough boards, fronds stacked on the roof, looking plunked down and ugly among the graceful palms, and farther on, taller than the palms, the square spire of a church.

It was too far to paddle to the wave, so, looking for access, Sharkey walked along the irregular edge of the lagoon, slapping at branches and stumbling on the rubble of broken coral. But even an hour of walking brought him no closer, and his walking convinced him that the wave was inaccessible from this side of the atoll. He knew the deception of sea distances, and even if he reached the promontory ahead, it was a mile or more paddle to the wave — too far. And so he picked some passionfruit from stringy vines that were twined on the spindly saltbush branches, and that was his lunch. He dozed for a while but was woken by flies on his face, and then — taking care

— made his way back to the pocket beach and the beaten trail and his little camp.

Telling himself it was wrong to hurry, he decided to spend another night, and again he gloried in the wildness of the place, the scrape of the palm fronds, the nameless birds that squawked in the night, the slosh that carried from the lagoon's edge, and he congratulated himself: surfing was not only the search for a great wave or a shore break; it was in its essence the discovery of a place like this.

After his early start the following morning he saw, with surprise and pleasure, something he had missed before — a profusion of rusted machinery, old tractors and dump trucks and bulldozers, their paint peeled off, falling to pieces in the jungle beside the road, disintegrating into heaps of reddish flakes, becoming part of the planet again.

But he could see they had been serious machines, perhaps the equipment of the coconut plantation, used for clearing and plowing the land. Some had metal tanklike treads rather than rubber tires. And as though defying their decay, the palms were heavy with clusters of unpicked nuts, and the fallen ones darkened the floor of the groves, some of them newly sprouted.

He drove on, satisfied that he had seen the wave and identified it as rideable. It was too hard to access from the inner shore beyond the camp he'd made, but it seemed approachable from the village on the far side of the harbor mouth. With this in mind he drove for another hour, past the airport and the hotel and some roadside settlements that might have been villages, and saw that he had rounded the atoll. This side was inhabited, with flimsy huts and fences, a few scrawny dogs sleeping in the road, chickens pecking under the palms, and children playing.

He was disappointed by the sight of the huts and the litter: it was not possible to be alone here, and he realized with his first glimpse of the children in the road and the men squatting among the trees, motionless, like vegetation themselves, that he had been buoyed at his camp in the palm grove because it was uninhabited. But idyllic was an unattainable state, even on this small atoll, and he told himself that it was the squalor and the idleness here and the skinny kids and the lame dogs that made it real.

Just ahead he saw the church he'd spotted from across the lagoon, and what had seemed like solid granite from a distance was gray-painted wood, simple clumsy carpentry on a large scale, the blunt and splintery steeple, the great flat front of the church mimicking a cathedral, and above the double doors a circular window painted green and yellow to resemble stained glass.

The priest he'd seen at the airport was standing with some children, peaceful in conversation, his hand on the shoulder of one of them.

Sharkey thought, as he had at his camp, what did it matter if there was surf or not? The rumor of a wave had enticed him, but what mattered was that he had found this peaceful island.

He greeted the priest and said, "I saw you at the airport a few days ago."

"Yes, I remember."

But Sharkey had been brisk with him, and he hoped the priest had not remembered his rudeness in wishing to get away.

"I was on the other side of the island," Sharkey said. "No people."

"Because of the bombs," the priest said.

"Right," Sharkey said. "I'm trying to find the best way to the wave."

The priest nodded, saying, "Your friend was saying the same thing."

Sharkey tried to hide his annoyance. Affecting to be casual, he said, "He's probably ridden it by now."

The priest's face gave nothing away. He said, "You can ask him. I saw him going into town this morning."

"There's a town here?"

"We call it a town," the priest said softly. "It's just over there" — and he pointed to where the road curved into more palm groves. "The bar and the dive shop and the boatyard where they do some repairs. Your friend won't be hard to find, though he seemed to be in a hurry."

Sharkey leaned toward the priest with a question in his eyes.

"People move slowly here," the priest explained, having read Sharkey's expression. "Your friend was walking fast."

Sharkey said, "Have you ever seen anyone ride that wave?"

The priest shook his head. "We have some divers and fishermen, all of them i-matang — outsiders. The people here seldom swim."

"What do they do?"

"They do what people do on small islands. They fish in the lagoon. They gather coconuts. They play. They quarrel."

The town was as the priest had said — one street, a few shops, a pier, a bar with a veranda that overlooked the harbor, some beached and broken boats, a low-tide odor of decayed fish and slime drying from green to black. Sharkey parked his pickup truck, and as soon as he got out and slammed the door he heard, "Joe Sharkey."

The man who called himself Doc had darted from the bar — and Sharkey was gratified to see that he was unchanged, wild hair and trampled flip-flops and the same aloha shirt but unbuttoned. Yet even under the rags he had the physique of a surfer — the shoulders, the legs, the burned hair, the hands pink and boiled-looking from soakings in seawater.

The man said, "Doc," as though to reassure him.

"How's it?"

"Insane, man," Doc said, but in a soft wondering way, and he went on, speaking in a disbelieving tone that was the more alarming for being a near-whisper. "The place where I was staying? It's just a hut in the palms. But the first night I'm there I hear these noises, someone getting hosed, that rocking sound and those unmistakable sighs. I think, 'Beautiful.' But at breakfast I'm talking to the guy — that one you saw, with the hat — and we're being served by this young teenaged girl — eggs, tea, papaya."

The man stopped and shook his head.

Sharkey said, "I'm listening."

"I said, 'Your wife's young.' He looks at me. 'My daughter. My wife's off-island.' I was thinking how I once had a daughter that age. So I left. I found a room here in town behind the bar. It's nothing, but the vibe is better."

Doc looked hard at Sharkey, sadness in his eyes, helplessness in his posture, his arms to his sides, flexing his empty hands.

Sharkey said, "You been on the wave?"

The man didn't speak, he was thinking of something else, but Sharkey was elated when with just the slightest toss of his head the man said, "Nah." Then he straightened and added, "I've been watching it. Grinds out some steep barrels."

"You stoked?" Sharkey asked.

But Doc just smiled that older man's smile.

Sharkey said, "I've been on the other side of the island. No one there."

"Because of the bombs."

It was what the priest had said. Sharkey said, "Was this place in the war?"

"I'm having a beer," Doc said, turning away and walking to the bar.

And that was another thing that older people did — didn't answer a question, said something else entirely, as though you hadn't spoken, to make you small.

"Soft drink for me," Sharkey said on the veranda of the bar, and when Doc ordered a beer, Sharkey had the urge to see the man drunk. He wanted to see him incapable of riding the wave today, too drunk to stand, hungover tomorrow.

"Big bombs," Doc said. He kicked off his flip-flops and rested his feet on the veranda rail. Now Sharkey saw a bandage on Doc's foot, but it was so dirty he had not noticed it until the foot was raised.

"How big?"

"The first tests were three-megaton H-bombs, but the yield-to-weight ratio made them more destructive — measured in terajoules, they were bigger by far than the one we dropped on Hiroshima. First the Brits in the fifties. Then us. In the sixties we set off twenty-four shots."

"I didn't see any craters."

"Atmospheric tests," he said, pointing upward with his bottle of beer. "Some from planes at eighteen thousand feet, some suspended from tethered balloons. No craters, unless you count genetic damage, genomic instability in DNA, birth defects, high levels of ionizing radiation, and radioactive contamination." He swigged his beer. "Cancer."

"There were people here on the island?"

Bearded, sweating, he went on drinking, but he was unexpectedly full of information. "Not many, a few hundred. They were instructed to put blankets over their heads so they wouldn't see the flash. No one told the birds. All the birds were blinded."

"And you know this how?"

"I'm a physicist, man. Cal Tech. I went to Hawaii to surf fifteen years ago and never looked back." He drank again but held the beer in his mouth for a moment as though in reflection. Finally he swallowed and asked, "This bombing is news to you?"

"I heard something. I thought it was Bikini where the tests were."

The man didn't answer at once, though when he did, he spoke casually, dismissively, disgustedly. "Way west of here, in the Marshalls. Another nuclear disaster."

"I saw a lot of heavy equipment on the other side of the island."

"Abandoned by the military. They dug huge holes and buried a lot of it, the rest they left to rot — too expensive to take it away." Now Doc smiled, a drunken smile. "It's a hole."

"What happened to your foot?"

"Gashed it on the beach yesterday when I was scoping out the wave."

"Coral's sharp."

"Broken bottle. There's glass everywhere. Rusty cans. Plastic."

"So," Sharkey said, and paused and nodded, "you make it to the wave?"

"Didn't want to risk it with this foot. The priest bandaged it — the clinic was closed." He smiled again. "This island is freaking me out," and what he said was the more disturbing for being whispered.

Sharkey said, "I was beginning to enjoy it. Now I'm not so sure." He leaned toward Doc and said in a low voice, "I got lost in the bushes by the lagoon."

Doc laughed loudly. "That's funny. When Captain Cook came here, some of his men went ashore. They immediately got lost — for a couple of days! It's the freaky vegetation. The island was uninhabited. It was perfect. But Jimmy Cook named it and put it on the map. Other ships visited. It became a coconut plantation. Then a bomb site and a junkyard. Now it's what you see — a dump."

Sharkey looked around and sniffed. "What's that smell?"

"Oil spill on the slipway — someone must have dropped a barrel." He finished his beer, then said, "Do me a favor? Help me move my board? It's still at that guy's hut."

"Are you going to surf with that foot?"

"Maybe not. But I don't want to leave my board with that criminal. His own daughter, man!"

So Sharkey drove Doc down the road past the church and into the palm grove on a rutted track to the hut, which was a tin-roofed plywood box, painted green, sitting on cinder blocks. A man sat on the front steps, smoking a cigarette.

"That's Dad," Doc said under his breath.

He was a dark frowning man in a torn T-shirt and shorts, his elbows resting on his knees, the cigarette in one hand, an open can of sardines in the other, and what Sharkey noticed was the size of his hands, the thick fingers, the way they dripped with oil.

"I'm here for my board."

The man hesitated, moved his mouth as though to speak, then went on chewing.

In its padded sleeve bag it leaned against the hut, but the bottom edge of the bag was torn, the stuffing pulled out.

"Who messed with my board?"

The man chewed, then, twirling one finger into the can of sardines, he said, "Was a rat," and went on chewing.

Nothing more was said. Doc lifted his board into the bed of the pickup, and as they drove away from the palm grove and were nearer the road, Doc said, "There she is."

A young girl in a school uniform, white blouse, blue skirt, was walking toward them. Sharkey slowed and stopped. Doc leaned out of the window.

"Remember me?"

"Yah."

The girl's thin face was set in a resentful, almost sulky expression, her underlip protruding. But perhaps she was shy, guarded, averse to questions.

"How's school?"

The girl made a face, not at the question but at the man who asked it, and said nothing.

"Everything all right?"

Now she did seem resentful, and she nodded, then turned and walked up the path where the man, her father, was waiting.

Doc sighed, and as he did Sharkey saw the island anew, as if for the first time. He had been thinking only of the wave and the best way to approach it. Nothing else had mattered to him. But now he was seeing the island with Doc's eyes, another place entirely, and he wished he had not known.

He had always surfed alone. History and customs and holidays didn't interest him, except when they impeded his surfing. He was proud of surfing every Christmas Day—the surf was always up in December. "Surf is my religion."

He did not want to know what Doc knew. He told himself that Doc was trying to impress him. Doc was a dropout, and like most dropouts he retained his old instincts and habits. He was not a competitive single-minded surfer. Doc's problem was that he knew too much.

But the next day, Doc with a newly bandaged foot helped him carry his board down the slipway, and he watched like a proud parent as Sharkey paddled out to the wave and sat rocking on the back of the swell, now and then riding it, exploding through the barrel.

And for Sharkey the wave was pure and ageless and eternal; no matter how badly the island had been abused, the wave remained the same, unspoiled, the same shape it had been centuries before, when it had rocked the sailing ship of Captain James Cook. Sharkey surfed for the remainder of his week on Christmas Island, claiming the wave as his own, rejoicing in it. Now and then he saw Doc onshore, a tiny figure in an aloha shirt sitting on the pier.

He saw that he'd been wrong—wrong about Doc. Wrong about the island, wrong in his judgments and his sarcasm, wrong about himself. But in this small, flat, crusted, and contaminated atoll, humming with flies, the itch of dog fur rising from its rotting coconuts, its littered beaches and reeking villages—the glowering man with the big oily fingers—in all this the wave was a muscle of water that lifted him and carried him forward, a thing deserving of a name. The wave at least was pure. He hadn't been wrong about that.

One of those nights, stinking of diesel and chattering with the racket of the bar's generator, under the glare of fluorescent tubes, Sharkey fist-bumped Doc and said, "Call it Jimmy's."

14

A House at Jocko's

Saving his money — the prizes, the endorsements, the annuity from his father's life insurance — he was able to buy a house by the sea on Pohakuloa Road, and saw Jock Sutherland's first ride on the break that he bestowed his name upon. With a house, his girlfriends stayed longer, weeks at a time. He grew fond of one, who called herself Sugar, because her Hawaiian name, Kaleoikaikaokalani — the Mighty Voice of Heaven — he found unpronounceable. Hawaiian-Chinese-Filipino, she was a beauty. He met her at a club in town.

"Not a surfer," he told his friends, "but she has other talents."

"All the wahine got those," was the usual response.

"Not like Sugar."

He could not imagine a future without her. "I'm done dogging chicks," he told himself. He married her in a ceremony on the beach, both of them draped with leis, flower crowns on their heads, all their friends attending — his were surfers in T-shirts and shorts, hers were from town, men in jackets, women in dresses. Their friends stood apart, and he could see at the reception afterward at the hotel in Turtle Bay that his friends, awkward in the formal gathering, kept together, got drunk, and left early.

A week later Sharkey called his mother from the pay phone at Foodland and told her his news. She said, "Oh, God," and sobbed, and he knew it had been the right decision not to invite her to the wedding.

Sugar wanted a baby. She said so, soon after they were married, indicating that there was plenty of room in the beachfront house at Jocko's.

"If we have a baby, we won't be able to travel," Sharkey said — he intended that summer to go to South Africa for the waves at Jeffreys Bay, their winter swell.

Sugar said, "I don't want to go."

"To South Africa?"

"To leave Hawaii."

She had been once to the mainland, to Las Vegas, and hated it. Las Vegas was the world. Hawaii had everything — why go anywhere?

Sugar and her friends and family distrusted the weather elsewhere, were comforted by their own food, reassured by the trade winds, and did not believe their sunshine could be duplicated anywhere else on earth. "Lucky we live Hawaii." Her family lived in Wahiawa; her father had once picked pineapples at Helemano and was now a civilian employee at the officers' mess at Schofield Barracks, her mother a cashier at the city tax office near the Wahiawa Police Station. They were proud of their haole son-in-law. They wanted a baby too, their first grandchild. No one had mentioned any of this beforehand: so much was revealed now.

Having grown up in a town in the middle of the island, Sugar was ill at ease living on the beach. The sound of surf kept her awake, and she told Sharkey about her fears of being flooded and drowned, imagining a wave rising up and breaking over the house. She was a poor swimmer, she never sat in the sun, she said surf meets were too long, she didn't drink or smoke. She yearned for a child.

An island girl, a simple girl, he'd thought; then he knew — no one is simple. Had she been a surfer, they might have spent their days together. Now even their nights were fractured by arguments, by silences, to the sound of the waves on the rocks in front of their house. In her sadness, and sometimes grief, it was as though a baby had been stolen from her, a phantom child she longed to possess.

Sugar's disappointment at their divorce was mixed with relief. He was not the sunny guy with money that she'd married but a selfish haole who cared only about surfing with his friends, nothing else. Her parents were angry: he'd let them down, he'd misled their daughter, and the divorce was a humiliation for them.

"And now all the paperwork," Sugar's father said.

But Sharkey hired a lawyer and gave them the amount of money they asked for, and his car, the furniture from C. S. Wo, and the cat. He kept his house at Jocko's, emptier now.

Sharkey's mother seemed grimly satisfied — perhaps she'd hoped he'd fail. The divorce was proof that she could not be replaced. And when he began avoiding his mother, in what seemed a self-destructive act of revenge — but it could have been a result of her drinking — she broke her hip, became housebound, insisted on a wheelchair until her hip healed, drank more, and demanded that he leave her alone.

"Go ahead, do what you want. I have Milly."

Milly was a middle-aged Filipina in green scrubs, who declared at the outset, "I am a licensed caregiver." She was gracious, attentive to the point of being a fussing hoverer, and she assured Sharkey that she would look after his mother as though she were her own mother. She moved in, slept in Sharkey's old bedroom, took charge, cooked, and cleaned, dragging a mop from room to room over the hardwood floors. Her cousin Orlando — Sharkey suspected him of being her lover — became a live-in handyman, bunking in the shed behind the garage.

Sharkey had seen enough of such arrangements to understand the ominous implications. Courts in the islands heard the cases all the time: the caregiver moves in, bonds with, and then dominates the employer, gets written into a new will, displacing the family. And the thwarted, disinherited family members litigate for what they believe is rightfully theirs, but in vain. The intrusive, usurping caregiver inheriting the house and the fortune of the employer was a common story in Hawaii; most moneyed families had a version of it — grotesque, melodramatic, farcical, or violent, depending on how much money was involved, but always with the same result, the servants ending up with everything. People who had much less, hearing these stories, clucked in sympathy but believed that there was justice in it.

His mother knew that, and the more she said, "Milly's a treasure, Ollie can fix anything," the more resigned he was to finding a renter for the house at Jocko's and moving back, enduring his mother's final years, simply to protect her.

Turned out of the house, Milly bared her teeth at him and hissed like a snake, certain proof that she was as greedy as he suspected. But she had beautiful teeth. She stole some of his mother's jewelry just before she left. Orlando growled and made vague threats, saying, "I'm not leaving this island," and made off with some tools from the garage.

"This is as it should be," his mother said. "Just the two of us."

Surfing calmed him, he competed more, and with his winning, his mother insisted on going with him to the North Shore, though she dozed in the car for most of the way, waking to the sound of the surf when he rolled down the windows at Waimea.

Sharkey was having his picture taken one day at Ali'i Beach and heard a familiar fluttery voice: "I'm his mother." She ran to his side and posed with him, girlish, waving to the camera.

She had been too young to be a widow, and she was now too young to be an invalid. She complained of obscure aches, and Sharkey hated her for what he took to be her dishonest complaints, for his captivity, having to spend every night under her roof. It was as though he were sitting on a swell, waiting for a wave to take him away, but there was nothing to ride.

He wished her dead, and one night she complained of chest pains. "And my arm!" Sharkey took her to Queen's Hospital in spite of his skepticism — she said she was in agony; he believed she was drunk again. She was admitted and wheeled away. At dawn the next day a nurse (he guessed) called him at home to say, "I'm sorry to tell you your mother has passed. We tried our best. It was her heart — congestive heart failure."

He was musing on the bland word "passed." She was hardly sixty. He had disliked her and doubted her, yet she had been telling the truth.

"Excuse me — did you hear?"

"Yes."

"Would you like to view the body?"

What was the point? And he feared the feelings the sight of his mother might provoke.

"No," he said, and asked for the body to be sent to Borthwick Mortuary.

In an unexpected turn, Milly and Orlando showed up at the cremation, loudly grieving, and later filed a suit challenging the will, which Sharkey fought off.

When people asked, Sharkey said, "It's tough — if you've been through a divorce and then your mother dies, you know what I mean."

Yet he was relieved; he'd ridden this wave to the shore, as he had with Sugar. He was unburdened, free to do what he wished. He tried to remember what it was that had impelled him to marry. But he knew the alluring woman he had proposed marriage to did not in the least resemble the unreasonable woman who became his wife — nor could he recall much about the allure. He gave thanks for his freedom, and five months later, just before he went to South Africa, he saw Sugar at the tax office visiting her mother; he was at the Registry of Motor Vehicles across the hall, renewing his driver's license. He was delighted to see that she was as pretty as ever, forgiving, dressed in a loose blouse. Beaming beautifully, she said, *"Hapai"* — pregnant. Not married, she said, but was planning to; her fiancé was a policeman — "Dispatch," she said — in the same building.

"He knows you," Sugar said. "Your career."

"Why are you smiling?"

"It's incredulous."

South Africa, cold in July, was strange and bleak. The long flight to Jo'burg, the connecting flight to Cape Town, and, as always, he looked for surf when the plane banked toward the city, flying parallel to the coastline and the great granite flat-topped mountain. He'd come alone—none of his friends could afford the trip, though all of them had heard of the waves at Jeffreys Bay.

The taxi driver who took him to his hotel said, "American?" and then, "You've got problems with your Blacks too."

"I live in Hawaii," Sharkey said.

"I saw that movie," and then, "Hula-hula."

"What problems?"

"Not with the Blacks as such," the man said, "but these whites who want to start trouble. Blacks aren't the problem. The whites who stir things up are the problem. All Blacks want is a push-bike and a little rondavel to raise their kids. What do they know about voting? They never had a vote. They obey the chief." Then he stopped at a red light and looked around. "And by the way, you want to stay out of this area—it's all Blacks and coloreds mixed in."

"What is this area?"

"District Six."

Sharkey then counted the streets from there to the hotel, and after he checked in, needing to walk, he went back to the area the driver had warned him about, District Six. It was a chilly evening, dark, with a damp wind from the harbor. Down a side street he heard loud music from a building and entered—a club that was filled with people dancing to a band. The men were dressed in suits and ties, and some women in bright dresses lingered at the bar, smiling at Sharkey in his sweatshirt as he passed them.

"Where do you come from?" a woman asked. She was tall, with a shaved head, in a long loose gown. Purple lipstick suited her blackness and shimmered in the light of the glitter ball.

"America."

"I want to see a real cowboy," she said, laughing.

"I'm a real cowboy," he said, and the woman laughed harder. "Have a beer."

At once the woman ceased laughing and raised her hand, gesturing as she spoke, in a marveling voice. "I was born in this city. I have lived here my whole life. I tell you no white man has ever bought me a bottle of beer." She ordered it in her own language, shouting at the barman and seeming to announce it to the women near her, and pushed a stool toward Sharkey.

They drank together in silence for a while, the woman smiling, then she said, "What are you doing here, man?"

"Looking for waves."

"None in this place!" Her laugh was full-throated, attracting attention, but the women who heard her laughed too, as though inspired.

"Jeffreys Bay."

"That is too far away. Eastern Cape. You will need a car."

"I'll get a car."

He needed to repeat it. The music was so loud they had difficulty hearing each other, so they listened to the music instead. The crush of people, many of them staring at Sharkey, pushed them closer to each other. Sharkey marveled at the fact that he had been in the city such a short time — an hour or so — and he was among lively people, getting drunk, drenched in sweat, smothered by loud music — happy, feeling he'd found out how to belong.

When he caught the woman's eye he lowered his head and said in her ear, "What's your name?"

"Thandi."

"Come with me to my hotel, Thandi."

"I will be arrested," she said, and grasped his arm. "Follow me."

She led him through the crowd at the bar and out a side door to an alley and, taking his hand, hurried him to the end of it, where in the semidarkness Sharkey saw a picket fence, higher than his head. Leaning against the fence, the woman lifted her long gown with one hand and drew Sharkey nearer to her with her other hand, tugging on his sleeve.

"What?"

"Jig-jig," she said.

Instinctively Sharkey looked around. A light burned over a doorway in the building they'd just left, but it was too distant and feeble to illuminate them. The alley was clammy-cold, the fence smelling of urine.

They were alone, he saw, but he was anxious, suddenly in this dark stinking place, and he began stalling, saying he was tired, he'd been on a long flight, and he was still talking as the woman groaned.

"Ach, we could have been finished by now."

The rental — a pickup truck the agent called a *bakkie* — came with warnings, some of them printed (*Do not leave valuables in the boot*) and some verbal. "No hitchhikers," the agent said. "And I'd advise you to hire a driver — you'll get there quicker. You'll have more time for surfing. Safer as well."

So Sharkey agreed and was introduced to Murad, a stocky man of about thirty, who volunteered that he was not Black. He was colored, he said — Malay and India, "and maybe a native, way back." He had gray eyes and his skin was sallow. He wore a thick sweater and a skullcap.

"They say the wave is a great right. The surf there."

"I know nothing about that," Murad said.

He was mostly silent after that, concentrating on the road, which was empty and straight in a landscape of low hills and thick bush, no villages, few houses, but here and there a glimpse of movement.

"What is that bird?"

"We call it a volstruis," Murad said. "You call it an ostrich."

Around noon, at a crossroads near a beach, stopping for gas — Murad muttering to the pump attendant — Sharkey suggested eating at the small restaurant across the road. Murad sighed and looked displeased.

"I'm hungry," Sharkey said.

"I will wait."

"Why not join me?"

"Do you know where you are?" Murad said.

Sharkey saw a sign at the crossroads: MOSSEL BAY — 2 KM. He said, "Mossel Bay."

"South Africa," Murad said through clamped teeth. "I am not allowed to eat in that restaurant. But go — ach, take your time, man."

Sharkey ate alone — fish and chips, in a booth, in the almost empty restaurant. He bought a sandwich for Murad, but lifting the top slice of bread, Murad sighed and said with distaste, "I don't take *varkvleis* — this meat."

Sharkey slept off his jet lag the rest of the way, and when they arrived felt fresh enough to surf — or at least to test the water, to paddle out to the break. He directed Murad to a parking lot facing the beach, where head-high waves were beating against the sand — smaller waves than he'd been expecting, but good enough to relax him and cleanse him of the sweat of travel. His wetsuit was in his duffel bag, his surfboard in its sleeve in the back of the pickup.

"Give me a hand, okay?"

Murad folded his arms and said, "I don't carry."

At the hotel Sharkey said, "Is there a bus back to Cape Town?"

"The night bus. It is slow. They will charge you extra for your board. You will not like it."

"I'm not taking it," Sharkey said. "You are," and put out his hand. But when Murad went to shake it, Sharkey said, "Keys."

A full week on the wave that was later called Boneyards: Africans gathered at the far end of the beach to watch him, but no other surfers showed up. "They'll come in the holidays," the owner of the hotel assured him — a man who also said, "You're putting on quite a show for the kaffirs."

"I guess that's a good thing," Sharkey said with a smile.

He took some pictures of the break, but without a telephoto lens it was impossible to do justice to the size of the waves, which had risen to twenty feet by the end of the week. From the beach they were like Sunset on a good day; on the break itself it was a huge and fickle wave, and his news was that it broke left and right.

What he remembered were the red roads and the cliffs, the syrupy gum-tree smell of woodsmoke from the cooking fires in the ramshackle village of round huts and their circular roofs at the back of the town, cigarettes sold in cans, the aroma of grilled fish, the dense flocks of shorebirds, the wide sky and the sunsets. He got cautious looks from Africans, their odd salutes and sidelong glances, their acknowledging grunts as he passed, and their rags — sensational rags, wool hats, torn trousers, and the malnourished faces of the children running on the stony paths on bare feet.

Travel in Africa made him feel small, it shook him, the rattle in his head affecting his balance; he longed to be home. After that journey he was glad to be back in Hawaii, and happiest on the North Shore, enclosed by the arms of the great bay. Everywhere else, even in Honolulu, the unpredictable happened, not necessarily bad but sometimes impossible to understand, because away from Waimea, he was among strangers.

An odd episode occurred the evening he visited a surfer friend, Trey, who'd begun to work in town at the Hotel Honolulu, at the seedy street-hooker edge of Waikiki. Trey supplied Sharkey with bags of Big Island *pakalolo* he called "killer buds," usually meeting him in Hale'iwa. But one day he said he needed to meet Sharkey at the hotel bar, Paradise Lost, at a specific time. Sharkey laughed at Trey's absurd insistence on being punctual, the stoner actually using that word. But he wanted the *pakalolo*, so he was on time.

"Meet Eddie Alfanta," Trey said when Sharkey arrived. "He's my Big Island guy."

Eddie was a dark squat man in sunglasses, with thick slicked-back hair, a heavy gold watch, a neck tattoo, and a gold tooth showing in his lopsided smile. His T-shirt said, WET WILLIES — TUMON, GUAM. He reached to fist-bump Sharkey's knuckles.

"No waves there," Sharkey said, pointing to the T-shirt.

"Fact," Eddie said. "Trey said you been around," and seeing that Trey had slipped away and was now behind the bar, he added, "Trey not so much travel. Hey, take a load off."

When Sharkey was seated, Eddie slipped him a soft, well-made blunt bulging with weed.

Sharkey wagged it. "Maybe they'll bust me."

"This the Hotel Honolulu," Eddie said, and clicked his lighter.

After one deep inhalation Sharkey said, "Primo."

"I get plenny. Trey tell me you doing a pickup." Then the man lowered his gleaming head, tugged down his sunglasses, and said, "Here's my proposition."

Sharkey had started to smile from the tickle of buoyancy swelling within him.

"My wife birthday," the man was saying. "I want to give her something special."

"Right on," Sharkey said in a strangled voice, holding his breath.

"I had in mind a surfer dude like Trey."

"Trey is cool."

"But Trey is religious kine."

"'Jesus was the first surfer, man — he walked on water.' I've heard all that. Trey don't surf on Saturdays. It's the Sabbath. His church" — Sharkey coughed and shook his head, and in a pinched voice said, "True Jesus Mission Church of the Latter Rain." Then he chuckled and remembered. "What special — catch some waves?"

"No. Make my wahine happy."

Sharkey wagged his head and stammered, but no words came out of his goofy smile as Eddie's face went in and out of focus.

"She stay upstairs."

"I hose your wife?" Laughing and levitating, a buzz in his ears, Sharkey remembered the punch line of an old joke. He said, "Like, what's in it for me, man?"

Eddie had not expected that; he drew back, and though his expression was unreadable behind his sunglasses, his cheeks shook, he tugged at his chin, then he licked his lips and said, "Killer buds. Where you think Trey gets his holy weed?"

"So what am I supposed to do?"

"Wait here."

Watching Eddie leave the bar, Sharkey, floating and imprecise, marveled at the man's efficient strut; and when Eddie returned, Sharkey clung to the arms of his chair, forcing himself upright, holding the crazy smoke in his lungs.

"You'll need this," Eddie said, handing him a key. "Five-o-eight. Just go on up." He helped Sharkey out of his chair and led him to the narrow elevator, punching the number 5 button on the inside panel and withdrawing his arm as the doors closed, calling out, "Be nice."

Sharkey squinted at the brass key tag, repeating the number. He found the door that matched it, feeling silly, poking the key at the lock but not managing to insert it, and as he tapped with the key the door opened and he was pulled into the darkness by frantic hands.

He stood murmuring softly as he was tumbled into a bed by a gasping, giggling woman with bony arms, who was yanking off his shorts, and he too was laughing in the darkness.

"I'm Cheryl — who are you?"

"Me, I'm the Shark."

"Don't bite me," she said in a small girl's voice.

On his back, rocking, then smacking the mattress, Sharkey said, "Far out, a water bed."

For a moment he was dazzled by a sudden flash of the bedside lamp and a small pale woman in black lingerie peering at him. "You're beautiful," she said, then switched off the light and sat on him. "You're mine," and she clawed at him, with either her fingernails or her teeth. "This belongs to me."

"Easy," he said.

"I can be scary," she said in a growly voice.

He struggled with her after that, as she pushed his head down, smothering him with her body, then riding his face. Pressed against the mattress, he heard the wavelike rumble and gulp of the water in the bed. Then the darkness was inside him, as though he'd drowned. But he was asleep, and soon she was shaking him. "Wake up, dude."

He was dazed. He could barely stand. The woman in front of him looked fragile, wrapped in a hotel robe, gaunt and blinking in the lamplight. Sharkey paused before her.

"Don't kiss me," she said, and turned away.

He stumbled to the door. He was so shaken he left the hotel by the back entrance, pushing past two men in hotel uniforms, without seeing Eddie or Trey.

In the next season he and Bingo, a surfer from San Diego, rented a van and drove the length of the California coast, stopping for days, and sometimes weeks, at surf spots, some of them well known, others known only to Bingo. Having made their reputation in Hawaii and been written about and photographed in *Surfer* and *Surfing World,* they were recognized, and either welcomed as celebrities or else threatened: "This is our wave, man. Take a hike."

"Bunnies," Bingo would mutter, seeing girls on the beach, and they took turns on the mattress in the back of the van.

In Mexico, in Baja and Puerto Escondido, the girls needed persuasion, some wanting money or weed; many said flatly no — a novelty to Sharkey that he was not recognized.

"They don't seem to know who we are," Bingo said.

"Maybe that's a good thing." Sharkey felt as he had on his first day at Roosevelt, when he'd been called a fucking haole, and mocked.

The Mexican girls knew nothing of surfing and stood on the beach and laughed, unimpressed, seeing Sharkey and Bingo sliding toward them on big waves. In the evenings, as they sat drinking beer next to the van, they were approached by Mexican boys, who demanded money or beer or cigarettes. The van was broken into one day when they were surfing, Sharkey's camera was stolen. They'd hidden their wallets inside a door panel. "It was a shitty camera," Sharkey said. "They can have it." They set off the next day for the border.

In Hawaii that March they learned that Eddie Aikau had drowned in an attempt to get help by paddling on his board from the overturned sailing canoe *Hōkūle'a* in the Ka'iwi Channel. The following year Sharkey won the Triple Crown and was regarded as Eddie's natural successor.

But by then surfing had become busier, more competitive — not the mellow fooling of past years but a fiercely contested sport, silent men jostling on waves. The prizes were bigger, the rivalries stronger, the endorsements greater.

It was in this period, early eighties, that Sharkey left Hawaii for California, telling the other surfers he needed a rest. But he confided to Bingo, who was in Santa Cruz, "It's not fun there anymore."

They surfed Mavericks and sold *pakalolo*, or gave it away, saying, "You looking for trouble?" inviting surf bunnies into the back of the van for weed and sex. They believed they could continue this way for years. "I'll be pushing forty one of these days, Bingo," was Sharkey's refrain.

But still in Santa Cruz at a coffee shop he met Stella, who said she was a teacher there, and got her into the van, and fell in love. He called it love. He thought he'd experienced the limits of desire before, but this was something new, a passion that turned him into a monkey.

She was small, pale, with full lips and ash-blond hair, and there lingered on her skin — her neck, her thighs — an aroma of overripeness, crushed flowers, stale ones, like musky vanilla, but creamy in their festering. It was sour sexual perfume that acted on him like a drug. Stella had no interest in surfing, but that didn't matter. After her classes she would breathe into the phone, "Come and get me. I'm horny."

And he laughed because she was a college professor, the backseat of her car full of books, and shelves of them in her apartment. After sex in her bedroom — books there too — her odor was much stronger, and when she parted her legs and he clutched her he was reminded of warm fish guts.

She flung her arms out and said, "I want to be like a man. I want to do what men do — anything I want."

"With me," Sharkey said, looking for reassurance.

"Of course, my darling," she said, sounding insincere.

Her recklessness impressed him and made him want to keep her for himself; it cast a spell, it made him — he told her this and her eyes glittered — cannibalistic. "I want to eat you and eat you." The feeling did not abate when he was back in Hawaii, away from her — it was passionate. She wrote him long letters. He never wrote back. She called, needing to talk. He hated the telephone. To satisfy her, and himself, he often flew overnight to San Francisco to meet her on weekends, spending two days in a motel room (pizza, wine, the shades drawn) without leaving. Then his return flight to Hawaii, and Stella back to her classroom teaching — "Women's Studies," "Gender Identity in Women's Literature," "Body Narratives in Feminist Films" — she who wanted to be a man. Her work meant nothing to him, yet he listened. He did not tell her he never read a book; he was grateful that she didn't ask.

Her big question was, "Where is this leading?"

"You want to be like a man?" He laughed and held her by the shoulders in a guy grip. He said, "Men never ask that question."

Yet he could not get enough of her. He told her he loved her, that he wanted to live with her, he promised her travel and adventure — all because he did not want to lose her. He would have told her anything just to be with her, to devour her, to watch her devouring him. He wasn't sure it was love — he had never known love; but it was unmistakably desire. And this small, smiling, almost plain but richly smelling woman with a great education in the heat of passion was foul-mouthed, the hot words burned into his memory a vivid gift to him that helped him remember, like a loop of wicked music, so he could savor what they'd done, and made him miss her. She had a word — some new to him — for everything, words he could not spell and some he could barely pronounce: "fellatio," "polymorphous perversity," "rimming," and "undinism." "What you just did?" she would say, stretching her nakedness, her fingers dabbing at her lips. "It's called irrumation."

"You so hybolic," he said, the one word she didn't know.

He took less pleasure in dominating her than in willingly surrendering, his body almost unrecognizable to him, unexpectedly awakened, with the same slippery completeness he felt when he plunged into a wave, all his flesh gripped and transformed by the water, his mind soaring. Sex with Stella was like that, capturing him; and she became more odorous afterward.

She believed his extravagant promises, but in the end, after months of this, finally exhausting himself of his sexual frenzy that was like an illness, and freed to think straight, he said he could not marry her — "I've already done that!"

He was relieved by the decision; she was maddened. In a crazed whisper, hot against his ear, she threatened to drown herself in their motel's swimming pool. He felt obliged to calm her, though he wanted to run — fear had killed his desire. Holding her, he was depressed, imagining the indignity of drowning in the small, shallow, fenced-in, and cracked motel pool. Her suicide in a big blue five-star hotel pool, he reasoned, would have been just as tragic but not as shabby and pathetic, and nothing like drowning in a wave. In her sadness she lost all her allure, and then became fierce, someone suddenly much older and indignant. Stripped by rage of her sexual attraction, she was powerless, and he pitied her but was still afraid of what she would do to herself.

He fled to Hawaii. She called him and screamed abuse and sobbed. Hating the phone, he forced himself to listen, trying to be patient; and noticing that she always talked for a full hour, he was reminded that she'd once told him she saw a shrink every week, always for one hour. He was relieved when she stopped calling. But the following Christmas the phone rang. Sharkey was serving turkey to his surfing buddies, spooning gravy onto his mashed potatoes.

"It's Stella," she said, announcing herself in a victim's voice, sounding sacrificial. She spoke as though addressing a large audience, loudly, like an exit line. "I'm coming apart!"

"Find someone else." He was in the house at Jocko's as he passed the gravy, looking out the window at the winter swell — another big day. "I can't help you anymore."

"You've got to do something," she said, pleading, with tears in her voice. "What are you going to do?"

"Catch some waves." And he hung up.

The sea never failed him. He was cured of his sexual obsession by fear, then boredom; but there was no end to the big waves. It was all he wanted, to be along the shore, alert, alive, afloat.

15

"I Want Your Life"

W hat's your secret?" was the usual question — seldom from surfers
     but often from hangers-on and interviewers. Saying he had none
sounded like an insincere denial, as though he were boasting that he had
many secrets he was keeping to himself. He sometimes said, and later in
exasperation pleaded, "I surf every day!" This was obvious, but who else did
that?

"The best training for surfing is surfing" was his mantra.

"And getting pounded," Garrett McNamara said. His North Shore neighbor, big-wave surfer Garrett, made no secret of the fact that he too was traveling the world, looking for the hundred-foot wave.

No one asked Sharkey's secret on the North Shore, where he was always
in the water, on a wave or waiting for one. He had done nothing else of value
in his life, had quit school at sixteen, avoided Vietnam by using the trauma
and disfigurement of his scar to gain a deferment, had never had a girlfriend
for more than a few months nor held a job for long — lifeguarding in Hawaii
was not a job but rather a privilege and a mission. Surfing was his obsession,
but perhaps like other obsessions an evasion, an escape — in his case an escape from dry land.

Water was his natural element — life-giving, offering him buoyancy,
weightlessness, purification. Except when attracted to a woman, in a sudden fever of desire, clutching at her, he was a slow talker, clumsy and torpid on land, like the clomping, gasping, flat-footed amphibian that glides
so smoothly when it slips into the water and flashes away just beneath the
surface.

He was silent in the water, like those creatures, and a talker onshore. Even
the surfers he knew well, who'd heard his stories many times, wanted to lis-

ten to him tell the same stories again in his slow confident voice, growly from smoking weed, always the same opening, the same pauses and plotty reminders, the familiar dialogue. "You should write them down," Bingo had once suggested. "No need," Sharkey said — they were better recited, like folktales, and would be repeated by anyone who heard them. "They give people something to say" — because his listeners were the stammering, inarticulate grommets with goofy smiles, hearing Sharkey tell of the strangeness of the world beyond the islands, or narrow escapes, and brutes, and heavy water, and especially of women. He was the adventurer, whose tattoos illustrated the risks he'd taken, the marvels he'd seen; the explorer, reporting back; the storyteller, the survivor, who always had the answer to the persistent question, "Got waves there?"

He'd flown back to Tahiti and Fillette. That was a story. He'd found a new break in Indonesia, and a woman named Putri. "It means princess," he said, and described some of their nights, and the danger of their nighttime lovemaking in the land of puritanical believers and honor killing for adultery. Another story. He'd surfed in Cornwall and Spain. "What kine language they speak in those places?" they asked in Hawaii. "And this Cornwall — it's like some kine country?" They loved hearing stories of islands that were small and seedy, with foot-high dumpy shore breaks, places that proved that Hawaii was the center of the world.

Sharkey realized in time that, random, selfish, and improvisational in his choices — "I'm a bum, I'm a surf gypsy" — pleasing himself, he'd created a personal style. His stories suited that style. Among the silent watchful surfers he was the talker, and without saying anything, his fellow surfers, especially the younger ones, began to dress like him, with the same shorts, the same hoodie and flip-flops, the same board, though he had a quiver of them. And in mirror imitation they seemed to acknowledge that his style was unique, the result of his travels and his romances.

And some, the visitors especially, didn't stop at imitating him. They wanted his life. They'd heard the talk about him, and — impatient, eager to learn the details of his career — they tried to befriend him, to know more. They told him about themselves, hoping to attract his interest, relating their exploits in the water, and with a penetrating gaze and their own stories seemed to insist, *Please, remember me.*

In this they tried, by being close, to live through him — never his fellow surfers in the *hui,* who were secure in their own lives and routines and single-minded in their surfing: they too were in the water every day — they were locals, whose lives were small and circumscribed by the islands. The surf bunnies and the wahine — most of the women — were seldom envious, and were happy simply knowing him, wanting nothing more than a casual hookup. It was a reassurance to him that many of these North Shore women were no different from the men, just as good in the water, just as unreliable onshore, just as hungry and horny, laughing among themselves on the beach in the day, as foul-mouthed as the guys, and prowlers at night, looking to be stoned. He was not a hero to them but rather a vortex of energy, a source of *pakalolo.*

But the surf tourists, the hangers-on, the groupies, to whom he was a celebrity — they could be parasitical. Incredibly — to Sharkey at least — the sponsors too, the big-money businessmen who funded the surf meets and flew in from California and Australia, badly wanted to be in his orbit. Men older than he was, millionaires, powerful in their dealings, who rented expensive houses on the beach for the surfing season and gave parties — they wanted his friendship, they praised his life, the life he had made out of accident and desperation and dumb luck, his whole existence a form of escape, fleeing to the water to be himself and protecting himself on land by telling lies about his life.

It seemed that the lives of these big, talky businessmen, many of them part-time surfers, were incomplete. Yet Sharkey saw success and risk and power in the men and felt puny next to them, as though they'd mistaken him for someone else, and he feared being found out and discovered to be an imposter. Or were they dazzled by his recklessness — for truly he had launched himself into waves as a boy and done nothing for years but ride them. Could this be called a career, or was it an elaborate way of avoiding any responsibility? He had no beliefs, no attachments, and had been sustained by an abiding confidence in himself. He had never considered his life worth imitating; he had succeeded through trial and error, through failure and near drownings, every wipeout a lesson in humility.

"You're an amazing success," he said to a wealthy man who wanted to sponsor him. "And look at me."

"You don't understand that you've just articulated a very critical thing," the man said — from California, his clothing and shoe factories in Vietnam.

Sharkey smiled his beautiful smile — that and his sunburned nose, and the pink ridge of the scar on his cheek, the fallen angel face of acceptance.

"You used the word 'success.' But success is a simple trick, it's empty — anyone can make money. You buy low, you sell high," the man said. His face was tense and urgent; he had large white teeth. "Success is different from achievement." And he held Sharkey by his shoulder. "I've made a pile of money. But you've achieved something."

Sharkey's wish, a form of rebuke, was that his mother could see the businessmen and hustlers and money men and hear them praise him, introducing him proudly to his friends: "This is my buddy Joe Sharkey . . ."

But his mother was dead, and anyway would have said, "I always knew he'd be a surfer. I used to drive him down to Ala Moana. I watched him surf at Sunset Beach. I worried about him, like mothers do, but I was sure he'd be the best."

Fables — he'd become a surfer to escape her. If he'd let her run his life and been denied the freedom of surfing, he'd have ended up a boozer like her, to ease the pain of hating himself.

Other surfers were better known and made more money on the circuit, but Sharkey was more photogenic, the face that these businessmen wanted as the face of their products — the scarred face, the Shark. He had burned blond hair, tousled and too long, his body was blue with tattoos, and even in furious water he had an easy stroke that powered him into the break. Most of all he had the smile. And as a result of having been an outsider, bullied at Roosevelt, snubbed by locals early on, having had to make his own way, he knew how to be a friend, to show humility, even when he resented having to be humble. His pretense of mildness made him approachable, and it worked with women.

Most money men were smooth and aloof, as smug and serene as magicians, and with that same well-it and unreadable face. You knew they were wealthy because they never looked hungry, they hardly smiled; they sat unmoved amid powerful silences, as though wreathed in clouds.

And yet some of these millionaires clung to him, wanted to be near him, wanted to know him, to have him as a trophy acquaintance, and after listening to his stories tried to impress him with stories of their own. But this bafflement became his muffled humility. He smiled to think he might have what they wanted, the thing that was lacking in their lives — and what was it? The freedom to spend every day exactly as he pleased, to paddle out and ride a wave, a boy's dream: a life of playing hooky. Maybe that was the dream of the money man — maker of sunglasses and T-shirts and bathing suits, owner of a mansion in Malibu: to be a carefree boy on a wave.

Grateful for the endorsement money but embarrassed by their frank admiration, Sharkey affected to complain — the breaks were getting crowded, the pressure to perform more intense; the meets were gangbangs; surfers had discovered Bali.

"I want your problems," one of the businessmen said.

"Seriously, it's getting harder," Sharkey said superstitiously, hoping he sounded sincere, because his life had never been happier.

"I'd trade places with you in a heartbeat," the big men said, and Sharkey felt pity for them, for having inspired such envy and making their success seem small.

Incredibly, they wanted his life, even the cagiest and the most worldly of them, who had everything, or so it seemed. They were persistent, often crassly demanding. "I've got to have more face time with you," one of his sponsors said, sounding like an insecure lover. And dealing with their attention, which seemed like clumsy wooing, he understood how a pretty woman felt, disgusted and repelled, dealing with the hot gaze and roaming hands of an unwelcome man — how did you fend him off without seeming like a complete bitch?

There was one exception, a man of the world, an occasional visitor to the islands, who wanted nothing from him but his friendship — one of the few whom Sharkey admired, someone almost unimaginable, a rogue and a pirate, shocking, confrontational, funny, infuriating, probably insane, but kept out of a madhouse by means of his wit and his medication — his drugs, *pakalolo,* acid, mushrooms, cocaine, whiskey. The drugs worked, they saved him, they were fuel, and finally, combustible, like fuel, they destroyed him.

This was how the friendship began. Sharkey, at a party, had been telling one of his stories. It was the tale of the Somali woman he'd met on a beach in Lamu, Kenya, after a trip to Jeffreys Bay in South Africa. The ludicrous racial rules, the obstacles and stupidities of apartheid, had depressed him and kept him from wandering freely, and apart from people he'd wanted to meet — local women especially. He'd flown first to Nairobi, then to Mombasa and Malindi, looking for waves, and found himself in Lamu, an island he'd reached by dhow, his surfboard lashed to the mast. There were no good waves in Lamu, but there were women, in black gowns they called hijabs, their heads covered by black shawls that wrapped across the lower portion of their face, only their eyes showing in the draping of all that black cloth.

"Her name was Aziza, she was waiting on the beach," Sharkey said. "But out of the sun, in the shadows beyond the palms. To tease her I said, 'What are you doing here?'"

"'Waiting for you,' she said.

"'You speak English.'

"'I was a teacher. They gave me the sack.'"

This was always the way in Africa, he said. You said hello, and they said they'd been waiting for you. Africa was a dream, a place without preliminaries. You were a white man. You'd been introduced long ago by other white men. Africans guessed what white men wanted, and they were seldom wrong.

But the strictures of South Africa had made him cautious, and he knew that Lamu was mostly Muslim, with strictures of its own. He waited until dark before continuing the conversation with the woman. He was staying at the only hotel on the island, an old whitewashed cube of a building called Petley's — a small bar, and all meals at a long common table of rough planks.

"The word for weed in Swahili is *bhangi*," Sharkey told the eager listeners. "A nice word, and a primo product."

After dinner he smoked a joint on Petley's veranda, then strolled onto the beach. As soon as he left the lights of the hotel he heard the crunch of coral behind him, slow footsteps, a chewing of soles — he was being followed, but he did not turn. Ahead, past a dinghy that had been drawn up on the sand, he saw that it was tethered to a fallen palm tree. The distant lights on the veranda illuminated the white eye painted on the bow of the dinghy. Sharkey sat on the palm trunk, and with a swish of cloth stirring warm air into his face, a black-gowned and partly veiled figure took a seat beside him.

"I didn't say a word. I was still smoking. But I knew it was her from the aroma, mingled sweat and perfume."

That she didn't move was a sign that she was interested. He reached for her, fumbled with folds of her gown, and found an opening, more warmth, as though inviting his hand.

"She was completely naked underneath. But when I stroked her thighs she pulled away. I said, 'Sorry.'"

"'Not here,' she said. That was encouraging."

She took his big hand in her small one and, her billowing black gown swishing against his body, led him back across the beach, avoiding the veranda lights, to the rear entrance of Petley's. The bar inside was so noisy it masked their sounds, their feet on the back stairs, his shutting the door to his room.

When he turned on the lamp beside the bed, the woman protested, a squawk, and reached for the lamp and switched it off. But he had seen two things in the flash of light — her Somali face in her Madonna's shawl, angular, her pinched nose, her even teeth, her thin dark lips, her small chin; and because in her hurry the hem of her gown had jumped, he'd seen a mottled yellowish scar, wide and matted like a patch of melted wax or hardened rags of flesh, on her thigh. She had once been badly burned, but she was lovely, and even her scar was bizarre and beautiful, like a weird medallion won by suffering.

"When she yanked her gown to cover it I turned on the light again and touched the scar on my face. Her eyes widened and she murmured a word, and a sigh of agreement. And that was not all."

In the hot room, in the narrow bed (Sharkey now had everyone's attention, and was speaking slowly), he'd slipped his hand between her legs and — so many secrets hidden by the gown — his fingers stroked an unfamiliar obstacle, more than one, a pattern of thin webbing, not flesh but raised sutures that were stiff to the fingertips, like an old wound or a scar, rough to the touch.

"She'd been sewn up," Sharkey said. "Somali style."

In the hush that followed someone said in a low greedy voice, "Hot damn."

"She rolled over and faced the wall, then reached behind and took hold of me. Slowly she guided me into the warm cleft of her *okole*. And then . . ."

His listeners, all men, were transfixed, sitting with their mouths half open, wanting more, as he teased them with a pause. But in the next moment a woman entered the room, and Sharkey hesitated.

"Go on," the woman said. She was young, fresh-faced, with sharp Slavic eyes and mocking lips, gesturing with a slender arm and beckoning fingers for him to resume his story.

Sharkey felt something hit his head and bounce into his lap — a bitten macadamia nut. Then another, which hit him harder, on his cheek.

"Hey — what the fuck!"

The woman laughed. "He's flirting with you!"

Turning sharply to confront whoever was throwing the nuts at him, Sharkey saw a balding man in aviator sunglasses and an aloha shirt, a cigarette holder clamped in his teeth, grunting as he flipped another nut. Sharkey caught it and tossed it back, hitting the man's chin.

The man laughed and staggered to his feet and hugged him.

"Then what happened with the chick!" one of the surfers yelled at him.

But the man had seized his attention and taken charge. The story was left unfinished, the party ended, and in the confusion that followed the man said, "I'm going to get you high." He packed a pipe and passed it to Sharkey, and when Sharkey later asked, "Was that heroin?" the man laughed a gasping convulsed laugh.

That hug, a form of bumping assault but clumsily tender, stood out in Sharkey's mind as the beginning of something important, the forming of his fame not as a surfer but as a celebrity friend — the acknowledgment of his power beyond surfing. The man saying "Nuts to you" had singled him out.

But that was an insight that came to him years later. At the time, in all the drinking and talk, it seemed to him that he was living in a turbulence of jarring and misleading colors, like being tumbled in the prismatic barrel of a dumping wave on a sunny day, spinning in a hold-down, then pushed aside, struggling to right himself to reach the surface. This was not fanciful: he spent many days in such waves.

"You're illusionless," the man said in a chattering voice. "That's radical."

*　　*　　*

That sweaty stranger's hug marked the end of one period, the beginning of another, young adulthood into maturity and beyond, golden boy to leathery waterman. And he saw that he was growing not only older but weaker — and so soon! — that this passage, this bridge in time, was the transition into middle age, the man helping him across to a time when he would be overtaken, obscured, outdistanced, and forgotten.

"Hunter," the man said that first night, after the hug, offering him the pipe that sent him into a drug stupor. It was, he saw, a kind of initiation.

The man was a reckless, delirious version of himself, and maybe Hunter saw Sharkey as the man he might have been had he not been a drunk, an addict, a show-off, a writer. But the man was brilliant. In his manic moods, screaming for attention, he was a monster, yet when he turned this energy into writing — and he could, the drugs and the whiskey fueling him — he had power.

Knowing nothing of surfing, he hero-worshiped Sharkey; and Sharkey, who never opened a book and had read none of Hunter's work, came to idolize the screaming man for his outrageous talk and his debts and his companionship — the friend he wished he'd had when he was a boy.

"We're both storytellers," Hunter said. "Except I get paid for it!"

"I'm just a surfer."

"I can't do it, man. I'm hydrophobic."

Sharkey began to laugh, because the word reminded him of dog bites.

"The lonesomeness of the ocean," Hunter said. "Heavy shit."

For Sharkey it sometimes seemed it was one of those periods, the Hunter years, he associated with indolence and stagnation and time-wasting and broken promises, hating himself for his laziness. But was it so? Looking back, he saw it was not an interlude of delay but important and pivotal, the making of him, the nearest he came to having an older brother.

And it mattered most because Hunter was rare in not wanting his life, as the others did; he wanted his friendship.

And Sharkey was admitted to another secret — that this careless, wasteful, mocking man, who raged, louder and crazier than anyone he'd known, this noisy man had a quiet, sober side that mumbled and was unsure and timid and bewildered and needed the praise of another hero.

16

Mr. Joe

The party in Kahala at a lumpy whitewashed Moroccan-style mansion that looked like large flood-lit sugar cubes tumbled at the edge of the beach was hosted by one of the tournament's sponsors — a new energy drink, Prime Fuel. It was always something cheesy, with a stark logo — the label, not the contents, that was intensively marketed. The sponsor himself, looking varnished, gleaming with a deep tan, welcomed the wild boys from the North Shore, who pushed past him, saying, "Yo, we're with Joe." Like two distinct species: the plump brown bearlike man, the skinny sunburned monkeys.

"Mind taking off your shoes?" the man said.

They pushed past him, laughing because they had no shoes, and hurried inside on dirty feet, howling, in torn shirts and tangled hair, the man's toothy smile becoming panicky.

"Never mind them," Sharkey said.

"This is a rental," the man said, pleading. "I don't want trouble. Are you Joe Sharkey?"

"That's me."

"I saw you surf today — awesome," the man said. "I'm Avery. Come on in." Then he looked warily into the next room at the pack of surfers crowding the tables, intentionally tripping each other, and snatching food. "If there's breakage or pilferage, I'll lose my deposit."

Sharkey gave him a smile lacking in reassurance, hoping there would be breakage or pilferage, delighted at the prospect of surfers walking across the white shag carpet on their dirty feet, teasing the other guests, monopolizing the sushi bar on the lawn, stuffing themselves and getting drunk on expensive wine or passing blunts and giggling. They were the poor gypsies from

Hale'iwa, admitted for one frantic night to a party on the far side of the island.

"Avery, the rich haoles here used to chase me off the beach when I was a kid," Sharkey said, swigging a beer and laughing. "The local kids chased me too."

Wandering past the buffet, he found Hunter hugging a bottle of Chivas Regal against his chest. "Son of a bitch," Hunter said, lifting it awkwardly with his forearms, then tipping it, leaning back, and drinking. He snatched at the bottle, holding it by its neck, and wiped his mouth with his free hand. "You're back, man." He mumbled and growled, working his lips. "You're needed here to keep the peace. All these rabid ferrets. Nice."

Hunter smiled at the wild boys, ragged and dirty but bursting with health, seeming to approve of their antics and vitality, as though acknowledging another breed of outlaw. "Weevils!" Hunter said. "Vermin!" and he yelped, seeing them giggling over the food, slopping sauce on their shirts, plucking with their fingers — hunger in their reaching hands.

"You drip gravy on my foot, *lolo!*" one shouted, kicking the other boy.

They were scarred and tattooed, and they kept together like a hunting pack.

"That the owner?" Hunter asked.

"Renter," Sharkey said. "He's one of the sponsors of the Pipe Masters."

"Going heavy on the bronzer. Looks like a fucking walnut."

"These guys pay the bills."

"Money's cheap," Hunter said. "Freedom's expensive."

His thickened voice gave his assertions a tone of authority, running words together and grunting when he was done, the grunt like a mark of punctuation.

"That's far out," he said, turning to some musclemen in grass skirts twirling thick torches and lapping at the flames, holding them like big fiery lollipops.

With Hunter distracted by the fire-eaters, Sharkey roamed through the house, searching for a bathroom, opening doors as he strolled down the inner corridors. In each air-conditioned bedroom a wide-screen TV set was on, but muted, and he was put in mind of these TV screens as fireplaces, flickering with color, giving a sense of life to the room, the comfort and reassurance of a hearth.

When he returned to the lawn he saw Hunter propped against a fire-eater, teasing him, chanting incoherently, swigging at the Chivas bottle. The barefoot surfers were awestruck, not by the muscular men twirling the flaming sticks but by the gibbering man in the aloha shirt attempting to light a doobie in his mouth by leaning into the flapping flames of a torch.

"Da guy so *kolohe*," one of the surfers said. "More worse than you, Shark."

"He's a famous writer," Sharkey said.

"You read da kine?"

Sharkey said, "No can read, brah," and the boy laughed crazily and bumped fists with Sharkey.

Hunter was now among the Tahitian dancers, mimicking the men's tramping and knee-shaking, and when the women ran onto the lawn, wearing high crownlike headdresses, Hunter whooped and snatched at them, egged on by the whistling surfers. Seeing him clowning, Sharkey thought, *He's a boy, an excitable boy, demanding to be seen* — and licensed in his disruption because he was, of all things, a writer. Hunter was the center of attention now, more conspicuous than the fire-eaters and the Tahitians with the shiny coconut-shell bras.

"Everything all right?" It was Avery, the sponsor, smiling in anxiety as Hunter humped the hip-shaking Tahitian women, the surfers cheering and whistling.

"Cool," Sharkey said.

"We're planning to showcase a new energy drink," Avery said. "Is that something that might interest you?"

"Oh yeah," Sharkey said, thinking, *Free money, that's what interests me — money without work, money without strings or office hours.* And the sight of Hunter swigging from the Chivas bottle and the words "energy drink" made him smile, because he knew it was water and syrup and a label.

"I loved those little flips you did coming out of the barrel today," Avery said.

"Off the lip. Tail slide."

"That's my dream."

"Not my dream. Just ways of getting points."

"What's your dream?"

"There's a wave — a perfect barrel in Indo," Sharkey said. "You can ride for three whole minutes in that barrel. That's one dream."

"You have more?"

Shouting to be heard over the drumming, Sharkey said, "The hundred-foot wave!"

"Where?"

"I'm looking!"

"Get in touch with me when you find it."

"When I ride it," Sharkey said.

Then Hunter intruded, hugging him — gasping, sweaty, looking smaller and misshapen, as drunks do, gabbling with spittle-flecked lips. After the beer, the wine, the Chivas, the *pakalolo,* the cocaine, it seemed he had out-lasted the others. Six surfers were sprawled on the lawn under the lights.

"Hundred-foot wave," Hunter said. So he had heard. "That's what I want to see, the monster wave — the biggest fucking wave in the world."

"Me too," Sharkey said.

"Show me some waves," Hunter said, stumbling.

Demanding, shouting, more like a badly behaved child than a rude man — loud and harmless, he made Sharkey laugh. Hunter stamped his feet and swigged again from his Chivas bottle.

"Wanna to see some waves!"

"Over there," Sharkey said, and pointed at the waves illuminated by spot-lights at the edge of the mansion's property, the break off the Kahala reef, far-off bands of tumbled froth, feathery in the lights.

"You surf there?"

Hunter, leaning to see better, was pink, glowing with sweat, as though he'd been pumped up with a drug, his eyes looking boiled, his shirt torn at the neck, buttons missing, his pale belly showing. He clutched the empty Chivas bottle with both hands, as though steadying himself.

Seeing that Avery the sponsor had slipped away, Sharkey said, "I came here as a kid. The rich haoles here set their dogs on me."

"You afraid of dogs?"

"No," Sharkey said sharply, then softly, "Yes."

"Where did you usually surf?"

"In town. Where I first learned — from a beach boy. An old guy, actually, Uncle Sunshine."

"Waikiki?"

"Magic Island."

"Fantastic," Hunter said. He was stirred by the name. He muttered, work-ing his jaws, keeping the words in his mouth. "I gotta see it."

And it was then that Sharkey remembered that he had come to the party with Winnie, his recent girlfriend. He whistled for her.

"This is Winona," Sharkey said.

"Tell him your name, honey," Hunter said to the woman approaching him.

"Call me Honey," the woman said, and gave Sharkey a kiss.

In the driveway, Sharkey thought, *Always that feeling of relief when I leave a party, always the anxiety at arriving.* The thought provoked by Hunter seemed the opposite: leaving, he looked defenseless, he was talkative, jumpy, furtive, seeming to look for reassurance, as though he'd been expelled, ban-ished to the darkness of the street.

"Where are we?" he mumbled later, crouched in the car.

"Passing Diamond Head."

The famous name calmed him, but still he stayed bent over, hugging the whiskey bottle, and he looked like a nervous child, now and then tugging at his baseball hat and still wearing sunglasses, peering at the road ahead.

Slightly tipsy, and buzzed from the *pakalolo,* Sharkey drove hunched on the steering wheel, overcautious and squinting into the glare of oncoming cars, Hunter in the passenger seat, grunting. Hunter's girlfriend — she insisted they call her Honey — in the backseat with Winona, who'd come for the party and been reluctant to leave. The two young women talked in whispers, like spouses determined to be friendly out of respect for their men, deferential but strong, hoping to find something in common.

"Old lady wants to join a biker gang," Hunter was murmuring.

At first Sharkey could not follow, there was no emphasis in the gabble, but he realized Hunter was telling a joke in a monotone.

"'Got a bike?' She says yeah. 'Any tattoos?' 'Yup.' 'Ever been picked up by the fuzz?'" And the rest was a succession of grunts and throat clearings.

Sharkey said, "What was that?"

"She says, 'No, but I got yanked by my nipples once.'"

"Hunter!" his girlfriend called out from the backseat.

Sharkey squinted out the window. "Waikiki."

"Far out," Hunter said, still groggy, his head down, swaying heavily.

After Sharkey parked at Magic Island, he helped Hunter out of the car — Hunter had been fumbling with the door handle — and led him through the palms to the far end. The two women followed, again like spouses, something tribal and old-fashioned in their trooping behind the men in the moonlight to the break.

"No waves tonight," Sharkey said. "All the action's on the North Shore. This is great in the summer, though — the south swell. I spent my boyhood here."

"The snot-green sea," Hunter said.

"True, you know, in some places. Not here."

"The sea. The snot-green sea. The scrotum-tightening sea," Hunter said. Then he grunted, "Joyce."

Sharkey considered the name for a moment. He said, "You don't get too many surfer chicks. Rell Sunn — Auntie Rell. Couple of others."

"What about me?" Winona called out behind him.

"And, yeah, this wahine."

A ship's lights winked in the distance, and the glow smoothed the ocean, shimmered on it and made it silky under the paler gleam of the moon, as they watched above the gulping lava rocks, amid the rattling palms.

"Mother ocean," Sharkey said.

"My mother is a drunk," Hunter said.

"Mine was," Sharkey said. "'Just a cocktail, darling. I can't move until I've had a drink.' Got drunk, broke her hip. *Make*-die-dead."

In a forced prissy voice, Hunter said, "Make mine a highball."

They were still standing on the grassy outcrop over the rocks, the two men, the women just behind them. Hunter mumbled, almost as though he were eating something, and then threw his arms out and leaned back and howled into the night. The two women stepped back, to give him room in case he did it again, but he rubbed his nose with his knuckles and mumbled some more, quieter now that he had released what seemed like a bellow of anxious rage.

Sharkey had not moved. He said, "My mother said surfing is a waste of time. Hey, it's my living. I never asked her for a penny."

"You can pick your nose but you can't pick your relatives," Hunter mumbled.

"She never watched me surf."

"My mother never reads my stuff. She thinks I'm a fuck-up." He laughed, the laugh gargling low in his throat. "She's probably right. I keep telling her it's part of my image." He then leaned over the ledge to where the small waves were slapping the rocks. "I saw you on TV today, surfing at Pipeline. I gotta hand it to you, man. They were some diabolical waves. I'm thinking, I could never do that."

Sharkey said, "I could never write a book."

"That reminds me, I've got a copy of my new book for you. *Curse of Lono*. It's at the hotel."

Sharkey felt a slight sense of oppression, of obligation, thinking, *He'll want me to say something about it, I'll have to read it, I'll never finish it.*

To change the subject, Sharkey said, "What about your father?"

"He died."

"Mine too. I was a kid."

"How old are you?"

Sharkey said, "Thirty-five."

"I remember when I was thirty-five. Good year. My first book, *Hell's Angels.*"

And Sharkey felt that oppression again — another book, a big brick of pages, daring him to open it, and his always thinking, *There's too much of it, it's heavy.* The mildewed smell of books in Hawaii made them seem poisonous — you couldn't open them without sneezing.

Talk of books, here especially, seemed irrelevant. What was the point of mentioning these inert objects while on the beach, facing the moonlit sea flickering with chop and now and then a wave bursting in blackness offshore and crusted in white; these palms, this mild air and moonglow — it was all beyond books. People who did not have this beauty in their lives found some strange squirrelly indoor comfort in books.

Sharkey did not know what to say, and was glad when Winona broke the silence, saying, "You guys going in?"

"Waiting for that monster wave," Hunter said. "It's bullshit, right? Hundred-foot wave?"

"No," Sharkey said. "People talk about them. Some people have seen them — you'd never forget a thing like that. The one west of San Diego — Cortes Bank. Other places — Tahiti, maybe Indo. They appear out of nowhere and then they're gone."

"Waimea," Winona said. "They come forty-five, some days in the season."

"Twice that size is what I'm looking for," Sharkey said.

"Perilous quest!" Hunter said, gagging. "The hundred-foot wave, holy grail of the ocean," and began to cough, batting his arms and tramping in circles as he fought to get his breath, spitting and choking.

"You all right, Hunter?" Honey asked.

"No!" he screamed and, trying to speak, gagged some more, then said in a pinched voice, "I'm drunk."

"Remember we're supposed to change rooms tonight."

"Shit!" Hunter shouted, and spat, then crossed his arms and looked helpless.

"You said you wanted a suite," Honey said. She turned to Sharkey. "Can you take us to the Kahala?"

In the car on the way back, Hunter found the empty Chivas bottle on the floor and cradled it like a doll and dozed off, snoring softly. But he came awake as Sharkey pulled away from a stoplight and cried out, "Hey, I could kill us all!" He lunged at Sharkey and grabbed the steering wheel and yanked at it.

But Sharkey held tight to it and raised his elbow, jamming it against Hunter's chin. He said, "But then we'd miss the weed, and the sex, and the waves," and slipped his elbow into Hunter's neck, applying more pressure.

"He's freaking out," Winona said.

"He's fine," Sharkey said. "Aren't you, buddy?"

But Hunter had sagged sideways. He had not heard; he was dozing again.

"That happens," Honey said.

Hunter emitted bubbly snores, but when they drew into the porte cochere of the Kahala he roused himself and said, "They're going to be driving me nuts," and looked again like a fretful child. Then in a plaintive tone he called to Sharkey, "Joe!"

Sharkey gave his keys to the bellman and guided Hunter to the reception desk, Hunter sleepily eyeing the clerk, a woman with a flower behind her ear and a welcoming smile.

"Name?"

"Thompson," Honey said.

Hugging Sharkey, Hunter said, "Put me down as Mr. Joe."

"You're moving us to a suite," Honey said, conferring with the clerk while Sharkey sat with Hunter on a sofa in the lobby, Hunter breathing hard, saying nothing.

When Honey had the key and Sharkey got to his feet, preparing to leave, Hunter said, "Come on up, check it out. Drink. Smoke. Hang out." And his voice trailed off as they walked to the elevator, Hunter clutching Honey now and limping. "After all that, I want a doobie the size of an Airbus."

They entered the suite — a large sitting room, bedrooms to the left and right. Winona whistled softly, murmuring, "I never seen anyting like this kine," but Hunter had begun to complain, not in distinct words but in a succession of grunts.

"It's a total bugfuck, this room," he finally said, shuffling toward the sofa. "Gotta move this thing. Give me a hand, Joe."

"Move it where?"

"There." He sounded petulant. "I need it nearer the TV."

"Maybe move the TV?"

"No — fuck, no. Then it would block the window. It would fuck up the view." He shoved at the sofa and barked at Honey, "Minibar!"

When they had moved the sofa, Hunter sat heavily and kicked his shoes off and slumped sideways. Honey brought him a drink, putting it to his lips in a mothering way and saying to Sharkey and Winona, "Help yourselves."

"Those flowers," Hunter said of a bouquet in a vase on a side table. "They're too tall. What are they?"

"Bird of paradise," Winona said. "Heliconia."

"They're going to tip over — move them." He put his drink down, took a twist of paper from his shirt pocket, and tapped some powder onto the back of his hand. He lifted it to his face and snorted it, and gasped, and tapped his nose, and said in a new voice, "Best ROA — route of administration," then, "Give him the book."

"*Curse of Lono*," Sharkey said, taking the book from Honey. "Cool."

"Captain Cook. Mayhem. Wild nights. Roast pig. Fishing. That's Hawaii."

Sharkey said, "Surf. 'Fucken haole.' 'Get off my wave.' *Hammajang* houses. Starry nights. And long mellow days."

"Insanity," Hunter said.

"It's all good," Winona said.

"Who asked you?" Hunter said, pushing his sweaty face at her.

Sharkey put his arm around her and said, "We have to split — long drive to the North Shore," but Hunter had begun to snort more coke.

"I need another bump," he said, and seeing Sharkey edging away, said, "Don't go!" He lurched to his feet, snuffling and rubbing his nose, and hugged Sharkey and whimpered a little, then let go. "I'm the Duke of Puke!"

"He so *lolo*," Winona said in the car.

"He writes books," Sharkey said.

"Since when you read books?" And she laughed and poked his arm.

But Sharkey said, "I'm going to miss him."

17

Reality Check

W hy miss him, this stranger? he wondered, because the man was a fid-
geting freak who talked without moving his lips, holding the growl
in his mouth, who hated sitting on a beach and would only watch surf on
television, in his suite, usually screaming at the set. And the book Hunter
had given him was a burden, like something a sponsor would give you — a
watch, a hat, a bicycle — that you'd never use and end up giving away. Sharkey had never met a writer before, and associated with Hunter, the word
"writer" seemed like an excuse for being half baby and half sage, living in a
world without rules — the writer made the rules and had the last word, or at
least Hunter said he did.

But when he was gone, Sharkey thought how Hunter was irreplaceable;
the other surfers were as flaky but wordless, and Sharkey had been bewitched
by Hunter's talk.

Hunter's enthusiasm for the monster wave — the hundred-foot wave out
there, breaking somewhere on the planet — renewed his desire to find it.
And it heartened him to see that Hunter, the writer, the reckless boy ten
years older than he, seemed as random and improvisational as he was — "I'm
a bum, I'm a gypsy" — and he remembered Hunter saying, "Perilous quest"
and "holy grail of the ocean," the powerful words justifying what he did every day and making it seem like it mattered.

But Hunter was gone now, and would not be back for months, or until the
next Honolulu marathon.

Sharkey surfed every day, and every day tried something new — a turn, a
cutback, swiveling on the face of a wave as though carving his signature

on it, writing on water. It was not practice or preparation; it was a way of
spending the day, easing the passage of time; a way of living his life, because
he made the moves his own.

And every night he went out, either to a bar or to a friend's house, to
drink and smoke on a lanai, telling his stories, reminiscing about his begin-
nings, remembering incidents from surfing distant waves, episodes in his
quest for the ultimate wave, the monster. Part of the drinking and drugging
was listening to the surf report on the radio from Bryan the Hawaiian and
planning where they'd go the next day. And that was useful, because he always vowed to go elsewhere, to have a wave to himself.

At some point in his smiling vacancy of mind a girl would rise from the
shadows and wander over to him, sidling like a cat, grazing his leg, and come
to rest at his feet. He'd reach for her; nothing would be said. She'd match him
drink for drink—they were island girls, surfers, boogie boarders, and the
ones with jobs had to be up early. But their nearness to him, leaning against
him, was an understanding that they would leave with him, laughing on the
way to his car, knowing what was to come.

No other preliminaries; they would kiss hungrily, become short of breath,
all the while slipping out of the T-shirt, stepping out of the shorts, and then
tipping themselves into the bed or onto the floor in a frenzied back-and-
forth that ended with gasps of animal satisfaction. Sharkey would wake like
a blinking monk seal in the early dawn, alone, ready to slide into the water.

He had everything he wanted except that wave, but his wanting it—his
search—gave a richness and direction to his life.

Hunter sometimes called, always at two or three in the morning, strangled
sounds, grunts, silences. Then, "It's madness here, man."

Sharkey could offer nothing of himself: he was content, no madness.

"We gotta do something together," Hunter often suggested, after a silence.

That was the plan—a promise. But the next time Hunter returned to
Hawaii he forgot the plan. He had the marathon to report on, and football to
watch. Sharkey saw how the eager fan, mumbling in a friendly way, "Mr. Joe,"
sitting in front of the TV, concentrating on a game, sipping whiskey, lifting a
powdery knuckle to his nose, could transform himself into the other Hunter,
crazed and incoherent, sometimes physically unrecognizable, shouting and
abusive, sweaty, bleary-eyed, hollering, "Bestial! Reptiles! Pigface!"

But each time Hunter returned to Hawaii was a reality check, both men
older: Sharkey, the reflective nonreader, watchful, cross-legged in a yoga
pose in the hotel suite, beside Hunter the writer, agitated and explosive. The
gypsy and the outlaw, Hunter said, the one man who admired him without wanting his life. Hunter's life was big enough, full enough, and Sharkey

looked forward to Hunter's arrival when, around Christmas, the Honolulu Marathon was about to start and the winter swell was building on the North Shore. Hunter eager too, so he said, to hear Joe's stories, to watch football in his hotel suite, to snort coke and drink whiskey, usually all at the same time.

"Mushrooms," Hunter said one of those times. "See if you can find some."

Sharkey asked Moe Kahiko, who said, "Got choke. Got plenny," and brought him some in a plastic bag, saying "They magic. Eat one or two." He took one from the bag, a damp gnome's cap, holding it by its stem, stroking the gills on its underside. "Try eat."

"What's it like?"

"Insane."

"Maybe later."

"More better when they not come dry."

Sharkey ate one that night, chopping it into small pieces and chewing a small handful. Then he sat, and the glow heated his head, he saw a sparkle in his house he'd never seen before, chairs and tables tingling. He was uplifted, he was on a wave, and the wave swelled, became phosphorescent and didn't break but carried him through the luminous air. He walked to the lanai to enjoy the entanglement of starlight, whirls and blobs blazing in the night sky, and his body shriveled so small his muscle was tissue-thin. He thought, *When have I ever been this happy?* He sat weightless on his favorite chair and was propelled, steering it through the widening room.

Overtaken by exhaustion at the end, he dozed, and the next day asked Moe where he'd found the mushrooms.

"You know where you get da kine cows in Mokūleʻia, near Dillingham? Plenny there, after one big rain. They growing around the cow shit."

"I want to see."

They went, Sharkey and Moe, one day after a sudden shower, hiking up the hill to the pastures where cattle were grazing. As Moe had promised, the small tawny gnome caps had sprouted on the fresh cowpats.

"Psilocybin," Hunter said over the phone. "Hot damn. That's the mother lode. Save some for me."

Sharkey anticipated an outing, a mushroom hunt, and planned it carefully to please Hunter. He'd take him for lunch in Haleʻiwa, he'd supply baskets for collecting the mushrooms, they'd go to Sharkey's house at Jocko's and eat them, getting high while watching waves — a field trip followed by an evening of visions.

"I hate hiking," Hunter said. "Fucking mosquitoes."

"It's an easy walk," Sharkey said.

But Hunter said, "Football," and "Got a deadline," and "Feeling shitty, man," and so there was no mushroom hunt.

Sharkey took some fresh mushrooms to the hotel. Hunter ate a handful them in his suite and trembled in his armchair and wailed ecstatically, gargling, his face gleaming, deaf in his delirium — and so Sharkey left him.

"More mushrooms," Hunter said the next day.

Before he left, he showed Sharkey the page he had written about it, then, seeing that Sharkey only nodded at it, Hunter read it, stabbing at it with his cigarette, crowing about how he'd hunted with Sharkey on the muddy hillside at Mokŭleʻia, among the cows and the marauding pigs, plucking the mushrooms from splashes of cow shit, as Sharkey had described. And there were wild dogs and loud parrots, and Moe was a tattooed Samoan with fuzzy hair and a war club.

Sharkey, who had thought of himself as unreliable, untruthful, a procrastinator, a committed stoner, a heavy drinker, now understood that in comparison with Hunter he was moderate in his habits. He loved the man for making him seem normal, because Hunter seldom kept his word, spent the whole day fantasizing and doping, sometimes chattered like a monkey, and might not leave his room for days.

I surf, Sharkey thought. *And Hunter hates the water.* But Hunter's mentions of writing were like a sorcerer's promise of magic. How did he do it? Where did it come from? What did it mean? Sharkey could not say. He had not read a word Hunter had written, not even the inscribed book he'd been given. All he knew was Hunter declaiming the outrageous adventure of the mushroom-hunting, and if in reality something never happened, what was the point of reading about it?

The man's evasions and untruths were obvious: he was in pain, he was lost, unable to cope, deranged at times. Yet Sharkey admired him for being able to turn his pain into something resembling strength, his weaknesses and his rage into a kind of heroism. That he was besieged by admirers for the books he'd written bewildered Sharkey — the sorcery in it; and Hunter allowed himself to be idolized by these hangers-on, who took charge of him and brought him to parties, to which Sharkey was swept along. Hunter was seen as a man of action, yet he was passive. He spent most of the time in a chair, watching TV. He hated to be alone. He could not manage without a woman, who — far from being a sexual partner — functioned as a nurse.

"Couldn't make it yesterday," he'd say to Sharkey. "Captured by freaks."

And behind him the nurse-girlfriend would roll her eyes or shake her head.

Hunter was sober most mornings. But when he insisted on Sharkey's driving him to the gun range at Koko Head he was drunk, and the range attendant, alarmed by his shouting, would not let him shoot. Hunter swore at him and, when the attendant turned his back, shouted at the man, his demon voice rising in his anger. He threatened the man, and only relented when Sharkey dragged him away. Later Hunter made it a story, added guns to it, and "demonic muzzle flip," and barking dogs, and Hawaiian chants. He read it to Sharkey. What had happened was embarrassing. But the story was funny.

That was his magic, to make an awkward episode into a kind of fable. Sharkey had not known that there was a public firing range at Koko Head, that Hunter was a gun nut, that he had access to pistols and assault rifles from his cronies on O'ahu. The sight of the guns in Hunter's pale trembling hands worried Sharkey. Hunter's moods shifted too; he complained of muscle aches, a bad back, insomnia — up all night, he needed a nap in the middle of the day.

"Great guy," he said to the nurse-girlfriend, this one named Bonnie.

"He's amazing," she said.

"I wish I'd known him years ago," Sharkey said.

She took it as a compliment to the man, but he meant that Hunter was faltering, in decline — repetitive, his memory misfiring. Even Hunter said so. "What do you expect?" he screamed into the phone one day — Sharkey guessed at an editor. "My brain's fried. There's a guy here who's feeding me toxic mushrooms!"

Sharkey wanted to show him North Shore waves. The marathon always took place in the big-wave season. "Monster waves!" he said. "Maybe something to write about."

"Scary waves," Hunter said. "I want to see who you are when you're scared. A different guy!"

"I'm myself on a gnarly wave. Not scared. That's who I am," Sharkey said.

"I'll be the judge of that."

But he couldn't pin Hunter down. No one could, not even the people who'd flown him to Honolulu and paid for his hotel suite. He was reckless, and like many reckless surfers Sharkey had known, he was superstitious.

"No, no, no," he'd say, entering a hotel room. "It's all wrong." And he would threaten to leave unless the room was arranged his way. He needed flowers, a view of the ocean, an ice bucket. And he was fickle, meeting Sharkey's friends. "I don't like the way your Samoan pal looks at me."

"Moe Kahiko. He's Hawaiian. He's mellow."

"No. He has a hairy feral quality. Ratlike cunning. Yellow eyes. He always looks like he's planning some kind of caper."

"It's called survival. He was raised by a single mom on the North Shore. They lived in a car for a long time. It was parked under a tree on the service road in Kahuku."

"See? I was right." Hunter sniffed the glass of whiskey he was holding, then downed it and roared, his mouth open wide.

"Being homeless made him resourceful. That's how he found the mushrooms."

"He leans over when he stands."

"You hate him for that?"

"He's not perpendicular, man!" Hunter sounded genuinely angry — not the fake anger that he used to be funny. With rage-spittle on his lips, he said, "I want him to stop looking at me with his yellow rodent eyes, like he's a fucking burnout!"

And not only Moe. Hunter took against surfers who were too tongue-tied to answer his growled questions, the woman at the 7-Eleven who, he said, "licked her prehensile fingers and then counted my change with them." Hunter did not want to touch the money. "Keep it!" Drugs made him see double, and he complained of crowds where only a few people were lingering on a beach.

He was a gentle grouch who needed friends around him, his Hawaii friends, the old, lame ex-football player from 'Āina Haina, a runner whom he'd profiled, a pair of strippers he'd picked up in his rented Mustang convertible (girlfriend-nurse driving), and a porn star he said was a celebrity, whom Sharkey had never heard of.

Sharkey, who hated crowds, understood Hunter best when he said, "Humans are an invasive species," but Hunter liked an audience, and Sharkey, committed to solitude, kept to himself.

"That porn star I was telling you about?" Hunter said.

Sharkey said, "Yeah" — he'd seen her once, but Hunter had never said anything more about her.

"She accused me of sexual assault. We went to court. I won!" He was lying on a sofa in his suite, a glass of whiskey resting on his chest. "And we celebrated! Didn't we, honey?"

"We sure did," the girlfriend-nurse said.

The next moment Hunter was asleep, poleaxed by the whiskey, like a baby grown overtired, shouting, then snoring.

"We sure did," the woman repeated sadly to Sharkey, twitching her lips in sorrow or regret, tearful, as though caught in a lie.

Sharkey knew from the tour that the surfers who were the most boisterous — the stylish ones — were the hardest to please, needing attention, like hyperactive children. A stoner would sit and giggle and be repetitive, but no one was more boring than a drunk. At his best, Hunter was appreciative and watchful; at his worst, unbearable.

Hunter was a container which when filled with drugs or alcohol became electric and lit up and began to vibrate, shouting, barking, throwing things, howling or going dark, looking like he was going to break something — a glass, a vase, a plate of spaghetti, the platter of cold pizza — as Sharkey had seen him do. Once, in a rage, he'd broken his leg; as a result he had developed an odd foot-dragging monkey walk, and often tripped and fell.

Hunter's girlfriend at the time covered her face and whispered, "It was terrible. He slipped on the tile floor in the bathroom. He screamed and screamed. He couldn't stop. They wouldn't sedate him because he was full of coke."

Never mind, Sharkey thought, Hunter was his advocate, he frankly admired him, he praised him to his friends, he listed him on the "Honor Roll" on the back page of two of his books, along with editors and athletes and rock stars he knew — he read the list to Sharkey, who wished he could have told his mother, *My name's in a book*. And Hunter wrote a short profile for a magazine, "The Shark at Sunset," and this too he read aloud — Sharkey smoking a joint and smiling.

"Going to Cortes Bank next month," Sharkey said. "My sponsor's paying. Fly over it in a helicopter. Film it first, then take a boat out and ride it."

Hunter wasn't listening, he was still talking. "I want to do a real profile of you for the magazine. They're big on surfers. Where've you been lately?"

"On some great waves in Mexico. Todos Santos, and way south — Puerto Escondido. But Cortes — that's a hundred-foot wave."

Hunter was nodding. He tapped cigarette ash onto a half-eaten sandwich. "You see the thing I wrote about Clinton?"

"I guess so," Sharkey said, though he had no idea. Clinton was a name to him, nothing more, one of Hunter's names.

Hunter was growling, mumbling, perhaps talking, and then he was snorting a bump of coke off the back of his hand.

"Gotta do something big," he said, adenoidal, gagging a little from the hit. "The whole surf culture deal. Like Hell's Angels — wild men on boards instead of hogs. Crazed outlaw gods!"

"It's not really like that," Sharkey said.

"Outrageous, insane, screaming island girls." He swallowed; he gasped and pushed at his nostrils. "Sex on the beach. Crashing waves."

Sharkey laughed; Hunter hadn't heard. He was preoccupied, drinking, drugging, determined to be high, paper twists of coke in his shirt pocket, bottles under his arms, amber containers of pills on the bathroom sink.

"Sometime I'll tell you about it," Sharkey said. "The ultimate wave."

"I don't have a lot of free time this trip," Hunter said.

"Whenever," Sharkey said, so as not to press him.

But his easy response put Hunter on the defensive, and he staggered to his feet and swayed in front of Sharkey, who stood up, fearing that Hunter might fall and thinking that he could catch him.

"I'm an addict," Hunter said. "Do you know how much trouble it is to be an addict? It's a full-time fucking job. I don't have time to do anything else."

He was writing less, he said — and, Sharkey suspected, perhaps not writing at all. Missing deadlines, he said. And when on a return visit Hunter invited Sharkey to his hotel and Sharkey said he was free to do the interview for *Rolling Stone,* Hunter said, "I don't do anything for them anymore. They're mainstream. I'm somewhere else, still tooling along, pedal to the metal, in the fast lane of the proud highway." He panted a little, short of breath from his shouting. "With the freaks!"

"The stoners," Sharkey said, because he was smoking a joint, midafternoon, assessing the waves off Kahala from the lanai of the hotel suite.

"Snorters," Hunter said. "Snorting makes me bounce off the walls, if it's good shit."

"Snorting what?" Sharkey asked, speaking through his teeth, holding the smoke in his lungs.

"Coke, speed, chalk, crank, smack," Hunter said. "Speed builds up dopamine, and that's a rush. Depends on the ROA . . ."

Route of administration — Hunter had mentioned it before: he was a pedant when it came to drug use, and his knowledge was immense and all firsthand.

"Tweakers in Hawaii fry their brains on meth, or they slam smack into their arms. The beauty of meth is that it can be smoked, but it's no good snorted."

"You're a snorter." Sharkey exhaled a pale but visible breath of weed.

"Big-time," Hunter said. "Like dabbing." He saw Sharkey squint, and explained, "Getting some concentrated weed and heating it on a nail and inhaling the vapor. Or hot-railing." Again he saw Sharkey frown, and said, "Heat up a glass tube end and snort a line through it, so it vaporizes up the tube. It's an instant high but it messes up my nose so bad I blow huge blood boogers that scare my girlfriend."

"Sounds like a trip," Sharkey said, alarmed by Hunter's intensity and feeling like a schoolboy with the damp roach of *pakalolo* in his fingers.

"Hot-railing — yeah. But you waste a lot of product that way. Still, I love blowing an insanely huge dragon cloud."

"Gotta go," Sharkey said. "Surf's up tomorrow."

Hunter said, "But either way you end up toothless."

Sharkey smiled, thinking how Hunter rarely listened to him, especially now, when he was winning on the tour, traveling, finding new breaks, getting better sponsors, and always in search of waves.

So he was surprised when Hunter said one day, "Remember when you said to me once . . . that thing?"

Hunter was lying on the sofa in his suite, his shoes on the cushions, wearing a misshapen fedora and sipping a whiskey. Sharkey shrugged at the question, which was unanswerable in its vagueness.

"I was telling you about the Ali-Foreman fight in Kinshasa." Hunter began to laugh, and his laughter gagged him.

The names meant nothing to Sharkey, even now, years later, this Ali Foreman—who could he be?

"You said, 'Kinshasa—any waves there?'" He hooted and coughed and choked, gargling phlegm, then leaned over and spat on the carpet. "Fucking heavyweight championship of the world, and you didn't have a clue! You didn't even know who Ali and Foreman were!"

Sharkey said, "They probably don't know who I am."

"I love that," Hunter said. "I mention people and you go, 'Who?'"

"Because I don't know," Sharkey said, to deflect the shouting. He had the sense he was being teased, and he resented it. He didn't understand what was behind it except the drunken ranting of Hunter, who was lying fully clothed —sweaty shirt, crushed hat, stained shorts—on the white sofa.

"Carville, Clinton, Wenner, Joe Montana, Ayn Rand, Carter, Ken Kesey, Johnson."

"Which Johnson? Kimo—the long-boarder?"

"Samuel Johnson."

"I guess I know Clinton. He stopped here once."

"But politics," Hunter said.

"Politics is a shit game. It's just winners and losers."

"Exactly. That's why you're focused. You're on your own wave."

"Where else would I be?" Sharkey said.

"Like Sherlock Holmes," Hunter said. "Watson tells him that the earth revolves around the sun. Sherlock thinks it's the other way around. Watson's incredulous at this dumb fuck. Sherlock says, 'So what? It doesn't matter to me.' He's on his own wave!"

"I've heard of Sherlock Holmes," Sharkey said.

"I tell people, 'There's this surfer dude in Hawaii. He's never heard of Joe Montana or Jimmy Carter.'"

"So?" Sharkey said in a faltering voice.

He was beginning to redden, his face heating with shame, and he was a child again at Roosevelt, being interrogated by a teacher and then teased by the local kids—"Haole! Panty! You not *akamai!*"—and for those hot moments he hated Hunter, the greedy, careless, wasteful man who knew nothing about Hawaii and yet wrote books about it.

Then Sharkey witnessed Hunter do something he'd never seen him do before. He put his drink down on the floor; he removed the smoking butt from his cigarette holder and stubbed it out by pushing it into a hamburger bun that lay bitten on a plate on the coffee table. He swung his legs off the sofa and struggled to rise. When Sharkey made a move to help him, Hunter waved him away and got to his feet, breathless from the effort, and tottered a little. He was big but bent, hunched over, broken, and looked crippled as he stood before Sharkey, trembling slightly. With a grunt he threw his arms around Sharkey and hugged him hard, surprising him with his strength, as though Hunter were clinging to life, with the exertion Sharkey used to wrap himself on a board and duck-dive under a wave.

"That's why I love you, dude."

Sharkey was too startled to speak; such tenderness from Hunter was new to him.

"I love you for what you don't know," Hunter said. "I love you for knowing the things that matter. Wave-riding. The lonesomeness of the ocean."

Just then the phone rang. Hunter answered, barking, hoarse, impatient. "The party's on the fifteenth. When I'm back in L.A."

His other world plucking at him, as it always did, the bigger world of power and celebrity and names that Sharkey did not know. Hunter was on good terms with everyone in that world — he needed them, they needed him, he was shamed by his need, or at least weakened, so he saw Sharkey as strong and solitary, because he didn't see that Sharkey had friends too — the water dogs, the surf gypsies, the barefoot freaks of the surfing world for whom only waves mattered. But you had to be on the water to see that.

The surfing world was small, loose, inward-looking, mostly silent, competitive, and illiterate; mostly kind-hearted, mostly mellow, eager to be on the cover of a surfing magazine but never intending to read it.

Football was Hunter's passion. He watched the games on TV and could not be torn from them. Interrupted, he swore or screamed, went red in the face, exploded. "Weasels! Vermin! Whores! Shut the fuck up!"

Seated, drugged, staring into space, wordlessly moving his lips, he was the Buddha of broken promises. "We'll do something together" and "I'll meet you there" and "I've got a plan." But he seldom followed through. He was indecisive, haggard, repetitive.

And at a time when younger surfers were winning and attracting sponsors, Sharkey wondered, *Am I like him?*

A shoulder injury from a wipeout at Jaws, when he was hit by his board coming out of a barrel, sidelined Sharkey for almost a year. In that year a number of new surfers emerged, and Hunter showed up limping — "Fucking hip replacement, can you believe it?" — and Sharkey said, "I've been out of action too," and thought, *But I have nothing else.*

Even limping, Hunter had an outlaw aura and a loud shout, was often pictured with a cigarette in one hand, a gun in the other, and the aura gave him a look of danger and celebrity. But more than that, his writing guaranteed that his achievement would last and be remembered — not the ride on water, leaving no trace, witnessed by a few guys onshore, but indestructible books, a legacy. Sharkey was dazzled by the very idea of a book. For the nonreader a book was a powerful fetish object, something magical, its creation a mystery. It contained secrets.

Even so, Sharkey was not provoked to read one. Reading made him feel like a child.

Their lives were parallel, and because Sharkey was ten years younger, he measured himself against Hunter, often gratified by the correspondences, or shocked when he realized that in ten years or so he might be like Hunter, angry, negative, raging, lame, because his youth was gone, his talent diminished.

"I can't write this," Hunter said. Another year, another week of the Honolulu Marathon, Hunter sitting at a table in the kitchen of his suite, his new girlfriend sobbing in the bedroom. "You have to do it."

"Impossible," Sharkey said. "No way."

"You're not high!" Hunter looked frenzied and resentful. He slapped his computer, avoiding the half-chewed slice of pizza that had dripped sauce on the keyboard.

"I'm a high school dropout, man!"

"All the better. It'll sound raw."

"I can't write," Sharkey said. "You have to do it."

"I'm buzzed." He licked his lips. "Can't see. Dope sick."

At times like this, his face gleaming with sweat, his skin pale, his eyes reddened, he did look sick and was probably feverish.

"Your friend, that guy Moe."

"Moe Kahiko?"

"Yeah. He can write it."

"Moe can barely speak English," Sharkey said, trying not to smile at the thought of Moe sucking on a blunt, his big dirty fingers tapping at tiny computer keys. "What is it you need?"

"Column for ESPN. The deadline's tomorrow." Still sitting, elbows on the table, head down, he called out "Patty!"

The woman who had been sobbing softly in the bedroom came to the doorway, wiping her eyes, looking sorrowful.

"Find someone to write my piece. Or else do it yourself." He had not turned or lifted his head; he spoke in animal grunts, crouched like a monkey, and then began to shout.

He was still shouting as Sharkey slipped out of the room.

The following year, after ten months of travel and struggle, Sharkey saw Hunter again. Both men were limping. Sharkey had injured his knee on a wave in Brazil — Cacimba do Padre — and the hospital in Pernambuco had discharged him with a knee brace that had split apart on the flight home. Hunter said he'd had back surgery.

But Hunter had a new woman by his side, attentive, lovely, much younger, nurselike in her concern. Hunter said, "This is the guy I was telling you about, the original Mr. Joe."

Anita had a beautiful smile, and while Hunter sat and smoked and talked, Sharkey watched her and envied Hunter for having someone so patient and pretty looking after him. She was knowledgeable too.

"I want Joe to see that thing I wrote about Nixon," Hunter said. "Where is it?"

"It's in *Better Than Sex*."

"That's surfing," Sharkey said. "Better than sex."

"Find him a copy," Hunter said. He tottered to his feet and hugged Sharkey. "You trigger-happy little shit. What have you been doing?"

"Blew out my knee in Brazil," Sharkey said. "But I met a guy from Portugal there. Apparently there's this humongous wave that breaks off a place called Nazaré. It's so gnarly they call it the wave of death."

"Yaaah!" Hunter's mouth was open wide. "I love it!"

"Not from surfers — from the local fishermen that have died in it. Their widows are in the town, lots of them, all in black, giving the wave stink-eye."

"You can ride it. I'll write about it," Hunter said. He sat back on the sofa and gave Sharkey a drowsy smile and mumbled, "Wave of death."

At his best Hunter was an enthusiast. He didn't know much about surfing, but he had a love of wild words and a frantic eagerness to please his friends, and he had always admired Sharkey's surfing. Surfing was celebrity, surfing was glamour to Hunter, but it was also risk. Because he was no swimmer himself, at least not in a choppy ocean, perhaps he saw it as flirting with death, in the way his own life was self-destructive, comic and macabre.

Sharkey was able to convince him that the opposite was the case, that he never felt more alive than when he was on a wave; that death was unthinkable when he was skidding through a barrel.

"Monster wave," Hunter said. "What if you wipe out?"

Sharkey said, "I'm a dog in the water."

"You're falling off a fucking cliff," Hunter said.

"In surfing you fall off the cliff and then the cliff chases you."

"Right. The wave is Mr. Death."

"No. The wave is a dumb force of nature. It's neutral. It's lifted from a reef or a rock. It rises and falls, then it's gone forever. A wave is a temporary shape. There's a shoulder and a lip and a face in wave anatomy, but there's no brain. You can measure its life in seconds or minutes. In the case of this monster wave, a lot of minutes. But no one has ridden it, because, like, how do you paddle your board into a hundred-foot wave? I figure if I can get towed in on a surf ski I might have a chance." Sharkey accepted a bottle of beer from Anita and clinked it against Hunter's glass of whiskey. "I've been looking for this wave my whole life."

In his excitement Sharkey did not notice that Hunter had dropped his head, and when Sharkey looked closely, what he took for intense concentration was deep sleep.

"He's had a long day," Anita said. "Plus he's on painkillers for his surgery. He's hurting."

Sharkey was abashed that he'd spoken with such enthusiasm and not been heard. He was chastened, and later, after Hunter had woken and revived himself with whiskey and a joint, Hunter asked him again what he'd been doing.

"The usual," Sharkey said, thinking, *True*. Perhaps the wave really existed, but he had not found it or ridden it.

Hunter was subdued, in pain; he moved slowly, snatching at furniture, and the one evening they went out Hunter needed a wheelchair.

"You'll be fine," Sharkey said at the entrance to the hotel, Hunter in the wheelchair.

Hunter plucked his cigarette holder from his teeth. "There's an answer."

Sharkey glanced at Anita, who smiled and gave Hunter's shoulder a maternal pat.

"There's rehab, which is like prison. But sometimes — again like prison — it works." He lifted his cigarette holder to his mouth and puffed, as though fortifying himself. "There's moving here to Hawaii — nice weather — and you and me, we can teach a course at the university."

"Me a teacher," Sharkey said. "What subject?"

"Writing is surfing, surfing is writing," Hunter said,

"That might work. As long as I don't have to read anything."

Chewing his cigarette holder, Hunter said, "And the subversion of young minds."

"You guys!" Anita said, and hurried to the curb, where a limousine was drawing up.

Hunter leaned closer to Sharkey, speaking in his growl. "And there's the nuclear option." He was still murmuring to Sharkey but staring at Anita in the distance, who was talking to the limo driver. "Lead poisoning. Death spiral. Bleed out. Die off."

"No, man," Sharkey said.

Hunter made a pistol of his hand, pointed the finger of the barrel into his mouth, and fired, his hand jerking back. He didn't smile. He trembled. He weighed the pistol-shaped hand and said, as though explaining, "Speed shakes. Chemical sweat."

"Move here," Sharkey said. "We need you."

Then Hunter called to Anita, "Cancel the car. I don't want to go. I'm not hungry." And he gestured to Sharkey, holding his arms out, still seated in the wheelchair. "Thanks, bro. You're a good listener."

A good listener, because with Hunter he never knew what to say. But "bro" struck him: yes, they were like brothers, Hunter both an inspiration and a bad influence, always going his own way but revealing his weaknesses to Sharkey, his younger sibling. Sharkey knew nothing of books or football or the cities where Hunter was celebrated as a hero. Their common pursuits had been drugs and women, but now Hunter had Anita and Sharkey the location of a monster wave.

Sharkey had recovered from his knee injury and was surfing again. But Hunter, always in pain, had not healed. No wonder he was stoned most of the time, or always on drugs. He got no exercise — he reveled in having a wheelchair to get him onto a plane. Yet he was humiliated by his limping, as he moved with effort from the chair to the bag on the counter where he kept his stash of coke. Addiction did not wear him down; addiction was his mode of survival.

When, after a few weeks, Hunter left, Sharkey realized that when he talked to him about surfing, his sponsorships, his quest for the wave in Portugal, Hunter only half listened, or did not listen at all. Hunter was thinking of one thing only, the cruel distraction of his pain. Compared to that, nothing else mattered.

The phone rang at two in the morning. It had to be Hunter. It was five in the morning in Woody Creek, Hunter's night of rocking or writing about to end; Sharkey knew by now that bedtime for him was dawn.

"Unner." He grunted something unintelligible, then said, "I know you don't care," and Sharkey realized his grunt had been a mention of football, the Super Bowl. "You're lucky. Just the essentials for you — it's all about the senses. I'm done, I'm a mess, physical wreck. My head is full of trivia, and useless shit. But you — all you think about is water." He paused, then gasped,

"You don't need books, you need water and women." He gasped and added, "You're a sensualist."

Sharkey said — his first words — "I'm waiting for you, dude."

A mumble, like chewing, then silence. Hunter was grunting again, but didn't say, "I'll be there," as in other years. He said, "That's cool. You're smarter than the rest of us."

"I'm a dropout, I'm a *lolo*, I'm not smart," Sharkey said. "Listen carefully, man, can you hear me?" He jammed the phone against his mouth and shouted, "I don't know anything! "

"I mean, staying in shape," Hunter said, unfazed by the shout. "Being in Hawaii. Riding the monster waves. Water is life, man."

"I believe that."

Hunter coughed — a terrible pain-filled cough, and when it subsided, he said, "Remember the time we went shooting at that outdoor gun range? And I was drunk, and they threw us out?"

"Yeah. They weren't happy. And you with a loaded gun."

"It was a forty-five-caliber Colt Buntline. Locked and loaded. Like me."

"You puked in my car."

"That'll happen," Hunter said. "Duke of Puke. My signature move. God, you put up with a bunch of shit from me."

"I learned a lot."

"So we're even," Hunter said, and began to cough again, and, gagging, struggled to speak, saying, "Gotta go."

Two days later, the news that Hunter, without warning, had shot himself; and Sharkey knew that in the phone call he had been saying goodbye.

He was a man who had lived his life explosively, in bursts. As he had weakened, dabbing and snorting, in the frenzy of fueling his habit, he had become inward, and Sharkey had not seen until the very end that in his inattention, his lack of interest, his not listening, he was withdrawing from the world that had lost its novelty for him, and, preoccupied with his pain, he was readying himself to die.

18

The Ultimate Wave

Your friend dies, Sharkey thought, and takes part of your being away, and you live on, smaller, with an unfillable hole in your life. The worst of it for the living is that the friend has vanished: the one person you loved listening to, the one who would have understood and taken pleasure in hearing about what you've discovered; the one person who'd believe you. Your well-wisher, dead.

The great self-pitying sadness for Sharkey was that he had found the wave but had no one to share it with, no one he trusted enough. It had to be a secret from other surfers, all of whom were looking for the ultimate wave themselves, the Big Mama. Just Sharkey's mention of its vast size had seized Hunter's attention — made him howl, his baboon bark of pleasure, because he was a man who celebrated the biggest, the best, the loudest, the weirdest, the craziest; someone who gloried in extremes. Hunter would have loved to hear of the monster wave, massive and strange and brief; an intrusion that swelled and broke and fell and was gone. He was like that outrageous wave, the one that Sharkey had searched the world for, that he'd prepared for throughout his surfing life; the one to crown a career.

In Pernambuco one evening after his knee surgery, Sharkey had seen a surfer sitting alone, having a beer on the veranda of a bar, and joined him. They talked of waves and travels — the out-of-the-way breaks. Sharkey mentioned that he'd surfed Cortes Bank but that it had been a bust — a long trip out to the wave and a disappointing swell when they got there, bobbing in the water a hundred miles from shore.

"We got a big one in my country," the man said.

"Where is it?"

"Place called Nazaré."

"How big?"

"Too big. You never seen one so big. Thirty meters sometimes."

Sharkey thought, *I've heard that too many times to believe it.* He said, "Who's ridden it?"

"So far, no one."

But I've never heard that, Sharkey thought: a big wave that has never been ridden.

"And not one," the man was saying, "but maybe four or five separate waves, breaking right and left."

"Why don't you ride it?"

"If I could ride it I wouldn't be telling you about it. I'd keep it for myself," the man said. "But this one has killed so many fishermen."

"Where did you hear about it?"

"I don't hear," the man said. "I see it."

His name was João Roque de Oliveira, he came from the city of Coimbra, sixty miles north of the bay of Nazaré, and the town Sitio on the cliff, above where the wave broke. It was a sad story, João said. Sitio and Nazaré were impoverished fishing villages, made poor because of the wave, which had swamped incoming boats and drowned so many men that the shore was known as a place of death. The stigma had doomed the villages, fishing had declined; the wave dominated its fate, looming over the place, threatening with death anyone who faced it.

"Wicked wave, bad wave," João said.

Sharkey laughed. "No. The wave is just a liquid, rising and falling, then gone forever. It has no character except its size and shape — and that's temporary. It has no morality. It's water, formed by the rocks beneath it and the wind behind it."

"But dangerous."

"Only if you're not prepared for it," Sharkey said. "If you fall off a mountain, it's not the mountain's fault. I've been surfing for many years and what I've learned is, never blame the wave. Look, I blew out my knee on Cacimba do Padre. Whose fault is that?"

"But I think," João said, becoming thoughtful, "if someone manage to ride the wave at Nazaré, he can bring luck to the village, and maybe tourists." He nodded. "Maybe money."

Surfers traded stories about waves all the time, and yet Sharkey had never heard anything of this one at Nazaré. Even surfers who'd ridden the waves at San Sebastián and the Spanish coast — Sharkey himself at San Lorenzo and Vigo, not far from the place João had described at Nazaré — even those watermen had never mentioned the wave.

Maybe they'd never heard of it. Or maybe it was that other factor in surf culture — the secret place, the special break, never to be shared. When Sharkey was interviewed and asked to name his favorite surf spot, he always said with a smile, "I'll give you my third favorite."

"I don't get it," the interviewer would say.

"Telling you my favorite will turn it into a gangbang."

Surfers were evasive when it came to talking about the great places they knew. They might swap the names of breaks, but the rare ones, the undiscovered waves, they kept to themselves.

So the fact that Nazaré wasn't mentioned did not mean it was unknown; it might be one of those secret waves in the world, known to a few, not to be revealed to the many, who would crowd the lineup.

"João, why are you telling me this?"

"Because you're Joe Sharkey."

Back in Hawaii he had a second operation on his knee and spent his days in physical therapy and cross-training. He said nothing of the monster wave, nor did he mention Portugal to any other surfers. He avoided telling Kailani, his girlfriend, suspecting that she might mention it to one of her friends at the health food store in town where she worked. All the women there knew surfers, and the wave would be revealed to the North Shore, and to Honolulu and the world.

What he said was, "I've decided to go with Prime Fuel."

"That cheesy energy drink," Kailani said. "It's junk. Just juice and chemicals and sugar."

"I need a sponsor."

"For what? You've got money, you got this great house in Pupukea now. You've got me."

She was pleading, indignant, and looked wronged. And she was outraged in the way only the young can be outraged, he thought — their innocence violated, with the knowledge of the jangle of money in the world, money as influence, a glimpse of business, seeing it — rightly — as the source of wickedness.

Sharkey said, "I have to do some traveling."

"If you take that deal, I'm not going with you." Her hair was black and lustrous; she tossed it as she threatened, and looked beautiful. "In fact, I won't want to know you."

"What's your problem?"

"You're selling out," she said. "You're not one of these stupid surfers who do anything for money. You're Joe Sharkey. You're *akamai*. You know more better than these guys." She began to cry, snatching helplessly at her eyes and her smeared cheeks.

"Traveling costs money. You've never been out of Hale'iwa. What do you know?"

Enraged by the question, by Sharkey's kicking her yoga mat as he said it, Kailani lost her tears in her anger and said, "That stuff is so junk. Is like poison. And you promised you never do it, and now you doing it. So you fake, and you make ass, and it have a bad ending — that's what I know, panty!"

And when she left, taking her tray of sprouts, her sticks of incense, her aromatic candles and her yoga mat, Sharkey was relieved. He had wanted to go alone. All the sponsors needed was his name and a photograph of him holding the bulbous bottle of Prime Fuel and smiling.

He flew via New York to Lisbon and rented a car. Passing the villages, the markets, the tile-roofed bungalows, the field hands pruning in the vineyards, he thought, *I am a stranger in their country. No one knows that I am on a reconnaissance mission. They too are unaware of the monster wave.*

João was waiting for him as he'd promised, at the church in Sitio, Nossa Senhora de Nazaré. He greeted Sharkey with a hug and said, "I obey what you said. I tell no one that you come here."

"I drove via Santarém — deliberately avoided the coast road," Sharkey said. "I wanted to be surprised."

"I show you," João said.

In the car, driving into the town of Sitio, he'd heard nothing, keeping the windows closed. And the church was in the town. But getting out of the car he'd become aware of a rumble — the sound not of water but of something more solid, like the movement of earth, the shifting of big boulders, the seismic tumble of their stone surfaces chafing, with the suggestion of a motor behind them; then silence; then the rumble again, a sequence of landslides, a mountain moving. He felt it under his feet, the vibration traveled up his legs and into his belly, he sensed it at the back of his eyes.

"We walk — we go to the *farol*," João said, leading him upward along a road, a fortresslike building in the distance, on the cliff at the end of the road, the cupola of a lighthouse surmounting it.

Approaching the cliff edge, Sharkey saw another cliff on a mountain headland beyond it, but this one was in motion — gray, still swelling, topped with froth, and the cliffside was not smooth. On its face were the toppling boulders in the landslide he'd heard. The mountain moved toward him in silence and then, slowly, it broke in a succession of loud collapses, some explosive, the shattering of rock, others aqueous sighs of sea spray, all these sounds at last subsiding in a rattle and smash, a swallowing of the sea.

João had been talking—the falling water had drowned out his words.

"It is the wave," he was saying. "And this is not the biggest day."

Sharkey said nothing for a long time, watching more sets rise and roll in and break.

"It closes out so near to shore," he finally said.

"Is a problem," João said.

"The problem," Sharkey said, and then watched more waves before he spoke again.

The problem was not in riding it, he considered—though that would be a long steep descent and maybe wiping out against the rocks. But more than that was the difficulty of paddling up this mountainside of the swell and setting up on its forbidding summit.

He said so to João.

"Sometimes we ride jet skis around the back of it," João said. "You know about towing?"

Sharkey nodded, still studying the wave, which, while he watched, parted in the middle, one wave breaking right and steeply, another portion breaking left in a barrel, and in the distance a swelling mound of gray ocean becoming bluer as it rose up, lifting and forming into a distant shapely hill and growing to a craggy cliffside before it rolled onward past the other waves and swelled and tipped and broke—and in a matter of seconds this stupendous work of nature was gone, collapsed, tumbled flat in a slosh of froth. Sharkey saw himself fighting his way to the sand, dragging his board behind him.

"I don't like the idea of being towed into a wave," he said.

"No other way to do it," João said.

"You know Mount Haleakalā?" Sharkey asked him. "On Maui?"

"I hear about it."

Sharkey doubted him, but said, "High mountain. Ten thousand feet. I saw it when I was surfing Jaws, and my buddy says, 'Let's go up the mountain some morning and see the sunrise.' So we got woken up at an ungodly hour in the dark and were picked up by a van. Then a long ride up a mountain road, and by the time we reached the top, dawn had started to break. We stood watching it."

João's face registered incomprehension, a wan smile, a slight squint, a twitch of impatience.

The sunrise in Sharkey's memory, impossible to describe to João, was an ocean of thick clouds whitening with silver light, the blown-open cheeks of the clouds defining themselves like the spindrift of waves, then pierced with shafts of gold — flames of it, blades of it, a gilded sea for minutes, and rosy light pricking it, an exploded ocean of billows filling the sky — big waves at last — and dispelling the darkness and warming his face.

"Awesome," he said, because he had no words for it. He was silent for a while and then said, "We'd brought bikes in the van. When dawn had fully broken we got on the bikes and rode downhill all the way to Paia — thirty-five miles, without pedaling."

"Nice," João said.

"Not nice," Sharkey said. "Cheating. Too easy. A ride up in the van. A ride down on the bike. Bad karma. I had to undo it."

"How you undo?" João smiled at the idea.

"A month later," Sharkey said. "I didn't want to wait — I didn't want this karma on me. I got a bike in Paia. I rode it to Makawao and kept going, up the hill, zigzagging, hairpin turns. I was gasping and that was good — I was suffering. And going slow, I saw things I hadn't seen before — orchids, geraniums, and the amazing silversword plant that only grows there — soft spikes, so beautiful growing in the lava gravel of this volcano. I saw this stuff because I was going slow, all uphill."

"Is the way," João said.

"I got to the top. And it was funny. The cars that had passed me on the road were parked on the summit, and seeing me, the people began to clap, and I started to cry. I had undone the lazy ride in the van. I rode back to Paia, happy."

"Nice story," João said. "But you never paddle into this wave. You never —"

He was still talking, but a much bigger wave was breaking and drowned out his words.

Back in Hawaii, Sharkey mentioned towing — just the word, casually, no detail — and Moe Kahiko said, "Laird wen' doing it. Garrett wen' doing. Braddah Skippy. Da guys."

"With a jet ski?"

"Ya. Da kine. Dey wen' try tow-in."

And when he asked further, it seemed that some surfers were being towed at Jaws, and on the biggest days at Waimea — a novelty, embraced by a few, spurned by others. Sharkey thought, *I would spurn it too, but I've seen the wave at Nazaré, and there's no other way to get onto it.*

In the same offhand manner, on one of those Waimea days, he mentioned to Garrett that he wanted to try being towed into a big wave.

"I can show you," Garrett said. "You'll feel great on the wave. You won't be tired from paddling in. You'll just sit there and wait for a beauty."

"Is it *pono*?"

"It's practical," Garrett said. "For some waves there's no other way."

"Give me a lesson."

"You don't need a lesson, brah. Just hang on to the jet ski. I tow you out and drop you on the wave." He bumped fists with Sharkey. "You do the rest."

It was that simple. The only question was when to let go, and Garrett gave him the signal, releasing him early, as the wave was sloping. And Sharkey found himself in a series of big sets that would have exhausted him had he needed to paddle into them. The others in the lineup that day, those who'd paddled out, eyed him and frowned, but they recognized him and said nothing. Only one of the younger surfers, a haole, hardly twenty, whom Sharkey did not know and who did not know Sharkey, called out, "Dude, you hitched a ride!"

To make a point, Sharkey took the next wave, paddling in front of the young surfer, crowding him, forcing him aside while he swore and spat seawater. Sharkey dropped in, surfing the right face of the wave that curled over him, and rode inside the barrel to finish, bursting through the overhanging foam at the far side of the bay.

"Two more rides," Garrett said, picking him up again, "and you'll have it down pat. Just a little softer on your release."

On the beach, toward sundown, Sharkey thanked Garrett for towing him. In his gratitude, he wanted as a gift to tell Garrett, almost twenty years younger, that he was learning tow-in surfing in order to ride the wave at Nazaré.

But he resisted sharing the name, and in the end they talked only of the day and the great surf and the vibe.

"Thanks for the rides," Sharkey said. "Who knows what monster waves you can conquer with a tow-in."

Garrett nodded. "Yeah, who knows," he said. "But we're not out to conquer, man."

Sharkey's smile was a query, a cue for more information.

"It's not about conquest, Joe," Garrett said. "We're just complimenting the wave."

But Sharkey saw it as much more than a compliment; he regarded it as a decisive statement, the assertion "I'm here, I'm on this monster wave, I'm still in the game" — and also as the last public flourish of a long career. No more trophies, no more contests, no more jostling; only the solitary ride down the greatest wave in the world, acknowledging the acclaim and then returning to his old haunts at Rocky Point and Leftovers and Pipeline. He hoped to leave his image on the memory of all the younger surfers: the old man bursting off the top of the wave at Nazaré and riding to the shore into obscurity, never to compete again.

The message he'd left for João was, "Call when it's predicted to be monstrous." And he advised his sponsor, Prime Fuel, that he was planning to attempt the biggest wave in the world; that the marketing team and photographers would need to be ready to converge at Nazaré in Portugal this coming winter.

When the call came, João saying, "Next week — gonna be huge," Sharkey alerted the team, told them of his plan, and had João set up a jet ski for the tow, and without telling anyone else flew to New York and changed at JFK for a flight to Lisbon.

I can do this, I have been preparing for it my whole life, he thought: this week, this day, this wave.

"Vacation?" the man in the seat next to him said as they landed in Lisbon.

"Sort of."

"Not good weather," the man said. "Come in summer. These months the sea is rough. Too cold. They close the beaches."

"That suits me," Sharkey said.

He drove the most direct route to Nazaré, calling ahead to João to warn him that the photographers and the Prime Fuel team would be coming.

"They here now," João said. "Lotta guys."

"No," Sharkey said. "They're just leaving New York with the crew. Some are coming from Australia."

"They here. They on the cliff. They setting up cameras and tents."

"Yeah, right," Sharkey said, and hung up, because the call was a distraction, the road was narrow, rain spattered the windshield, and he had no idea what João was talking about.

As before, João met him in front of the church, the Portuguese man conspicuous in his yellow slicker and his deeply tanned face framed by his hood. Instead of walking, they drove to the lighthouse on the cliff and saw the tents and the windbreaks.

"Those aren't my people," Sharkey said.

"I know now, "João said. "They tell me. Is the news."

"What news?"

"Good news is the wave is coming big tomorrow. Bad news" — he punched Sharkey playfully — "your friend is here."

"What friend?"

"Mr. Garrett."

"McNamara's here?"

"With his team. He going out tomorrow."

There was something in João's poor pronunciation that Sharkey found especially annoying, his slurring delivery of this unwelcome news.

"What about my team?"

"Maybe they come soon."

"But I want to ride the wave tomorrow." Sharkey heard a plaintive tone in his voice, almost a note of helpless pleading.

"You ride the wave," João said. "Is come big all week."

Sharkey did not have the heart to say, "I want to be first."

"Where's Garrett staying?"

"Here. Nazaré. Same hotel." Joao took it all as a joke, an irony, a coincidence.

Lingering in the lobby after he checked in, Sharkey heard the familiar friendly voice: "Aloha, Joe — how's it? Hey, this is great. You here for the wave? Of course you are, why not?"

"You didn't say you'd be here."

"You didn't ask."

Garrett was kneeling over a unblemished surfboard bag, longer and fatter than any bag Sharkey had ever seen. He'd unbuckled the tension straps and was unzipping the sides.

"You hungry? There's good grinds at a little place near here." Still he worked the zippers open, poking beneath them with his fingers. "I'm meeting Nicole there pretty soon."

"That your board?"

"Yeah," Garrett said, and lifted the upper flap of the bag, revealing a gleaming silver thing, a Mercedes medallion, stamped near its top end, and a pointed tip that made it seem more like a dagger than a surfboard.

Sharkey said, "I'm not hungry, man."

He slept badly, but when at last he subsided into sleep, his phone rang in the darkness — João, excited, fully awake, barking in his ear.

"It coming big, Joe!"

"Where's the team?"

"They leave a message. They say tomorrow for sure."

"Who's riding today?" Sharkey asked, but he knew the answer.

Joao said, "Your friend."

"Right."

"You can maybe watch."

Sharkey was not used to being a spectator, idly watching and whistling among people turned away from him, anonymous in a crowd. He backed off, sliding around the photographers, the cameras, the paraphernalia of umbrellas and tripods and billowing windbreaks, all Garrett's team and well-wishers. His own team—the Prime Fuel people, his photographers—had still not arrived. He had asked João about the tow-in, and João had smiled and pointed to Garrett on the beach below, setting off on a jet ski, and said, "Only got one."

And now the crowd on the cliff was calling out to Garrett as he was being towed from the harbor to the left, into the dark slope of the swell. Their faces were tight with fear. They were not cheering, they were appealing to him, offering piteous encouragement, as though to a man in grave danger, and could not help sounding sorrowful.

Sharkey did not think of himself as a jealous man, yet he felt an unexpected tug of resentment, as of being betrayed, cuckolded by a friend, seeing Garrett clinging to the back of the jet ski, dragging his board, climbing at a sharp angle up the wave, carving a streak of white into its belly, like a tear in dark billowing silk. And he was glad when Garrett was towed beyond the break and was hidden by the high foam-trimmed tops. Sharkey raised his binoculars and peered. He saw black water brimming against the sky. The man was lost to view, in the distant sea, behind the huge swell.

Hearing several anguished cries from the crowd, Sharkey looked up and was strangely consoled, and a moment later hated himself for it.

The sound of the sea helped: it smothered him. Falling water had never sounded more destructive, the early sets sliding toward the cliff and breaking like boulders cleaving—not the slop and splash of liquid but the shattering of rocks splintering to smallness, the whole great mountain of water smashing and draining away to a swirling reef of bubbles; and then another, louder.

Three more swelling waves, with wide irregular faces, almost vertical, and then hollowing and scooped and toppling; but no sign of the surfer. Sharkey turned his back on the wave; he kicked at the stones on the cliff, hating the ugliness of the land, feeling stifled and disgusted, stumbling slightly as he gasped for breath. Then a sudden shriek from the crowd, and more yelps, some agonized cheers, and he spun around.

A tiny figure had slipped across the top of the wave and dropped in, and was speeding across its face, carving a narrow furrow of froth.

The wave was still rising as the man grew smaller, cutting sideways—and when Sharkey looked through his binoculars again he saw something even more unusual than this dwarf tumbling down the wall of water. On the face of the wave were more waves, some like moguls on the black run of a ski slope, others like ridges, still more of them formal waves—surfable waves on the wave itself—taller than the surfer who was carving his way around them, speeding toward the bottom of the trough.

Sharkey willed him to stay upright, and when at last the man was struggling in the massive collapse of the wave, then lost to the fury of the foam,
Sharkey cheered with the rest of the watchers on the cliff, the photographers,
the exuberant locals, the sponsors in their distinctive jackets and caps, the
team hurrying down to the beach.

João rushed to Sharkey and hugged him.

"Tomorrow your turn!"

He had no fear now. Seeing Garrett master the wave convinced him he could
ride it, and if the wave was bigger tomorrow, so much the better. Yet he slept
badly, remembering how the face of the wave had not been glassy, how there
had been ridges and head-high waves protruding from it, the phenomenal
scowl of the water monster, its vast bumpy face seen up close.

He was up and in his wetsuit before João's wake-up call. The weather that
early morning was bleak, a low sky of woolly gray clouds, a wind thick with
the sourness of kelp and the tang of the deep sea.

He had his surfboard, he was dressed to surf. But his team, the sponsors,
the film crew and photographers he'd expected, were nowhere to be seen.
João stood with a warmly dressed woman and man, their faces scarcely visible inside their hoods.

Futile, surprised into his own language, João said, *"Muitos carros."*

Sharkey was disconcerted to be among strangers and was aware of their
indifference.

"Conferência de imprensa," the woman remarked, pointing to a platform near the hotel that had not been there the day before, people gathered
around it.

"Incrivel!" an old woman in black shrieked. *"Grande onda!"*

A group of eager hurrying boys pushed past him. Sharkey hated being
able to understand what was said, and that he did so imperfectly made it
worse for its truth being blunter — traffic jam, press conference, a mass of
excited chattering people turned away from him.

The news was of Garrett's ride, the man himself being interviewed, the
lights singling him out in the early-morning gloom. He stood straight, a
small glowing man on the improvised stage, holding his magical board, the
board glinting in the photographers' flashes.

Looking fascinated, João and the others drifted toward the press conference, and Sharkey slipped away. Seeing a pickup truck passing, he stuck out
his hand, and when the driver smiled in a wondering way, Sharkey pointed
to his board and said, "To the beach — okay?"

His words were barely audible over the booming of the waves, but the
board said enough.

As they drove down the hill to Nazaré and the beach, Sharkey glanced at the cliff at Sitio and saw a pack of children, not looking at the wave but kicking a football, and felt a pang for his insignificance.

A jet ski was parked on the slope of the beach, a man astride it, eating a small circular pastry.

"Take me out," Sharkey said, slapping his board.

The man smiled — he understood but looked doubtful, narrowing his eyes.

"Yes, yes, yes," Sharkey said. *"Grande onda."*

Shaking his head, the man finished his pastry and licked his fingers, then began to drag his jet ski the short distance down the slope into the flop of the shore break.

No one saw Sharkey yank the zips, sealing himself into his wetsuit; there were no witnesses to his splashing toward the jet ski and fastening his board to the rear bracket. The man revving the engine did not speak English but used gestures — his voice could not be heard in any case in the loud surf.

That no one was watching made it easier; without witnesses Sharkey was so negligible as barely to exist, half submerged and insignificant being towed across the harbor and into the steepness of the swell, up and over two rising waves, and disappearing behind them.

And then he was at sea, in the middle of the channel, his back to shore, facing the incoming waves. When he let go of the tow rope and was released from the jet ski and was alone, he was a mere wisp on the water, ghostlike, no more than flotsam, perhaps not even visible to anyone on the cliff. And the jet ski was tipping past the crest of a wave and growing tiny, then gone.

For fifteen or twenty minutes Sharkey straddled his board, wondering if the sets were diminishing but keeping to the back of the wave, slipping away when it built and rolled beneath him. He was content in the lift and push of the swell, and unobserved he felt a great stillness, buoyant in the black water, too small to be seen, calm in his smallness.

But he felt himself lifted higher and higher now with each successive wave, the sets rising and giving him a better view of the cliff at Sitio — the crowd had dispersed — and of the ocean. He saw a bulge at sea, like a whale surfacing, its enormous gray head emerging, losing its roundness, its mouth opening, its jaws widening , becoming cavernous, resolving into a formal wave, still rising as it neared him. He recognized it as his longed-for wish; he smiled in greeting, thinking, *Yes.*

This was the wave he'd been yearning for, finally reaching him from the far ocean, long awaited, the wave at last coming to meet him. He was glad to be alone for this, the intimacy of this rendezvous, relieved that no one was watching, liberated by being no more than a speck in the sea.

No one saw him being hoisted and flattening himself on his board, no one saw him paddling like mad into the spume on its crest at the edge of its lip, no one saw him make the final push and drop in. No spectator stood on the cliff as he drove left down the face of the wave, using all the strength in his legs to steer himself across the sudden ridges and creases of steep water toward the thickness of yellowy froth and sea scum on the shore — only small boys on the high cliff, kicking a football, but they were looking at their bouncing ball. And then he was tumbled, blinded, fighting for air.

19

The Kiss of Life

Sharkey's whole back smarted like a blistered sunburn with his fresh tattoo, UNDER THE WAVE, his skin still hot, stinging with the welts of a mass of unhealed needle punctures and bright ink. He stifled a gasp as he was nudged by someone pushing behind him. He stepped aside on the lanai to let the young chattering surfers pass by, and he growled in annoyance at their clumsiness, bumping him, oafishly and unlikely, unsteady in their gait, pigeon-toed and toppling, like amphibians — so sleek in the water, so awkward, stumbling on solid and unforgiving wood planks.

None glanced at him, none spoke, none saw him or commented on the blood that had leaked into the back of his T-shirt. He was old and inanimate. They were big reckless boys, with a scattering of pretty girls, wide shoulders, crazy hair, and bruised feet, pushing past him in a scrum of energy and health and, what was most remarkable, their youth, their gusto, a heedlessness that made them risk the biggest barrels at Pipeline or the winter swell at Waimea.

I was a punk like you once, he thought. *But I surfed Nazaré, and no one here knows it.*

The bungalow belonging to Hunter's friend Franco faced Rocky Point — not large, but the lanai was wide and roofed, surrounding the whole house, and when it became obvious to the surfers that there was not enough room for them to circulate inside they spilled back onto the lanai, laughing, teasing, swigging beer and smoking joints in the sharp burned-vegetable smell of *pakalolo* and sour beer suds.

"That's a man-sized blunt," one of the boys said to Sharkey.

Sharkey showed his teeth as he held the smoke down, saying nothing, wondering whether he would be recognized. But the boy merely nodded in the torpid, seemingly slow-witted way of an uncertain sea animal, sleepy-eyed and tottering on a clod of earth. He seemed to look past Sharkey's head at the breaking waves at Gas Chambers, animated by the sound of water sloshing on the shore, like pebbles swilling in a barrel.

"Custom-made," Sharkey said, and tried to think of something more, but he was too buzzed to come up with anything clever. And talking to surfers involved the challenge of thinking in another language.

"I seen you with Moe Kahiko," the boy said. "He got da kine. Killer buds."

Sharkey was about to reply when he realized the boy was not listening, had begun to lurch away in the direction of four young surfers at the rail of the lanai, whooping at the arrival of someone from the street.

"Hi," he said to a young woman, who looked surprised to be greeted.

"Hi," she said guardedly, and hurried past him, her surprise becoming a kind of anxiety.

I look like an old man, he said in his mind, speaking to himself in a tipsy way, his nose full of smoke, his back burning with the unhealed tattoo. *But I have surfed the monster wave at Nazaré.*

Then he was alone, and looked inside the house through the big window on the empty lanai. But he saw nothing but a thin man, gaunt-faced with falcon features, in a stained T-shirt, one blue tattooed hand raised to his mouth for a hit on a sparkling doobie. The man's face was creased, his neck leathery, his hair spiked and going gray, his mouth half smiling in puzzlement, the lips cracked and stung by salt, the long upraised fingers also sea-soaked and pink and pickled, holding the burned-tipped joint — a weatherbeaten man peering back at him from the inner room, a stranger, his own reflection.

Then he knew why no one recognized him: he was sinewy, too watchful to be trusted, lurking like an outlaw, an idle predator, not hungry but hopeful and alone, a nonentity but old. His skin was blackish and blotchy in places, and the tattoos on his hands and arms were no longer blue but grayish and porous, his skin tissuey from decades of waves slapping it, of sun scorching it. He was a scarecrow haunting the party, a wraith among the pretty girls and golden boys.

The man in the mirror of the window was crowded by gesturing boys, hooting, whistling.

"He's here!"

"Yo!"

"Aloha!"

And he saw, still reflected in the window, the slight, smiling, crop-haired figure of Garrett, garlanded with leis, and his pale lovely wife, wearing a crown of blossoms, advancing behind him across the lanai, greeted by Franco.

"Here's our hero," Franco said.

But entering the house, Garrett looked aside and saw Sharkey standing by the rail of the lanai — he had backed away from the window and the cheering boys.

"Shark," Garrett said, and reached to bump fists, but before Sharkey could meet him with his own fist, Garrett staggered, surrounded, and was pushed into the house, the young surfers following.

In an unexpected hush, the music shut off, Franco began to speak, praising Garrett, provoking bursts of laughter and some boyish hoots; and then Garrett, to applause, haltingly thanked Franco and the partygoers, who cheered as he introduced his wife. The awkward enthusiasm, the inarticulate hollering, were like a tribal rite, but a happy one, of simple celebration.

"Really happy to be part of the paddle-out," Garrett was saying. "Though I never knew him."

Franco interrupted, saying, "Hunter was one of us. He'd understand why it's taken us so long to pull this thing together. How many years, eh? Try wait, doc! But we'll give him a real sendoff, with lots of aloha."

Sharkey sensed the bewilderment in the room, felt it on his skin, the murmuring, the confusion. They hadn't known Hunter either. And he smiled, thinking how he and Hunter were either unknown or forgotten. But he couldn't blame the new generation of watermen for their ignorance, because he himself had never read Hunter's books and could hardly believe that such a restless man could sit still long enough to write anything.

Dusk was falling, lending a fragile luminescence to Franco's garden, the white petals of the plumeria, the crimson torches of ginger, and he was studying them in the mild stupor of *pakalolo* when he was nudged — Garrett.

"Why didn't you come inside, man? I wanted to introduce you."

"That's good. I like that. Introduce me." Sharkey was thinking how, as a stranger now, he needed to be identified and his history explained.

"You did it! You surfed Nazaré!"

Sharkey said, "No one saw me."

"Wrong! They told me — they saw you from the cliff, they saw you from the beach. Diogo, the jet ski guy, saw you."

"Was that his name? Garrett, what I did isn't news."

"That's better, that's humble."

"Everyone saw you, man — the whole world."

Garrett said, "The only one who mattered to me was Nicole. She saw me. That was all I wanted."

Hearing this, Sharkey became tearful, and blamed the blunt in his fingers. He hid his sorrow with sudden anger, saying, "My team didn't show up!"

"You didn't need them! If I'd done that with no one watching, I'd be stoked."

"I could have wiped out bad. I only realized it when it was over."

Garrett said eagerly, "Yes. Did you sense it? That you might die?"

"My mind was empty. I felt" — Sharkey took a hit of the blunt and held the smoke down, then exhaled — "I felt that because no one was watching, I didn't exist. That I only came alive when I was in the shore break, pounded in the soup. And no one was waiting for me."

"Your wave might have been bigger than mine," Garrett said, teasing Sharkey with a poke in his arm.

"They're gone — your wave, my wave. Gone forever," Sharkey said. He put the blunt to his lips and drew on it.

Garrett nodded slowly. "You going back to Nazaré?"

Sharkey did not reply, he was holding his breath. Finally he said, "That was the one I was waiting for," through clenched teeth. "I'm done."

"Me too. But I want more. What're you going to do now?"

The question was vague and ungraspable. It was like being asked, "Who are you?" He had not thought of *What next?* And in his confusion he became aware of a commotion inside the house, a swelling of shouts and bumping floorboards, as of sudden knocking feet. With that too, being crowded by hearty boys and laughing girls, the golden youths, jostling to get near Garrett as Garrett laughed, fending them off, calling out, "He did it too! The Shark was at Nazaré!"

But no one heard, or if they did, no one recognized his name, and Sharkey stepped aside as the surfers pushed past him.

But beyond this were the other cries — yelps, urgent shouts from inside the house, as Franco appeared at a side door and called out, "Olive — we need you here!"

Sharkey watched like a sleepy child as Franco called the woman's name again to the next house, another bungalow behind the hedge of torch ginger and heliconia stalks and crooked plumeria branches.

A small but certain voice in the twilight responded, "I'm here."

"Bring your kit. I think we have a situation."

A woman in a pink patterned pareu parted the flowering hedge, a black valise under her arm. She brushed past Sharkey and he got a whiff of her, not perfume but a soapy aroma of damp hair and glowing skin and a tangle of sweetness, maybe from the crushed petals on the hedge.

"In here," Franco said.

"Call 911," the woman said, entering the house.

Sharkey in his semidaze drifted to the window and looked inside, relieved that it was open, no glass now to reflect his face. A boy lay doubled up on the floor and the woman knelt beside him and began talking to him, urging him to wake, taking his pulse, putting her ear to his chest and mouth. The boy was eerily bluish, his shirt unbuttoned, his toes feebly twitching.

"I just found him here like this," a girl crouching nearby said.

"Did you see him take anything?"

"He does a bunch of stuff. China Girl. Tango. *Batu.* I don't know. Is he going to be okay? Hey, what's that?"

"Narcan," the woman said, adjusting her pareu as she waved away the fretting girl. "Move, please."

"They're coming," Franco said.

And Sharkey watched, breathing slowly, as the woman in the pareu bent over the boy, her face against the boy's, her mouth locked on his in what seemed sudden passion, heaving her breath into him, pressing on his bare chest. The kiss of life. Then she sat up and frowned, her hands snatching at her bag, unwrapping a syringe, biting the tip off, holding it to the light, the window where Sharkey stared, drunk with fascination, a humming in his head, half smiling.

Half smiling — because of the kiss and the craziness. At the other side of the house loud music had started, with shouts and laughter; and here in this shadowy room, the little crowd of silent anxious faces, the boy on the floor, his chalk-white face and blue lips, the woman hovering and inserting the syringe into his right nostril, depressing the plunger, the boy's head moving as though in protest, and then the left nostril, penetrating a bubble of snot and shooting the Narcan up his nose.

The music was still thumping the walls and the floor as the boy opened his mouth. No sound came out, his mouth was simply gaping, but he wagged his head in a sort of sluggish resistance and he gasped, choked a little, and, attempting to raise his head, he drooled on his chin.

"He's moving," Franco said, a flutter of panicky relief in his voice. "Is he all right?"

"No — this is going to take a while." The woman was peering with a small flashlight into the boy's eyes, then wiping his chin, brushing his hair out of his eyes, tidying his shirt. "And if he's been on fentanyl he's going into withdrawal."

Just then, over the sound of the music and her voice, and the shouts from the other room, and the laughter, the wail of a siren, growing louder, nearer.

"Tell them to take him to Kahuku. I'll go with him. He needs to detox."

Still slack-jawed and doglike in his stupor, Sharkey now filled the window, watching the frantic figures, admiring the efficiency of the small woman in the flimsy pareu—pretty wahine, he was thinking—and she seemed the only person in the house with a working brain, someone with a gift, in the sudden visitation from next door, a ministering angel taking charge.

What he first noticed from her physique was that she was not a surfer, and that confounded him, because this slight, small-boned woman had obvious power. She had flown into the room and hovered over the boy in his distress —muscular, blue-lipped, frozen in a convulsion, pale twitching toes—and she had kissed him with force, as insistent as a lover, pressing her mouth against his, and breathed life into him. Lifting her face from his, she had worked magic on his nose with a syringe while caressing him, all this time Sharkey gaping at the window. Even in his half-buzzed state, dead-eyed, his mouth open, his flesh like clay, Sharkey was aroused, as though a voyeur at a scene of unembarrassed passion.

"You're blocking the light," the woman called out to Sharkey.

"Sorry," he said, and heard his voice as goofy.

But the woman had gotten to her feet and was shaping her hands in the air as though trying to grasp something.

"What's all this fuss about?"

She meant the music, the shouts, the laughter from the other room.

Franco said, "Planning a paddle-out. You're welcome to come along, Olive."

"Anyone I know?"

Hunter, Sharkey said in his mind, and at the same time Franco said, "Hunter Thompson. It's taken six years to arrange this."

"My hero," the woman said, putting the last of the vials and the syringe back into the small box and slipping the box into her bag, deft with her beautiful fingers. "I always fancied him."

She looked around the room, at the tall tattooed girl crying in relief, another girl wearing a dog collar, the giggling surfer boys, the solemn face of Franco clutching his cell phone, the spilled food and vomit, the clutter of beer cans, the racket in the next room, brutal music and cackling laughter. All this with the slowing siren of the ambulance outside the bungalow, the gagging boy on the floor, and the sizzle of breaking waves just beyond the hedge at Rocky Point.

Then, staring disapprovingly at Sharkey, she tossed her head and said, "Hunter Thompson. How staggeringly appropriate."

Silent, heads bowed, in the muted light of early morning, the young surfers gathered on the beach at Waimea, holding their boards under their arms, as Franco—old, limping, white-haired man—distributed the leis. Dawn was a milky gleam in the ragged clouds above Waimea Valley—no sunlight yet

— and a pinkish vapor lifted and lightened at the horizon to the west, where the wide ocean looked flattened by the sky.

"Nice to see you, Shark," Franco said, handing Sharkey a coil of soft yellow blossoms.

"Wouldn't have missed it for anything. Too bad we couldn't have done it sooner."

But Franco had moved on, still distributing flowers. The surfer next to Sharkey spun his lei on his wrist and turned to Sharkey looking baffled — freckled, pinched face, flexing his toes in the sand. He said, "This guy — what's his name?"

"Hunter."

"From the mainland?"

"From all over."

"Where did he surf?"

"Everywhere."

"Gnarly?"

"You bet."

"Sweet." And the boy twirled his lei over his head, adjusted his board, and started down the beach, kicking the damp sand.

He had no idea. None of them did. And he would have been disillusioned if he'd met the man, especially in his last years, the frenzied, injured, addicted Hunter, who could barely walk. And the woman, Olive, who had said, "My hero," looking up from the boy whose life she'd just saved — she too would have been bewildered by the wreck of a man whose books she obviously admired, whom she'd never met. He was a man who had never surfed and ended up baffled by the sea — crippled by pain, buzzed on drugs, stalled in his writing, hating his body — who'd blown his brains out. But he was a hero.

So that's how it worked, Sharkey reflected as he flattened himself on his board and paddled toward the middle of the bay. Hunter's physical self didn't matter. His books stood for him — that madman genius, people called him, his furious voice of defiance — the man in the books was the one people loved and talked about; the man himself had vanished into his myth now.

None of these paddlers knew him, the nurse — Olive — at the bungalow, the spectators here on the beach — none of them could have had any idea of Hunter's timidity, his vulnerability, his whispers, his frailty, his clinging to life, and with a gunshot his letting go, dropping himself over the falls for an eternal hold-down.

But though no one in the paddle-out knew him, they would remember him, as a spirit, at the dawn of this lovely day, in the imagery of floating flowers, the surfers ranged in a great circle on the bay while the long-haired Hawaiian priest, seated on his board — a blossom behind one ear, a crown of flowers on his head, a *haku* lei of pikake — chanted prayers in full-throated Hawaiian. All the surfers slapped the water, pounding the sea with open hands, and cheered. Then it was over, a formal effort ended, the ritual creating someone to remember, a bit more of the myth.

Sharkey turned as soon as the slapping stopped and the water was stilled. Paddling to shore, he saw her waiting on the beach, a small figure in green hospital scrubs, holding a lei, looking helpless, but smiling when she saw him slipping off his board and approaching her.

"I was at work, in surgery — they wouldn't let me off. I'm sorry I missed it. A paddle-out is so awesome. I cry sometimes."

"It's all *pau*," Sharkey said. "It was beautiful — a good turnout. He's been honored. A good memory."

"What to do with this?" she said, lifting her arm on which the lei hung. Then she smiled and lifted the lei and, standing on tiptoe, looped it over Sharkey's head.

"You're supposed to get a kiss with a lei."

"I know that," she said, and kissed him, warming his lips with hers on the cool morning.

"Don't go," he said, seeing her turn away.

She faced him then, squinting, dipping her head, an exaggerated *What now?* smile.

The panic Sharkey felt just then was the urgent need he experienced when he wanted a drug or a drink, a thirst he felt convulsing his whole body. It was not lust, it was a need much deeper, a desperate sense that he was being abandoned, that at last he'd found someone who could save him.

"Don't leave me," he said.

She took it to be a joke and smiled again.

"Please," he said, and with that word Olive lost her smile and took a step closer to him.

PART III

The Paddle-Out

1

Lies

S he'd hoped for dirty rain and just a scrub of moonglow, but the visibility was poor enough to suit her, the car's headlights diffused by misshapen ghosts of drifting sea mist, one of them twisting like a wraith in the road. Beside her, Sharkey sighed and squirmed like a small boy in a big chair, kicking to get comfortable, wishing to be elsewhere. Two weeks after his wipeout he was still too rattled to get behind the wheel. Struggling to break free of the hold-down, snatching at his leash, he'd somehow whipped his hand and sprained his wrist. He was gripping the wrist now, cuffing it with his good hand as he fidgeted, discontent obvious in his cramped unwilling posture.

"This sucks."

But Olive did not reply. She drove downhill to the shore in silence, then along the narrow road next to the slosh of the sea.

At last she said, "Bloody right. That's why we're here."

Near Waimea a pothole the size and shape of a manhole opening shone in the lights of an oncoming car, water from the morning's rain shimmering silver in the hole.

"I hate being here."

"Ask yourself why." When he didn't answer she went on. "And yet you pass this spot practically every day on your way to town or surfing."

"I don't stop."

"That's why we're stopping."

"I don't even look."

"You have to — now."

He struggled in the seat. "I don't want to do this."

"Pull your finger out, mate!" she said, and gasped in frustration.

That got his attention. When he sensed the car slowing down he covered his face, but clumsily, favoring his injured wrist.

"It was right here," she said, "on a night a little like this."

She rolled onto the shoulder of the road, a narrow strip of sand, broken coral, and stones grinding beneath the tires. Her yank on the handbrake had a force with the sound of a demand in it, in the ratcheting a jerk-squeak of finality.

Sharkey sat in silence. After a deep breath that he expelled as a sigh he said, "I didn't see him."

"That was your first lie. You did see him — you said, 'Oh God' — and then you hit him."

Olive unclicked her safety belt and got out of the car, Sharkey following her, slowly, in reluctance. Now Olive was kneeling in the dark, the sound of waves breaking in Waimea Bay, sea-slop draining from the deep fissures in the lava rocks on the low cliffs.

"He was lying here," she said. "I could see his neck was broken. Head trauma. He had no pulse."

"He was drunk."

"You were drunk," she said, standing up to face him.

"I was buzzed."

"Buzzed is drunk."

"He was riding down the wrong side of the road."

"You're blaming him. A lot of bike riders ride that way."

"I didn't mean it," Sharkey said softly.

"I know it was an accident. But it might have been avoidable if you'd been sober. Remember, I wanted to drive."

"Why didn't you say so?"

She stared at him, a passing car lighting her face, her expression of defiance.

"Don't tell me you don't remember — please, not another lie," she said. "The cop came and asked for details."

"I knew his father. Ray-Ban. Goofy-foot."

"You didn't tell him you'd been drinking. He asked you if you'd been buckled up. You lied about that. He asked you how fast you'd been going. Another lie. How many lies so far?"

"People say those things all the time."

"Yes. But a man died," Olive said. "You killed him. And there's some sinister shadow over you — over us. And you think it doesn't matter? You don't eat, you can't sleep, you hardly surf these days." She paused and took his hand. "Your life has somehow gone into reverse." She tugged his hand for emphasis. "We have to make it right."

He turned away from her and clutched his face again. "I said I was sorry," he whispered into his hand.

"A lie. You never said that."

"I want to go home," Sharkey said. "My wrist hurts. I feel terrible. I'm tired."

They stood in darkness, hearing the sea, the low breaking waves at Waimea, seconds apart, like a vast tureen of thick soup somewhere beyond the palm trees, the plopping sound of it being slowly emptied. And when a car approached and the road was lit, they saw the ugly broken pavement and the loose stones, the litter of soda cans and plastic bags snagged on low bushes, and their own car, parked at an angle on the sand, tilted on the shoulder, the pothole like a brimming sewer, the nearby tree trunks slashed with initials.

"It was right there," Olive said. "That hole filled with rainwater. I hadn't realized how deep it was."

Sharkey squinted past the palms to the bay, scowling at the dribble of moonlight on the blobs of froth. No wind, only the slop and plop of the soupy sea on sand and rocks.

"Kneel down with me," Olive said.

"All the drama," Sharkey said, and made a sibilant scoffing, seeming to spit.

"A man died here," Olive said. "On this spot."

Sharkey glanced to the left and right, and seeing no cars, he walked near the pothole, kicking his flip-flops. Then he lifted his swollen wrist with his good hand to favor it and knelt next to Olive.

Bowing her head, Olive said, "Three beers at the bar and a hit of *pakalolo*. 'We'll get your car tomorrow,' you said. No seat belt. Driving in the rain, you began that long story about Moe Kahiko. Then 'Oh God.' You hit the man and kept sitting. You didn't get out of the car. I did, and saw that he was dead."

"I checked him out," Sharkey said in a tone of protest.

"Wait. The cop comes," Olive said, still narrating the order of events. "You tell him that you weren't drinking. That you were buckled up. That you didn't see the man on the bike."

In the distance beyond the curve of the bay a car's headlights lifted from the surface of the road, making a tunnel of the trees. Sharkey rolled back to a squat and began to get to his feet.

"Stay where you are," Olive said. "Is that what happened?"

"Something like that."

"Is that a yes?"

Sharkey sighed — the small boy's sigh, a whimper with a yes fluttering through it.

The oncoming vehicle slowed down—an old pickup truck, a surfboard slung in the back—and when it rolled to a stop the driver cranked down the window.

"You guys all right?"

"We're fine," Olive said.

But the man was watching Sharkey, who had dropped to his knees again.

"Sure you don't need any help?"

Olive said, "We lost something."

"Eh," the driver grunted, with confidence. "Joe Sharkey—how's it?"

Sharkey lifted his hand slowly, a tentative salute. "Like the wahine say, we wen' lost something."

"Some bugga cockaroach you stuffs?"

"Nah." Sharkey touched his face, keeping his hand against it as though he didn't want to be scrutinized. "Was maybe my fault."

When the man had driven off and they were in darkness again, Olive said, "How many lies is that?"

"I don't know. Couple, three."

"Seven," she said. "But there were more."

Back in the car, she pulled onto the road and drove toward Hale'iwa, then onto the bypass. The tension of visiting the scene of the accident, her intense concentration, her anxiety—all the emotion—nerved her to be efficient rather than uncertain. And Sharkey's halfheartedness stiffened her resolve. It was like being in Emergency, hyperalert at midnight, receiving a casualty on a gurney, controlling the moment, in triage.

"Where are we going?"

Home was in the opposite direction. Olive had taken the way through the cane fields and was ascending to Helemano on the steep country road, no streetlamps, little traffic, twelve miles of darkness.

"Wahiawa," she said. "The cop shop."

Sharkey nodded; he seemed to accept the logic of retracing their steps, reconstructing the timeline of the accident. But he didn't speak; he lapsed into the dullness Olive had come to see as his usual mood since killing the man, not unwilling but bleak and detached and luckless.

"When did it happen?" she asked.

He bobbed his head as though marking time. He said, "I honestly don't know."

"Think," she insisted.

She could hear a slow growl of frustration. Sharkey didn't speak, only made an audible gripe, but it was a grunt of futility, not as distinct as a word.

"Over a month," she said. "It'll be five weeks on Thursday."

"That long?" he said in a whittled tone of loss, his voice trailing off.

"And in that time nothing good has happened. You've gotten repetitive. Incoherent sometimes. I lost the baby — your baby. You almost drowned."

He was slumped, holding his hands to his eyes. She wanted to say more but was overcome by pity, the big tattooed man with muscular shoulders sitting hunched over in silence, his posture that of a child sorrowing for a wrong he'd done.

He was fragile, he was broken, she had to be careful, and she drove as steadily as she could, so as not to jar him with sudden acceleration or braking. She lulled him with the monotony of the straight road and, on the outskirts of Wahiawa, just before the bridge at Lake Wilson, she slowed the car.

Sharkey still slumped, Olive looked over and saw scattered rags at the base of the embankment, a tipped-over supermarket shopping cart, a baby carriage, and she knew that this was not junk or discarded but the elements of primitive domesticity, the camp at the top of a steep path where, beneath the eucalyptus trees and the Norfolk pines, there were people in dirty tents or under tarps, a cluster of homeless people, cooking over wood fires, muttering in the dampness, and children too, living like jungle folk, hidden by bushes — the Hawaii she hadn't expected, of bad days. The woodsmoke and tang of burned meat from those huddled poor gave off the misleading odor of a picnic.

After the bridge, another light and the low town, she turned left and at the top of the hill another left, Sharkey groaning with each turn.

"Oh God."

"We have to do this."

The police station was a one-story, flat-topped building at the street's dead end, behind a well-lighted parking lot.

"I don't want to go in."

"Just try to remember what happened, and we might not have to."

She parked the car and led Sharkey to the open terrace where, on the night of the accident, she'd approached him, the rain falling hard, and he'd said, "I ran into a drunk homeless guy."

That is wrong, she'd thought, but she hadn't acted, hadn't corrected him. And afterward his life stalled, went sideways, seemed to drag to a halt, and he'd become hopeless.

I have to revisit that scene, she'd thought, *his dishonest statement.*

They climbed the stairs to the terrace where the police station sat like a fortified building atop a swale of sloping grass, a lava-rock wall at its perimeter. Seeing her pass him on the stairs, Sharkey paused, but she gestured for him to follow, insisting with her beckoning hand.

Sharkey obeyed, digging his toes ahead of him — the reluctant child again — and when he drew near her he whispered, "I'm not going in there. You can't make me."

She turned to him, took him by his two hands to calm him, brought him closer, and as he bowed toward her she touched her forehead to his and said softly, "All you need to do is tell me what you said in the accident report."

"You mean what happened that night?"

"What you claimed happened that night," Olive said. "The lies, the half-truths, everything that got you off the hook."

He hesitated, then said in a small shallow voice, "I explained the accident."

"Was it the truth?"

"It was what I remembered."

Olive said, "Joe, listen. If you don't tell me the whole truth, I'm going inside. I'll get a copy of the report and I'll show you that it's full of lies."

He stood flat-footed and solemn on the terrace, glancing at the station entrance, then turning to look outward, beyond the rock wall, to the parking lot — the lights in a nimbus of drizzle, the wet street, the night glow over Wahiawa, the air muddy and chilly, a twinkle of red lights and the stutter of a rotor, a helicopter bumping low in the sky in the distance, going lower to land at Schofield Barracks. Sharkey pretended to be interested, he fidgeted, rubbed his arms in the chill, sniffed a little, blinked and breathed hard, unsure of what to say.

Olive said, "You told them you hadn't been drinking. Was that true?"

"No. I've already said that."

"But you dictated it to the cop who was writing it down in the accident report. You saw him writing it."

"Okay, I'd had a few drinks."

"Three drinks. Over the limit. And the *pakalolo*."

Still watching the starless and indifferent sky, Sharkey nodded.

"You were in a good mood — talking — but you were toasted."

"Yeah."

"Seat belt?"

Sharkey jerked his head, an unwilling negative.

"So the cop wrote another lie on the report."

"Guess so."

"Did you see the man on the bike?"

In a thin breathy voice Sharkey said, "I guess."

"Former lifeguard, trained in first aid. Did you administer help to the victim?"

"Kind of," Sharkey said, beginning to object. "Okay, you got out of the car and checked on him."

"What did you do, Joe?"

He took a deep breath and with an effort of will that was audible said, "Nothing."

"But in the report it says that you hurried to his side and checked his vital signs."

"I meant that you did."

"All those lies," Olive said.

"The cop never asked the right questions," Sharkey said. "He saw who I was, he mentioned his old man — I knew the guy. And here at the station the same deal. 'You're Joe Sharkey.' It's happened lots of times before — you've seen it. Locals respect a waterman. They know the risks I've taken." He muttered a little, then said, "My rides."

"They gave you a pass. They were dazzled. You could have set them straight." Olive stepped away from him. "The worst of this isn't that you lied to them, or concocted a false accident report. The kicker is that you lied to yourself." Her voice frail and tearful, she said, "I loved you — and you lied to me."

He walked away from her, into the half-shadow at the corner of the station. She watched him for a while and, standing there, she saw a squad car pull in. After a slamming of car doors, a policeman marched a barefoot, handcuffed man up the stairs to the terrace. The man's long hair was flopped over his face, his shirt torn. Another policeman met them at the station entrance with a flashlight, which he shone on the face of the handcuffed man, who averted his gaze.

"This the ten-sixteen?"

"Yah. Lemi Street. Domestic."

Seeing Olive, the cop with the flashlight turned it on her and called out, "Can I help you?"

"I'm fine, but can I ask you question?"

"Make it quick — we gotta book this guy."

"When you get a fatality — accident or homicide — you send the body to the medical examiner, am I right?"

"Yeah. In town — Iwelei."

"How long do they hold the body?"

"Till they ID it, so they can issue the death certificate," he said, standing against the door, propping it open for the other policeman to lead the handcuffed man into the lobby of the station. "That all you need to know?"

"Thanks. That's it."

When they had gone inside, Olive walked over to Sharkey, who was still half in shadow, his upcast face peering into the darkness.

"That night," Olive said, "you were standing right there on the terrace. Do you remember what you said?"

Sharkey began to speak, then sighed, an irritable fumbling to make a reply, thought better of it, and finally lowered his head.

Using his careless voice, Olive said, "I ran into a drunk homeless guy."

Sharkey nodded, rubbing his face with the back of his hand, chafing his mouth with his knuckles.

"Tell me what you did."

"Killed him," he said. "I killed a guy."

"Who was he?"

Sharkey's hands went to his face as though to mask it.

2

"Unidentified Male"

His frailty was one thing — as a nurse, she understood that, he'd experienced some sort of psychic trauma; but he was infantile too in a way that baffled and provoked her. He had been like a child at the scene of the accident at Waimea, yawning anxiously, looking away, shuffling his feet. And he was childlike too at the police station, hesitant to speak, tongue-tied and touching his face; he had squirmed in the car like a brat, and back home had curled up, hugging himself, buried in pillows. Olive struggled to be patient. The stark truth that he had no one else — that his behavior would have antagonized most people — brought out a maternal side in her, the one that had softly throbbed in her body when in a pool of blood she'd miscarried in the surf. And so she reclaimed the child in Sharkey.

They were back in the car the next day, heading into town on the freeway, Sharkey bent forward as though he'd been scolded, and she could hear his long slow breaths, like sighs of woe, as he made himself small in the passenger seat, spitefully compact, holding his head in a lamenting posture.

In the heat and glare of Honolulu, on the dusty concrete of the back streets of Iwilei, he seemed smaller still and looked stricken, among the industrial buildings tagged with graffiti, the lowered shutters, and the corrugated iron warehouses behind padlocked fences. He was no longer the bold waterman who rode the big waves. She wondered if his childishness was a reversion, his way of sorrowing. It was not his physical size she was assessing but the diminished aura of strength, his way of standing, one shoulder lower than the other, that made him oblique. He was now like a man seen in profile, turning aside, shy and unthreatening. Because of that impression, she — who was delicate and so much smaller — loomed larger as a force, giving directions, vibrant with nervous energy, taking command but maintaining a mode of motherly protection.

Sharkey lingered behind her — "I'm with her," he said to the receptionist, who singled him out because he was a man — while at the counter Olive unfolded the paper with her hospital's letterhead.

"I've got this for the medical examiner," she said.

"Stickney not here at the moment. He wen' stay in conference."

The clerk fingered the paper. She was a fish-faced woman, her black hair drawn back so tight the contour of her skull was evident under it. Her fingernails were long and glossy green, and one nail tapped a line on the paper.

"Who Olive Randall is?"

"That would be me."

"I'm need for see you photo ID."

Olive handed over her driver's license and at the same time signaled for Sharkey to show his.

"This is my partner — he's mentioned in the authorization. We're here to get an update on one of your pending cases, a body that was brought in."

"I'm reading all that here," the clerk said peevishly, prodding the paper, head down. "Take a seat."

"The medical examiner," Olive said. "We need to see him."

"Chief medical examiner," the clerk said, still pondering the paper, and without looking up added, "We real backed up today. If this letter approved I check if anyone free to assist you in your requess. You need see Stickney." Only then did she raise her eyes. "Sit, please."

Sharkey had already found a chair and was staring vacantly at the floor. Olive drew up a stool next to him. A framed announcement on the wall was headed FREQUENTLY ASKED QUESTIONS (FAQS) ABOUT AUTOPSIES, the first question being, *Where is our loved one being taken?* Olive looked away.

"It's going to be all right," she said in a voice so raw it was like a surrendering statement of utter hopelessness.

She raised her hand to touch his cheek, and he reacted as though he were about to be slapped and, wincing, looked pained. That made her all the more tender toward him. Her instinct was to hold him, caress his head and whisper reassurance. When he bowed as though in despair, clutching his hands, his tattoos looked frivolous and mocking, like graffiti.

So they sat, side by side, slightly apart, small mother, big boy, twitching at times, saying nothing, as though grieving, while people came and went, murmuring at the counter, taking no notice of them, rattling papers, and it seemed they were perhaps in mourning too.

Olive glanced up. *Can we come and see him/her?* was the second question in the framed announcement.

After twenty minutes or more—Olive couldn't tell; she had begun to meditate, relishing the silence of the wait—the door to the inner office was thrust open by a man who held it ajar with one hand, a clipboard in his other hand.

"Joe Sharkey," he said with a summoning shout.

"And I'm Olive."

"You Braddah Joe?" the man said, a smile forming on his lips. "How's it? I'm Stickney."

"Are you the chief medical examiner?" Olive asked.

But the man—potbellied, in green scrubs—was awkwardly hugging Sharkey while still clutching the clipboard.

"Hi, Stickney. Aloha."

"I think maybe you know my cousin Wencil Makani. Big surfer. He seen you on the Pipe so many fricken times. He say was awesome—he so stoked."

As the man backed away to behold Sharkey, Olive reached and flicked the clipboard, saying, "We're here to see the death certificate of this person."

"You make us proud, brah," Stickney said, jerking the clipboard Olive had touched and holding it against his loose shirt. "At your age, still riding monsters."

"Riding monsters," Sharkey said in a small ironic voice.

"Dis way, guys." Gesturing with his clipboard, Stickney indicated that they should follow him through the door. He led them along a corridor, past offices to a stairwell leading to the basement, talking the whole time. "No death certificate for this case as such. Before we issue official-kine death certificate we need one ID, and so far cannot—got no hits so far on the ID."

"What have you got?" Olive asked.

"Got autopsy report."

"Can we see the remains?"

"That's where we going, sister. Like I was telling you. To da kine—morgue." And to Sharkey: "Surf up today morning?"

"Head-high."

"Is that the coroner's report?" Olive asked, because Stickney, wagging his arms in the stairwell, was rattling the pages.

"Pathologiss," he said.

"What do you do?"

"Medical examiner. I do some assisting. Like, I helped with this case."

"The accident victim?"

"The assumption is accident, but who knows the real true reason for decease. Look like he got smoosh pretty bad by one car. But, hey, what led up to it is the question."

Sharkey looked away, his hands flying to his face.

Olive asked, "What's the answer?"

"Autopsy," Stickney said, chewing the word. "Or you can say necropsy."

They had come to the bottom of the stairway, where a windowless corridor led to a heavy door. Stickney poked some numbers onto a keypad on the wall, then pushed open the door.

The smell of disinfectant was strong — stronger than anything Olive knew at the hospital, stinging her eyes. When Stickney flicked on the inside lights, she saw what might have been a bank of filing cabinets, a gray wall of handles and labels. Stickney tapped the paper on his clipboard, all the while glancing at the labels. Then he bent over, and in one graceful motion, saying "One-two-tree," caught hold of a handle and pulled at it, sliding out a long platform on chuckling rollers, a shroudlike cloth on it, lumpy from the body beneath it.

"Here one decease," Stickney said, and swept away the cloth, bunching it and tucking it under the gray bony feet, a plastic band around one ankle and on the other foot a toe tagged and scribbled with a number and a date.

The rest of the body was as gray as the feet, but in places with the dull yellowish pallor of old rubber. It was damaged in places, deeply scored — slashed and stitched, like a big mended monster doll, part of the skull broken open, a piece of the cranium missing, a Y-shaped scar running from the shoulders down the chest, the stem of the Y ending at the lower belly.

Sharkey had turned away and was staring wildly at the floor.

"We're wondering who he is," Olive said.

"The one thing I cannot tell you," Stickney said. "Because we never find out."

"Did you take fingerprints?"

"Always we take — if got fingers, the body."

"Sometimes no fingers?"

"Or more worse, sometimes hands no got. Sometimes feets no got."

"In that case, dental records?"

"If got teeth. Buggah came here last week, no hands, no teeth. What can we do?"

"Crime victim?"

"Coulda been, was decompose, one month, maybe more, in Keʻehi Lagoon, was dredge up by one fisherman."

"If you can't ID a body, what do you do?"

"Keep ʻem here in the locker. Wait for *ohana*. Maybe they mention a tattoo or a mark or scar." Stickney consulted his papers. "Just one small tattoo on this body, like a name."

"Show us, please."

"Left arm — forearm."

Stickney used his ballpoint to indicate the inch-square mottled patch, bluish on the shriveled skin.

"Looks like a Chinese character," Olive said, and photographed it with her phone.

"I never think of that," Stickney said. "In the file, the tattoo."

"What happened to the head?" Olive asked, and heard Sharkey softly groan.

"Was autopsied. I open it myself. Vibrator saw. Brain was took out for lab work."

"Did they find anything?"

"They look for abnormality. Tumor. Toxic substances, all that. Same with chest cavity. The guy got hit by one car, but why? Maybe he drunk? Maybe drugged out? We start with external metrics — weight, length, identifying marks." He chopped with his clipboard. "Then we cut."

"All those stitches. I mean, I work in a hospital, but that much suturing is pretty rare for us."

"Remove front of rib cage, expose trachea and lungs and remove. Then abdominal. Liver, kidneys, intestines, what-not. Inspect da kine, send every-thing to lab." He nodded, widening his eyes. "We more thorough. Reason you never see in your hospital. Autopsy is a big money loser."

"I've seen enough," Sharkey said, and crept to the door, retching.

"We put everything back. Then we sew up."

"What did you find here?"

"Says here no alcohol. Not much food. Traces of drugs — suspected meth. Complete toxicology report no come through yet. But homeless."

"Why do you say that?"

"I can always tell by da kine dirt."

"Just that?"

"Skinny guy, needs shave, condition of hands and feets. Signs of negleck. Poor people, you can always know. Plus, no one claim him up to this point in time."

"What about personal effects?"

"Nothing that we found. Nothing in pockets."

"So what happens now?"

"Wait and see. I thought maybe the reason you come here with this con-sent authorization letter was to give us some help. Maybe you know him. Maybe you saw him."

"We don't know him," Sharkey said in a choked voice, leaning against the far wall.

"What we're maybe going to do is get the sketch artist from HPD to come over and do a picture. Like how he looked when he was alive. We'll put the

sketch in the *Advertiser* or *MidWeek* and see if anyone get memory jogged."
He turned to Sharkey. "What kine board you got? Wencil gonna ask me."

Olive said, "Didn't the fingerprints help?"

"Like I said, we run them on the database. No hits yet. You know, sometimes we never find out. Couple of guys last year, no hits at all. Still unidentified."

"Where are they?"

"At the mortuary. Over at Affordable Caskets off the freeway, Moanalua.
Got cremated. Ashes in a box. But we kept some DNA in a file, just in case."

"He has a sweet face," Olive said.

"Haole guy," Stickney said, and with pride he added, "We autopsy more
akamai, so no disfigurement."

"Looks like wax," Sharkey said.

"Because more worse exsanguination," Stickney said, proudly licking the
word on his lips. "Bleed out when we work on him."

All this time the dead man had lain as gray as dead meat, his withered
arms to his sides, the fourth person at the conference, a silent, futile presence around whom all the talk had circulated. By degrees, as though daring
himself, Sharkey had inched nearer, blinking at it, until the body became
less fearsome, its color less shocking, and at last familiar, but tragically so,
contorted like a martyr's.

The man looked drowned, though it took an effort of Sharkey's dulled
imagination to see him as a whole man. He was a fragment, not only in the
sense that he'd been cut apart and sawn open and stitched back together,
but a fragment as an aura of emptiness, this body as a shell, no more than
a carcass — a sad wrapper of dead and folded flesh, its tubes and pipes and
organs hauled out and poked over and shoved back in. Its essence was gone.
Its essence was life. Its blood had been drained away. It was a spiritless bag
of skin and bones, and the skin itself, bluish yellow in places, its limbs ashen,
its hands — Sharkey was nearer them now — enclosed in small paper sacks,
fastened at the wrist with pale tape.

A surfer held down under a succession of monster waves, pawing not
at water but at a smothering boil, ended up this way, suffocated and finally
pushed to the beach — pale skin, corpse meat, staring eyes, soupy seawater
spilling from his gaping lips. Sharkey had seen them in the sand at the shore
break, at least ten drowning victims in his life, young men vital in every way,
powerfully built and yet defeated, stiffened by the rigor mortis that seemed
to come so quickly. His gaze was always drawn to the hands and feet, perfectly formed and useless, the sad still fingers and toes. But those poor dead
men — and one small pale Japanese woman with a fixed face of terror, her
mouth rigid, gaping in a silenced howl — they had been whole, newly dead.

Yet this nameless man, UNIDENTIFIED MALE printed with an inked number on his toe tag, was mangled, incomplete, grotesque, like a botched crucifixion, a mass of cuts and crude sutures so widely spaced they were like the stitches on a rag doll, the swollen edges of skin and flesh a child's learning-how-to-sew project, a blob of laced-up guts.

Only the man's face was whole, and though it had bristly unshaven cheeks, the blue lips slightly parted showed excellent teeth, even and of an unlikely whiteness, the face itself unmarked — thin, slight, indignant creases around the eyes, an expression of affront, of being wronged — the suddenness, the unfairness of death. The man was not old or ugly, as Sharkey had expected. He was perhaps in his early sixties, and there was a suggestion of athleticism in his sinewy legs, gone gray now but retaining their shape. His hair was long but neatly arranged — Stickney's doing; he looked tidy and compact, taking up a narrow length of space on the shelf of the morgue drawer.

The face was mutely accusatory, and Sharkey saw *I am here because of you* in its eyes and its crumpled form: *I belong to you. I am your responsibility. It is your duty to lug me into the light.* And so Sharkey felt burdened and afraid and helpless, and he sorrowed for the man and for himself, encumbered by having to drag this dead nameless corpse along wherever he went from now on.

He saw himself lying there — he'd come near enough to death so many times it was easy for him to project his own body into the drawer. But what shocked him was that the man looked so small and lonely, naked and discolored and bloodless, unrecognized, friendless, the best of him — the miracle of life — gone. Not obscurely leaked away but taken from him, his life knocked out of him. And he looked unloved.

But turning away from the corpse, Sharkey felt an uprush of energy, joy bordering on rapture, a feeling of miraculous survival, and needed to calm himself from his exaltation. *But I'm alive!*

"I'm going to take some pictures," Olive said, raising her phone.

"Can take. But cannot publish without family permission," Stickney said. "Which family?"

Stickney reacted, jumping a little as though teased. "Good question, sister!"

Stickney went on talking to Olive, skidding his thick fingertips on the papers on his clipboard, his jowly face full of life — his presence made it for Sharkey a study in contrast, the dead man looking deader, more futile, like a scabby log tossed by a wave to the beach among the broken shells and splintered driftwood and webs of dried sea froth, the corpse twisted into that same mass of sea-washed flotsam in a tangle at the tidemark.

"So you can't tell us anything about him?" Olive was saying.

"I can tell you everything," Stickney said, wagging his finger at the body with each assertion. "What he ate. What he drank. If he smoked. If he done drugs. That he was probably homeless. How did he die. Plenny more." Then he smiled, but grimly. "Only one thing. No name, as yet."

"How did he die?"

"Not from the drugs, but he had drugs in his system. Cause of death was blunt-force trauma to the cervical and spine. Skull fracture. Internal bleeding. Say hemorrhage here on the report."

"From the accident," Olive said, and took Sharkey's hand and held it, clutching his cold fingers.

"Hit by car," Stickney said. He grinned at Sharkey. "Wait till I tell Wencil I seen you. Insane, brah. He gonna freak out."

3

Kapu

In the distance a glowing canopy of high leafy boughs in a grove of brittle albizia trees, rising rags of oily smoke, the flare of a campfire, light without much illumination, the whole of it hidden by tall scrub and guinea grass, enclosed by evening shadows. At the edge of the road next to the guardrail a supermarket shopping cart lay on its side, with a rusted broken baby carriage, the limbless torso of a child's plastic doll, a burst-open plastic bag of trash, its contents strewn and picked over, probably by feral cats or wild pigs. And painted on a board in the goop of what looked like peeling nail polish, the word KAPU.

"We should have come here sooner," Olive said, but disgustedly turning aside. The junk pile had an aura of hostility and violence, and the sign meant go away.

"Probably weeks ago," Sharkey said.

But they knew, standing there at the head of the path, why they hadn't. The place looked forbidden, if not haunted. There was no road. The path was narrow and seemed to lead into the pinched darkness of an ambush.

It was almost six o'clock, an hour from sundown, the day after their visit to the medical examiner's office. On the way home, passing this spot, Olive had said, "Homeless camp."

"What do you think?" she said now, lingering at the roadside — the bypass road, cars flashing past. She kicked at the shadowy overgrown footpath, near a tulip tree in flower, its fallen blossoms littering the ground like red rags.

"It's getting dark," Sharkey said, in the insincere, too-emphatic tone of an excuse.

"Maybe come back," Olive said, fumbling for a reason not to enter the path and stepping away. "Maybe earlier next time."

They got into their car and went home, into the dying light, not saying what was on their minds, the thought they shared, that a place so near and so familiar, just a few miles from their house, close to Haleʻiwa and the main road, not far from the beach, some of it visible — the woodsmoke, some patches of plastic tarp and laundry on some of the branches of the bigger trees — here was a place that was unknown and maybe dangerous, like a jungle village in Indo, away from the beach.

But these people were poor, they were homeless and unemployed and ragged; they were the filthy bearded men and gaunt women that drivers saw crossing the bypass road at that point, hurrying on dirty feet, slipping into the muddy rut of a path, elusive and seemingly desperate, clinging to the edges of the town, crouched in the tall grass. They washed, if they washed at all, in the sinks in the changing rooms at the beach park and scared the tourists. They didn't panhandle, they didn't beg, they were reputed to be thieves yet were seldom caught in the act. Their overwhelming intention, it seemed, was to remain hidden, anonymous, out of reach, and in the uniformity of their raggedness they preserved a kind of anonymity — no one could name them, they looked alike in their poverty, they were a constant presence. Yet they were unknown.

And that was odd in a beach community where everyone had a name, or at least a nickname.

On the night of the accident the policeman had said, "We seen him near the homeless camp on the bypass road." Stickney too had said, "Homeless. I can always tell by da kine dirt."

Without saying so, both Sharkey and Olive had avoided going to the place, but they knew — once they had stopped on the road and studied it — that they were committed to paying a visit. Stickney had said he'd found no personal possessions other than the man's rags, the policeman had found no ID. But there was more to know, more to uncover, which might lead to their learning the man's name.

So after that first tentative assessment of the place — their glimpse of the smoke, the path, the junk pile — they went again, heartened by a sunny morning and fewer cars on the road. The passing traffic the previous time had made them conspicuous and self-conscious, standing by the guardrail. They were embarrassed to be seen there by passersby, raising suspicions, and they felt awkward too, being in a place where they didn't belong and — since *kapu* meant forbidden — were not welcome.

More rejection. Sharkey felt the awkwardness more than Olive. He'd once

been welcome everywhere, living his surfing life as the Shark. He was accustomed to being recognized and greeted, as the policeman, as Stickney
had done; and it surprised him — bewildered him — when someone asked
him his name and didn't say, "The surfer," as soon as Sharkey spoke it. He'd
taken it for granted that he would get a smile or a hug. But this had been so
frequent in the past few years that he now saw it as indifference, confirming
his sense that no one knew him anymore, or if they did know his name, they
didn't care — dismissed the risks he'd taken, the prizes he'd won, the monster
waves he'd survived.

The thought of trespass was unformed in his head, just a pulse of hesitation, but it became clearer when, starting down the path, his bare legs cut by
the sharp edges of the tall grass, brushing it aside, walking ahead of Olive, he
saw the bobbing head of a man approaching — bearded, with matted greasy
hair, sunburned in blotches, pushing a rusty bike.

"Hi — how's it?" the man mumbled through cracked lips without a smile.
He prodded with his bike, shoving the handlebars before him, nudging
Sharkey and Olive. Then they were beside him, close enough to smell the
man, his dirt-sweat, his damp hair, the stink of his rags. A decaying haole,
blocking the path.

Sharkey reached for the man's hand and shook it and gripped the hard
dusty fingers and said, "Joe Sharkey."

The man squinted at him, sizing him up, then frowned, looking toasted
or tipsy — vague, anyway, in the bright sunshine. Breathless, unsmiling, he
opened his mouth, then closed it, swallowing his name as neatly as a cane
toad snaring an insect.

"We're visiting," Olive said.

"Looking for someone," Sharkey said, his right hand humming with the
man's dirt.

The man leaned back and scratched his neck. The tattoo on his neck was
large but unreadable. He spoke to Sharkey. "You a cop?"

With a surprised giggle of incredulity, Sharkey said, "No, man, we're just
cruising."

Extending his hand, his yellow fingernails upright, making a cup of his
palm, the man said, "Give me something."

Olive had been preparing for this, clutching a dollar. She handed it to
him.

"Come on!" the man said sourly, pinching the dollar bill and gesturing, as
though handing it back. "Give me five."

The man was thin, and smaller than Sharkey, yet there was about him an
air of menace — his teeth, his dirty, demanding fingers — and a twitch of the

unpredictable. Sharkey knew he could shoulder him aside, push him off the path, but the man would howl and push back, scratch like a cat, maybe bite, and what was the point of fighting him?

Handing him another dollar, Sharkey said, "It's cool — we'll just slide by," and slipped behind him.

"You ain't going to find anything," the man said. "You on the wrong road, buddy."

"Where's the right one?"

"The one that leads somewhere," the man said, and jammed his handlebars against the overhanging grass and pushed into it, calling out behind him, "This one don't lead nowhere."

When he was gone, Olive said, "I don't like this."

"Might as well check it out," Sharkey said, without conviction. He was glum from the encounter but walked on, shoving at the grass, taking the lead.

The air was hot and windless on the path, enclosed by the tall grass, but further on — only minutes, slapping at the insects whirling in the stillness — they were at the edge of a clearing and saw the tents, the blue tarps stretched on poles and slumped like heavy awnings. Two cars were parked on flat tires under the big tree, one car with a whole wheel missing from its back axle, and it was obvious from the cardboard taped on the windows that they served as shelters. Tipped-over cereal boxes littered the top of a wooden picnic table; a cat was asleep on a tin tray.

A woman in a baseball cap poked at a pot propped on boulders, the pot and the boulders blackened by the fire.

"Yaw," she called out, and opening her mouth in objection showed her blackened teeth. A man who had been sitting camouflaged by the leafy shadow on a sofa stood up and became visible — not a sofa, Sharkey saw, but a whole car seat askew on the stony ground. The man was fat and fierce-faced, his head enlarged by a frizz of hair in which tiny white scraps of lint were entangled.

Two small children stirred inside one of the cars, and a woman in a beach chair waved her arms and shouted, "You no see the sign?"

"What sign?" Olive said.

"Da *kapu* sign."

"We never see it, sister," Sharkey said.

"I telling you," the woman said. "Dis all *kapu* here."

This woman was younger than the others, with thin hard-muscled legs, wearing a man's shirt and old faded surf shorts, and yet for all the tears and stains in her clothes and her dirty feet, she had lovely eyes — greeny-blue

— and an appealing manner, coarse and up-front, that suggested the willing surf bunny she might have been thirty years earlier.

Now the man said loudly, "You haoles gotta go."

The children roused inside one of the cars began to laugh, jostling each other, perhaps playing a game, and then flinging toys through the car's open door — broken toys, fragments of plastic.

The fat man took a few steps forward. His dirty T-shirt was lettered ALOHA FUN RUN. He opened his mouth, worked his big jaw in reflection, then said, "What you want?"

"We're looking for someone who maybe used to live here," Olive said in a reasonable voice.

"He got a name?"

"We don't know — we're not sure."

"You don't know who you looking for? Is insane," the woman in the ball cap said from her creaking chair. She shrieked at the children, yelling for them to be quiet, and the children sank into the darkness of the car's interior.

In that moment of distraction, Sharkey looked around and saw the fat man leaning against a tree, his arms folded on his potbelly.

"The man died," Olive said. "We think he was staying here at the time."

"Ask 'em what they got for us," the fat man called out.

The woman in the baseball cap stepped forward. "You hear him. What you got for us?"

"If you have any information, we'll help you," Olive said. "The man was riding a bike and got hit by a car just over a month ago on Kam Highway at Waimea."

"He wen' *make*?"

"Yes."

"I know dis buggah."

"What's his name?"

The woman smiled. She put her hand out and twitched her fingers. Olive folded a dollar into the woman's hand and she made a fist, enclosing it.

"That Jeff. Haole guy."

The children in the car began to scream in the backseat, kicking the seat back, one beating the other and pulling his hair.

The other woman spoke up, not whole words but denying noises, a kind of whinnying, as she sidled close to Olive. "He not Jeff. I know the guy wen' *make*."

Olive held out a dollar. The woman took it and held it to her face in two hands, examining it. "He name Oncle Mack."

"Did he have a bike?" Olive asked.

Watching Olive closely, the woman said, "He have one bike. He ride dis bike."

"This Uncle Mack," Olive said, "was he a haole?"

"Jeff da haole," the first woman said. "She a bull liar."

"Oncle Mack, he a fucken haole too."

"Dis all *kapu!*" the fat man shouted from beneath the tree, and gestured, spreading his arms. "Time to go." He pointed to the path. "Show's over."

Before Sharkey could react there was a commotion in the dense grass and four children emerged, walking into the clearing, a girl and three boys, all of them neatly dressed, wearing small backpacks. Seeing them, Olive smiled, feeling somehow reassured by their solemnity and neatness, the way they nodded at the strangers as though showing respect. Just as quickly the children became shy, averting their eyes, awkward in the disorder of the camp.

"We not homeless," the fat man called out, protesting. "We houseless. Big difference."

"Who is this Uncle Mack?" Olive asked the woman who was fluttering her dollar bill.

"This our home. They try to kick us the hell out. How you can kick people off their own *'aina*?"

"Uncle Mack not the man. Jeff the man," the woman in the baseball hat said.

"All *kapu!*" the fat man shouted, waving his arms, his gesture taking in the whole camp.

"We're going," Sharkey said as the man started to walk toward him and the woman in the baseball hat pressed against him. He said, "Joe Sharkey." He said it distinctly, as though uttering a formula for protection, but it had no effect.

"Give me something," the woman said.

At the picnic table the four children had slipped off their backpacks. They seated themselves, two on each side, and were sorting books and papers as though preparing to do homework. It was hard for Olive to tell through their dirt and their gaunt faces if the adults were haole, but these children being young, in clean T-shirts and shorts, were certainly haole, and the tallest of them, a boy with a splash of ink on his arm, had a thatch of light hair, streaked blond by the sun.

"They go to school?" Olive asked.

"Yah. Elementary — by the old cane fields, pass Ali'i Beach," the fat man said. "Give me some money — buy books, buy stuffs for them."

And now Olive considered the schoolchildren seated and scribbling, and the two small children in the car playing again, reciting in singsong voices, and the first woman back stirring the blackened pot, raising her ladle, lifting white bones and black meat and slimy greens.

"Is that soup?" Olive asked.

"Is not," the woman said in an indignant tone, chucking her chin upward in a gesture of superiority and twisting her lips. "Is adobo."

In that moment, with that word, Olive saw it anew, as a whole coherent settlement. The place had come into focus. What had seemed random, makeshift, a thrown-together huddle of shelters and junk, cast-off people and their broken things, now seemed unified, something fixed and whole. It had a purpose, and a sense of permanence. Was it the neatly dressed children that completed it? Tarp shelters side by side, beach chairs, the car-seat sofa, the inhabited cars, the cooking fire and the pot of adobo, especially that — a meal with a name.

It was primitive but it served them, and in the trailing smoke and the trampled earth, the bypass road out of sight, the camp existed in a parallel world, a dirty improvised version of the other one, self-sufficient. And the trash pile — old bottles and plastic bags — like an anchor, in the shape of a great scab of indestructible squalor.

Frightful, Olive was thinking, *impossible to clean up,* and also, *We don't belong here.*

Glancing back, she saw the fat man leaning against the big tree, cradling something in his arms, a creature that came awake and raised its head: a small dog, but with the pinched face and the flaring ears of a bat.

Sharkey seemed to be loitering, looking around, as though at any moment he would be recognized and admired. He then passed a barrel and looked in, seeing empty bottles and cans. Someone had collected them to redeem at the supermarket.

"This is all money here," he said, praising them.

But, hearing him, the man holding the small dog made a pushing gesture that was unmistakably "Go away."

The completeness of the camp disturbed Olive — being purposeful, it seemed more of a threat, more tenacious and potentially hostile. She signaled to Sharkey, and he followed her to the path, making a shaka sign to the people, but it was not returned. Then, a few steps into the path, they looked back and saw high grass and nothing of the camp.

In the sudden heat of the narrow path, its humid confinement, the bunched upright grass blocking the breeze, the whole passage a stifling tunnel of razor-edged grass blades and thornbushes, Sharkey tripped on a low post, regained his balance, then kicked it in fury.

It was another signpost, another splintered board daubed KAPU.

"We should have obeyed it," Olive said.

Sharkey sniffed. He said, "Did you see those kids doing their homework? They go to school! School costs money — where do they get it? I wanted to give them something. That boy, the older one with the hurt eyes — I saw myself in him."

"What do you mean?" She was ahead of him, calling over her shoulder.

"Haole kid. He has a tough time at school. He has to stick up for himself. Fight for everything he has."

And Olive remembered the children, the big boy with the solemn face, the tense way he sat, like a boy on a bike, a little apart from the others, his sun-scorched hair, his delicate hands, and that was not ink on his pale arm — her memory came into focus — but a blue bruise.

"Joe Sharkey got bullied at school?"

"Every fricken day."

"Must have been horrible."

"Made me want to win," he said. "They were local punks. All I cared about was surfing. I'd never be able to fight them — too many of them. But there were the waves. They took me away. You could be a very tough guy and wipe out on a wave. I learned to ride monsters. It was my way of escaping from them."

But Olive had hardly heard that, or rather, she'd heard that boast so many times she was deaf to it. She was thinking of the bruised boy with the conspicuous blond hair and the wounded eyes and *I saw myself in him.* And a surge of love and sorrow for Sharkey that she'd never felt before made her throat ache, a constriction that kept her from being able to say she loved him. So instead she paused on the path and rested her head against his chest briefly, chafed it with her cheek, the clumsy touch of mute animal tenderness.

At the end of the path, just ahead, where it gave onto the bypass road and their parked car, they saw a woman from the camp — the younger sinewy one, with the wild hair and the man's shirt and dirty surf shorts. A bath, a comb, and clean clothes might have made her desirable — she wasn't old, late thirties maybe, and though she had the leathery look of the others, and their watchfulness, she had health, a sturdy posture, and an air of defiant confidence.

She called out "Hey!"

"How did you get here so fast?" Olive asked.

"I take the other way. We got a quick way out in case the cops come and we gotta make a quick escape."

But they walked past her.

"I can help you. I know the guy."

Olive turned to face her.

"Give me some money and I can find his stuffs."

Olive said, "You know the guy that was killed?"

The woman squinted, pursed her lips, looking grave, and nodded slowly. "Was a great guy. Haole guy. Was a shame he pass."

"The other woman back there said his name was Jeff."

"Rhonda stupid. She don't know nothing."

"What was his name?"

"They don't have names here, just nicknames."

"What was his nickname?"

"I forget — my memory junk. Being as it's my medication."

"You have his things?"

"Most of them. I was afraid the other ones might cockaroach his stuffs, so I hide them. Even the cops, I didn't show them."

A smiled floated at the woman's lips and trembled there, and when she winked at Sharkey, she seemed younger, flirtatious, a look of canny calculation altering the light in her complexion. Then she turned to Olive, fixing her eyes on her — sisterly, conspiratorial, seeking an answering smile. The woman was about Olive's height but bony, legs apart, her dirty feet in frayed flip-flops, her posture insistent. She put one hand out, level with her waist. The dirt was dark in the ingrained lines of her palm, her fingernails black — a skinny hand asking to be filled.

"What's your name?"

The woman pressed her lips together, hesitating. Then ungummed them and said, "Lindsey."

Olive put a twenty-dollar bill into her hand and the fingers trapped it and closed over it.

"When?"

"Give me a few days. And another twenty."

"We'll be back Thursday. To the camp," Olive said. "You'll get the other twenty then."

"Thursday's good," the woman said, and she jammed the money into the pocket of her shorts.

In the car Sharkey said, "The cops could have done that. Why didn't they?"

"Because the man didn't matter," Olive said. "Don't you see? Homeless, poor, living under a tree. Why should they care?"

"But you heard the woman. They went there looking for personal effects."

"She probably figured they were worth something to her."

"She guessed right. I promised her forty bucks. I'm sure she'll hold out for more."

The two days they spent waiting to return to the homeless camp they speculated on what the woman might bring them — clothes, papers, books; not valuables, but items they could use to identify the man she had called Mack.

Having emboldened themselves — Sharkey smoking a joint — they went back, choosing midafternoon, a time when they imagined the children would be home from school, counting on their presence to bring an air of calm to the place that was menacing in its clutter and stink.

And the children were there, as they'd hoped, seated at the picnic table over their papers and schoolbooks, doing homework, looking diligent, though they'd slipped off their flip-flops and kicked the dirt beneath them as they worked. The way they sat, with their backs turned to the world, seemed their way of shutting out the sight of the disorder. Nor did they glance up when Olive and Sharkey entered the clearing, not even when the small dog with the batlike ears and the pinched snout began to yap, shaking its head.

"Ola," the fat man said, and scooped up the dog, smiling at the tense expression on Sharkey's face. He said, "You got big *maka'u*. Is the dog or me?" and showed his teeth.

"I'm not afraid," Sharkey said, but he stepped away.

"Ola wen' smell you fear." He snorted, affecting superiority. "You panty."

One of the children gasped, then looked away.

"We're looking for Lindsey," Olive said.

"No names here. We like the Foreign Legion."

"Lindsey had a name."

"She split. Not in the legion anymore."

"We were supposed to meet her."

"You got appointment, yah?" The man mocked them with his body, dropping the dog and crossing his arms while the dog darted at them, yapping.

Olive said, "Do you know where she is?"

"She high somewhere," the man said — he hadn't stopped smiling in his grim way, though it wasn't really a smile, it was a scowl of defiance. "I think maybe someone give her some money. Wonder who?"

"She junk." The words were distinct and near, but whose?

It was the other woman. Now they saw her, so still on the torn car seat under the tree that, camouflaged by her rags, she seemed like a lumpy part of it, or a heap of rotting cloth. The children at the table crouched with lowered heads, averted eyes, scratching at open notebooks, ignoring the strangers, the dog yapping and slavering.

Olive saw again that the disorder of the camp was fixed and featureless, and so it was not a camp at all but a settlement, like the ruin of a scattered household. The burst cushion was left where it had been, those empty cans had not been picked up or kicked aside, the beach chair, the chewed boogie board, the mildewed mattress, the shredded plastic bags — all of it remained as they had seen it before, nothing moved or cleared, giving the squalor the look of solidity. The same piercing smell too, as before, woodsmoke and damp rags and decaying food. Olive was struck — not that it was ugly but that it seemed indestructible and everlasting.

The fat man had not moved, though at some point he must have unfolded his arms, because he was pointing at the path and mouthing the word *kapu*.

4

Pau

They drove home and told themselves they weren't shocked — that it was
a dead end, they'd been misled, they'd allowed themselves to be persuaded by the woman Lindsey because they were so intent on finding the
identity of the man who died. They'd keep looking, they said; they wouldn't
let this stop them. They were devastated, yet they wouldn't admit it, and the
failure ate at them.

For a week or more of shapeless days they hardly left the house. They
said there were chores to catch up on, repairs to be made, animals to be fed
— the geese, the chickens — all the maintenance that living in the country
required, vines to trim, windows to be washed, rats to be trapped.

"So much to do," Sharkey said.

"We'll deal with it."

What was unspoken between them was the bleak experience of the homeless camp. They'd been shocked, more than they could express in words. The
sight was not just dreary, it was unexpected; it was appalling, like looking
into a pit of poverty and hostility and being hated for it. Sharkey, who prided
himself on being fearless on a monster wave; Olive, who dealt with blood
and death and who believed herself unshockable — they were frightened
and intimidated by the homeless camp, by the sight of junk and improvisation, by the physical threat of the fat man and his yappy dog, and they felt
helpless and bereft in the presence of the earnest schoolchildren.

It could have been a jungle clearing in a poor country — it was no better.
Given its proximity to the well-traveled road, to the world of money and
tourists and restaurants, it seemed worse than something they might have
found thousands of miles away. Sharkey had seen such slums on his surfing

trips, in Africa and South America. but none of them had depressed him like this. And yet it was a fifteen-minute drive from their house — easily walkable, a hike down the highway, then the path through the tall grass and there it was: desolation.

So easy to get to, so miserable; and the logical next thought: how simple for those desperate people to climb out of their stinking encampment, carrying a slasher, and find their way to houses up the hill or along the beach — to the lovely pole-house that Sharkey and Olive shared — and take revenge for being so poor. The experience of the homeless camp made them keenly aware that they had so much that these people wanted, running water and shelter and good food, what seemed like luxury.

How was it that on this lovely island such a blighted place could exist? And they knew that there had to be many such places. The homeless who camped on the beach or pitched tents on the side streets of Honolulu came and went, usually moved along by the police; but this camp in the clearing under trees, with the dog and the children and plants growing in pots and junked cars serving as shelters — this camp was immovable.

Olive envied Sharkey for his faulty memory — his response was a general feeling of woe, the detail fading. All she saw was detail, the ugliness of it, the resentment on the people's faces, the village of dirty feet, just down the road.

They weren't imagining that the dead man might have lived there. They had the policeman's word for it — DeSouza, whose father had surfed with Sharkey, had said that he'd seen him "near the homeless camp on the bypass road" and added that he knew him by sight. And those people — the fat man, Lindsey, the woman she had called Rhonda — they had known something of the man, but they'd been suspicious and they'd calculated that any information they had was worth something. It was easy to understand their reaction — unhelpful, aggressive, mocking, threatening. They lived in an insecure world of leaky tarps and old cars and junk piles, of struggling to get by, always in a survival mode, scavenging or thieving.

The thought that the dead man could have lived there gave Olive a little glimpse into his life. Sharkey shrugged when she mentioned it, saying that the man was probably headed there when Sharkey had killed him. And now it was as though he'd never existed.

Sharkey and Olive stayed home, and in the ponderous way he went about his chores now Sharkey avoided discussing his reasons for abandoning the search for the dead man's identity. Olive, who remained his motivator, kept to herself, stunned by the sight of the filthy homeless camp so near to where they lived in comfort.

They were afraid, not so much that they would be tempted back as that the people there, seeking them, conning them with "We got news ... we know the guy," would find out where they lived and rob them.

And there was always the chance that the dead man had a relative—a lover, a wife, a child—at that homeless camp or another, someone who would find out why Sharkey and Olive were asking about the dead man and would stalk them and take revenge. So they were afraid, cowed by what they had seen, and kept to themselves. Olive had taken a short leave of absence from the hospital but she worked a few days, filling in for someone who was sick. It was a relief for her to be back in the hospital, dealing with trauma and fractures and wounds and seizures, rather than at home with Sharkey, who had become more withdrawn, or on futile searches for the identity of the man he had killed, the corpse with the tag on his toe—a number, no name.

On one of those days, after working at the hospital, Olive returned home to find Sharkey on the lanai among the potted plants—ferny feathery *pakalolo*—his legs drawn up beneath him, more like royal ease than a yoga posture. He was staring at the sea beyond the treetops. His empty gaze, his motionless head, his slack body, reminded her of how his life had contracted and narrowed, his vitality drained away—the image no longer of a surfer but of a drowning victim, propped upright. The pity of it was not that his life had stalled and become smaller but that he was indifferent to it—the melancholy fact that he didn't seem to notice it. This became normal now, the sitting, the blank expression, his silences, a kind of dying that had set in the night he had killed the cyclist, and this an effect of it, the thud to his memory acting on him like an anesthetic. On this night Olive pondered his slack egotistical posture—not like a man watching a sunset but rather like a big stupid boy distracted by cartoons—and thought, *I can't leave you like this.*

"I'm back," she said brightly, to get his attention.

He didn't respond, but when she repeated it, he said, "Where have you been?"

"The hospital. I did Keola's shift."

"That's cool." Spoken without emphasis through barely parted lips, it was no more than a two-syllable grunt. Now she saw a joint in his fingers.

"Should you be doing that? I thought you were cutting down on the *pakalolo.*"

That had been the agreement—that he would try to stay sharp, regain his health, and resume surfing to build his confidence after his near drowning at Waimea.

"This is only number six."

"That's what I mean."

"Six is cutting down."

And with that he reached and stroked the feathery leaves of the *pakalolo* in the pots. It was the caress he might have used on the fur of a beloved animal. She forgave him his selfishness — he seldom touched her that way these days.

"Did anyone call?"

"I think so."

"You think so?"

"I didn't pick it up."

She was beside him, hovering. He saw that she was stern.

"I was busy."

But she knew it was his stunned condition — he was slow and uncertain, and maybe it was his fear, a result of the visit to the homeless camp, the sense that those ragged desperate people who'd mocked his fear of the dog might find him and demand — what? Money, explanations, attention. "Busy" was the one thing he was not. She told herself he was in shock and resisted blaming him for not seeming to care.

She picked up the phone and heard the pips that indicated a message had been left. Dialing the access number, she got the robotic voice: *You have two new messages.*

The first was from her, one she'd left the previous day, saying she'd be home soon. He hadn't heard it, he hadn't noticed she was late; she erased it.

Yah, Joe, the second message began. *This Stickney Medina at the medical examiner office, referencing da kine, that guy you was inquiring about. Just to let you know we got some hits.*

They had phoned ahead — Olive had made the call, and Stickney was excited, not about the news he had to share but that Sharkey would be paying another visit. He asked Olive, "Joe — he's coming too, yah?" And when Olive said yes, he'd be there with her, Stickney said, "Thing of it is, my cousin Wencil, he wants to meet him. He so stoked."

The two men were waiting in the lobby, Stickney gesturing in green scrubs, Wencil in a torn T-shirt and board shorts, at attention on bare feet, a small stocky man, about thirty, unmistakably a surfer — the wide shoulders, the thick neck, bruised water-soaked hands and pinkish fingers, the slim bandy legs, tribal tattoos on his stomach and the nape of his neck, tattooed names on his arms, with dates — his children. And he had a surfer's way of standing, feet planted flat, leaning back and canted slightly to the side, as though balancing on a board.

"Joe Sharkey," Stickney said, with the gusto of a boast. "My cousin Wencil Makani."

Sharkey said, "Aloha."

"And his wahine," Stickney said.

But Wencil did not take his admiring eyes off Sharkey, and he smiled as his gaze traveled from tattoo to tattoo, from his gray-flecked sunburned hair and his freckled forearms to his tattooed ankles and knobby toes. There was about both men a look of having been soaked and scrubbed and dried out thousands of times, the abrasive effect of seawater on skin, a roughened and eroded texture, a raggedness around the fingernails, a chronic redness in the eyes, bruised toes and broken toenails, a saturated and salt-rubbed body made leathery by the sun, one water creature sizing up another from the barren solidity of land.

"Insane," Wencil said, and stuck his hand out to initiate a complex surfer's handshake, hooked fingers and fist bumps, and a final, ritual thumb tug.

Olive watched. Wencil had not even glanced at her.

"I seen you at the Eddie when I was a kid," Wencil said. "Then later — when? Ten-something years back."

"I didn't win," Sharkey said.

"We gotta go." Stickney consulted his folder, more to impress the others with its seriousness than to gather information. "We got some paperwork."

"I hate paperwork," Sharkey said. "I hate the word."

"Try wait," Wencil said to Stickney, with a flash of anger. And to Sharkey, "No, you didn't win — not the biggest wave. But you catched a more better ride. Was a triple head-high monster and you throw yourself at the lip, you in synch on the floater, the lip bang." He raised his arms, turning his hands. "Come down the face, make a cut back to rebound. Then find the barrel as the whole thing's closing out on the beach. Was insane."

"*Mahalo*, brah. It was a Thursday."

"I get it — just another day. But was a gift to me," Wencil said. "*Mahalo atua.*"

"I can see you're a waterman."

"Not like you. Nevah like Joe Sharkey." Wencil dropped his arms, pushed his face forward in helpless admiration, breathing hard. "When you go out — you surf today morning?"

"No."

"Was killer," Wencil said. "Plus was killer yesterday. You catch some waves yesterday?"

"I can't remember," Sharkey said.

"He's taking a break from the water," Olive said.

"How you knowing, sister?"

"I'm his friend," Olive said, but gently, because Wencil seemed excitable — he had barked at Stickney and was badgering Sharkey, twitching on his bare feet.

"I got one Sharkey T-shirt—you face and DA SHARK," Wencil said. "I always want one pair Sharkey shades."

"He doesn't do those endorsements anymore," Olive said.

"Waugh!" Wencil twisted, looking fierce, his teeth clamped together, and drew his arm back as though to prepare to throw a punch. "I talking to the Shark!"

"Wen-boy," Stickney said, "we got to go to the office."

"Bodda you?" Wencil took Sharkey's arm. He said, "You was like a god to me when I was a *keiki*," and he nudged Sharkey to the side, bumping his shoulder, and when they were out of earshot of the others he said, "Gimme a coupla bucks, okay. Man, you like one hero to me."

Seeing Wencil whispering to Sharkey, Olive glanced at Stickney, who shrugged and rolled his eyes, then walked over to them.

Before he could speak, Wencil said, "Who dis fricken wahine?"

Sharkey said, "We have to go," but mildly, chucking Wencil on the shoulder with a friendly fist.

This talk, the back-and-forth, had attracted the attention of the people seated in the lobby waiting area. Olive was aware that they were making a scene, that Sharkey was being ineffectual and that Wencil was in the way, paddling his hands as though swimming toward her.

"I say, this guy was one hero to me," Wencil said.

"He can't give you any money," Olive said.

"I never ask for no money. You think I like one beggar?" Then he jumped aside and spoke indignantly to the room. "You think I want to cockaroach you money? That not me. That not how I roll. You want beef? Bring it on, sister."

Olive steered Sharkey away from the chattering man and toward Stickney, who was waiting at the office door. Sharkey wore a half-smile—of vagueness, of inattention. He seemed to register Wencil's agitation but not the reason for it, the man clinging and making demands, then yelling at the bewildered people in the lobby. He paddled toward Olive again.

"What's wrong with him?" Wencil said.

"Nothing's wrong with him."

"Tell him I nevah want his money."

"I'll tell him," Olive said, Sharkey shuffling beside her as though sleep-walking.

"My whole *ohana*, all my surfing buddies, I tell them I coming to see da Shark," Wencil said. "I even wear my Shark T-shirt."

"That's good."

"No, it not good, because now this shirt is humbug, and now I tell my *ohana* that Sharkey wen' *pau!*"

"Sharkey's not *pau*," Olive said.

And somehow the repeated word stung Sharkey—he seemed to come awake, and turned, lifting his arms, batting Olive aside, making room so that he could face Wencil.

"I killed a man—he's in the storage room here," Sharkey said, indicating the stairwell by jerking his head to the door that Stickney held open. "I could kill you too."

5

Unclaimed Remains

S tickney pawed the papers with his big outspread fingers, like a visible process of thought — dim comprehension, stumbling from line to line with his splayed hands, resembling a beginner at a piano, planting them hard on the keys, producing sour notes. He sat with Sharkey and Olive in the conference room at the medical examiner's office, at a table strewn with files and manila folders, apologizing distractedly as he sorted the papers, saying, "Wencil-boy — he mean well."

"Is he okay?" Olive asked.

"Sometimes he so futless."

When he had the stack in order, Stickney squared it upright with his clutching hands, tapping the bottom edge level on the table. He looked up and said, "You kill this buggah?" — holding out the thickness of papers that stood for the dead man.

Sharkey's eyes, heavy-lidded and dulled by his outburst, seemed to peer beyond the papers, beyond Stickney, beyond the wall, and the glaze that shone through the slits beneath his lashes seemed to indicate that he was lost in thought, not recognizing anything but looking inward.

"It was an accident," Olive said. She'd been surprised by his sudden admission — *I killed him . . . I could kill you too* — and the effect it had on Sharkey. It had scared her; it had hardened his features, it had made him seem dangerous, especially in the fierce way he'd turned on Wencil.

"We get all kine accidents in here," Stickney said. "Plenny bike-related. Plenny unattended death. But I thought you was *ohana* to the buggah."

Sharkey considered this, nodding a little. "If I was *ohana*, would I be asking you his name?"

"He was riding down the wrong side of the road, in the rain, on that bad patch at Waimea," Olive said.

"And he was probably stoned," Stickney said. "The toxicology tests came back. He tested positive for lots of stuff. Alcohol. *Pakalolo.*"

"I would have tested positive for that," Sharkey said. "At the time. If they'd run tests."

"And crank — more worse. Traces of *batu*. This guy was full of illegal drugs." He was nodding, repeating the word *djrugs*.

"Can we see the test report?" Olive asked.

"Got it somewhere here." Stickney sorted through the papers again with his fat skidding fingers.

"Never mind," Olive said. "What we need to know is if you got a name."

"Got two, tree names," Stickney said. "But we got some solid hits too. Mainly from his prints. We ran his prints and got stuff from all over."

"Such as?" Olive said, and saw that Sharkey was glaring across the table at Stickney as though demanding an answer.

"Far-out stuff. We get some from the mainland, a place called" — he scrabbled at the paper with blunt finger pads — "Santa Clara."

"Near Santa Cruz," Sharkey said.

"You probably surfed Mavericks — Half Moon Bay. Awesome waves, yah?"

Sharkey said, "What was he doing there?"

"Say here was speeding."

"He got a speeding ticket?"

"Yah. This long time ago. A moving violation ticket. Doing a hundred forty-two in a forty-five-mile-limit zone. They booked him, printed him."

"What was his name?"

Stickney snorted and said, "The buggah name was not the thing that jumped out at me."

"What jumped out?"

"One forty-two," Stickney said. "What kine car does one forty-two?"

"A fast car," Olive said.

"A spendy car," Stickney said. "So I read the whole report. Turns out he was driving a Ferrari. All the specs are here."

"He stole it."

"Was new kine. Registration in his name," Stickney said. "One of his names."

Olive leaned to look at the police report, and Stickney put his fingers on the paper and spun it so that she could read it.

"Max Mulgrave," she said.

"But we also have this," Stickney said. "From the gun registry database —

all gun owners in California get fingerprinted. Got a different name. Maybe he come up with a new name because he was turned down for a drug conviction. We get that sometimes."

He showed the *California Department of Justice Firearm Ownership Report,* and the name, Robert Ray Low.

"What else have you got?"

"Plenny. Got hits from the VA. He was in the DOD file. That's not Low, that's Mulgrave."

"What about date of birth, place of birth? Father's name?"

"Got," Stickney said. "All that." He pushed the papers aside. "Too much to process. Look like he born somewhere on mainland." He tapped a line with his fingertip. "Kansas."

"Arkansas," Olive said. "Even I know that."

"Look the same to me."

"Different state," Olive said, lifting the document. "Floristan."

"Got waves there?"

"No waves," Olive said.

"And this," Stickney said. He opened a folder and removed another document — photocopied, they could tell from the way the signature was printed, and the signature was *Mulgrave.*

"Looks like a property deed," Olive said. "He owns a house?"

"Used to own a house — this is a transfer of ownership. Look at the purchase price."

"Three million and change."

"Ten years ago, in San Fran. What you suppose it worth now?" Stickney said, seeming to gloat.

"He was homeless," Sharkey said.

"Not then," Stickney said, and flicked the document. "He riding high then."

"So what happened?"

"Something heavy. And there's more."

"Can we have copies?"

"Some of it classified, like military records and police stuff. Or get limited info, for family only. But the rest — okay." He stood, as though for the dramatic effect of showing his big body. "Some amazing stuff here — like stuff I never see before. But there's something more amazing."

He leaned and planted his hands on the papers, breathing hard, seeming to believe that he was creating suspense out of his clumsy delay.

"Please go on," Olive said.

But instead of replying, Stickney carried the sheaf of loose documents to the photocopier and began to feed papers into it.

"All these numbers, all these names, all these hits," Stickney said, teasing a document into the slot. "We send out bulletins and emails to the next of kin, even letters." He bent over and sniffed at a copy sliding from the chute into the tray. "And what do we get back?" He was still feeding papers into the slot. "Nothing," he said. "Nothing."

"No one to claim the body?"

"Nobody reply!" He turned and widened his eyes. "We cremate him. We send him over to the morgue. Now it up to them to find out next of kin. And they have the rest of the paperwork. The protocol stuff, not the personal."

"Aren't you still looking?" Olive asked.

"Out of our hands now. We ID'd him. We got prints. We got identifying marks and scars. The tattoo."

"I have a photo of it."

"Good, 'cause we burned the body."

"I thought you kept it downstairs."

"Got to make room for more human remains. We kept some DNA in the file. Dental records and that. That's the policy. Once we ID someone, the case sent to the morgue, where they store the ashes."

"How long do they store them?"

"Until they're claimed. So far it's classified as 'unclaimed remains.'" He had finished feeding the last of the paper, yet the photocopier continued to chatter, shooting out and sorting the copies into the tray. "So far it looks like no one wants him."

"We want him," Olive said.

Just before Red Hill, on their way back to the North Shore, they passed the morgue, which was visible from the freeway — a windowless building beyond a stand of flowering trees, and the sign that Stickney had mentioned, AFFORDABLE CASKETS.

"We could stop."

Sharkey was driving, badly — but he'd insisted. He accelerated — his way of replying — and past Red Hill said, "Let's look at these papers first. Get acquainted." He said nothing more for a few miles and then, at the Pearl City exit, "He's just ashes now."

Sharkey drove on, pondering. That the man was reduced to ashes was both a solution and a dilemma. He was no longer a whole corpse, with the scars of the accident — not a stitched carcass and cracked staring head, yellowish, waxen, wounded, looking offended in death, the fatal embodiment of blame. He was now dust. As a pile of ashes, probably a few scoopfuls in a small box, he had less power to haunt.

But that was the paradox. Pulverized, he seemed impossible to identify.

He was not a man anymore, he was less than ashes, he was powder, like a heap of coarse-ground pepper. You could scatter him over a bowl of noodles and who would know the difference?

Sharkey was silent the rest of the way, the sort of silence that was more and more his mood, his demeanor, as though stunned and enfeebled, bringing darkness wherever he went, and at times a sudden irritability, as when he had shouted at Wencil, "I could kill you too." It was shocking to Olive because it was just what she feared, that he was dangerous, not only to himself but to anyone near him — and she was nearest.

"Are you sure you're okay?" she asked in traffic at Wahiawa.

He did not answer until a mile farther on, at Helemano.

"I can drive," he said, looking grim, because the shoulder of the road there was loosely paved with crushed lava stone that had the appearance of ashes.

Afraid of angering him, Olive said nothing more. She knew, as a nurse, that it was a provocation to remind a patient, especially a frazzled one, that she was a caregiver. Better to promote the illusion that she was a friend, that he was not fragile, that whatever issue had arisen could be solved; and above all, never to suggest that his mind was shattered, that he managed to survive only by groping and being ignorant of the truth of his condition and not acknowledging that she was doing most of the work, propping him up and humoring him, as she did in the hospital to the most damaged patients.

They had descended to the coast road, he'd seen the waves, the white rollers of surf and the incoming swell. Sharkey gripped the steering wheel in both hands, as though in the cockpit of a plane, pulling it out of a nosedive, his forearms stiffened, pale with effort, making his tattoos bluer.

The waves were bawling. Olive could see from Sharkey's reaction that the waves were speaking to him, rolling to the shore, daring him to ride them. She knew that Sharkey never saw a wave without imagining himself on it — and not merely on it, but crouched in a posture that suited that particular wave; and he often criticized the technique of the surfers who were on it. But these loud waves mocked him for driving past, reminding him that he'd once mastered them and that he was powerless now.

The wash and chuckle, the lap and swirl of breaking waves continued to Waimea, where Sharkey finally said, "Talk to me."

"We're almost home. We're fine."

He hated that she was trying to reassure him, as though he were weak; he hated most of all the suggestion of being weak. Approaching his driveway, he was surprised to see the big gate of solid boards sliding sideways on its rail, as though he'd given a signal. Then dark fingers on its edge dragging it and a face in shadow under the visor of a ball cap.

Moe Kahiko. He stepped from behind the gate and waved the car in, kicking a fat goose out of the way.

"I feed the chickens," he said when Sharkey had parked, speaking to him through the car window. "Give some pellets to the gooses. Change the water — the water real dirty. And this," he went on, reaching into his pocket. "I pick you some mountain apples — ripe, the apples. It's all good, brah. You want me close the gate?"

These favors, this fussing, and his toothy smile: he stood at attention. Olive said softly, "This numpty wants something."

He snatched the door open for Sharkey, clumsily deferential, while at the same time showing him a mountain apple, weighing the small pinkish fruit in his hand as though awarding a prize.

"For you, braddah."

"He's tired, Moe," Olive said from the far side of the car.

"It's okay," Sharkey said. "You need something. What is it you want?"

"Nothing, brah!" And Moe laughed, mirthless and shouty. "I never want nothing. It Skippy, he need. I asking for Skippy Lehua."

"Asking what?"

"That you go over to his surf *hui* and say something. Talk story."

"But why are you asking?"

"I owe Skippy one favor. He help me out udda day, get me some products. But I have no money for give him. Can only pay when I sell 'em. But in the meantime I still owe him, like I wen' say. He say if I no pay he give me lickings. 'I come looking for you!'"

"I still don't get it, man."

They were standing among the lemon trees beside the garage, the two men sparring near the fallen fruit, in the sticky odor of bruised citrus.

"He give me one condition. He give me a break if I ask Sharkey to talk to the *hui* guys."

"If you ask?"

"If you wen' agree, brah."

"You're the favor, Joe," Olive said. She'd picked some lemons; she held them in her hand, and she kept herself a little apart from the men, smirking at them, trying to be patient.

"Ass right," Moe said, startled into truthfulness. "I promise Skippy you wen' do it."

Sharkey frowned at Moe's pleading eyes, the guilelessness of his appeal, imposing on their friendship because of the debt, to help calm Skippy, buying time for Moe to sell the *pakalolo*.

"'Cause matter of factly, I tell Skippy I never for see you surfing these days, which mean you probably have plenny more time to talk story."

Moe's hopeful face was the face of a child, and even the apple he clutched to propitiate Sharkey was offered like a child's tentative gift.

"You got something else to do, brah?"

The simple earnest question stung Sharkey into confusion. "No — nothing."

Relieved, and in a careless reflex, Moe raised the apple and took a bite, filling his mouth, showing Sharkey a bulgy smile.

"Community center," he said. "Hale'iwa."

He prepared himself for a crowd and, resentful in anticipation, said to Olive, "Better not keep them waiting." But he was saddened by the few cars in the parking lot at the community center, and humiliated, seeing no more than ten boys on the folding chairs toward the front, and a few girls sitting in a group on chairs behind them, all of them grommets. They were very young and awkward, as though unused to the rigidity of chairs, sprawling or seated sideways, uneasily balanced, hugging themselves, none of them sitting upright.

"Here the man," Skippy said, scuffing toward Sharkey, looping a plumeria lei over his head, giving him a hug. "This my *hui,* all surfers. They waiting to hear your *mana'o.*"

Sharkey raised his hand, making a shaka sign. They mumbled their greetings, and he was dispirited again — so few of them, so young, mostly haoles, slung like monkeys on the chairs, barefoot, with wild hair.

"Guys, *e pule kakou,*" Skippy said. "Say a prayer. *Aloha ke Akua* — God is love."

The chairs creaked as the youngsters bowed their heads, clutching their spiky hair in an attempt at piety.

"*Ka mana o ke Akua e ho'opakele mai ia kakou,*" Skippy intoned, then, "The power of God proteck us." He glanced up. "Say *Amenay.*"

"*Amenay.*" The growl filled the hall, then died away.

"Okay, this guy been on the North Shore since fo'ever," Skippy said in a new voice, chirpy, his enthusiasm causing him to stammer. "He know Eddie Aikau, he know Jock, he know Sunny, and all the Hawaii *ohana.* He wen' surf the big monster in Nazaré, but you never hear about it, 'cause Garrett he get all the credit — for true!" Skippy turned to Sharkey and slow-clapped in appreciation. "I admire this brother so much, and thanks for his *kokua,* showing up here. Let's hear da kine he got for us. Give it up for surf legend da Shark — Joe Sharkey!"

Instead of applauding — which he expected — the youngsters shifted and gabbled in their seats, thrashings that made the metal chairs creak.

"Aloha," Sharkey said.

In the murmur of response, he saw that Olive had taken a seat several rows behind the little group. Pale and apprehensive, she looked in her concern more than ever like his nurse, and he was reminded of his last glimpse of Hunter, feeble and flustered, attended by his nurselike wife.

"Thanks for that introduction, Skippy — but, hey, please don't admire me. Yes, I knew Eddie. He died in a super-heroic attempt to reach shore from the *Hōkūle'a*. He's known more for that than for any wave he rode or prize he won. His sacrifice made him a god. And Jock — a great surfer. He still fixes roofs. Sunny Garcia — he made a million bucks in prize money and he's one of the most depressed people I know."

"Triple Crown, brah," Skippy called out.

"But winning the Triple Crown didn't keep him from trying to kill himself. And look at Andy Irons — how many titles? World champion. And he drugs himself to death, thirtysomething, in a hotel room in Texas." Sharkey paced back and forth before the youngsters, whipping his hand at them. "You guys are groms — you need to know this. Maybe you've got the moves. Hey, you'll probably blow your knee out hotdogging in a tube. Maybe you think you can get famous by riding a wave, even a monster wave, like me and Garrett. But let me tell you, it's a very brief ride, even on a monster. A few minutes at most, and then it's over. That's not a sport, that's a kind of play — surfing is playing in the water. And what do you do the rest of the time?" He paused and stared at them, then growled, "My hero, Greg Noll — da Bull — rode a monster in Makaha, or did he wipe out? No one ever saw it. He was spooked and gave up surfing."

"Some guys, they wen' see him," Skippy said. "Just no picture."

Sharkey leaned at them and hissed, "You're stoked. Then you get old. Then you lose the stoke."

"Wait, wait," Skippy said, standing up, clutching his T-shirt in his distress. "You're bumming them out, brah."

"I want to hear more," one of the girls yelled from the back. "Let the dude talk."

"The wave," Sharkey said. "Consider the wave. You think because you're riding it that you're superior to it. But you're not — the wave is one of a kind. It's unique — but you're not unique. The wave has not existed before. It comes out of the sea, rising on an unseen reef. It lifts you, gives you a ride, and then it's over. It's dead and gone. Or maybe you're not on the wave. Maybe no one's riding it. Maybe no one sees it. Think about that."

Sharkey defied them, facing them, his crazy hair making him seem a wild man. They looked scolded. Skippy was murmuring to the boy next to him. Olive seemed to be suppressing an urge to tell him to stop — he saw a kind of panic in her widening eyes. He had not known what he was going to say, but something in Skippy's prayers and praising introduction, saying how he admired him, filled him with shame that had become anger.

"Get rid of the contests!" he shouted. "I know what you want. You want to win prizes. You want respect. You want to compete. You want to win and be a hero." He took a breath, and panted, saying, "But winning is nothing—it doesn't help you. You get to my age and you're *pau*. No one knows you. No one remembers. Look at me—you don't know who I am!"

Out of breath from his rant, he thought of the purity of the waves, how they were shapely and brief and neutral—neutral most of all. And with the waves rolling toward him in his mind he saw the oafs jostling in the lineup, who splashed into them and tried to wrestle themselves upright.

"I've done nothing, I've made no difference, yet the wave always leaves a mark," he went on, because his pause had created an awkward silence. "Even a small wave reaches the shore, disturbs the sand—grains of it—or shifts a whole beach, or chews at the dirt of an embankment, and maybe undermines and collapses a house. Then it vanishes. The perfect crime. And maybe in its short trip to shore, it tips you over and drowns you."

Someone called out, "Sweet!"

"Like life," Sharkey said. "You drop in, you ride for a while, then you die. The ultimate hold-down."

The word seemed to excite a boy in the front, who pulled his finger out of his mouth and wagged it at Sharkey and said, "Like, did that ever happen to you, man—a real bad hold-down when you thought you were drowning?"

Sharkey said fiercely, "Yes, I've been under a wave—hold-downs, tossed by a boomer, caught in a cave in a reef, over the falls, the duck-dive into oblivion—all of that, shacked in the impact zone. It's like being waterboarded."

"But, like, I mean drowning," the boy said, gnawing his finger.

"I'm drowning now!" Sharkey shouted into the boy's face, and the boy looked slapped.

The chairs creaked, there were groans, they were startled by the shout, by Skippy raising his arms and yelling, "It's all good, brah." Olive staggered to her feet, kicked her chair aside, rushed to Sharkey, and took him by the hand and led him away, Skippy calling after him, "Next time, brah, for these *keiki*, I hope you have a more better message."

6

Paperwork

"All this fricken paper," Sharkey said in a blaming and aggrieved way, stepping back at the sight of the separate piles of folders Olive had set out on the long koa dining table. She stood at the head of the table, as though presiding over a meal she'd prepared.

"I tried to make it chronological," she said, and hearing Sharkey swear under his breath, she reacted sharply, smacking the table in frustration, shaking the nearer stacks.

She'd been up early, sorting the papers, leaving Sharkey in bed, undisturbed in his stupor. After the fiasco at the community center, Sharkey had gone to bed, and he had not woken until long after Olive had finished her work, tidying the documents, creating files.

"Start as we mean to go on," she said.

"What does that even mean?"

"Be meticulous in creating a profile."

"What's the point?" Sharkey said, turning away.

"There's a man buried somewhere in all this paper."

What Sharkey mumbled in reply was indistinct, but his tone was dismissive.

"The man you killed," Olive said, and Sharkey reacted more forcefully than when she'd smacked the table — it was as though she'd smacked his head. "The man you don't know, whose ashes are sitting in a box, jinxing you."

"I hate paper," he said with disgust. "I hate documents. People say, 'We have to do the paperwork,' and I want to puke at the word."

In a pitying voice, and looking sorrowful, Olive said, "You're afraid."

"Out of my element." He pushed at his face with his fist.

"What would that element be?"

"Surf."

"You almost drowned in the surf at Waimea, mate."

"Maybe I'm not used to this." He wandered back to the table and flicked one stack with his finger. "I'm not into paperwork." He saw that Olive was still watching him with pity. "I never wrote a real letter," he said. He hated the precision of paper, its stern language, the obligations it imposed, the formality of it, the demands. "I never read a real book."

"That's the sort of thing a little kid might say," Olive said. "A lazy little kid."

He wasn't insulted. He shrugged and with a stubbornness that hinted at pride he said, "I never had to."

"You have to now," Olive said, edging toward him. He was so big when she was near him, her head below the scorpion tattoo on his biceps. But her anger gave her courage. "If you don't, you might never surf Waimea again. Or anywhere."

She could see that he was intimidated by this, or at least daunted by the prospect. And so she walked past him and went to the first pile, then lifted the folder and slid out a formal document that looked like a diploma, framed with a blue ornamental border.

"Birth certificate," she said, pinching it. "Forget the other names — this is our man. Max Mulgrave, born in 1950, Floristan County, Arkansas. A southerner. I looked up Floristan. It's somewhere in the Ozarks. And here's his diploma: Floristan, the Crusaders."

"Class of '69," Sharkey said. "I was lifeguarding then. What was his sport?"

"No mention of sports here," she said. "But Stickney did the donkey work by getting all these documents."

"What's this pile?"

"Military."

Hearing the word, Sharkey involuntarily came to attention. He saw the Colonel. He hadn't thought of him in years. As a father, yes, but not the man in uniform, peering down at him, a cigarette burning in his fingers. *Stand up straight* and *Elbows off the table* and *You need a haircut.* The smoker's growl.

"He was a soldier," Sharkey said in a wondering way, his voice trailing off, daunted again but this time by the fleeting apparition of a stranger in uniform, faceless, looming a little, a shadow, someone like his father. He looked aside, wincing.

"So it says. Stickney must have got his records through the Freedom of Information Act — or probably his department applied." She was holding a manila folder. Opening it, she said, "This is all public domain stuff, but it's something." And she read, "Official Military Personnel File — service number, dates of service — July 1969 to May 1971. Branch — Unit C-Troop. Final

Rank E 7, Gunnery Sergeant — Staff Noncommissioned Officer. Place of entrance, Fayetteville, Arkansas. Place of separation, Fort Irwin, California."

"And what does that tell us, other than he was a grunt?"

"Look at the dates. He enlisted at eighteen, at the height of the Vietnam War."

"My father's war," Sharkey said, and saw the man again, his severe face and upright posture, reeking of cigarette smoke, implacable in his order-giving.

"Straight from high school."

"What was his outfit?"

"Says here Eleventh Armored Calvary Regiment. Look," she said, passing the file to Sharkey, "a kind of insignia."

"They call that a patch. Black Horse. What was his rank, did you say?"

"Gunnery sergeant."

"Not all these guys went to Vietnam. He might have spent the war driving a desk in Omaha."

"Turn the page," she said. "Look at 'Assignments and Geographical Location.'"

"You read this already?"

"There's not much to read. Bare facts. But look where he served."

Sharkey lifted the paper to his face. "Bien Hoa. Operation Fish Hook."

"Operation Fish Hook — I mugged up on it," Olive said. "May 1970, an incursion into Cambodia, less than a year after he enlisted and was shipped over. It was pretty famous, because it was an invasion, probably illegal. But it was on the Ho Chi Minh Trail — a big depot, just over the border. A huge firefight and the destruction of a whole arsenal of weapons — lots of American casualties, but obviously not our boy."

Chastened by her quiet recitation of facts, Sharkey said, "Where did you find this out?"

"This morning — ten minutes on my computer. It's all online."

"'Go online.' That's another expression I hate. Like 'Do the paperwork.'" He began to sigh in frustration.

"Calm down. Look what else I found. This is the man. Check out the next page."

Sharkey lifted the page. He read, "Awards and Decorations."

"Out loud, Joe."

"National Defense Service Medal. Vietnam Service Medal. Vietnam Campaign Medal. Expert Badge Rifle M-16. Presidential Unit Citation Award for Ninety Days or More in Combat." Sharkey's voice had slowed and softened as he'd gone down the list. "Purple Heart with Oak Leaf," he said in a whisper, and handed the file to Olive.

She said, "He wasn't driving a desk in Omaha."

"My father would have loved this guy."

"There's more," Olive said. "It gets better."

She flicked through another file folder and brought out a document, this one more elegant than the birth certificate, with an etched border and the man's name inked in the middle, ennobled in ornate script.

"University of California at Santa Cruz, Class of '74. Bachelor's degree — electrical engineering." She handed the certificate to Sharkey, saying, "Do the math. Born in 1950. After his tour in 'Nam he's still a kid. He gets the GI Bill. Finances his education. He's only twenty-four when he graduates."

"Could have been at Mavericks. That's what I was doing around that time."

The mention of Santa Cruz, his memories of Half Moon Bay, helped him see the man more clearly — not his features, not as an individual, but the sort of young man — student, stoner, skateboarder — who gathered with friends at the edge of the bay on big days, peering from the parking lot or standing on the beach, looking admiringly at the surfers. Sharkey had always been eager to flash a shaka sign at them, to show he was from Hawaii.

"But he couldn't have surfed it. Very few guys did then. I knew most of them."

"Maybe he wasn't into big waves," Olive said.

"He ended up in Hawaii, though."

"We don't know when. That's not in these docs. But there're a few clues. Remember what Stickney said about the speeding ticket?"

Sharkey glanced at the paper in his hand as though he might find the answer on it. For a moment the name Stickney meant nothing to him, but Olive had said it earlier, and he knew it was connected to the documents on the table. His mind was not a blank; it pulsed with movement, a swirl of bubbles in water tumbling above him, twisting him deeper, the daylight dimming in the water as he was pressed beneath the wave, losing the ability to know which way to swim, buried alive in the turbulence.

Dazed by the vision, he said, "What was the question?"

Olive repeated it: Stickney. California. Max Mulgrave. The speeding ticket. Clocked at 142 miles per hour.

"That's cranking," Sharkey said.

"Remember? Stickney asked what kind of car goes that fast?"

"Muscle car."

"Look at the ticket," Olive said. "All these documents contain bare facts. But some facts are more telling than others."

Sharkey was reading in his usual way, like a blind man, his fingers tracing the surface of the ticket, moving from line to line as though touching Braille dots.

"Ferrari. An '84 Testarossa," he finally said. "Where do you get a car like that?"

"The letterhead on the next page might offer a clue."

Sharkey slipped the photocopy of the ticket aside. His fingers crept toward the bold print at the top of the page, *Max Integer* — but except for that name, the page was blank.

"Max Integer," he said, touching the name. "Some kind of company?"

"An integer's a number. His software company. See the address? Santa Clara. He was one of the pioneers in Silicon Valley. God knows what sort of stuff he made — some kind of software. He must have started the company sometime in the '70s, after he graduated. The speeding ticket says a lot about his income. It gives his home address in Cupertino. Still there — I Googled it — a mansion behind a wall. And I looked up Max Integer. Symantec offered big money for the company in '82, papers speculated the purchase price in the tens of millions."

"He was rich," Sharkey said, and saying so, he did not know him anymore. As a possible surfer he had a presence, a hard body; as a soldier, a uniform; as a student too he had a certain substance among books and was almost recognizable. But as a millionaire he was an elusive wisp camouflaged by expensive clothes, or sitting in a sports car, or hidden in a villa. That's how the rich lived — they hid themselves, they were almost unknowable, they were their possessions, cars and clothes and real estate. You never saw one in Hawaii without humungous sunglasses, you never saw one on the North Shore. They hid in Kahala, surrounded by walls, and their gardeners chased you off the beach.

This man had no face, no physicality, he was not flesh; he was money, and money said nothing. Money was camo, it made him inaccessible.

"Really rich," Olive said.

"Riding a junk bike in the rain at Waimea." He handed the file folder to her.

She placed the folder with the others on the table, handling it with care, a sort of dignified formality, as though concluding a ritual, one that Sharkey was relieved to see ending. The mass of paper had confused him, the documents were hard to read, the print was small, some of it made no sense to him. Such documents needed to be interpreted, studied, comprehended, turned into basic English, and even then they hardly hung together.

Sharkey was relieved to see Olive gathering the loose paper, making a single pile, a stack of folders. He smiled when he saw her slip the stack into her canvas tote, the one she carried to the hospital. He thought, *Take the paper away from me.*

"So what do we know?" she said.

"We know who he was. Max Mulgrave. That was the guy."

"That you killed."

Sharkey clawed at his face, rubbed his eyes; he sighed; he said, "Yes, yes. Okay, I know. It's all there, in the paperwork."

"The drunk homeless guy," Olive said.

This silenced Sharkey, because just as the man had begun to come into focus, as a surfer or a soldier, he had dissolved and become indistinct, lost and distorted in the thick green camouflage of money.

"You know his name. His military record. His university. His business. But you don't know who he is. Think about it — if someone knew your name, what would they know about you?"

"A lot," Sharkey said. "That I won the Triple Crown. Endorsements. That I surfed Tahiti and Nazaré. Rocked the Pipe. Shredded Waimea."

"And what would that add up to?" she said.

As she was speaking, with those school-teacher questions, Sharkey thought how she had lost her looks, become plainer and plainer with each demand, not the woman he had loved. Her questions, the way she asked them, her flat voice, her pinched face, made her a stranger, an unattractive one, someone he wanted to run away from.

"Those bare facts" — she was still talking — "is that you?"

"I'm Joe Sharkey. The surfer. The whole world knows that."

"You're a sixty-two-year-old man," Olive said, holding him still, piercing him with her stare. "You're selfish, narcissistic, and ungrateful. You've spent your whole life doing whatever the bloody hell you've wanted to, living on your mother's money. All I've ever heard from you is how awful the human race is, why most people are worthless, and why do women have children. You've had every advantage and you're still a misanthrope — and for your information, that's someone who hates people."

"Say what you like. You're trying to hurt my feelings. I don't care."

"I'm trying to save you," she said.

"All those things you're saying about me — selfish, ruthless — listen, if I hadn't been like that, I would never have become a great surfer."

She backed away, laughing, and her laugh shocked him — it was a hoot of defiance he'd not expected, and he raised his arms as though to deflect its mocking sound.

"You're no bleeding way a great surfer," she said. "Eddie was great. Kelly's great. Garrett's great. And you — you're a good surfer. You told me you lost your endorsements a few years ago, when you stopped cooperating. You got lucky at Nazaré. Then you got lazy, and now you don't surf at all. There are plenty of guys like you on the North Shore. Plenty in the world."

"How many of them surfed big days at Waimea?"

She didn't laugh this time to caution him. She whispered instead, saying, "The last time you surfed Waimea you got pushed under the wave. You nearly drowned."

As though slapped by her, Sharkey sat down on the floor and held his head, seeing only a swirl of bubbles, the dimming light in the depths of the wave, a growing sense of helplessness as it darkened.

"No one knows you," Olive said, unrelenting. "Though I know more than most people. And this man — the man you killed — all we know are the few facts of his life that anyone could find out on the Internet. A lot of them don't fit together. Born in a kiss-me-arse town. Then the army. Then school and a business and a big speeding ticket. A ton of money. And the next thing we know is he's riding a bike in the rain, drunk and stoned, just like you, at Waimea."

Still holding his head, Sharkey said, "I'm sorry — I'm so sorry."

"We don't know this man — we really don't know anything." She knelt and embraced Sharkey, holding his head, consoling him in a way that killed his desire yet comforted him, more like a mother than a lover. "We need to know."

"It was an accident," Sharkey said, moaning, his mind still on the man on the bike in the rain.

"Think of what we don't know," Olive said, not scolding now but spirited, with a hint of promise, as though beginning a folktale. "The missing years. Between making a fortune on the mainland and ending up homeless in Hawaii."

"Lots of stoners come from the mainland and end up on the beach here."

"When did he come? Where did he live? What did he do here? Who did he know? What happened to all his money?" Still holding him, she let this sink in. "Maybe he was married. If so, did he have children, and where are they, and do they know he's dead?"

Sharkey said, "Maybe he was like me. No wife. No kids."

"No one seems to know, or care, that he's a box of ashes on a shelf in the mortuary in Honolulu."

She released him then. He got to his feet, staggered a little, and bumped the table as he backed away.

"But it's not only him. I'm worried about you. Joe, nothing has gone right since that happened." She thought a moment, looking pained, thinking, *Voodoo death.* "Sometimes at the hospital a person checks in. 'Don't feel good.' We run tests, we review the paperwork, we do what we can. But we know what's going to happen. There's this horrible shorthand expression we use. 'He's terminal.'"

Sharkey began to speak but thought better of it. He wandered to the lanai and sat in his usual chair, the bentwood rocker, and stared at the chickens pecking on the lawn. Olive did not join him at once. She watched him from a little distance, and it seemed to her that he was diminished — older, somewhat shrunken, the shadow on his face giving him a look of sorrow. Tattoos on such a man looked absurd, the big man reduced, the man of action in repose, very still and smaller. The impression she'd had weeks ago, that his body looked uninhabited.

She went to him, softly. He shut his eyes when she touched his shoulder.

"Think of it as a quest."

He nodded and spoke in a whisper, as if to himself. "I know what a quest is. I used to look for big waves."

7

Floristan

On a day of heavy traffic, on their way to the airport, they took a side road, Olive driving, Sharkey slouched in the passenger seat, his head lolling like an invalid's. But his eyes were alert to the shanties half-hidden in the trees, the ragged tents off the bypass road, the cluster of huts aslant in the muddy valley just before the bridge at Wahiawa, the shelters of blue plastic along the bike path at Pearl City, the lean-tos and piled-up cardboard buttressed by rusted shopping carts and splintered crates under the freeway at Nimitz, and at each scattered rat's nest of sticks and plastic, bearded men and women with greasy strings of hair, sticklike themselves, skin burned to leather, in sweaty rags, in the glare of sunshine, standing in tall grass or under shade trees. The homeless of the island.

"Those shonky huts," Olive said.

On a hot stretch of the freeway, a shirtless man in torn shorts pushed a shopping cart piled high with rags along the gravel shoulder, a dark futile figure scowling at passing cars.

"Samuel Beckett," Olive said.

"You know him?"

"Figure of speech. Lost soul."

"He came here like them," Sharkey said after a while, approaching the airport road. "From the mainland. Like them — when he had nowhere else to go."

He seemed to speak in an accusing way to a man crouching slack-jawed on the sidewalk, his skinny arm flung around the neck of a dog with stiff dirty fur and a fat twitching tongue.

Seeing Sharkey, the man extended his arm, cupped his hand, begging. But Olive drove on.

"We don't know that. Right?"

He grunted, an unwilling no.

"All we know is that he had a life. We owe it to him to find out what it was, and why he ended up at night on a bike in the rain and then dead in Waimea."

"I hate going to the airport here. Every flight you take is so long. I'm not in shape to fly."

"If we don't do this, your life won't be worth living. It's awful now. Look at yourself. You don't eat, you hardly sleep — and you don't surf anymore."

"You think I'm cursed," he said, giggling mirthlessly to show he didn't believe it.

"Wrong word."

"What would you say?"

"No one did anything to you. The thing's inside you." She was glad to be driving so that she didn't have to see his face when she spoke. "I think you're in trouble."

"Whatever." He covered his eyes, masking himself, feeling nagged again.

"The worst of it is you don't know it."

"Arkansas," he said. "It's so far away."

"You've flown to South Africa. To Portugal. To Indo."

"There are waves in those places. There's no waves in Arkansas."

He spoke softly, keeping the words in his mouth as though he were chewing, so that what he said was a vibration rather than a clear statement. He objected to the trip but, weakened, he was docile, mildly stubborn, too slow in his movements to object. It seemed to be his usual state now, ineffective, more like a child than a man.

But Olive was used to that — with Sharkey, and in her work. The sick at the hospital who raised their eyes piteously to her as she made her rounds from bed to bed — they were childlike. Fearful, helpless, haunted, they needed her to soothe them, to encourage them and make them hopeful.

Sharkey had become like them, a semi-invalid, dependent on her. And so he hated going to the airport and whispered his objections and said the homeless people by the roadside disgusted him — "Why don't they go back where they came from?" Still, he did not have the strength to oppose her with any conviction. He followed her because he needed her.

What heartened Olive, and appalled Sharkey, was the knowledge that he would follow her anywhere now. But it was not love — it was need. He had nowhere else to go.

In the terminal, the woman checking them in held up his driver's license and said brightly, "Joe Sharkey," then handed him the license with his boarding pass, beaming as though presenting him with a gift.

Sharkey rallied a little at the thought that she'd recognized him; he stood straighter and managed a thin smile and snatched at his belt, pulling up his pants — his weight loss meant that his clothes bagged and flapped.

"Gate five," the woman said, then looked past him, raising her hand. "Next in line."

She had no idea. Sharkey said, "I hate being with all these people," and gestured to the other travelers, jostling him. They oppressed him, he was one of them, he found them clumsy and slow, burdened by bags and cases. You left home and then you were in the world, and the world was full of people pushing past you who didn't know who you were. And it was as though you didn't exist.

He was muttering, on the verge of cursing out loud, when he saw a woman approaching with a wheelchair.

"Is that thing for me?"

"I asked for it," Olive said. "We'll get through quicker."

Sharkey was at first confused, but he sat, and, pushed by a Filipina attendant, a young woman in a uniform, her nametag LAKAMBINI, was eased through the security zone. When their flight was called, the woman wheeled him down the jetway and tipped him through the doorway, then helped him to his seat. As Olive had hoped, he was calmer as a result; the efficiency quieted him.

In the window seat beside him, Olive said, "This is the right thing to do." She took a folder labeled FLORISTAN from her bag and began to flick through the papers inside: travel brochures, hotel and rental car confirmations, lists of offices and locations. On top, in a separate stack, the papers that Stickney had copied for them, the details of the dead man's history. "You might think it's melodramatic for me to say this, but your life depends on it. That's how I feel."

Sharkey grasped the folder and opened it on his lap. He looked at the top sheet of paper, running his eyes over it but not reading it, merely allowing himself to be impressed by the close print and the detail. It was as though he were not looking at words at all but rather at a thickened mass of complex equations that amounted to a kind of formal magic for those with the time and patience to separate the lines and translate it. But the idea of doing that himself — reading it — fatigued him.

"We'll make a schedule from this."

"Shed-jewell," he said, mocking her.

"Plonker," she said.

But he was comforted by the fact that Olive understood the challenge — the quest — and was taking charge. He placed his hand on that top sheet as though drawing warmth from it.

"I've mentioned Hunter Thompson," he said.

"Many times."

"I really related to him."

"You told me you never read his books."

"Right," Sharkey said. "But it's not about reading his books. It's that he wrote them. Lots, I think. He did journalism. Writing — that's all he really did. The drugs, the women, the crazy — yes. But the writing was all he really cared about. That one thing."

He was nodding, jogged by the movement of the plane, which had begun to speed down the runway, and suddenly lifted. Then they were in the air, tilted over Waikiki, in the distance the vast hollow battlements of Diamond Head, which when they passed it seemed like a gigantic barnacle. Sharkey was murmuring, his hand still pressing the papers, as though rehearsing what he would say next.

Olive leaned nearer to him. "Where are you going with this?"

Sharkey did not look at her. He seemed more earnest facing forward, squinting in the roar of the plane. When he spoke it was with a voice of certainty, raised to be heard above the noise of the engines.

"My one thing," he said, "the only thing I ever did, was surf. That was my life, all I cared about. That's all I did. Monster waves."

He smacked the folder and pressed again, and in its thickness it seemed to pulse with life, to hold more warmth than when in his hand.

"Unlike him," he said.

"He's got a name, Joe."

Sharkey lifted his hand and lowered his head to the label at the top of that stack of papers. "Max Mulgrave."

"The man you killed."

Sharkey bent his head, inclining it closer to the name, his eyes squeezed shut, his lips twisted in confusion.

"We'll find him."

In a pained whisper of self-reproach, Sharkey said, "He did so much in his life."

Olive stroked his cheek but, daunted by the howl of the air rushing against the plane, could not think of anything more to say.

"All I did was surf."

Then he slept, and they flew into darkness, waking hours later with a sudden bump of turbulence and the pinpricks of lights below them, meaning they'd crossed into California, and he dozed again. Dawn over the desert woke him. A wheelchair was waiting for him in Dallas, and the next flight, to Little Rock, was short. They were soon in a rental car, Olive at the wheel, in the paler light and bushier trees of the mainland, flatter hills, a chill in the air, October in the Ozarks.

Always, away from Hawaii, the world looked older and darker, in muted light under a lower sky, the landscape lumpier, and fenced, much of it gouged by plows. But the trees were taller, the houses bigger and more solid and severe than any in Hawaii. The road through the flat-topped hills was lined by blackish woods, and in some hollows they saw a white-painted house and what looked like a farm, planted fields or a tethered horse, a dog rushing to the perimeter fence when they slowed the car.

"Parts of the West Country look like this," Olive said. "Devon. Dorset."

Meadows, rivulets running through them, browsing cows. The woods were leafier and softer, the trees agitated by the breeze, and where the land was low-lying it was muddy. Yet it didn't have a visible edge, as Hawaii did —you weren't confined, you could keep driving.

"I'd die in a place with no water."

"Voilà, there's some water." In the depth of a valley the shining folds and corrugations of a shallow river tumbling over water-smoothed boulders.

"How much farther?" Sharkey asked, then sagged and slept.

It was early evening when they reached Floristan, Sharkey coughing himself awake as the car stopped. They found the motel Olive had booked, and, too tired to eat, heavy with jet lag, they slept, waking before dawn, lying in each other's arms.

Sharkey said, "What would I do without you?" in a whisper. "I'd be lost without you."

She had no reply to this. She was too moved to speak, grateful for his acknowledgment.

"I've never said that to anyone." He breathed it into her ear. "I've never felt it."

"Lovey," she said.

"My father used to tell his men, 'Consider yourself already dead, and you'll be fine.'"

He'd told her that before, numerous times, fixed in the trauma of his repeating-himself phase. She did not remind him. She kissed him; she said, "Buck up, mate, we'll muddle through this."

But over breakfast at a diner next door to the motel — "A real breakfast," Olive said — he sat, looking futile once more. Olive took a sheet of paper from her folder and pushed it across the table to Sharkey, who was licking pancake syrup from his fingers.

"Read it to me," he said.

She didn't need to consult it, she knew what was written on it. She said,

"We're going to his school, to the town hall, to the registrar of deeds, to the police station — all the places that might have a record of him or his family."

"We could have found records online, like that *moke* Stickney did."

"Just bumf."

"Bumf?"

"Bum fodder. Paperwork. You say you hate it and you're probably right. We have to talk to people who might have known him — family, friends, anyone. We need to find out who he was."

"Where do we go first?"

"Swings and roundabouts," she said, with a shrug. "Cop shop, I reckon."

Sharkey felt small and ineffectual in her presence, admiring yet intimidated by her conviction. She was brisk and downright, in the English way — "Buck up, mate" was her mantra, and, now and then, "Pull your finger out." No wonder she was such a capable nurse: she was decisive, dealing with injured and suffering people, always conscious of time passing, motivated by a sense of urgency, her whole being possessed by the necessity to save a life — to rescue; and now she was rescuing him.

But though he was grateful, and murmured his thanks, he was helpless, as when, under the wave at Waimea the last time he'd risked surfing, he'd been trapped in the water, aware both of drowning and of being surrounded by swimmers, unable to help himself. And that helplessness had terrified him, because he'd thought *I'm drowning* and yet could not move, as in a dream, paralyzed by sleep, and surrendering to the heaviness of the water, rolled in the coffin of the wave and, looking up, was taunted by the dim daylight far above, on the surface.

Seeing him brooding, Olive asked the waitress for directions to the school, the town hall, the police station. Removing a pencil from her bun of hair, the waitress circled them on the map Olive had printed from the Internet. After that — the waitress saying, "Y'all come back, hear?" — they headed down the main street, Sharkey tagging along behind Olive. Passing a whitewashed house with green shutters and an old wheelbarrow serving as a planter, geraniums spilling from its tray, and on its own island in the center of town, surrounded by flowerbeds, the granite statue of a Civil War soldier clutching his musket, Olive said, "Pure Americana."

"Mulgrave — sounds familiar," the desk sergeant said at the police station. "I think there was a kid at our school with that name."

But when Olive spelled it, the policeman said, "That's not it. It's your Yankee accent, ma'am."

"Hear that, Joe? My posh Yankee accent."

The sergeant agreed to tap the name into his computer, but found no matches.

"Anything before the early nineties, it won't be in our database. We didn't get computers hereabouts till then. You could check at the town hall — right across Main Street."

The lawn fronting the Floristàn Town Hall was planted with apple trees, some of them still hung with fruit, and the façade of the building was shaded by a high-roofed porch lined with white columns. Inside, the lobby was cool, a fluff of dust on the varnished floorboards. Seeing TOWN CLERK lettered in gold on a door, Olive entered and greeted an elderly man in a swivel chair, reading a newspaper at a desk.

"Nice trees out front."

"Floristan's famous for its flowering shrubs. You have to come in springtime."

Olive asked see the voting rolls. The man selected a ring binder from a shelf, saying, "This is up to date," but the name Mulgrave did not appear in any of its pages.

Olive said, "The family definitely lived in Floristan."

"They own property?"

"Yes, I'm sure."

"Registrar of deeds — down the hall, just past the drinking fountain. They might have something for y'all."

Olive rapped on the counter and a powdered white-faced woman appeared, her cheeks crimped like piecrust when she smiled at them. She was kindly beneath her makeup. She wore a yellow silken dress, a floppy bow at her collar, a blue flower pinned just beneath her billowy shoulder. She said she didn't hear too good — "Hearing-impaired," she clarified. When Olive wrote the name Max Mulgrave on an office *While You Were Out* pad, the woman said, "Give me some time-frame idea of the date you think he lived here, please."

"Could have been fifty years ago."

"That's a help," the woman said. She was perhaps sixty — old enough to be a contemporary of Max Mulgrave's. But when they asked, she said, "I'm from Fayetteville. I married a Floristan boy." In a softer voice, "He passed."

She went to a cabinet and pulled out a drawer. Using the fingertips of both hands, she flicked through the cards, searching for the name.

"Little bitty old cards," she tut-tutted.

The process took so long that Olive and Sharkey sat down in chairs by the wall.

"Y'all check the voter rolls?" the woman called out, still looking down at the cards.

"Yes. They sent us here."

"No one by that name presently owns a residence in Floristan district."
The woman shoved the drawer back into the cabinet.

"But thirty or forty years ago, or more?"

"If they did, the records would be in the annex, where we keep the old
files. I can look. I'll let you know if I find anything. I'm fixin' to do that after
lunch. I'm Rose."

"Thank you, Rose."

"I love your accent, miss."

"I love yours," Olive said.

"But yours is like the movies."

They traded phone numbers and set off for Floristan High School. Brick,
squarish, as stately as the town hall, it was two blocks down Main Street.
They walked, Olive wondering whether she should simply stop when she
saw anyone of sixty or so and ask whether he or she knew the name Max
Mulgrave.

"All this way from Hawaii," Sharkey said, wondering at the town, shaking
his head.

The receptionist at the high school took them to the office of the deputy
principal, who was Black — a tall man in a dark suit and floral tie who introduced himself as Dr. Johnson.

"Those records would be in storage," he said when Olive told him the
graduation date. "You need to go online."

Sharkey lifted his hands to his face and groaned into his fingers, turning
away.

"Is he all right?" Dr. Johnson looked sour in his sudden confusion.

"We've come rather a long distance."

"This is the new high school." Dr. Johnson had turned away from Sharkey. "Your friend might have attended the old high school."

"Where's that, Doctor?"

"On Cherry Street. It's a museum now."

"How old are you, Doctor?"

"Forty-seven — and by the way, please call me Purnell."

"Purnell, did you know a family named Mulgrave when you were a teenager?"

"I take it they were white folks?"

"Yes, sir," Olive said, and heard Sharkey mutter "Haoles" through his teeth.

"I didn't know any white folks at all when I was a youngster. I lived out at
Yellville — but not in Yellville proper. Countryside. First white person I ever
got to know was at college. I was around twenty then."

"What about the yearbooks? He might be in one of them."

"Maybe have a look at the school library. What did you say was the year this gentleman graduated?"

"'Sixty-nine."

"Ancient history," Dr. Williams said in a pained voice, tightening his face. "Library's the big room on the second floor. Miss Ruffin will be glad to help you."

Miss Ruffin, a soft-faced woman, chalky with makeup, was seated at a computer; her welcoming voice said, "Come right on in." She tapped the keyboard with a gesture of finality, stabbing at it, then turned to face them and listen to Olive's question.

"Excuse my apron," she said. It was starched and white, with yellow flowers embroidered on the bib, and made her look like an elderly child.

Olive wrote Max Mulgrave's name and his graduation year on a slip of paper and handed it to Miss Ruffin.

"Tell you one thing for certain," Miss Ruffin said. "You won't find anything of that kind on this here computer. All the yearbooks is over on those shelves. Ain't got but one file copy on hand, and none of those early years been digitized."

"So we came to the right place," Olive said.

"Yearbook-speaking," Miss Ruffin said, "you're at ground zero."

"That's a lovely apron."

"It's to keep the dust off. Books are just a caution for dust."

"Apron? Dust?" Sharkey said. "What is all this talk? What are we doing here?"

Hugging him, to comfort him, to restrain him, Olive felt the tension in his body, his hard arms tensed as though about to lash out. Soothing him, she heard Miss Ruffin speaking.

"The *Apple Blossom*, 1969," the woman was saying in a new tone — brisk, efficient — selecting a blue volume from the far end of the shelf. "You can use it on the table yonder. Just return it to me when you're done."

Sharkey's outburst had spooked her, stung her, made her wary, and impelled Olive to hold on to him until she felt him relax, a softening of his posture. She led him to the table, where they sat side by side, Sharkey with his head in his hands as Olive leafed through the yearbook. She turned first to the section headed SENIORS, the graduating class, and there he was, blond, thin-faced, solemn, in a white short-sleeved shirt with an oversized collar, a stain on the pocket. The other boys on the same page wore jackets and ties, and most were plump and smiling. He looked forlorn.

The caption under his photograph read: *Max Mulgrave . . . "Buzz cut". . . Good with numbers . . . Slide Rule Club . . . "I'm real busy" . . . "Hey Joe" . . . Future astronaut.*

Olive read it to Sharkey in a low voice, but he remained holding his head and did not react. The entry was much shorter and less detailed than any of the others, and unlike them there was no listing of his participation in sports or student politics or the prom. Others mentioned football, baseball, Apple Blossom Achievement, Future Farmers of America, cheerleader, cadet.

But two items stood out: "Hey Joe" and the Slide Rule Club.

"It's a song," Sharkey said.

"Fancy that, Joe," Olive said. "Not in my repertoire."

"Loved that song," Sharkey said. "Kind of an anthem for me. 'Hey Joe, where you gonna run to now?'"

Olive had found the page headed SLIDE RULE CLUB and the group photo, eight students, four girls seated on chairs, knees together, their hands on their laps, fingers laced together, and standing behind them, four boys, Max Mulgrave on one side, pale, haunted-looking, a face of apprehension, the same short-sleeved white shirt with the big collar, the same stain.

"Some of these kids might still be alive," Olive said, writing their names in her notebook.

When she was done — there were no more mentions of Max Mulgrave in the yearbook — she handed the volume back to Miss Ruffin, open to the Slide Rule Club page, and thanked her, saying, "Do you know any of these people? They'd all be late fifties, early sixties now."

Adjusting her apron, Miss Ruffin settled the book on the counter and studied the page, touching each name with a pale finger, murmuring to herself.

"Those girls is most likely married," she said. "Probably grannies by now. But this Terry Baggett, he's in town — Baggett Insurance. And this fellow Ray Siggins, you'll find him somewhere. It's a good family, lots of Sigginses hereabouts. Curtis Rickards — lots of Rickards too. Could be one of the Rickards at the dairy, or the filling station."

Baggett Insurance was nearest, on Main Street, beyond the Civil War memorial, but Terry Baggett was not there, the secretary said. Olive said it was urgent. The secretary offered to call him, saying, "This about a policy?"

"In a way," Olive said.

The woman hesitated, and then Olive saw that she had been eating a sandwich, which she still held in her right hand, half concealing it below the level of her desk. A bit breathless in her confusion, she said, "Missed my breakfast," then placed the unfinished sandwich on her blotter and dialed the number. She handed the ringing receiver to Olive.

"This is Terry," came the voice.

Sharkey had been staring out the window at the planter on the sill, the browned late-season blossoms. But as though to turn his back on Olive, he crept to an aquarium bubbling on a shelf, the yellow and blue fish flashing at his approach.

"You don't know me," Olive said into the phone. "I'm at your office, inquiring about a man named Max Mulgrave."

In the long silence that followed, Olive wondered whether she'd been cut off.

"Hello?"

"I'm thinking," the man said. "I haven't heard that name for years. You kind of blindsided me with it."

"You were in high school with him."

"Coon's age ago."

"Were you friends?"

"What's this concerning, miss?"

"My name is Olive Randall. I'm trying to trace old friends and acquaintances of Max Mulgrave's."

"I don't reckon you'll find any."

"Why would that be?"

"He didn't have but two or three to begin with. And when he left town he never come back. Or maybe once, but not more than that."

"So he did come back?"

"That was the talk. It would have been years ago. Maybe it was to see his mother."

"Is she still in town?"

"She passed." The man sighed, a scraping sound in the phone. "I'm sorry, miss. I don't have time for this."

"Can I run a couple of names past you?"

"Do it real quick."

Olive read from her notebook, "Curtis Rickards. Ray Siggins. Mary Lou Gordon."

Interrupting her, the man said, "Mary Lou's married. Moved long ago. Ray's still in town, but he's busted up about his wife's passing. Curtis, you might find him at his garage. Gotta go. Bah now."

The phone went dead. Olive handed the receiver back to the secretary, who said, "Mr. Baggett's real busy."

"Curtis Rickards," Olive said. "Could you direct me to his garage?"

But the secretary was looking fretfully at Sharkey, who was twirling his finger in the bubbling aquarium, poking at the darting fish, his tongue clamped in his teeth in concentration.

"Sir, y'all mind leaving them fish be?"

Sharkey, still with his finger in the water, said sharply, "Do I tell you what to do?"

"Joe!" Olive said in sudden fury, and Sharkey shrank like a scolded child and sidled away from the aquarium.

"Rickards' Garage," the secretary said. "It's set back a piece, behind the Piggly Wiggly, big ole Texaco Star up top. But he don't pump gas no more," and seeing Sharkey creeping back toward the aquarium, said, "Sir!"

Olive led him outside, but before she could warn him to behave he said, "Something about this place. You get the feeling that half of it is buried." He meant the state, what he had seen of it, the sense he'd had on the drive from Little Rock. The life of the land was hidden under the hills and hollows and the trees thrashed by the wind, in the muddy creeks, an inner darkness of ghosts and corpses and bones, the dirty water and stagnation in the road-side ditches, the faded shirts and ragged underwear hung out to dry on the laundry lines of the poor farmhouses, a haunted landscape of secrets and resentments. He did not have the words to explain this vision to Olive. He said, "I found that fishbowl a relief."

Farther up the street, passing Belle's Diner, she saw the Piggly Wiggly store and smiled at the name — "Extraordinary," she said — and behind it the Texaco sign the secretary had mentioned.

"I'm hungry," Sharkey said, pointing at Belle's Diner.

"Let's see this guy first."

Inside the open-fronted garage a man in blue overalls was tinkering with a car upraised on a block lift.

"Looking for Mr. Curtis Rickards," Olive said.

"In the office," the man said, and seeing Sharkey behind her, added, "You got some serious tats, bro."

"You too," Sharkey said.

In the manner of someone surrendering, the man lifted his arms, show-ing his forearms, in one of his greasy hands a socket wrench that he held like a weapon.

"Four years in Cummins Unit," he said. "That's where I learned to do this," and wagged the wrench. "What's your excuse?"

"Surfer tribal," Sharkey said, but Olive was at the office door, calling to him, and when he joined her inside, she said, "This is Mr. Rickards. He's going to tell us about Max Mulgrave."

"Call me Curtis — pleased to meet you," the man said, reaching for Shar-key's hand. He wore a battered baseball cap and a T-shirt with red lettering, GO HOGS. The man spoke slowly, with a lazy mouth, his lips so loose and awry Olive couldn't lip-read his words. "So you know Max?"

Olive said, "In point of fact, we don't know him at all. We're doing a bit of research on his background."

"Something happen to him?"

"He passed away."

"Sorry to hear it," Rickards said, and adjusted his ball cap in a formal reflex of grief.

"Mr. Baggett told us where we could find you. We understand you were in high school with him. The Slide Rule Club."

"Oh boy, that takes me back." He sniffed in reflection, then seemed to remember something. "Please have a seat. Can I offer you folks a soda?"

"No thanks," Olive said, sitting, Sharkey pulling another chair next to her. "And we don't want to waste your time."

"This is Floristan," Rickards said. "All we got is time."

"Max Mulgrave," Olive said, prompting him.

"Very smart — supersmart. Very quiet, grew up real poor. Clothes all tore up. Got teased at school."

"For being poor?"

"For being smart," Rickards said. "Got whupped by his pa." He tugged at his ball cap again, leveling his visor, the visor stained from his tuggings. "One thing I recall is he was restless — set on leaving Floristan. And he did. Joined the army out of high school. I believe he served in 'Nam, like some others in our class. Never came back."

"We heard from Mr. Baggett that he might have returned to see his mother."

"That could be so. But old Widder Mulgrave, she's long gone."

"Where did she live?"

"Off Seven South. One of them roads that crosses the creek. That'd be Indian Creek. I don't get over there unless I have to tow someone or light up a battery."

"Do you remember anything else about Max Mulgrave?"

"Math whiz. A brain — imagine that, a brain in Floristan. Real quiet type. Could have gone to Fayetteville, but he didn't have the money. And look at me. I had the money, but I took over my daddy's business instead."

Sharkey cleared his throat to get Rickards's attention. He had been staring at the man's head as though trying to locate a thought inside it. He said, "He was teased at school?"

"You know how kids are," Rickards said.

"I sure do," Sharkey said.

"Had to fight his battles."

"I know all about that."

"What about other friends like you?" Olive asked. "Are there any of them in town?"

Rickards's half-smile drooped on his loose lips, rueful in reflection. He said, "I can't rightly recall if he had a girlfriend. Smoked a lot of weed after school, but that was no big deal. All of us was stoners then." He tapped the ragged blotter on his steel desk as though indicating that he was struggling to think hard. "It was so long ago. I wish I could tell you more, but darned if I can remember." Then he glanced up but looked severe, narrowing his eyes. "One interesting thing. I went over to his house once. It was to bring him a book — it was a little old book of logarithm tables, like we used before computers. Max was sick in bed, and we had a test coming up. This was his old house, shotgun shack, not the one his mother moved into later."

"You took him a book," Olive said. "What was interesting?"

"Interesting in a sorry way," Rickards said. "The house was all cattywampus. Max was ashamed. He hadn't expected me. He didn't like me seeing it — the house cattywampus, and his life no better. His ma smoking on the front stairs. Off to the side a beat-up Eleanor."

"Eleanor?"

"Outhouse — privy. Particular kind. They didn't have no plumbing, the Mulgraves," Rickards said. "By then his daddy had run off. And after that visit he avoided me, like I'd seen things he didn't want me to see. Out of shame, I guess. He stayed away from me. I wasn't too surprised when he joined the army. Folks from Floristan, that's one way to move up — the service. I imagine he was a lot better off wherever he went."

"After the army he went to college in California," Olive said. "Started a successful business. Then sold it. Relocated to Hawaii."

"I'm so fetched to hear that," Rickards said, and choked a little and fussed with his cap, then pressed his fingers to his eyes.

Olive saw that the man was weeping, using his fingers to stop his tears, murmuring but not able to speak clearly, his effort showing in his crumpled shoulders.

"I'm sorry to upset you."

"No, I'm happy," Rickards said, but in a suffering voice. "It's just remembering his poor old shack, and Max sick in bed, and how ashamed he was. I'm glad for the happy ending."

"Thanks for your help," Olive said, rising from her chair and moving to the office door.

Just as they were leaving, Sharkey turned to face Rickards, his mouth opening wide, his neck reddened under his tattoos.

"I killed him," he said, keeping his mouth open, panting furiously. "I killed Max Mulgrave."

Rickards huffed and seemed to swell, and stood up at his desk, kicking his chair back. He snatched at his hat, and out of his pain-filled face, his bulging eyes glazed with tears, came a strangled helpless honk that might have been an anguished word.

Too tired to look further, they went back to the motel, telling themselves they needed a nap, but they slept on, waking in the dark, bewildered by the strangeness, the stale breath of the air conditioner, the smell of the decaying carpet. They lay in silence, open-eyed, until the stained ceiling became visible in the next morning's daylight.

At breakfast Sharkey was silent. Olive said, "I know what you're thinking. Waste of time. Wild goose chase. But this is where he came from. This town made him. These people, these streets, that man. We know him better. This was his world."

Her cell phone sounded, its ring and vibration causing it to fidget on the table.

"Is that Miss Olive? This is Rose, from Deeds. How you folks doing? I just found something."

The woman was where they'd left her, in the small office, a folder on the desk before her. She plucked it open with satisfaction.

"This is the title deed we found in the annex. For a house in the name of Ebba Mulgrave, Indian Creek Trail, right here in Floristan. And this here, another document certifying payment in full, some serious money, with the notarized signature of the gentleman you inquired about, Mr. Max Mulgrave. And his address."

Olive examined the names, mother and son, impressed by the flourish of the son's signature, in great contrast to the mother's irregular scrawl, less a written name than something pictorial, a doodle in blue ink.

"Funny old address," Rose said.

"Kaulawaha Road," Sharkey said.

"You know how to say it. What kind of word is that?"

"Hawaiian."

"That zip code," Olive said. "It's in a place called Wai'anae."

Rose clapped her hands and said, "Looks like you found what you was looking for."

8

The Leeward Side

Y ou look happy," Olive said. "I can tell you're much better."

Crap. Sharkey, blank-faced, too tired from the return flight to speak, thought people said those empty words to sell their hopeful delusions and to be blameless.

He was not happier, he was not better, getting back to Hawaii on the long flight from anywhere was like a hangover, he still felt weak and alienated, like someone fighting the grip of turbulent water. The memory kept repeating. He'd been drowning in the outflung arms of Waimea Bay when they found him and hauled him to shore. But the fright had not abated, and now he knew that in such close calls, something much worse than he'd experienced before, the fear did not leave him, even in the clods of red dirt in Floristan: he went on drowning.

"Glad to be back here anyway," was all he said after Olive prodded him.

He could not tell her why, though he knew. He never had the words for the images in his head and didn't want to sound stupid trying to describe what he saw, the stifling sense of confinement he felt on the mainland, the chill on the sunniest days, how he craved the freedom he felt in Hawaii, the beauty of the light skimming on the ocean, the empty space most of all.

Everyone stupidly believed it to be the other way around — "the mainland's huge, man" — the cities and long roads and distant hills in places like Nevada and Utah, or where they'd just been, in the bushy woods and low hills of Arkansas. Those places pressed on his head and imprisoned him with bad smells, the air thick with sour vegetation and decay, with diesel fumes that reeked of poison, the cities stinking with too many people. He had hated the dark woods on the drive to Floristan, the disorder by the roadside, the junked cars rusting in tall grass. In every crowded town he'd imagined witchlike faces staring from the windows of houses. The mainland was a place of muffled voices and intimidating buildings and overdressed strangers, all those baggy clothes and big shoes — you never saw flesh, never bare feet.

He could not rid his mind of the sense of failure he felt, trapped in mainland narrowness, suffering an obscure thirst, the dust like a disease. The mainland was a place of threat, of danger, of whispers — yes, the roads were long, but they were all dead ends, the mainland was an underworld of shadows and strangers.

Hawaii was huge and sunlit and sweet. It was not just the mountains and the cliffs and the green vertical *pali,* rising like organ pipes, under the sky-high arches of enormous rainbows — it was the water. The sea was also Hawaii, the sea was its world. The islands did not end at the shore. They were part of the luminous ocean, and the ocean was endless and life-giving and, just offshore, empty of people. No one on the mainland knew that. "Cali's got waves," they said, but the rest of California was jammed against all those other states, of wreckage and desert. Hawaii was a gorgeous green woman reclining on her side, sensual, sloping, allowing you to rest against her softness.

So he was where he wanted to be. Yet he knew he was fractured and feeble, stumbling at times like an old man who could not swim to save his life. And he was exhausted too — all that way to a dot on the mainland map, only to discover that the plot led to Wai'anae.

Guessing at his frustration, Olive said, "We needed to go. We know him better now, because of that trip. We have something to go on."

They were in Olive's car, passing Chun's Reef, barefoot grommets crossing the road, their boards slung under their arms.

Sharkey said, "What do we know." It was not a question, it was an exasperated remark.

"That he was poor, and restless — you saw his sad face in the yearbook. That he wanted something better. That he was determined to leave. That he's not the corpse in the mortuary now — he's a man in motion."

"That he got teased at school," Sharkey said with feeling.

"You saw that he bought a big expensive house for his mum. He ended up with money."

"He didn't end up with money. He ended up drunk, on an old bike, in the rain at Waimea. He ended up dead."

They had passed Weed Circle and the narrow track to Snake Road, which Olive took to avoid the traffic at Helemano. She cut through Schofield to Kunia Road, a ribbon of pavement across the lower slopes of the hills and the mountain, the old volcano, deeply scored, its tubes of lava cold and densely forested. Concentrating on the narrow road and avoiding potholes, Olive had not answered, so they were passing the plowed fields at the Ewa end when Sharkey spoke again, as though finishing his thought.

"And I'm dying too."

"We'll find him," Olive said, in her hearty bucking-him-up tone.

"I used to drive this way to go to Wai'anae and Nānākuli to surf," Sharkey said. "I was strong. I knew I'd get hassled by *mokes* in the lineup, but I'd think, 'Bring it on, brah.' I earned respect."

"I wish I'd known you then."

"Good thing you didn't." He seemed cheered by the memory. "I was a dog."

"Lucky me," Olive said. But she thought how she hated the way men boasted of their stupid maleness, the way they thought that women were impressed by the boasts. But only other men cared, or laughed, while women concluded, *Another reason not to trust you.*

He was not a man, he'd become a child again, and she felt sorry for him, especially at those times, more frequent now, when he admitted he was afraid.

"It was all different when I came this way before," he said. "Because I was different."

"We'll go straight to his house," Olive said, to change the subject, because she knew that he'd talk about how everything was different, and that would lead to him talking about being old, then he'd talk about dying, and she hated that. She wanted him to understand that they were still on a quest and that a new life for him might be possible at the end of it.

"I'm staying in the car," Sharkey said, suddenly deadened—the fear was physical. They had passed through Wai'anae on the highway, the shops on the right—yellow walls, scrawled signs—the sea shimmering on the left, the waves like enemies, the thresh of water scooping at tree roots, toppling palms—they lay across the beach—and cracking cement revetments, tossing gouts of sand on the highway. The glare of sunlight exposed the squalor of Wai'anae and made it sinister, the graffiti more hostile for being so visible, the detritus—driftwood, household garbage—like mayhem. The gray coconuts piled in the high-tide trash on the grassy dunes looked to him like severed heads.

Having turned into a side street, Kaulawaha Road, Olive slowed the car in front of a chain-link perimeter fence, a black dog head-butting it and making it rattle. The dog yelped and slavered, speaking to Sharkey in accusatory barks.

Industrial fencing and a guard dog, but the house was lovely, two stories faced in redwood, in contrast to the bungalows, small behind their faded paint, that lined the street near it, the big house like a symbol of a powerful man towering over the poor.

The fence was recent — shiny, out of character in the funky unfenced neighborhood. A covered lanai on the second floor faced the sea, allowing a view of the town, the ocean — sunsets, waves, the green flash.

"He lived here in the 1980s," Olive said. "When he bought that house for his mum." She slipped out of the car and, sensitive to Sharkey's hesitation — the barking dog, his fatigue and anxiety — said, "Come on, mate. I need you."

Just as they got to the edge of the fence, they saw a man striding from the house in the direction of the barking dog. He did nothing to calm the dog, allowing it to leap at the fence, making the chain links clang against the steel posts.

"You want something?"

He was dark, local, Hawaiian or Tongan, with black slicked-back hair and a wet jowly face, in a sweatshirt with cut-off sleeves that showed his beefy arms. He carried a thick wooden club in one hand. He wore shorts that came below his knees and flattened flip-flops on his tortured-looking feet. The dog gnawed at the club, coating it with slobber.

"Nice house," Olive said.

But this pleasantry seemed to anger the man, and his anger was highlighted by the perspiration on his face. Still holding the club, he lifted the front of his sweatshirt with his free hand and mopped it, showing his belly, a four-inch appendix scar upraised like a purple welt.

"Nevvamine." He flexed his big jaw; he had dog teeth and a scummy tongue. "You selling stuffs? Something like that?"

"We just have a few questions."

"What department you from?" The man put his head against the fence, facing Olive.

"Take it easy," Sharkey said.

"Eh!" The man's grunt rumbled from his belly. "Bodda you?"

Olive said, "We were wondering about a previous occupant of this house, that's all. Someone we're researching."

"I stay here ten-plus years!"

"What's your name?" Sharkey said.

"Who wants to know?"

"Me — I'm Joe Sharkey."

The man shrugged, and went on poking at the dog, goading it to growl and nip at the wooden club. "You don't need to know any names, okay, ha-ole?"

Sharkey stepped back, not because of the man's rude reply but because the dog had tired of gnawing the club and had leaped, thumping the fence with his front paws and opening his mouth wide to bark.

"This house was once owned by a man named Max Mulgrave," Olive said.

The man frowned. He turned away and walked a few steps, then he paused and called over his shoulder, "Time to go — I mean, for you."

"Dead end, dead end, dead end," Sharkey chanted as they walked back to the car.

Olive said, "No — another revelation. Look at this lovely house. He lived here. He looked out of those windows. He stood on that lanai and watched the sunset and the waves. Maybe he was a surfer. Why else would he come here?"

Sharkey could not match the dead broken man to a surfboard — he barely imagined him upright. But he was rattled by the visit for another reason. He took a deep breath, then said, "That dog freaked me out." He was relieved to see that the dog had followed the man into the house.

"This is the address that was on the payment form — the one he signed," Olive said. "This has got to have been his house."

Kicking at the weeds by the roadside, Sharkey said, "I hate unfinished business. We don't know anything."

"We know masses," Olive said. "We found his hometown. His photograph. His friends. We know where he came from — that's crucial."

"We don't know enough," Sharkey said, and gasped, feeling helpless and lightheaded and lost. "It's making me worse, the not knowing."

Drowning out his moan there came two blasts of a siren's bloated buzz, a police cruiser heading toward them, stopping directly behind Olive's car, blue lights flashing, its buzz dying. A burly policeman in a tight shirt got out and stood facing them, his thumbs hooked onto his belt — the belt weighted with gadgets, phone, Taser, cuffs, mace, and a thick black pistol.

"This is private property, folks. We've had a complaint."

"We were just leaving," Olive said.

"That's good, because I don't want to get involved in any paperwork."

He didn't blink. He kept his mouth open, teeth showing, as though to warn them.

"Paperwork," Sharkey said, spitting the word.

Hoping to lighten the mood, Olive said, "We're day-trippers from the North Shore, making an inquiry. We think a man named Max Mulgrave used to live here."

The policeman brightened; he let go of his belt and stepped closer, smiling. "You know Max?"

"In a way," Olive said. "Do you?"

"Everybody in Wai'anae knows Max," the policeman said — impressed, eager to oblige. "Rich haole. Good guy. Haven't heard anything about him for quite a while. I know he took some hits."

A crackling sound in Sharkey's head kept him from speaking.

"So this was really his house?" Olive said.

"One of them. The first one, best one. The others were more worse. One was junk. But Max — he stay humble."

"The man who lives in this house now doesn't know him."

"He from Maui — got money, got some food trucks. He know Maui things. He don't know the Leeward Side. He buy this from another guy. He so lucky to have Max house."

"What can you tell us about Max?"

"I can tell you he was bulletproof. I can show you his friend — he knows everything. They were buddies. But, hey, you gotta move your vehicle."

"Where is this guy?"

"Follow me."

In the car, following the cruiser, Olive said, "He doesn't know. He thinks Max Mulgrave is alive."

Sharkey sighed, as he often did hearing the man's name, the name like an accusation; and he knew that saying he was dead would mean his having to admit he'd killed him. He resisted saying anything; his guilt burdened and weakened him.

"This policeman is taking an extraordinary route."

The cruiser had moved through a neighborhood of small bungalows, along back streets of junked cars, to the highway, but instead of reentering the residential area the policeman headed to the beach on a service road patched with softened tar that ran parallel to the main road, past overflowing trash barrels and piles of litter — blue plastic, discarded tires, rusted bicycles, and shattered toys. They came to what looked from a distance like a campsite, a huddle of tents atop a steep sand dune, surrounded by windbreaks of canvas, and twiggy lean-tos wrapped with tarpaulins, the twigs protruding like bleached bones. A small Hawaiian flag flapped upside-down on a stick secured to one of the tent poles.

That was the foreground of improvisation and disorder; in great contrast the background was a forested ridge, the old twisted lava flow showing in its folded slopes, the green dignity of a Hawaiian mountainside, its sweet aromatic woods.

The policeman waved them forward, and when they drew beside his cruiser, he called out, "Ask for Frawley DeFreeze. Is his friend. He mention Max to me other day."

Olive parked, and they walked up the ramp of sand and tussocky turf into the littered area of the tents, where three men were seated in beach chairs, facing the sea, the small waves flopping against the shore, rolls of scummy foam draining into the sand, some shrieking children kicking at it.

"Aloha," Olive said.

The men leaned back, scowling, their chairs straining under their weight. Two were very fat, bulked against the frayed webbing of the chairs; the third was gaunt, holding a small flattish can under his chin. They wore dirty T-shirts and torn shorts and baseball caps. Now Olive could see that the gaunt one was eating, flicking food from the can to his mouth with chopsticks. At first glance they were like a trio of ragged clowns, harlequins in patches who at any moment might get up and dance and distract her with their foolery, but she saw they were inert and stubborn and colorless in their squalor.

"This whole area private property," the fattest man said, gesturing with his cigarette. His face looked roasted by the sun, blackened and peeling in places, his lips cracked, but he wore a good pair of aviator sunglasses, which obscured his eyes. As though for emphasis, he canted sideways and spat into the sand. His hat was lettered LOCAL MOTION.

Sharkey said, "You guys surfers?"

"We look like surfers to you, haole?" The man plumped his belly with his hands, and the others laughed.

"Reason I ask is I'm a surfer." He put out his hand. The others did not move to shake it. He said, "Joe Sharkey."

"Here's a stick," Local Motion said. A bruised and chipped surfboard was jammed in the sand beside one of the tents. "Give me twenty bucks for rent. Go surf."

Sharkey hesitated, digging his toe in the sand, hating the man for his hostility. "Not today."

"Haole say he one surfer dude. Now he say he no want for try surf." He nudged the man next to him, who obliged, expelling cigarette smoke with his laugh. The gaunt man went on eating, now making scouring motions inside the can with his chopsticks. The yellow label on the can said WAHOO. He stared at Sharkey, then opened his mouth wide to clamp it on the chopsticks. He sucked the fish fragments from them, then tossed the can aside.

"Frawley," Olive said. "We're looking for him."

"He at the food pantry," Local Motion said.

The gaunt man, dabbing at his lips, looked closer at Sharkey. He squinted and said, "Sharkey," and chewed the word with his lips, because he had no teeth. "Sharkey," he said again. "You was at Roosevelt. You was a Rough Rider."

"Yeah. Long ago."

"Old days," the man said. He jabbed his thumb at his sunken chest, snagging it on a rip in his T-shirt. "Fonoti. I stay Roosevelt."

Sharkey knew the name as one of his antagonists but could not discern the muscular wild-haired boy in this skinny toothless balding man squeezing his chopsticks with bony fingers and staring out of deep-set eyes with his mad monkey face.

"I was in da *hui*," he said. "Wilfred Kalama and Bradda Jay and them."

"Wilfred — what happened to him?" Sharkey said, remembering his tormentor.

"He wen' *make*. Too much of drugs. Ice, he smoking."

"*Batu*," Local Motion said, as though clarifying.

"Vai and Nalani, they got grandkids. Nalani stay in Vegas."

"You know this fucken haole?" Local Motion said.

"We was at Roosevelt," Fonoti said. "Hey, good old Rough Rider days, brah." He saw a fleck on one of the chopsticks and lapped at it. "So where you stay — what kine job?"

"Like I said, surfing."

"Except," Local Motion said, gesturing with a fat finger, "I offer him one stick and he back off like a panty."

"He's tired," Olive said, provoked by the man's mockery. She had kept a little behind Sharkey, listening to them, surprised by the sudden names and the reminiscence of school in the squalor of the camp, the flapping tents, the litter, the tossed-aside Wahoo can sunk in the sand.

Not tired but anxious, needing relief. The names had fluttered through Sharkey's memory as distant and dark. He was looking at the sea, gazing beyond the men and the scattered camp and twists of paper and broken plastic as of shattered toys, easing his mind with the afternoon light on the water, the far-off waves, silvery corrugations at this distance. The sun was so low a fishing boat crossed in front of it and blocked it, winked it away for seconds. The incoming swell was a consolation, the ocean seeking him. He had known struggles in the water, but in the end the sea had always befriended him.

Clearing his throat, Fonoti struggled to his feet, staggering a little, then kicked past the two other men and approached Sharkey and straightened. In a strangely formal ritual, he opened his arms and hugged him, jarring Sharkey hard with the itch of his sweat-stink. He released him and beheld him, his dark eyes deep in their sockets.

Local Motion clapped his hands to his knees, a decisive gesture. "Me —I'm Frawley. What you want to know?"

He folded his thick arms across his shirt and turned his sunglasses on Olive, and she saw on his roasted face the pitted scars from chicken pox or acne.

"Max Mulgrave," Olive said. "What can you tell us about him?"

"Max!" the man said. "Bradda Max," and reached to bump fists with Olive. "He down on his luck now, but he one great guy."

"When did you first meet him?"

"Early days — eighties — when he came here after the big buyout deal with his company."

"That he sold?"

"Not to Symantec, though they made a big offer. He sell it to his employees," Frawley said. And now, losing his aggression, he lost the lilt of pidgin and the gabble of synthetic English, becoming more grammatical as he gained in pride. "He did the right thing for his workers."

"I take it his company made software," Olive said.

"You don't know?" The man laughed in a surprised, superior way, blowing out his cheeks. "Max came up with one of the first and best software programs for finding glitches in operating systems. Debugging was his thing. Bug fixes. Software patches." He reached to scratch his blunted and damaged-looking big toe, then heaved himself back in his chair and went on. "He devised the Max Patch — you don't know that, and he famous for it. Max had the formula. But he wasn't satisfied, so he made the smart move. He sold everything and came to Hawaii."

"For any specific purpose?"

"For the specific purpose every haole comes to Hawaii — to chill, to smoke *pakalolo,* to catch waves."

The word "waves" woke Sharkey. "He was a surfer?"

"Maybe better than you," Frawley said. "You know the Big Board Classic — Buffalo Keaulana's competition? Max competed two, tree times."

"So did I," Sharkey said.

Lighting a cigarette, Frawley eyed Sharkey sideways, blowing smoke, the smoke swelling, seeming to represent the widening cloud of his doubt. "Max got major points."

"I got points," Sharkey said. "Did he win?"

"Didn't have to win. Surfing for him was all the time fun. He was *pono.*"

Olive said, "How do you know so much about his business?"

The man next to Frawley, who had not spoken, poked him and laughed, and Frawley said, "I see what you're thinking. Big fat babooze, living on the beach, dirty clothes, dog life." He wagged his finger at her like a wiper blade and said, "I was senior accountant with the biggest firm in Honolulu, office on Bishop Street. I serviced clients from all over, high-end clients — Max was one. I had a nice house like Max, nice car, wife and kids. I was kicking ass. I'm not the buggah you see. Hey, I was Frawley DeFreeze, CPA. I had a life."

"So what happened?"

"Internal audit. Forensic audit. Big *shibai*. Some downtime in O Triple C. Insolvency."

Olive said, "Cooked the books?"

Scowling, Frawley pinched the dirty bill of his cap with one hand and lifted it. He scratched the scurf on his bald patch with his other hand, grubbing his scalp with his bitten nails, grunting, as though audibly reflecting. Then he smacked his lips.

He said, "Defalcation."

"I'm not sure what that means."

He settled his cap again. "Made some bad choices."

"What about Max?"

"Made some more worse choices — went all *hamajang* with no receivables and no liquidity," Frawley said. "But before that he did some great things — righteous things. Touched people's lives. Ask anyone."

"Tell me about his company, this amazing invention of his," Olive said.

"You're interested in his company that he sold" — Frawley puffed his cigarette in defiance — "and you don't care nothing about the people he helped?"

"I'm just curious about where all the money came from," Olive said in a subdued voice, to calm the man.

"Guess you're not computer savvy — the whole fricken world knows about Max Integer. Kids at the high school here use the Max Patch — updated one. You got a computer, brah?"

Sharkey said, "Yeah. I don't use it much. Just for Surfline or Windguru, to get swells and wave heights."

"There's books about his debugging. Real hybolic stuff. You read books?"

This challenge from a fat man wearing a LOCAL MOTION cap and a chewed shirt, sitting over his swollen belly in a twisted and slumping beach chair next to a stained and torn tent on a littered dune in Wai'anae.

"Books," Sharkey said. "Not much."

"Go online," Frawley said. "Big surfer, try surf the 'Net."

"And we'll find out about Max Mulgrave?"

"Not the Hawaii stuff — he was low-profile here. But you'll find out what he created, the company he sold." The man concentrated on his cigarette, puffing it, tapping ash. "But listen up. If you want to know what he did here you won't find it on Google. You have to ask people in Wai'anae." He turned aside. "Fonoti — true or not true?"

"True, brah."

"What about his wife?" Olive said.

"You ask all the unimportant questions."

"What are the important ones?"

"About his *kokua*," Frawley said. "You know *kokua*?"

Fonoti said, "It da kine, like help."

"Alex?" Frawley said.

And the other fat man, who had been silent all this time, nodded a little and wheezed and heaved himself out of his chair. He stood unsteadily and said, "Not so, Fonoti. It mean more than help. It mean give everything, make sacrifice — you do something and want no more nothing in return. It mean unselfish, really caring for people, never ask for nothing."

The man was passionate, almost preaching as he'd risen from his creaking beach chair, gesturing while Sharkey and Olive backed away. He was still talking.

"Some people Max *kokua* never know his name. But the people who matter, big people, they know him."

"Alex, he know," Frawley said as the man tottered and sat down again. "This is why I'm kind of surprised. You asking about him. Funny you don't know all about him, asking these questions."

"Like I said, we're just making inquiries."

"Computers to the high school," Fonoti said. "Max geev 'um. Money to the community health center. Max geev 'um."

"He give me these," Frawley said, tapping the lenses of his aviator sunglasses. "These real high-end."

"And plus," Alex said, as the others joined in.

The competing voices, hectoring, growing shrill, praising Max Mulgrave, some of them strangely scolding, seemed to berate Olive for not knowing about all the good that Max had done. They went on listing his accomplishments, and the worst of it was that they did not seem to know the man was dead. He was still alive, spreading joy, uplifting the poor, easing pain. Each assertion of praise Sharkey took as an accusation, something physical in it, like a slap, turning him sideways, pushing him away.

He found himself shuffling down the dune of salt-bitten grass and cast-off beer cans. To rest his eyes he looked ahead to the shoreline, where the wash of waves lapping the sand caught the last of the sun, the fire on the sea, a flash on each small wave like the memory of light.

A fisherman stood on the beach, whipping a line from his long pole, casting it in successive slashes until with a scissoring sound it looped and plopped in the trough beyond the surf zone, where the water glittered like fish scales. Nearer the shore, small children pretended they were drowning, screeching for help, startling the plovers strutting at the edge, where the slop of the small waves seemed to speak to Sharkey in cautioning stammers.

Seeing the swirl of the bits of broken coral, Sharkey backed away. Rolled in the agitated shore break, the coral was smoothed and made small, knuckles chalk-white from the beating of sun and sea, sluiced together in a great mass, and not like coral at all but a gathering of sea-whitened bones separated from a lost body, a skeleton somewhere, and smashed and smoothed in the greenish stir of a tide pool, among sea blooms and the gray fur of algae on the slabs of lava rock.

It was a broken skeleton rattling in the black sea wrack of the shore break. Sharkey stepped away from it. The push of small waves beat a froth of bubbly spittle in a ridge that straggled along the dark sand near the chips and splinters of bone-white coral. Sharkey was startled by the accusatory sound of the bones in the water, lisping at him. The sea had always spoken to him, but never so severely, nagging with the monotony of malice.

"No," he said distinctly, shielding himself with his hand. "Never."

But the single syllables of the slop and the sight of bleached bones and clicking knuckles were inescapable. He stepped back from what he took to be the complaint of a broken man he vaguely knew, his corpse washed ashore, all his bones scattered.

"Joe, you've got to hear this," Olive said as he approached the little camp from the beach.

"Going home," he said in a haunted voice, and walked past her to the car.

9

A Dog Off His Leash

I n the morning, exhausted by the shocks in his dreams — always over the falls into heavy water, under the wave, and suffocating just before he woke — his body was like clay. But he was grateful for sunlight. After he got up and sat in his rocker on the lanai, soothed by green tea Olive had brewed ("Cuppa," she said, and kissed him), he became alert to the sounds of the morning, the roosters' crowing, the twisted chirp of the myna birds, and the geese fussing, a chorus of competing squawks beneath the house. The fragrant breeze rattled the bamboos, in the blaze of sunshine the dew winked on drooping grass blades. But he thought, *Why am I so sad?*

"I promised we'd go back," Olive said.

Sharkey shut his eyes as though to expel a memory. He said, "Fonoti, from long ago. Crazy Samoan."

"He told me what happened to you at school — the gang. He said he was sorry."

"Apologies are funny shit. I laugh whenever I hear one." He looked at her with a faint smile. He said, "Those punks made me strong. They made me want something better. They gave me a purpose. All my life I wanted to get away from people like that — to swim out and catch a wave. And dismount before I got to shore, and paddle back and find another wave. Stay in the water, live in the water."

Olive knelt and took his hands to comfort him, not submissive but concerned, a gesture Sharkey always took to be a nurse's reaction, steadying an anxious patient, and his hands had a patient's tremors and sick pallor.

"And now I'm afraid of the water," he said, not consoled, feeling trapped by her touch. "That guy Frawley knew it. He dared me to surf with that crappy board, all those dings on it. I couldn't do it. He knew I was chicken."

"I talked to him, the roly-poly one," Olive said. "He's down on his luck, he pongs something awful, but he's pretty clever — a bright spark. He kept saying Max was *hamajang*. What is that?"

"My life these days," Sharkey said.

Olive kept her hands on his. She said, "In his telling, Max was a boffin. He wants to show us where he lived, introduce us to people he knew. Fill in the Max Mulgrave details."

"Max was a boffin?"

"Techie," Olive said, and squeezed his hand, "Supersmart."

Sharkey went quiet after that. Without any further explanation or prodding, he allowed himself to be steered to the car.

On the way back to Wai'anae, Olive stopped at Zippy's in Wahiawa, leaving Sharkey in the car. She came out carrying three Styrofoam boxes, which she put in the backseat. When they got to the camp on the beach she presented them to the men, who hooted when she handed them over.

"Plate lunch," Frawley said, flipping up the hinged lid. "Spam musubi. Portogee sausage. Two scoops macaroni. Egg something. Good grinds, sister."

They ate, Fonoti laughing softly, pushing aside the food he could not chew, Alex stabbing at the meat on Fonoti's plate, Frawley grunting as he swallowed. Sharkey stared at the sea.

"The tour," Olive said, seeing them finishing, gasping with satisfaction.

"The walkthrough," Frawley said, cocking his head. "I show you the whole Max thing. Due diligence."

At the car, Alex saw them off, standing at attention and saluting. Frawley snatched open the front door and sat next to Olive, so Sharkey took the backseat with Fonoti, who elbowed him, saying, "Like old times, brah. Too bad Wilfred and Nalani not here. Nalani, she liked you, man!"

Sharkey turned to the sea again, for relief, though Fonoti went on chattering. His stink filled the car as he scratched his scabby knees.

Frawley reached for the dashboard and fumbled with some knobs, bumping them with his knuckles.

"What are you playing at?" Olive said.

"Turning on the AC. Hot in here, sister."

She resisted remarking on the fact that he had just come from pigging it in his ragged tent on the beach, exposed to the morning sun. She said, "I'll be delighted to turn it on, but in that case you can't smoke. If you insist on smoking, we keep the windows open and the AC off."

Frawley shouted into the backseat, "The wahine one hard-ass!" He lit a cigarette and said to Olive, "You see the original house?"

"That two-story house — yes," Olive said.

"Was one story already when he bought it. He put on the second floor and made a major renovation." And as they passed it, Olive driving slowly, the black dog stalking them along the chain-link fence, Frawley said, "He lived up top. He let all kine people crash on the first floor — surfers, homeless people, families from the beach. Was like a hotel." He leaned out the window and yapped, mocking the dog's bark. "Back then was no fence."

"He didn't charge them anything?" Olive said.

"No charge. He had overhead costs and they sleeping and sitting on his tangible assets! Some stayed for weeks, for months. That's how he got the name."

"What name?"

"Uncle, the rich haole."

"They called him Uncle?"

"Out of respect. Even later, when he had no receivables, like the past few years, always Uncle. Maybe he got money now, passive income or something. Smart buggah."

"The cop said he was bulletproof."

"Oh, yeah."

"Why would he say that?"

"Ask the cop," Frawley said. "The cops know him."

Fonoti spat out the window and said, "Kind of insane, us showing you the Max world here. More better he showing you himself."

To fill the silence that followed, Olive said, "But we're here."

"Keep going straight," Frawley said. "To Makaha."

"He lived in Makaha too?"

"No — we pay respects. Uncle Buffalo stay there. Plus his *keiki*."

"Buffalo Keaulana?" Sharkey asked, lurching forward.

"Was his *kupuna*," Frawley said. "Take this right."

As Olive drove slowly through a grid of sleepy streets to a back road of small flat-roofed houses, Frawley leaned over to look out her side window. He squinted and said, "His car not there. Maybe in town. Keep going."

Sharkey said, "Buffalo. I met him a few times."

"He respect Max so much," Frawley said. "And Max, he respect him back. Go *mauka* here."

It was a side road, which after fifty yards became a country lane, jogging the car with its potholes, a scattered herd of cows swinging their tails and chewing behind a wire fence as they watched the slowly passing car.

"That van," Frawley said. "Max stayed there for almost one year."

A blue van was parked under a tree at the edge of a field of wet greasy clay, its tires flat, the rims sunk into the dirt, its side windows punched out, shards of glass glinting on the ground beside it, cardboard stuck into the window frames, the windshield painted black.

"The rich haole," Olive said.

"This van was later — I'm giving you evidential matter. He stay here around the time he got busted."

"What was he arrested for?"

"Never got booked, as such," Frawley said.

"Cops respect Max big-time," Fonoti said.

"Even though drugs maybe a significant factor," Frawley said. "Or speeding, or vagrancy, or whatever. Always gets off. If you do due diligence, you'll see he got no rap sheet. If you ask him, he'll tell you. He didn't even get a misdemeanor. Me, like I said, after the external audit, I ended up with a fraud case. Fonoti here, he got a felony. But Max, he'll tell you straight, 'I'm clean, brah.'"

"Hang a U-turn here," Fonoti said; then, in an affronted voice, "They calling it a felony. It was a bad rap, relating to the so-called abuse of a family member. Would have been one misdemeanor, but they claim it happened in the presence of a minor." He spat out the window again. "Making it upgrade to one felony. But that part about the *keiki* watching the beef was bullshit."

Back on the highway, Frawley pointed to a compound of yellowish buildings with red roofs behind a chain-link fence and said, "Wai'anae High School. The Seariders. Max gave them all computers, he set them up with software."

"Buggah should be doing one victory lap," Fonoti said.

"Maybe that's why the police gave him a pass," Olive said. "Because he was generous."

Frawley said, "Sister, a lot of people generous. I did estate planning, way back, when my life was normal. Before bad choices."

"White-collar crime, Fraw-boy," Fonoti said, and giggled, his discolored gums showing greenish in the car. Something in his slushy toothless delivery made the expression even more mocking in its absurdity.

"Back then I knew plenny generous clients. They still had to face the music. But Max — he never. Go ask him."

"Drugging?" Olive said.

Frawley shrugged. He looked peeved, he sighed, he blew out his cheeks. "All kine."

"What happened to his money?" Olive asked.

"What always happens to money? It goes away. Doesn't stay still." He lit a cigarette as though to allow himself time to reflect. "Gave a ton of it away. I set up trust funds for him. Some of his money got cockaroached."

"That little humbug house," Fonoti said—it was a small weathered shack, surfboards propped against it, a Hawaiian flag flying upside down on a pole in front—"Max stay there for a lilly bit."

"After the van?"

"Was before," Frawley said. "We not giving you chronological sequence. Like Makaha—he lived in the nice hotel there for a long time—luxury, writing checks. He had a big life."

"What about his family?" Olive said. "A wife?"

"You gotta ask Max."

"He had one?"

"Maybe still has one," Frawley said.

"Plenny wahine," Fonoti said. "The wahine like him."

"Because of his money?"

"Because he's a good guy," Frawley said in a stern correcting tone.

In that mood, Frawley was the dominant CPA again, his pen tapping a ledger, niggling at a detail, not the fat man in the dirty T-shirt but an authority figure, strict and forbidding. Olive was reminded that the man he had been was the man he was now, in spite of torn clothes and sweaty arms and tangled hair. He still saw the world in terms of "receivables" and "passive income" and "evidential matter." Beneath the dirt and sweat and cracked fingernails, a certified public accountant.

"I wish Max was here now, so I wouldn't have to explain. You'd see, you'd know." Frawley hitched in his seat as though suddenly finding the car too small for his body, his knees jammed against the glove box. "Past couple of years he came, he went. But never mind—good guy, *pono* guy."

Back on the highway, in traffic, halted behind a bus picking up passengers, Olive said, "Where do you think he is now?"

Frawley folded his arms and frowned and did not look at her. He said, "I think I showed you enough. Pull over here at the stop, after the bus go."

"What about the rest?"

"Max can show you the rest."

In the backseat, Sharkey began to stammer, half-formed words like urgent breaths failing in his throat.

"We don't have a lot of time," Olive said, hesitating, then pulling forward and parking at the forward end of the bus stop.

A berm at the roadside formed the edge of a dune, and when Olive switched off the engine, killing the fan, they sat in heat and glare. Even with the windows open the car was hot. Just ahead, beside the berm, an old woman trawled through a trash barrel, selecting soda cans, while two boys on dirt bikes seemed animated by having something to watch—the car of gabbing people, pretty haole woman at the wheel. A shirtless man wearing a wool hat and surf shorts lay on the sandy berm, his body perfectly still, only his toes twitching, tickling the air.

"Not a lot of time," Frawley said mimicking Olive's English accent, smacking his lips, fingering a cigarette, preparing to light it. "You know we say, 'Try wait'?"

Sharkey said, "What she means is —"

But Frawley cut him off. "We're not like you, sister." He lit the cigarette and savored the pause he was creating and blew smoke out of the side of his mouth. "We stay waiting. We do nothing but stay wait. Our whole life is wait — from little *keiki* to big adult, always wait. I sometimes try due diligence to figure out the difference between locals and haoles. The simple answer I come up with is, haoles no wait. And all we *kanaka maoli* do is, what? Fricken wait. Even when I stay in my office on Bishop Street, the haoles come and go, never wait. And Frawley at his desk — wait. You got no idea what it's like. You always have what you want. We never. Fonoti?"

"We never," Fonoti said, amplifying the word like a cry, *Nevah.*

Olive allowed them a respectful silence, and then said, "I didn't mean to rush you."

"And plus, the other thing," Frawley said. "What are we waiting for?"

Fonoti said, "I waiting for Max."

"Ass right," Frawley said. "We used to say 'Max — he to the max,' like an expression. Maybe we waiting for him."

In his aggrieved rant about waiting, his talk had shifted from his accountant's precision to a blunter lingo, more local, especially on that last word, *heem.*

He sat grunting, as though digesting the meaning of what he'd said, the echo of it rumbling through his big body.

"In the meantime, we *hoʻomau*," Frawley said, and looked at Olive. "Push on. Persevere for Max sake."

Sharkey turned to look out the window, seaward, where the surf had risen, chest high, and beyond the gouts of foam in the breaking waves a boy at sea, swaying on top of the water, too far out for Sharkey to discern his board, the disjunction making it seem as though the boy was dancing in the ocean.

"Hot like hell," Fonoti said, breathing through his nose, a crackling sound.

"Give me twenty bucks," Frawley said.

"For what?"

"For the" — he puffed his cigarette — "for the indenture. What we call the agreement."

Olive fumbled in the bag at her feet and brought out the money.

Crushing the bill in his hand, Frawley said, "And Fonoti. For his knowledge. His *manaʻo.*"

"Funny old lot you are with the wonga, twenty bucks a bung," Olive said, holding a twenty-dollar bill between the two front seats until Fonoti pinched it in his fingers and flicked it away from her. "I still have a few more questions."

"Tanks."

"So does Joe," she said. And in a deliberate way, as though formally introducing him, "Joe Sharkey."

Frawley humped and heaved in his seat until he was turned around, staring at Sharkey.

"One more house," he said, and directed Olive back into the traffic and up the main road past the high school to a junction where he said, "*Mauka* here."

Olive turned inland on a wide road rising on a long slope to a bluff of two-story houses. They were faced in stucco, pink and pale yellow, some with pillars and porches, all with lanais projecting toward the ocean.

"The one with the big breadfruit tree in front," Frawley said, as Sharkey ducked to get a better view through the windshield.

Olive said, "Max lived here?"

"No," Frawley said. "I did. That was my house. That was my *'ulu* tree. I lost it all when I had some issues. Nice place, huh?"

"Smashing," Olive said.

"When you see me at my tent at the beach, I know what you're thinking —the guy's a bum. This was my house once, but it wasn't me. That tent isn't me. I'm still me. So you want to see all the places Max lived in, but it's a goose chase. Those places aren't him—those houses and shacks. He's still himself, no matter what."

Olive began to speak, but Frawley raised his hand.

"Take us back to Pokai Beach," he said, and as she drove away he kept talking. "Most of us are alone in life. But if you're real lucky, you got one person you can talk to without staying afraid they'll judge you. You can say anything to this person. He's true to you—I don't say 'like a brother,' because a brother can let you down. My brother was a buggah. This person, this true friend, is someone like your own self. It's not love I'm talking about—love is insane. No, it's trust." He used his whole face to utter the word, making it sizzle, as *truss*. "Max is that guy for me. I wish I knew where he stay. I miss him. There's so much I want to tell him that I can't tell no one else."

Fonoti said, "Hey, you don't know trouble till you lose your best friend."

By then they were back at the parking lot, Frawley sighing and snatching at his face, his voice having gone croaky and sorrowful from his talk.

Sharkey put out his hand. He said, "Joe."

But Frawley's hands stayed in his lap, obscured by the protrusion of his belly. He said, "I know who you are. Big Joe. North Shore guy, da Shark. Fonoti so stoked to see you because you went to school together."

Fonoti said, "Plus hung out." He sniffed, remembering. "Wilfred Kalama. Nalani. Vai. That little psycho haole, forget his name."

"But I'm not stoked," Frawley said, not listening. "I seen you surfing — you're nothing special. Lots of guys like you — long board, monster wave — some of them more better."

He straightened in his seat. All his talk — some of it lapsing into pidgin, some of it preachy — had given him dignity. Now he seemed to have an air and a presence approaching grandeur, in spite of his burned face and scarred arms, his dirty clothes and frizzy, dusty hair.

"I know that," Sharkey said, looking beaten.

"They don't get endorsements. No big life for them. Just *mokes* and ba-boozes in Makaha, waiting, like locals always wait. But Joe Sharkey — big fricken deal."

"It's not what you think."

"I seen you at the Big Board Classic, way back. You got points. But I'm not impressed. You was junk. Max got less points, but he surf with heart." Frawley put his face closer to Sharkey's and said with force, "He was a dog off his leash."

Looking pained, his features crumpling, Sharkey said, "He was at that meet?"

"Sure. But you snobbed him."

Sharkey tried to speak, to acknowledge what he'd just heard, but he was unable to make a sound. He had no breath in his mouth to form a word.

"So maybe you got more questions?" Frawley said. And now, reflective, he took the twenty-dollar bill he had crushed and placed it on his thigh and smoothed it against his sweaty flesh, pressing the wrinkles out of it. "Ask Max."

With a retching hack, like the onset of nausea, Sharkey began to sob.

Frawley loosened the car door, then thrust it open with his elbow, saying, "Go boo-hoo somewhere else, haole."

10

A Protected Species

The stranger had shimmered into focus, a flat shadow at a distance, a silhouette swimming to shore, the dark speck in the far-off chop, simple as a water dog bobbing in the fetch of waves, slapping the water and swelling to a muscular body with reaching arms and, closer, becoming lighter, swifter, almost angelic, trawling with cupped hands in the sun-splash, making his way across the pleats of water in the bay, and finally a buoyant creature resolving itself to a man with a face — eager features, wide eyes, beautiful teeth, gasping in the shore break, calling out, "It's me — Max."

The dead man had a name now, and a past, and friends, and a community — those other shadows swimming from the depths behind him, the man in Floristan, the camper Frawley, old Fonoti, who knew so much and who wondered where Max was now.

No one had known anything of the dead man, and then it seemed everyone did — or enough people to provide a profile. And what struck Olive as odd — and she emphasized this to Sharkey — was that though he had served nobly as a benefactor to many people, he'd also had run-ins with the police. According to Frawley, he'd been stopped, reported, written up, and warned but never arrested, never charged with any offense. And so he'd remained unknown and out of official files.

"It would have been ever so much easier for us if he'd been convicted of something," Olive said. "Frawley sort of hinted that he'd committed some serious offenses. But nothing stuck. He'd slipped away — blameless. And why?"

"Bulletproof," Sharkey said.

"How does that happen?"

Max Mulgrave had been stopped, he'd been cautioned, but he'd always been let off, it seemed. A man living on the edge — a vagrant — subjected to stops or searches, with a history of drug use, who'd never been busted. He had no rap sheet, and yet if he'd had one, how simple it would have been to add detail to his life in Hawaii.

That he'd been stopped was a help in knowing more, but he was blameless as far as the law was concerned.

Ask the cops, Frawley had said, with the smirk of admiration some men have for lawbreakers who escape arrest. *The cops know him.*

Olive reminded Sharkey of that. Sharkey said, "My memory's junk."

"What about that cop who wrote the report — the one that came to Waimea the night it happened?"

"My head's not right."

Sharkey had thrown himself onto his sofa, looking broken, in an odd twisted posture of visible discomfort, his eyes turned toward the window, his body slashed by sunlight, something sacrificial in the way he lay slumped and vulnerable, like a man abandoned. He was staring at a tree in the gully below his house.

"I saw an owl there once — a pueo," he whispered, too softly for Olive to hear. "It's good luck to see one, because they're endangered."

Olive said, "He told us his name."

"I totally spaced."

"He said his father was a surfer."

"Ray-Ban," Sharkey said, after a long silence. "Goofy-foot."

"I don't even know why I'm asking. That guy Stickney made us a copy of the police report. His name will be on it."

New to the United States, a *malihini* — a newcomer — they called her at the hospital, and still new enough in Sharkey's life to be insecure, often surprised by his moods, uncertain of the depths in his mind, and uneasy in the disorder of the house — his house, his plants, his chickens, his geese — she kept her composure by using her nurse's training as a meticulous re-cord-keeper. You did not exist as an alien without paper to prove it: every scrap added to your identity, every ticket and receipt to your plausibility. And since the accident she'd begun to regard her attention to the details of her life with Sharkey as the diagnostic notations at the top of a fever chart.

She was a girlfriend, without provable status, and she often thought of Sharkey dying in his bed and the authorities saying to her, "Who are you — what are you doing in this house?"

She saved all the bills she'd paid, the receipts for household items, all the hospital bills, and the prescriptions in one file, the insurance claim in an-other file, and in that a copy of the police report, "Details of the Accident," "Action Taken," "Summary" — paragraphs of evasions and half-truths and outright lies, signed by Sharkey and the reporting officer, the lines under

"Victim" — name, race, physical appearance, date of birth, home address, marital status, Social Security number — all blank. The only item entered, the one certainty, was the "Injury Code," 04, in a box: fatal.

Beneath the reporting officer's illegible signature, a blue scrawl, his name printed in a child's block letters: Ronald DeSouza.

"We have to see this guy."

Sharkey's expression was unreadable, perhaps one of boredom, perhaps one of agony, or he might not have heard. Preoccupied, he sometimes seemed breathless or deaf, as patients in pain often were. But Sharkey's absence was extreme, as though he were underwater.

Rounding Waimea Bay, late afternoon, in the southern quadrant of the sky billows of soot-black clouds dragged long gray curtains of rain across the distant ocean. To the west was a gaudy flare at the horizon around the crimson mouse hole of the setting sun, its hot ferocity puddling the sea around it, the fire blazing on the water of its finality. The waves were distinct — backlit as they advanced — and Sharkey thought, *Waves are thresholds.*

Sharkey resisted saying this, and adding, *You learn to step over them and become someone else on the other side.* But what did that mean? Thoughts like these bewildered him, and kept him silent.

Olive was driving again, with thoughts of her own she could not share. On the way to Wahiawa, through the darkening pineapple fields, in the traffic at the bridge, and then parking at the police station — near the entrance steps, because it was raining — she was keenly aware of Sharkey crouched beside her. She hoped he wasn't sulking. Guiding him through the parking lot into the station, she had felt a heightened sense of him as someone fragile, and another little glimpse of what motherhood must be like. Sharkey was reduced, he was numb, he needed to be reassured and humored and reminded to be careful. He scuffed next to her, obedient but vague, his arms swinging loose, unusually conspicuous in his tattoos and yet looking fraudulent, shuffling shyly with all that outrageous ink. In the rain, sudden gouts of it lashing him, his wet face framed by his lank hair, he bent over in a futile effort to avoid it, the big clumsy child.

"Officer DeSouza," Olive said to the desk clerk.

But the man in uniform looked past her and spoke to Sharkey. "He expecting you?"

Sharkey's feeble smile of confusion indicated that he had not registered the question.

"I called this morning," Olive said. "I was told he'd be off-duty at six."

"Please take a seat."

They did so, not speaking, just breathing audibly as they waited, the breaths like marking time. But when, at a little past six, DeSouza appeared at the desk and waved to the clerk, he walked past Olive and Sharkey, his workday done, with an air of someone fleeing.

"Excuse me."

DeSouza compressed his lips in impatience, and before Olive resumed he was already backing away, as though hoping to avoid a further question, straining to go home.

"I'm off-duty," he said in a peevish voice.

"Joe Sharkey," Olive said.

The name stopped him. He cocked his head in concern and leaned closer to Sharkey's expressionless face.

"Shark?" He still looked uncertain, as though the name might wake Sharkey and make him familiar.

Instead of speaking, Sharkey slowly nodded.

"You been sick, brah?"

In a whisper, his head bowed, confiding to the policeman, Sharkey said, "I'm drowning."

Alarmed — she had last heard him say that in a panic to the grommets at the community center — Olive took charge, saying, "We need to talk to you."

DeSouza took them to the outer lobby, where they sat in a corner, Olive showing DeSouza the accident report with his signature on it, DeSouza tapping the lines with his fingers, saying, "Sure I remember. Waimea. All that rain. The guy on a bike. The fatality. No ID. Open case — there was no follow-up."

"We found out his name. You can fill in the blanks now."

"This report's already been filed. We'd have to make out a new report, refile it, or maybe file a supplement. Try come back tomorrow."

"It was a man named Max Mulgrave."

DeSouza sat up straight, jerked his head back, then smirked in disbelief. He said, "You're joking, right?"

"For real."

"That was Max?" DeSouza said. "You sure?"

"The mortuary ran a check on his prints."

"He's still in the morgue?"

"He's ashes now," Olive said. "We're looking for his next of kin. We went to the mainland — his hometown."

"Better off looking in Wai'anae."

"How do you know that?"

"Max was famous there."

Sharkey said, "Famous for what?"

"Famous for being a good guy," De Souza said. "But he kept a low profile.

We knew he was down on his luck, but we didn't know he was on the North Shore."

"You told us you'd seen him — you'd picked him up before. That's what you said at the time."

"The guy you hit, yeah — he had no ID. How was I supposed to know? I seen him around the camp near the bypass road, but it was just vagrancy, looked like a bum. Not worth the trouble of a ticket. And that night, the rain, the guy lying all bust up."

"But the prints," Olive said.

"That's the medical examiner's thing, at the morgue. We sent them the remains."

"I killed him," Sharkey said in the same confiding whisper.

The whisper startled the policeman more than a shout would have done. He turned away from Sharkey, to Olive, with a plea tensed on his face.

"Max," he said, sighing a little, snatching at his ear. "Not many people knew him by sight, but everyone on the force knew his name. Like a monk seal."

"Good swimmer," Olive said.

"No — no. A protected species."

Olive saw the man on the ground at Waimea in the rain near the black brimming pothole, broken, twisted, pale in death, unprotected.

"Forbidden by law to harm or destroy," DeSouza said. "You can do serious time, plus a big fine, for messing with a monk seal. Any cop bust Max Mulgrave, he gonna get serious lickings from the chief." He turned to Sharkey and studied his gray grieving face. "Funny thing. As far as HPD was concerned, he was more better than you, Shark."

"In what way?" Olive said, because Sharkey was stunned by the words.

"In a good way. Long time ago he did some kind of favor — some *kokua.*"

"That's what we were told in Wai'anae — he helped people, bought computers for the school."

"Not that. This was something else — something major. Big-deal *kokua.*"

"What was it?"

"I don't know — before my time. But I can hook you up at headquarters with the guy that put out the word. Maybe he'll tell you."

"The chief?"

"Deputy chief, field operations. Name is Malo. I'll make an appointment for you. He probably doesn't know that Max wen' *make.*"

"I was real sorry to hear he pass," Deputy Chief Malo said when they told him they'd come to discuss Max Mulgrave. The man's simple statement did not match the sorrow and incomprehension that showed on his face, convulsed in grief. Sitting behind his desk he was an imposing Hawaiian presence, with an enormous, oddly geometric head, as though carved in wood by an amateur, with odd flat planes on his skull, his black hair lustrous in the sunlight from the window, and under his bony brow eyes shining with tears. He lifted his big hands to his face and held on, stifling a sob, gagging a little, loosening a lock of hair that dropped past one ear.

"Good guy," Olive said.

"*Pono* guy," Malo said, insisting. "The best."

"You know how he died?" Sharkey asked.

"I saw the report — DeSouza just sent it. Was, what? Coupla months ago?"

"Yeah, Waimea, that bad corner. It was raining," Sharkey said. "All my fault. I killed him."

"You was sober?"

"Half drunk," Sharkey said.

"You was driving impaired," Malo said, losing his grief in a rush of anger and regaining his voice of authority, pushing his hair back. "You killed a good man."

Olive said, "Joe is trying to make it right. We want to know as much as we can about him."

"So much to know," Malo said. "He was in 'Nam. Had a business on the mainland — sold it for big bucks. He came here to live a great life — so many friends. So generous. Everybody loved him. Never mind he's a haole, the guy was so *pono*." He paused a moment, then added, "Plus a surfer."

Olive said, "I'm sure all that is true, but Officer DeSouza — and other people, his friends — say he had some issues."

Lowering his head, shortening his neck, looking bull-like, Malo said, "No clouds in your life, sister? And this guy —"

"Joe Sharkey," she said.

"No clouds in Joe Sharkey's life?"

"Plenny clouds," Sharkey said. "And one of them a big cloud."

"As far as Max goes, I could show you the logs," Malo said. "Excessive speed, controlled substances, DUI, vagrancy, loitering." Malo folded his hands and placed them on his blotter. "But so what?"

"The charges were dropped — all of them?" Olive said.

"On my orders."

"I'm sure you had a reason."

"I had a lot of reasons," Malo said.

He pulled out a drawer in his desk and pawed the objects inside with the wide rake of his thick fingers, finally alighting on a disk encased in a square of plastic. Rising from his desk with a grunt, he crossed the room to a DVD player and fed the disk into the slot with one hand, then manipulated a remote control the size of a candy bar with the other hand.

"Show you something," he said as the monitor brightened. Without any prologue or narration the exterior of a church with a pencil-point steeple flickered into view, buttery in sunshine. "Central Union Church," Malo said. "Most holiest church on O'ahu."

Men wearing aloha shirts and women in colorful dresses, carrying garlands of flowers, walked among the royal palms, hundreds of them in a procession, filing into the church. Mingling among the bright shirts were police officers in blue uniforms and white gloves, many of them with armloads of blossoms.

"Some kind of service," Olive said.

Malo shushed her, and as he did so the interior of the church filled the screen, white pillars lining the sides, an altar decked in flowers, and a clergyman, decorous in a white surplice trimmed with lace, standing before the congregation, holding what had to be a Bible.

A dark bare-chested man wearing a crown of flowers approached the altar rail, a red cloak knotted on one shoulder and billowing across his body as though he were wrapped in a flag. He carried a wooden staff, which he raised to silence the congregation. In a clear piercing voice he began crying out in his own language, a lilting litany that echoed in the church, that at some moments sounded like praise and at others like a sustained and lyrical denunciation.

"*Oli mahalo* — the chant for thanks," Malo said. "Hawaiian kine."

When the man's cries died down, a hymn sung by an unseen choir began. The camera angle was positioned from the choir loft, the church spread out below. While the hymn continued, a procession made its way down the central aisle: a priest with a tall gold cross, altar boys holding candles, and following them an elaborate casket, part of it draped in silk and stitched with orchids, purple and white.

"Please be seated," the priest with the cross said, facing the congregation and standing a little apart from the priest clutching the Bible.

To the rattle and thump of seats and kneelers, Malo said, "Church was packed. Standing room only."

"We gather here to celebrate the life of Daisy Lokelani Hino," the priest said.

As he spoke, the camera tracked among the pews, going closer, finding grieving face after grieving face — more women than men, and the women looked especially stricken. They were lovely women, masked in sadness, most of them young, Hawaiian or Asian, some of them Black, all in vibrant feathery dresses, weeping as the priest spoke of the life of the woman in the casket.

"*Lokelani* means heavenly rose," he said. "The thorns of a rose remind us of Christ's suffering at the hands of the soldiers at his crucifixion. The rose itself tells us about hope and resurrection in the eternity of heaven."

Raising his voice, he spoke of love, of forgiveness, of Christ's compassion — of Mary Magdalene; and he told the story of the woman with the alabaster jar who wept before Christ, her tears falling on his feet, how she wiped them away with her sweet-smelling hair and covered his feet with kisses and then massaged them with the ointment from her jar. Pausing between elements in the story, which was tinged with sensuality, he invoked the name of Daisy Lokelani Hino, using it as a sort of chorus, until it seemed she too was a biblical character, another follower of Christ.

Praying in Hawaiian — "She will hear us, it is her mother tongue" — the priest urged the mourners to understand her immortal soul and to consider that she was not dead, that she lived in the arms of God, that her spirit dwelled within the hearts of everyone present, to guide them.

"Grief is holy," he intoned. "Lokelani is not dead. She is showing us the way to salvation."

And so for the next half-hour Deputy Chief Malo sat before the monitor, absorbed in the funeral service, as alert as though he were seeing it for the first time. At intervals, covertly, he pressed his fists to his eyes, and when he took them away his eyes were puffy and reddened with tears.

Moved by the display of mourning and by the sweetness of the hymns, the harmonies echoing in the church, Olive took Sharkey's hand. It was cold, as lifeless as a slab of meat, and yet he was attentive, watching closely the progress of the service.

As the organ swelled, cascades of urgent chords drowning the choir, the pallbearers guided the casket down the aisle, the mourners nearby in the pews reaching out to graze it with their fingers or place a flower on it, as though caressing the body inside.

The last vivid shot was not of the casket or the church; the camera veered and swung to capture a tight shot of a young man with a deeply tanned face and tousled blond hair, standing half in shadow, staring sadly in the direction the casket had gone.

"That's Max."

Malo aimed the clicker, froze the moment — the handsome man in profile — then switched off the machine, and the screen went black.

Olive said, "That was quite a funeral."

"Like royalty," Malo said. "Like when Bruddah Iz pass. Cost tens of thousands. Maybe hundreds of thousands. All those flowers. All that music. The band."

"Who was she?" Olive said. "Someone special, I imagine."

Malo hesitated, perhaps for the drama of the pause, and he lingered a bit longer, but when in the stillness he had their attention, he spoke with grave solemnity.

"A prostitute," he said. "Sex worker. Wahine got murdered."

In spite of herself, Olive groaned, then swallowed and went silent. Sharkey emitted an involuntary cluck, a twig-snap on his tongue, like punctuation.

"Was a big event — was historic," Malo said. "Everyone in Honolulu knew about it. Was in the *Star-Bulletin* and the *Advertiser*. Big stories and pictures. The wahine had no family, just those *popolo* hookers and sex workers you see in the church. Wahine had no money. Body was unclaimed. The papers wrote about that, how that big funeral happened with mystery money. What people didn't know was that Max Mulgrave, when he found out the body was unclaimed at the morgue, he paid for the whole thing. Was a whole bunch of money — the flowers, the choir, the musicians, some big-name Hawaiian performers, like Don Ho and Danny Kaleikini and the Makaha Sons of Niihau. You seen them, no? The Hawaiian *kahu* chanting, the hearse, the headstone, and afterward big luau at Paradise Cove, with hula, and they *imu* a bunch of pigs. Hey, the whole nine yards."

"Murdered," Sharkey said. "Did they catch the guy?"

"Max involved in that big-time," Malo said. "Was a guy with a Taser. Tased half a dozen Waikiki hookers in hotel rooms, then raped and robbed them. They injured bad but they survived. One was from HPD, a decoy cop, policewoman plain clothes, Officer Ah Wong. She get heart trouble from the electric shock of the Taser."

"Cardiac arrhythmia," Olive said. "A stun gun sometimes captures the heartbeat and causes ventricular tachycardia."

"You got it, sister. Officer Ah Wong had to quit the force and retire on disability. Daisy Hino not so lucky. She get tased and go into cardiac arrest. Then a coma for weeks. Finally they take her off life support."

Olive said, "So who was the guy with the Taser?"

"The murderer," Malo said, widening his eyes, in a voice of correction, "was one haole college professor. No joke. Leading a double life — classroom life and low-life. He thinks he can get away with it, because, hey, who cares about hookers? Plus the perp had good cover — who's gonna look in a college for a haole murder suspect?"

"But you caught him," Olive said.

"Because we got one tip. A lady ID'd his car. We trace the car to the college, over Windward Side. Max gave us the technology to track him. This was early days of GPS — testing stage. But Max had friends in the business, because he's a tech guy. We followed the guy's every movement without him knowing, and one night — maybe two a.m. — we bust him. He's with a hooker, he got a Taser, he's ready to pounce, but we pounce first. All those ladies you see at the funeral? Three or four of them testify against him. He have a good lawyer with a bullshit story of how he carry a Taser for protection. But we have something special in our favor."

He smiled and paused, as though to encourage Olive to ask what the special advantage was. She glanced at Sharkey, who was slumped in his chair but facing the TV monitor as though replaying the elaborate funeral in his memory, like a glittering succession of afterimages.

"So what did you have in your favor?" Olive said.

"Money," Malo said, savoring his reply. "Big money. Money for lawyers, money for Officer Ah Wong's medical bills, money for the force to upgrade our surveillance." He smiled again. "Max's money."

"When did all this take place — the arrest, the trial, the funeral?"

"Early on, when Max was one *malihini* in Wai'anae. But we never forget it. He stay in our good books, like a hero. He tattoo her name on his arm — Chinese kine."

"Do you know anything about Max's ex-wife?"

"She threaten come stalking him. That's why he applied for a handgun license, because she verbalizing threats. He took out a TRO — we have her contact address. My secretary, Mable, has all those details, but it could be out-of-date. Was long time ago."

Snatching and straightening papers on his desk, Malo made a show of being busy, ignoring Sharkey and Olive, and then, when they displayed signs of leaving, Sharkey stretching, Olive groping in her bag for her car keys, Malo got up and went to the door of his office and opened it.

"Amazing story, eh?" he said. "Like a legend. Max Mulgrave legend. Okay, gotta get back to work, folks."

Olive was still sitting, though, with her keys in her hand, stilled by a struggle with logic, too preoccupied to stand up.

"I'm bothered by one thing," she said as she tugged at the arms of her chair and got to her feet. "If you never convicted Max Mulgrave for his DUIs or drug possession or vagrancy or all the other mentions in the logs . . ."

She swayed slightly, unsure of how to finish her sentence.

"Yeah, so what?" Malo said, as though anticipating an accusation.

"Maybe you contributed to his downfall," Olive said. "Maybe you could have saved him."

"Maybe *you* could have saved him," Malo said, and now he was staring stony-faced at Sharkey. "But instead you killed him."

11

Smack

The rain had stopped; the land swelled with sunlight, alive now, limpid, dripping in the soft late-afternoon glow, a fattening rainbow arched in the cloudless sky over Haleʻiwa, its luminous stripes textured like tissue, or threadbare cloth spun across the town. Olive was at the wheel, Sharkey fixed in one of his silences, as they drove along the soaked and blackened bypass road, the big trees sparkling, their boughs still wet, the tall grass sodden, glistening from the purification of the downpour, the day washed clean.

And then a sudden ugliness. "The camp," Olive said as they passed the tulip tree and the break in the roadside fence. "I don't have the strength to face those people today." She answered herself, as she often did these days, because Sharkey seemed numb and deaf. "Maybe some other time."

But Sharkey was alert at the surf breaks. At Lani's and Chun's, and later at Leftovers and Alligators, he marveled at the storm-driven waves, ragged from the aftermath of the rain. The day was serene, but the chop still churned, an effect of the westerly that had dragged over the sea.

A solitary figure appeared at Waimea, and his darkness got Sharkey's attention as they rounded the bay — a man, his back turned, but familiar, plodding down the bluff of sand to where it shelved and was undercut by the shore break. The man wore shorts but did not carry a board, nor did he hesitate to dip his toe first but walked into the low wall of surf and stepped into the sea and vanished as though into a hole.

Sharkey mouthed the words, "Gone under."

At home Olive was talkative, seeming to reassure herself, her characteristic and chatty back-and-forth, the way she muttered when she was alone, thinking out loud, more slangy and British when she talked to herself—

"Mustn't grumble . . . Cuppa tea would do me a power of good . . . Get crack-ing" — all of it unintelligible to Sharkey.

She said, "That Chinese character tattooed on his arm that we couldn't fathom — it was her name."

The storm was still swirling in Sharkey's head, the surf like wild applause. He was silent, but he was not calm; his brain was frenzied, needing relief, rehearsing the mute panic of being underwater, tumbled and struggling, caught beneath a wave. But instead of fearing it he saw it as a form of rescue — an answer, a painkiller.

"Maybe tomorrow, crack of dawn," Olive said, still quizzing herself over the homeless camp. "Start as we mean to go on."

The idea filled Sharkey with dread, the uncertainty of "maybe," the hor-ror of "tomorrow." He felt punished by time; he wanted no more days of pain.

"I'm sure you're as knackered as I am," Olive said, speaking on his behalf, because he was lying on the bed, the last of the daylight dimming on his face, decaying to a shadow passing over his eyes. He had not spoken aloud since the police station, his "Gone under" had not been audible. But he was awake — more than awake, his body buzzed with anticipation.

And when, stimulated by his sleeplessness — Olive asleep and turned away and lightly snoring — he slid from the bed, left the house, and started down the hill.

Sometime in the night, in the twitch of a dream, yawning and roll-ing over, Olive threw her arm beside her and was woken when it flopped against the emptiness of the bed, her arm unexpectedly loosened by a miss-ing body.

"Joe?"

The silence clarified her mind. She called again, dressed and quickly looked from room to room, and then dashed to the lanai, where Sharkey often sat, his legs extended, when he could not sleep. There she saw his phone on the side table. She picked it up, thinking, *If he left it behind, he's not coming back* — finding something reckless and final in his leaving it, like abandonment.

On an impulse, because it was late, because he was forgiving and mellow and she easily found his name on the phone, she called Moe Kahiko.

"Yah." His voice was phlegmy, clotted with sleep.

"It's Olive from down the road — I can't find Joe. Will you help me look for him?"

"What time is it?"

"Two, or nearabout."

"Where he stay?"

Waiting for his laborious sighlike yawn, like a groan, to cease, she paused, then said, "I don't know. Moe, that's why I'm asking you."

"Give me a minute. I put some clothes on and pick you up."

Two-twenty by her watch as she slid the gate open; a moony night of stillness, the only sound the drone of surf from down the hill at Waimea, audible confusion, strangely mechanical but out of sync, like the stammer of a pump misfiring, a sequence of interrupted thumps, the waves.

The lights of Moe's pickup truck entered the gateway, and she ran to the vehicle, the sound of the surf immediate in her consciousness. She said, "Let's try the beach."

"It come up big, the surf today night."

She remembered her chuntering monologue, how Sharkey had said nothing, made no reply even to direct questions; how he had looked past her at the storm surf as they'd rounded the bay.

They were down the hill in minutes, the road silvered by the moon, and Moe ran the red light at Foodland, passing Rubber Duckies and Three Tables and then the overlook above the lava rocks of the bay. Olive strained to see Sharkey. That the beach was empty, the sand whitened by moonglow, did not reassure her. She thought, *We're too late — he's gone.*

Moe pulled into the parking lot, close by the changing rooms, where another car was parked aslant on the grass verge. Two people were visible inside, smoke trailing from a cracked-open side window, the mildewed aroma of smoldering *pakalolo*.

"Ask them if they saw him," Olive called out.

But failing to get their attention by rapping on the car window, Moe pulled the door open. The man at the wheel said, "You a cop?" The woman beside him ducked, hiding her face.

"Looking for my braddah," Moe said.

The man grunted and switched on his headlights, illuminating the beach, and at the ledge, in the slosh of the shore break, Sharkey stood facing the bay in water to his knees.

"Joe!"

Hearing his name, Sharkey plunged into the waves. He did not swim. He thrashed and fought the water, as though attempting to sink himself under a wave.

Moe sprinted to him and caught one of his flailing arms, while Sharkey protested, trying to yank his arm free, hitting Moe with his other arm.

"What you doing, you *lolo*?"

Olive approached, sinking in the wet sand, howling with a force that startled Sharkey, stalling him; and he surrendered to Moe's embrace, looking defeated and ashamed as he was led to the car.

At the house Moe helped him through the door to his bed, Sharkey stumbling, and held him while Olive sedated him with two capsules, urging him to drink from the glass she tipped to his lips.

"What kine meds?" Moe said.

"Xanax."

"We like snort it." He allowed himself a cluck of recognition.

"He'll be okay in the morning."

Moe said, "He just flipped out."

"Maybe he was afraid. We're supposed to visit that homeless camp on the bypass road."

"Kimo's *ohana*," Moe said.

"You know them?"

"I been there," Moe said, sounding vague. "I wen' sell some merch there."

"Come with us."

"Okay — you got it."

She kissed him; he held her. He stank of dirt and sweat and seawater, and she began to cry, from the pent-up anxiety of the day — the police, the video of the funeral, the vanishing of Joe, and what she was certain was a clumsy attempt at suicide.

Over her sobbing, Moe said, "Smoke one joint, sister. Or maybe smash and snort one of them Xanax. You feel more better."

"I'll feel fine if you come with us tomorrow."

"This my *'aina*. This my turf. I know the way."

In the morning Moe whistled from the driveway, then called out on the stairs and on the lanai flattened his face against the sliders, wearing the same T-shirt and torn shorts as in the night, his hair kinked and mud-matted, a big dark dusty angel, the oily smear of his face on the glass.

"We go in my truck, crew cab. Your car, they think maybe you're cops."

Moe drove; Olive sat in the cramped backseat with Sharkey, her feet deep in clutter, one door wired shut, the upholstery fuzzy with dirt, the engine coughing as it labored up the road amid the hum of gas fumes and burned plastic, Moe grunting each time he shifted to a new gear. The sensations of these details reminded Olive of the night before, her panicked search for Sharkey in that truck.

Sharkey said nothing, and Olive wondered what she would do if he tried to throw himself into the road. She'd managed to restrain agitated patients, but never alone — it was usually a group on the flailing person, a nurse on each limb. But he sat next to the door that was fastened shut by thick twisted wire. He'd have to fight past her to kill himself now.

Moe said, "How you doing, brah?"

Olive took Sharkey's hand, out of tender affection but also to test his mood. His dry palm, his slack fingers surprised her — his loose grip was not that of someone possessed by any urgency. It was like holding a child's helpless mute hand.

"How am I doing?" Sharkey said. In the same searching whisper he went on. "I feel I am someone else. I just don't know who."

"You da Shark, brah."

Olive tugged his hand to reassure him. They were passing Waimea Bay, near the entrance to the parking lot. They did not need to mention the drama of the previous night — the groan of the waves lamented it, the rip and ruck from the shadow zone of the far-off storm was like a feverish memory of desperation.

It seemed that Sharkey heard it that way, yet his voice was reflective, rueful, when he began to speak again, interrupting himself to start over several times, to make himself clear.

"I did it because I felt ashamed and guilty," he said. "And now I'm bummed and more ashamed because I did it."

What he'd done was understood. No one spoke, and after that pained confession, Olive thought, what could one say?

"Thanks," Sharkey said. "You saved me." He was studying the ocean; they were at Chun's Reef now. "When I was a lifeguard I never had to save the same person twice."

At the bypass road, Olive said, "Maybe park by the fence — near that big tulip tree."

But Moe had slowed and turned and nosed the truck into a half-hidden driveway that led through the tall grass, and when he came to the broad scrawled sign — KAPU — he kept going.

"I know this place. I know these people."

Then they were at the edge of the clearing, a dog barking and straining on his long leash.

"Aloha," Moe called out, and strode to the man seated near the dog.

In a blue haze of smoke from a smoldering fire pit, the man was sprawled on the car seat set on the ground that served as a sofa, his baseball cap resting on his frizz of hair, the same T-shirt, ALOHA FUN RUN, on his torso. He got to his feet and crouched in a threat posture, but his look of ferocity vanished when he recognized Moe. He shouted, "Mr. Kahiko, mushroom man — what you got for me?"

"Anything you want, Jimmy."

The two men hugged. Still in the hug, glaring over Moe's shoulder, the man said, "Why these fucken haoles here?"

"My friends," Moe said, disengaging himself and, with a little chivalrous bow, "And now your friends."

A movement from beyond the barking dog—two women stirred, one scuttling on all fours like a puppy from beneath the shelter of blue plastic, the other unfolding herself from the old car's backseat. Both women looked damaged, one of them fattish, her hair twisted in gray braids, the other squinting from under slatted lids, in a ball cap and apron. The one with the ball cap went to the fire pit and kicked the smoldering wood, sending up sparks.

"Where the kids at?"

"They got school, yah."

"I know this guy," the woman with the braids said to Sharkey. "I see you before."

Olive said, "We paid you a visit about six weeks ago. We were looking for someone. You told us to go away."

"My short-term memory is junk," the woman in the apron said.

The other said, "I thought you was from Child Protective Services. Come to take my kids away."

The big man approached Sharkey, who was scowling from the fury of the barking dogs. The man said, "Yeah—you. I remember."

"We brought you some malasadas," Olive said, presenting the woman with a cardboard box, the sides of the box stained by the grease from its contents.

"Still piping hot, the malasadas," the woman with the braids said. She offered the box to the big man, who waved her aside, and then she took one out and began chewing.

"I'm Olive."

"This Winona," the woman with the braids said. "I'm Rhonda."

"Kimo," the big man said, extending his hand to Sharkey's and gripping it. "Normally, like I always say, we the Foreign Legion—no names. But if Moe say you friends, we got names."

"I'm Joe Sharkey."

Rhonda giggled and poked Sharkey's arm, like a small girl's awkward greeting.

"The first time we were here we met a woman, Lindsey," Olive said. "She claimed she knew the man we were asking about."

"Lindsey a meth head," Winona said. "She gone."

"We didn't know the man's name then. Now we know. Max Mulgrave."

"Max gone too."

"You knew him?" Olive said, flustered by the sudden revelation.

"He stay here for a while."

"I know the guy?" Moe said to Kimo.

"Sure. The guy you call Smack."

"Smack," Moe said, and turned to Sharkey. "I know Smack. Why you didn't tell me you looking for Smack?"

"His name is Max," Olive said.

"I sell him all kinds of merch. *Pakalolo. Batu.* You name it. That Smack is hardcore. How he get the name is he using smack, no needles — he smoke it and sniff it and sometimes eat it."

"We hear he pass," Kimo said. He turned to scream at the barking dogs, and the dogs whimpered and crouched in the dirt. "Someone run into him at Waimea."

"That was me," Sharkey said. "I killed him. That's why we came here before. I didn't know his name. I was trying to find out who he was. He wasn't carrying an ID."

"You the guy wen' kill Max?" Kimo asked, and stepped so quickly toward Sharkey that Sharkey backed away.

Intimidated, weakened by the question, fearful of what might happen next, Sharkey said in a faltering voice, "Yes. I ran into him."

"You can prove it?" Kimo was leaning at him, looking eager.

"The cops know it."

"I mean, you can prove he wen' *make*?"

"His body's in the mortuary," Olive said, to distract the man. "Ashes now. He was cremated."

Kimo had turned to Rhonda and was nodding vigorously. Her expression was ambiguous, at first sorrowful and slack, and then a faint smile, with something like satisfaction, flickered on her cracked and sunburned lips, which made her reaction macabre.

"It was all my fault," Sharkey said, strengthened by the sight of the two people silently communicating a sense of pleasure. He'd expected to be assaulted by Max Mulgrave's angry grieving friend, but the man had turned away from him.

Olive took Sharkey's hand. She said to Kimo and the women, "I don't blame you for being upset."

Kimo shrugged, wiping his hands on his T-shirt. "We hear he wen' *make*, but where the proof?" He gestured to Sharkey. "You did a bad thing, mister. He was a good guy — he live over there with Rhonda for, what? Year or so."

"More," Rhonda said.

"He set up her kids in school. Those kids you saw before. Smart *akamai* kids. He organize a trust fund for them."

"He had money?"

"Not much left. He spend most of it on drugs."

"I never charge him much," Moe protested. "Smack like a braddah to me. But the trouble was the *batu*. The cheap stuff, it can wreck you. But . . . was his money."

Kimo said, "He put some aside for those kids, to give them one chance in life. The bank in Hale'iwa got all the papers. They know he wen' *make*?"

"Probably not," Olive said.

"You can tell them — show them the death certificate and all that."

"We'd be glad to do that. If it's important to you."

"Important for the will," Kimo said. "Rhonda in the will. The *keikis* in the will." He went to Sharkey and held him by his shoulders. He said, "I know you upset. But was an accident. Max was high a lot of the time. He fall off his bike, sometimes he half drown. He safe now, in heaven. No more pain."

Hearing this, Sharkey feared he might cry, and he blinked away his tears. He could endure anger, but any expression of forgiveness made him weepy.

Kimo faced him, and although he was ragged and smelled of the smoke and the camp, he was precise in his instructions, saying, "Go to the bank today. Take the documentation. Rhonda need that will. The kids too. After probate they have a chance. Like the lottery, brah."

All this time Rhonda had been smiling at Sharkey. At the mention that Max Mulgrave had been living with her — in the car or the blue plastic shelter, it was not clear — she'd assumed a sly expression. But now she raised her hand and poked his arm again, the small girl's teasing face in her old woman's battered features, her red eyes and gray braids fixed on their ends with tattered ribbons. She tugged his arm and then spoke softly, a braid in each hand, wagging her head like a coquette.

"Way back, you was one lifeguard."

"Long ago," Sharkey said. "I was a kid."

"I was one of your girls," the old woman said in the same low voice. "You fuck me on the beach at Waimea. You call me your seal pup."

The other woman, Winona, had not heard. She walked over to Sharkey with the greasy box of malasadas and said, "Try one. They junk when they come cold."

Standing under the trees, the smoke from the fire pit blowing past them, the dog lying in the dirt biting itself, Kimo and the others took turns hugging Sharkey and Olive, who promised to meet them again and to submit the death certificate to the bank.

"Maybe fix us up with a lawyer," Kimo said. "And then you gotta come back and see the *keikis*."

In the truck, driving away, Moe said, "I know this guy — Max, Smack, whatever. Long time ago, he want so choke *pakalolo* from me I cannot receive it in my mail can, because the post office they get more suspicious. So I do a bad thing. I send it to your mail can — and, shoots, it come lost."

"I've heard that story," Olive said, her hand flying to her face to cover her smile.

"Yeah," Sharkey said. "You were supplying him?"

"Big-time — when he had bucks, and an insane spendy car," Moe said. "Later I see him all over on his junk bike. All the time when the surf up we sit on the beach, smoking, talking story, tripping, watching you shred the monster wave. You his hero, Joe — he so stoked, seeing you surf."

12

The Release

Onenpersonnremained — faceless, distant, spectral, but necessary. Maybe she was stricken with grief, or maybe not. The quest to know the dead man had turned up so many surprises. Yet when Sharkey mentally rehearsed the confrontation, his confession, the okay he required on the release form, he stalled. She was the ex-wife, in California, next of kin. She knew from a message from Stickney at the morgue that Max Mulgrave was dead, but nothing further than that. She had to be told who was responsible for his death. And Sharkey needed more than her signature; he needed to see her face. But he went on procrastinating.

"The mainland," he said, tasting the word, wincing at its bitterness.

All of Hawaii's ugliness and none of its beauty comes from the mainland, he thought — every sack of cement, every piece of paper, every plastic bag and soda can, every hard drug, every chain-link fence and pane of glass and rusted rebar, every roll of barbed wire and yellow crime-scene DO NOT CROSS tape. The cheesy Christmas ornaments, every plastic toy, all the hats and T-shirts, the high-rises at Kakaako, golf clubs, TV sets, books, Styrofoam cups, every car, every gallon of gas, every bicycle, the fiberglass and epoxy for surfboards, every single haole. Me.

"You have to go."

"I feel futless there," he said. "And everything's wrong."

He meant, away from the surf — and miles of mainland surf were infected with runoff, sewage contamination, needles in the shore break, oil slick. And the traffic, the talk, the foul smell and freeways. He remembered the fleeting visit to Floristan. No wonder Max Mulgrave went to Hawaii! The mainland was bewildering and intimidating and uncomfortable; and you had to wear shoes.

"But even after fifty years in Hawaii, I'm still a fucken haole," he said, his head in his hands. "The only people who really belong here are Hawaiians. The rest of us are from somewhere else."

"What are you saying, Joe?"

In a grieving whisper of reproach he said, "That when I killed that drunk homeless guy, I was also a drunk homeless guy."

In the two weeks it took to visit the bank in Hale'iwa and provide the death certificate and call the ex-wife to ask her to sign the form for the burial — her name was Libby Aranda, she'd remarried, she lived in Santa Monica — in those two weeks Olive was called back to the hospital; the leave of absence she'd taken to help Sharkey through the crisis was over. He'd have to go alone.

"You're better," she said.

No, he thought — it's always pressure when people say that. Even she, who knew him so well, had no idea. And he thought, as he often had, without the words for it, *If I don't know myself, how can you possibly know me?*

"You can do this. Then it's over."

Nothing was certain. Every wave had a hidden contour and something like a mystical muscle in it that could trip you; every succeeding wave had the capacity to hold you down and suffocate you to death. The world was a wave, a wave was pitiless.

He'd counted on Olive's affection, she'd mothered him in a way that showed him what mothering meant, encouragement and protection his own mother had never offered. But Olive's attention, her patience, her uncomplaining support he'd taken for granted, pretending to object to it. He hadn't realized until now that love was something practical, a tenderness in the day-to-day that made the day better.

He'd become, through all this, since the crash — no, since killing Max Mulgrave — utterly dependent on her. Love was liberating, but love was also a mode of concern. Her love was taking his hand and steadying him, driving him when he was too distracted to hold the wheel, being his friend, waking Moe in the middle of the night and saving his life at Waimea. He would be dead without her love. So when she told him she was going back to work, he panicked. He loved her, but he was too self-conscious to repeat *I'd be lost without you,* as he'd told her once. But that was how he felt.

He'd never needed anyone before, he valued the necessity of finding his own waves; being a loner had always been his boast. He'd pitied Hunter for being helpless without an entourage of fixers. But his life had gone wrong, and becoming weak he regarded as his curse; yet Olive had stayed by his side. She was lovely, she could be passionate, but he saw that what mattered most was her compassion, her help in getting him through the day—that was love.

She was not a saint. He knew how he exasperated her, how she turned away and murmured, "Bugger," "Crumbs," "Knickers," "Blast." The times she'd said, as though in resentment, "You're like a wet weekend." But they were words so foreign to him it did not seem like impatience or anger but British and silly, the mantra in a weird little foreign amusement, like a chant in a children's game.

His first sight of Olive had been at the party long ago in the house at Rocky Point, when she'd knelt on the floor and rescued that stoner who'd overdosed, and he'd been aroused and inspired and greedy for her. So they became lovers. But their lovemaking, wild as it had been at times, mattered less than her instinct for living, her good heart and her ingenuity, her willingness to help him through this crisis. Now he could not remember when they'd last made love, and yet he knew he would drown without her. In those places, the homeless camp, the shitshow on the beach in Wai'anae, when he was tongue-tied or freaked out by a barking dog and Olive stepped past him and asked a direct question of a stranger, he had never loved her more. She was stronger than he was, and stood by him and was patient. Only kindness mattered.

"I'd go if I could," she said. "I'd like to meet this ex-wife and get the drift. But I'm needed at the hospital. I'm back in surgery."

She hugged him and was surprised by how tightly he held her, how he hung on, the big helpless man burying his face against her neck. He seemed to be moaning, *No.*

"I think it's a good thing you're doing this alone."

"I don't want to."

"You'll do fine, baby."

He loved her for saying that.

Olive dropped him at the airport, giving him a folder with his ticket and a sheet of paper with his itinerary, his hotel, the details of Max Mulgrave's exwife, her address, her phone number, and then she kissed him and patted his cheek, saying, "Gotta go."

But inside the terminal, at the check-in counter, when the baggage handler placed his duffel on the scale, he heard the ticket agent say, "I'll need to see your ID, Mr. Sharkey," and the man yelped, "No way!"

"Joe Sharkey," the baggage handler said. He was an islander, Hawaiian or Samoan, with a neck tattoo, a shaved head, a jutting jaw enlarged with bulging teeth, his big body strapped in a corsetlike brace of straps and webbing. "Da Shark!"

The ticket agent peered at Sharkey's license and then at the baggage handler.

"Where your board at, Joe?" the man said, hooking his thumbs into the straps of his brace.

"I don't surf anymore," Sharkey said in a subdued voice, feeling small next to the man.

"You lost some weight, brah."

"It's not that."

"He da weenah!" the man shouted at the ticket agent. "Triple Crown! Monster wave. He came top in the Eddie. Dis man da Shark!"

He reached to bump fists, but Sharkey was slow to respond, and said, "Last time I surfed I nearly drowned."

"Not true, brah." But the man dropped his arm and stepped back.

"I should have drowned."

"You da Shark," the man said in a querying and uncertain way.

"I killed a man," Sharkey said loudly. Then in a hot whisper, "Ran into him at Waimea. He wen' *make*."

The baggage handler put his hands up and thrust with them, as though repelling a bad smell. He parted his lips and stammered, then with force said, "Shoots!"

The ticket agent said nothing, simply passed Sharkey his baggage receipt and boarding pass, but when Sharkey got to the security checkpoint he was ordered out of line — "This way, sir. Just a few questions" — and frisked and interrogated, then made to wait in a windowless cubicle while his carry-on bag was searched and whispered phone calls were made.

Finally the TSA man handed him his driver's license and said, "You're good to go."

On the flight — overnight, five hours, not long enough to sleep — he sat awake in the dark as though dazzled by an afterimage.

A woman in the seat next to him said, "You got masses of attention back there."

"Do I know you?"

"Parool Verma," she said. "Travel writer, I'm here on assignment. You might have read my things."

Sharkey said, "I don't read."

"What do you do?"

"Surf."

She wagged her head from side to side, and though he could not see her clearly, he inhaled her, a sweetness he was unused to — perfume, a syrupy fragrance that formed a kind of aromatic shape in the semidarkness and defined her body.

She said, "I was wondering. I saw them at Waikiki. It's mainly white guys, is it not? No people of color. I mean, minority communities."

"Many," Sharkey said.

"But not African American, to be sure."

He snorted and got a powerful whiff of the perfume. He said, "You from L.A.?"

"I can say L.A. was our portal."

"Nick Gabaldón — L.A. guy, great surfer. Black. Crashed into the pier at Santa Monica on a big day — wen' *make* shooting the pier. But, hey, we don't color-code surfing."

"Maybe that's the problem with the sport, not so?"

"There's no problem. It's not a sport."

"What is it then, if I may be so bold?"

"I don't know." He was too weary to think of words. "It's a kind of life."

"Just that alone, selfish life."

"Yes!" Sharkey surprised himself with the force of his reply, then fell suddenly asleep, waking just before the plane landed in daylight. The woman hurried away from him. He roused himself to collect his bag and dozed in the taxi, waking when they arrived at the hotel, and slept until noon.

The arrangement Olive had made with Libby, the ex-wife, was that Sharkey would meet her at her house for a drink. Sharkey would tell her that he had killed Max Mulgrave, he would explain that Mulgrave had been cremated, and he'd ask her to sign the release so that he could organize a proper burial. Or, if she insisted, this ex-wife might want to take care of it — maybe an interment in Floristan? The ashes would remain in the mortuary in Honolulu until a decision was made. But he needed to tell her what he had done, driving drunk, ending the man's life.

After a shower and a sandwich, and wearing an aloha shirt, he went to the porte cochere of his hotel, where a man in a white uniform with gold braids and epaulets approached him. He looked to Sharkey like the leader of a marching band.

"Taxi, sir?"

"I'm going to this address." Sharkey showed the man the card Olive had written in block letters.

"Alta — it's six, seven blocks. You could walk it."

"Taxi," Sharkey said with such bluntness that the uniformed man grabbed his whistle and blew it hard until a taxi appeared.

In the taxi he felt fragile, afraid of what was to come, his head ringing, his skin like tissue. He wanted this to be over and then after the night at the hotel to get the early flight back to Honolulu.

The house was large, two stories, Spanish style, creamy stucco, yellow cornices, windows covered by wrought-iron grilles, a wide porch, surrounded by a deep green lawn and flowerbeds, a mainland house with thick walls and a red tile roof and a varnished door of golden timber. It advertised itself as a rich person's house. He knocked.

A swarthy man in a dark suit opened the door.

"Joe Sharkey."

He put out his hand, but the man, who was wearing white gloves, stepped back, saying, "Mrs. Aranda is expecting you. Right this way."

So it was the butler, and he felt fearful again, as though tricked, out of his element — easily fooled.

She was seated in an armchair, clutching something in her lap, at the far end of the living room — flowered cushions, flowers in vases, a coffee table with a bowl of blossoms floating in it. As Sharkey approached her, a man entered the room quickly and stepped in front of him.

"Cesar Aranda," he said. "I'm Libby's husband."

"Please sit down," the woman said. "I get nervous when people are standing while I'm sitting."

She was blond, her hair clumped and curled, a mass of it on her head and falling to her shoulders — bony shoulders and thin arms. She wore a yellowish blouse of shimmering silk, opened to reveal a chunky necklace as thick as a lei, and on her skinny wrists heavy bangles. Sharkey saw the mounded hair and jewels before he saw the woman's face. A pinched face, a half-smile, reddened glistening lips — a brittle indoor beauty, of a glamorous sort he always thought breakable.

And what he took to be a cushion or a purse on her lap under her hands was a small dog, with white fluffy fur and wicked black eyes.

"What will you have to drink?"

"No drink," Sharkey said. "Thanks — I'm all set."

"I was told you came for a drink."

"Soft drink," Sharkey said in a choked voice.

The woman spoke to the man in the dark suit, hovering in the doorway. "You heard him, Diego. Juice."

The woman's husband approached her, pushed a cushion aside, and sat next to her, taking one of her hands from the dog — the dog growled — but it was less a gesture of affection than something proprietorial, a way of uniting with her against Sharkey, as they faced him from across the room. When the dog growled more loudly and swelled in the woman's lap, Sharkey stiffened and sat back in the sofa.

"So how did you know Max?" the woman asked.

"I didn't know him."

With a satirical smile on her red clown mouth, she giggled and said, "What are you doing here, then?"

"I came here to tell you I killed him." Sharkey had rehearsed the words so many times it was as though he were hearing a hollow echo, and he was scarcely aware he had spoken them aloud.

But the woman had heard. Slowly a twitch animated her face, which had seemed small and unfriendly, and her pretty lips at first parted, seemed to prepare to speak, but said nothing and curled in a smile.

"Someone had to do it," she finally said, and glanced at the man, tugging his hand, as the dog yapped twice and settled its head deeper in her lap.

The man in the dark suit and white gloves brought a tall glass on a tray to Sharkey and said, "Lemonade, sir."

Sharkey took it but didn't drink. He held it in both hands and said, "It was terrible. I was drunk. I crashed into him with my car. He was on a bike. It was a dark rainy night, the road was gnarly. He didn't have a chance. He had no ID. They kept him in the morgue. I've spent the past two months trying to find out his identity and piece together his life."

The woman wagged her head, jogging the curled clumps of her thick hair. She said, "What kind of bike?"

"What kind of bike?" Sharkey said, repeating it, because the question was unexpected. "An old bike. A junk bike."

"The kind of bike a bum might have," the woman said carelessly.

She's trying to shock me, Sharkey thought, *but she does not know that after what I've been through I am shockproof.*

"That man had a Ferrari—he had millions," she said. "And he threw it all away."

"You pieced together his life," the man said. His slight accent made him seem slow and skeptical. "What did you find?"

The man's voice was self-important; the woman's was sour. They sat side by side, giving Sharkey the sense that he was being questioned in stereo, the woofer on the left, the tweeter on the right.

Why should I tell them what they probably already know of his life? Sharkey thought. *They're testing me.* But he had come for a purpose: he needed a favor from the ex-wife, so he began.

"He was, in the beginning, just a dead man lying in the road," Sharkey said. "He was surrounded by people, the strangers who slow down when they see a car crash. Most of them knew my name, but none of them knew his name. I was stupid. I didn't bother to find out who he was. He was a drunk homeless guy I'd crashed into. I even started to tell myself it was all his fault." He sipped at his lemonade and continued. "But then things started to go wrong in my life — accidents, illnesses, bad-luck things."

"Such as?" The woman seemed to be smiling again.

"My girlfriend had a miscarriage. I almost drowned."

"You look perfectly all right to me," the woman said. "And by the way, Max always wanted tattoos like yours."

"Inside I was dying," Sharkey said. "My girlfriend convinced me that it had something to do with killing that man and not admitting it. Maybe bad karma."

"Or guilt," the man said. He pursed his lips and added, *"La culpa."*

"Yes, or that — it doesn't matter. People say 'I conquered the wave' and the next time they surf they wipe out, or face-plant, or die."

"Anyway, you did detective work," the woman said. "Pretty easy in the age of the Internet."

"Right, it's not hard to find facts, but facts don't tell you enough. We got his name from his fingerprints, and then his military record, his high school stuff, his hometown. But that's just paperwork — I hate the word. Books, documents, photocopies. That's not a man's life. That just a bunch of paper."

"It's how the world works," the woman said.

"That's the trouble with the world," Sharkey said.

"What's the alternative?" the man said.

"I went to his hometown."

"Jesus, you actually went to Floristan, that shithole." The woman abruptly shifted in her seat, disturbing the dog, and as the dog squirmed and yapped she stroked him. "Go on, what's wrong?"

"I'm glad I went," Sharkey said, leaning back. "I met some of his friends."

"He hated that place."

"He built his mother a house."

"Don't I know it! And she was such a bitch to him."

The man patted her hand and said, "Let him finish, darling."

"You see where someone comes from and you understand them a lot better," Sharkey said.

"Where do you come from?"

"I was an army brat. My father wanted me to attend West Point. Go to 'Nam, like he did. I quit school, I quit everything and surfed. Your husband, Max —"

"Ex," the man said sharply.

"Ex-husband — enlisted. That got him out of his hometown. He was in Vietnam at the worst time. He got medals. He used his military service to go to college. Started a company, a big company."

"That's where I come in, darling," the woman said to the man beside her.

"We had a beautiful home in Palo Alto — I did the decorating and landscaping. Max Integer was a short drive away. We had friends, we had a fabulous life." She sighed. "For about six years. And then Max decided that what he really wanted was to be a surfer."

"I get that," Sharkey said.

"I don't," the woman said. "He threw everything away. The business, the house, the friends — me."

"You could have gone with him to Hawaii."

"Really, can you see me in Wicky Wacky Woo, sitting on a beach while Max is falling off a wave? Plus do you know what the sun does to your skin?"

"I guess so."

"Look at yourself. No offense, but you haven't spent much money on sunblock, my friend."

The man laughed — too hard — and patted her hand. "Be kind, darling," he said, but his gesture roused the dog, and when it began to yap furiously Sharkey blinked and was unable to reply to the sunblock remark.

"You know all about Max's service record and his company," the woman said, restraining the dog. "But do you know what he had in his luggage? Probably ten million dollars."

Sharkey said, "When you think about it, it's really not that much in Hawaii."

"He sold his company to his employees for twenty-five — like a fool. He could have gotten ten times that from Symantec. He gave five to his alma mater, Santa Cruz. I got the other ten, and look what I did with it. This house, a great life, a wonderful guy."

The man lifted the flopped-over locks of hair from her forehead and they kissed as the dog twitched and fussed. When the man withdrew, touching her lips with his fingertip, Sharkey said, "I have just one favor to ask." He slipped the document from Olive's folder and handed it to the woman.

She lifted the paper and read, "Declaration for Deposition of Cremated Remains," and handed it to the man, who studied it, running his finger down the page. But the woman was still facing Sharkey. "Why me?"

"Your name was listed as next of kin. If you sign it, I'll take care of the rest. I was thinking of arranging a paddle-out, traditional kine. Flowers. A bunch of surfers. Some of his friends."

But the woman had begun to talk over him, saying, "I know what happened in Hawaii. He turned into a bum. He bought a big expensive house on the beach, he gave money away. His friends were deadbeats and leeches, but he didn't care. I suppose they gave him drugs. He always had a thing for uppers. Coke, when we were married, but it was mainly recreational.

He probably got into speedballs and freebasing. Meth, crack — he probably tried everything. The wonder is that he got away with it."

"Putting junk like that in your body," the man said. "It's just poison."

"Listen," Sharkey said, "I like drugs as much as the next man. Maybe more than the next man."

"Bet you're proud of yourself," the woman said.

"I'm not proud of myself." Sharkey tried to suppress his anger, but his voice was tortured. "I was zorched when I killed him."

Unmoved, the woman said, "What do you do besides surf? What kind of work?"

"Just surf."

"What have you accomplished — what have you made?"

"Made moves," Sharkey said. "On water."

The man smiled and made a mocking noise in his throat. The woman said, "Like I said, how did he get away with it? He was famous for his speeding tickets in Palo Alto. But as far as I know he never got one in Hawaii. It would have shown up on his insurance. Never got arrested. No drug bust — they would have told me, as next of kin."

"*Mordidas*," the man said knowingly, smoothing his hair. "Must have bribed the cops."

"The cops totally respected him," Sharkey said, and thought, *I'm not going to tell her about the prostitute's funeral, or Wai'anae, or the homeless camp, or his will, the trust for the schoolchildren, nothing about his lover Rhonda. She'd just mock him for it.*

"Say five or ten thousand," the man said. "I'm curious. How much cocaine does that buy?"

Sharkey cupped his hands, he shaped them, forming a small pinched pile, saying, "More or less."

"He gave all that money away," the woman said. "He blew it, like a fool. He was reckless when we were married. Easily bored. 'I was a soldier,' he used to say. 'Burned out that self. Then I was a student. Burned out that self. Then a software geek. Burned that out.'"

Sharkey listened intently, wishing to remember the words. He said, with feeling, "I totally get that."

"A wasted life," the man said.

"What do you know?" Sharkey said, enraged again. "You got a job?"

"I'm a stylist," the man said. "I have my own salon."

"What is that?"

"Hairdresser," the woman said.

And Sharkey lost his anger; he laughed — hooted, clapped his hands to his knees, and gagged when he tried to respond. He had not laughed for months, and it was more than laughter — he was purging himself of his sadness, expelling the misery he'd accumulated, ridding himself of gloom in a yell of pleasure. "Hairdresser!" He caused the dog to explode in a torrent of yapping.

Sharkey could not sit still in his hilarity. He got up and walked in circles, bumping the furniture, disturbing the flowers; and it was as though he were laughing on behalf of Max Mulgrave, because he was sure that Max would let out a mocking scream if he heard that the man sitting beside his ex-wife — her husband, Cesar — said he was a hairdresser. He was laughing for himself, he was laughing for Max — laughter was health and strength.

"Do you need a glass of water?" the man said, raising his voice because the dog was still yapping. Sharkey seemed to be choking. But it was a spasm of hilarity.

Sharkey raised one hand, indicating no.

"Take your declaration," the woman said. "I'm not signing."

Sharkey sat on the sofa, he wiped his eyes — his laughter had produced tears. He was quieted by the woman's refusal. He said, "The ashes are in the mortuary."

"They can stay there."

"If you don't sign, they'll likely be put in a common grave."

"Maybe that's where they belong, with the other bums."

The man put his arms around her, but when he hugged her she seemed to stiffen and go sad.

"Call him a cab, Cesar," she said, and as she stood up the small fluffy dog jumped to the floor and frolicked at her feet. But she was unsteady, and, seeming determined to leave the room briskly — in her cold, uncooperative mood — she stumbled and had to grip the doorjamb to regain her balance.

"Darling," the man said. But she ignored him. He said to Sharkey, "You upset her!" Seeing that Sharkey had gone mute, he added, "I'll call you a cab. Where are you going?"

In his hotel room he turned off the air conditioner; the droning died, the air went warm and stale, penetrated with the rank smell of sofa cushions. Sharkey sat on the bed, feeling helpless again. It was midafternoon in Hawaii. He thought of calling Olive, but he didn't want to report another defeat, and besides, she was probably saving someone's life in surgery. Then he remembered how, hearing "hairdresser," he had laughed — great loud healing laughter — and he smiled at the memory. It had been a beautiful moment, and all the better for having those two people as witnesses. Yes, it probably spoiled everything, but it was wonderful, an assertive statement of belief. He was vindicated, knowing that his friends would have laughed, Hunter would have laughed, and he was sure that Max Mulgrave would have laughed.

He flung open the French windows to the small lanai attached to his room and stood, considering the ocean — the familiar voice of water on the move, threshing the shoreline, and was soothed by its whisper, as though by a hit of weed.

Then what he took to be an answering sound — the *ding-dong* of recognition — was the telephone by the bed.

"Yes?"

"I'm in the lobby." It was a woman. Who? She sighed and said, "Bring the paper."

"Be right down."

She was standing by a pillar, wearing a long coat, probably to look inconspicuous, but all it did was make her stand out. It was pink, and her hair was tucked into a big blue hat. When Sharkey got near her, she reached out and clutched his arm and drew him closer. In this harsh lobby light she looked older, lines visible beneath her makeup. It seemed she'd been crying and the traces of the tears had aged her.

"Let's sit."

Beside her on a sofa by the wall Sharkey said, "Where's your dog?"

"I left Corazon at home." She touched his nose, a teasing gesture. "You're afraid of him. Funny. Max was afraid of dogs too."

"That's good to know."

"I'm sorry," she said. "I was a bitch to him. I was a bitch to you. Never mind Cesar. To him, Max was a freak. He doesn't know I'm here. Where's the paper?"

Sharkey unfolded it and smoothed it on the arm of the sofa. "Here's a pen."

She read it through, murmuring, "'Shall be disposed of in the following manner,'" then signed it, adding her address and her phone number.

"Where's this place" — she put her finger on a line — "Waimea?"

"A beach. A bay. A surf break. A wave," Sharkey said. "Sometimes monster."

"And what's the idea — scatter his ashes?"

"Something like that, with prayers, with flowers."

She handed the paper back. She looked tearful, her lips tremulous. Her fingers were thin, the skin loose and crepey; her fingernails were long and lovely, pink, pearly, like polished shells, and she wore an enormous glittering diamond ring.

"I didn't mean those things I said."

"You were upset."

"I wasn't upset. I'm a bitch." She said it ruefully. "Max was kind."

"That's what I discovered."

"All that trouble you took to find out about him," she said. "Max would have done that."

"I don't know what to say."

"Then kiss me," she said.

He leaned over to kiss her cheek, but she held his head and grabbed his hair and kissed him fiercely on his lips and forced them open and moaned hungrily into his mouth. When she was done, leaving the sweet creaminess of lipstick on his tongue, she rested her head on his shoulder and sighed.

"You remind me of him — you laughed like him," she said. "A free spirit, reckless as hell. But a good heart."

"Yes, I know him now," Sharkey said in a tearful whisper. "I'm so sorry he's gone."

Sharkey woke buoyant, motionless, as though floating on his back, then with a whiff of the sea from the lanai realized where he was. He smiled at the ceiling. Remembering that his flight to Honolulu was not leaving until late that evening, he slipped on his board shorts and hurried out of the hotel, waving away the man in the white uniform and gold braids at the porte cochere who saluted and said, "Taxi?"

"Not today, chief."

He crossed the main road and walked toward the pier, descending from the narrow cliffside park to the beach just beyond the pier. He kicked off his flip-flops to feel the heat of the sand rise from his soles to glow in his legs. The surf was hardly more than a foot, and yet it chuckled and beckoned as he flexed, preparing to enter the water at the break he knew as Bay Street.

Stretching, canted sideways, he saw three small boys seated near him, watching the novice surfers, unsteady on their boards and toppling into the waves. The boys sat crouched in attitudes of exclusion, three explicit silhouettes, stark against the whiteness of the beach, a coating of sand sugaring their arms and legs.

"Hi, guys."

The boys twitched at his voice and looked warily at him, as though bringing him into focus, but said nothing.

"Why aren't you out there catching waves?"

One boy laughed, averting his gaze; another said, "That's hard, man."

"You good swimmers?"

"Pretty good," the biggest boy said.

"Then you can do it."

They all laughed and, still seated, swayed, showing indecision, then leaned away from him.

"I'm Joe. Tell me your names."

The big boy was Junior, the boy next to him Matisse, the smallest whispered, "Tavious." Their faded shorts and battered flip-flops, their torn T-shirts, their hair dusted with sand grains, made them seem like waifs.

Junior said, "I want tats like you, man."

"Go for it," Sharkey said. "But listen. Those kids out there are using the wrong boards. The waves are better suited to body boards, which" — he turned to glance back at the stalls at the margin of the beach by the cycle path — "you can rent."

"If you got enough bones," Matisse said.

Sharkey snapped his fingers. "I got the bones."

"Yo, cool," Junior said, wheezing with admiration.

Sharkey said, "Me, I'm the Easter Bunny."

This made them laugh, and they scrambled to their feet as he beckoned them up the beach to a stall with an awning and a stack of boards and swim fins hung on hooks. They were silent and watchful as he spoke to a deeply tanned man slouched in a beach chair.

"I'm going to need four boards with leashes, and three sets of swim fins for my friends here."

Using the back of his hand, the man tipped up his ball cap and turned his beaky face to Sharkey, not saying anything but sniffing, interrogating him with his nose. He said, "You're going to keep an eye on them?"

"I'm giving them lessons."

"I mean my boards, man. I lose a lot of inventory to kids here."

Sharkey rocked slowly, flexing his toes to calm himself, considering his reply. The man's nose was burned pink like a peeled shrimp. He said, "That's harsh on my friends here." He smiled at the boys, who straightened and smiled back. "But tell you what. I'll pay you a deposit, and if the boards are cockaroached, you can keep it."

"These are quality boards," the man said, heaving himself out of his chair, his sigh conveying reluctance. "I'm putting eight hundred on your card. If I don't see the boards again, consider it forfeited."

Sharkey murmured "High finance" to the boys as he handed the man his credit card.

Carrying the boards and fins down the beach, Sharkey heard one of boys say "Cockaroach" and giggle.

At the water's edge Sharkey said, "Put your board down flat and climb on top, your chest on the upper half. You're a turtle, right? Now show me how you're going to paddle."

They practiced paddling on the sand, scooping with their cupped hands, then holding the nose of the board, duck-diving, and for the wave breaking right, grabbing the left rail with their left hand, their right hand on the nose, and kicking with their fins.

"Tryin' to remember," Matisse said.

"Let's boogie."

Sharkey led them into the surf zone, among low advancing sets, blue frothing to white, the sprawl of foam scooping toward shore. He showed them the moves again and then urged them on as they shouted and tumbled, flailing in the suds. But after five or six tries, they grew in confidence and balance and rode the waves, tumbling when Sharkey signaled, then heading back to ride again. Flattened on his own board, Sharkey watched with pleasure, thinking, *There is nowhere I would rather be,* and reflecting on how the day was transformed for him by the sight of the three boys gleaming in the sea, exulting, the small boy, Tavious, squealing.

They continued until early afternoon, when Sharkey said, "Let's eat, guys." Passing the rental shed, Sharkey called out to the man in the beach chair, "We're cockaroaching them!"

He bought the boys burgers at an outdoor café nearer the pier. Watching them eat, he thought of mentioning Nick Gabaldón; but they were happy, they were hungry, they ate with gusto, and why remind them of their race?

"You guys are good. Stay unsinkable."

Holding his burger, wiping his mouth with the back of his hand, Junior said, "You ain't no Easter Bunny, man. Who you really?"

"I'm nobody — average Joe," Sharkey said. "Just passing through. But I want you to promise you'll come back here again and practice. Take my board — give it to a friend. Hey, I don't know what you feel like where you live, but let me tell you, in the water" — he lowered his head, he spoke fiercely — "in the water, you're somebody special. Remember that."

13

The Paddle-Out at Waimea

A beautiful North Shore early morning, a sweet whiff of damp foliage that had the freshness of lettuce, and a gauzy veil of greeny-gold heat haze like a halo of pale light over the stillness of Waimea. A fuzz of reddish gnats and tiny jeweled flies stirred in the warmth. A troop of surfers, thirty or more, their boards under one arm, batted at the insects with their free hands as they loped barefoot toward the beach. There, the pale sprawl of bay glowed as smooth as a lake between the arms of spiky black lava on either side, the Leaping Rock on the left, the boulders at Pinballs on the right. One of the surfers muttered, "Total glass."

A few distant corrugations, the twitch of a ribbed swell toward the horizon, but near to, this dawn, the sea was a white whisper.

In the parking lot, gilded by the sun striking through the haze, Sharkey reached to his roof rack for his board, Olive beside him, the surfers passing.

"Give him a hand, guys."

"No, I'm cool."

His will was strong, yet trembled with the weight of the board when he clapped it under his arm. But he was determined not to be helped.

Around him, in the lacework of sun-flecked shade, the surfers young and old, the young ones chattering, the older ones solemn and silent — Jock, Garrett, Brock, Ryan, the Florence brothers, and others on the beach sitting cross-legged, some pacing. Sharkey recognized Stickney and Wencil, Alex, Fonoti and Frawley, and from the *kapu* camp Rhonda, Winona, and Kimo, the schoolchildren gathered near them. Skippy Lehua had come with some of his grommets, and Sugar with her three children, May and her Chinese husband. All of them tense and tearful in their gaudy shirts. Moe was there. So was I.

"Insane," Sharkey murmured.

As we gathered on the foreshore, three black-and-white HPD police cruisers drew up at the edge of the parking lot. Six officers got out and marched to the beach, where they stood in a line, at attention, and saluted.

Onlookers too, early risers, rock jumpers, beachgoers, gawkers, tourists, crowding the surfers.

A hoarse haole voice: "Some kind of Wayan ceremony?"

The *kahu* had been waiting on the beach. He was wrapped in a priestly green gown and wore a lei of niihau shells, his long black hair under his crown of flowers drawn back and braided. He strode to a dome of sand and beckoned to Sharkey, who handed him the small green bundle, the ashes wrapped in sacred ti leaves. And then the *kahu* faced the bay and recited a chant in Hawaiian that silenced all the whisperers. It was not a lament — it sounded more like a plea for mercy.

"*Lehu kane*," he said when he finished, and sprinkled the green bundle with water from a coconut shell. A robed Hawaiian man stepped next to him, carrying a conch shell. He was also wearing a flower crown, and fastened to his neck a heavy russet cape. He blew a long sputtering trumpet blast on the conch.

Sharkey accepted the green bundle and fixed it with a strap to the nose of his board. The plop of a small insistent wave snatched at a length of sand and turned it to a rim of gravel. A golden plover, its head down, strutted past, its beak lowered to stab at a sea bug, as Sharkey set his board in the fribble of the shore break.

He flattened himself on it. He cupped his hands and paddled slowly into the whispering water of the bay, breathing the tang of the sea, liking the salt, the familiar taste of surfing. The surfers massed behind him and dropped to their boards and followed on them, staying together, a flotilla of them, stomachs pressed against the boards, rhythmically stroking the water.

At the center of the bay they fanned out, making a great bobbing circle, an eccentric lineup, Sharkey in the center. And when he sat and straddled his board, they did the same. He picked open the leaf bundle, cradled it in his hands, and held it close to his eyes, improvising a prayer, asking forgiveness, muttering, "Max," as though to a friend, and then whirled it, scattering the cloud of ashes. Acting as one, the surfers slipped the leis from their necks and flung these flowers into the center of the circle and slapped the water, a clatter of smacks and splashes, wrinkling the sea.

In the silence after that, they parted the circle, like an entry break in a reef, allowing Sharkey to paddle through the gap.

As he stroked alone toward shore, a thickening ripple from the incoming swell rose behind him, lifting him a little, and the next was a big enough bump, gulping under his board, to get his attention. He crawled to a kneeling position and rocked himself into the following wave, a small one, the sort he called a threshold, like the first wave he'd ever ridden, at Magic Island.

He tipped his board into the wave's shallow sloping face and got to his feet. Without effort, like a hero on a flying carpet, not tensed in a surfer's stance but standing confidently upright, a fearless boy again. Hands on hips, he slid to shore, and to Olive, on the chuckle of a wave that was freaked with froth.